THE PULSE OF DANGER

Jon Cleary, an Australian whose books are read throughout the world, is the author of many novels including such famous bestsellers as *The Sundowners* and *The High Commissioner*.

Born in 19—  —teen to become a com—————————————— even a laundryman a——————————————— won second prize in ——————————————— and launched him ————————.

Seven of his ————— have been filmed, and his novel *Peter's Pence* was awarded the American Edgar Allan Poe Prize as the best crime novel of 1974.

Jon Cleary's most recent novels have been *The Golden Sabre, The Faraway Drums, Spearfield's Daughter, The Phoenix Tree, The City of Fading Light, Dragons at the Party*, also *Now and Then, Amen* and *Murder Song*. He lives in Sydney and travels the world researching his novels with his wife Joy.

'Mr Cleary is a most expert novelist. His scenes slide noiselessly into gear.' *Times Literary Supplement*

'The man has a noble gift for storytelling and a nice dry humour' *New York Times*

'Jon Cleary has the ancient skill of the harper, creating a store of rich fabric and breathless tension' *Los Angeles Times*

'Jon Cleary's books all bear the stamp of craftsmanship and quality' *Sunday Telegraph*

'An author who just seems to get better with each book' *Canberra Times*

JON CLEARY

The Pulse of Danger

Fontana
An Imprint of HarperCollins*Publishers*

First published in 1966 by Collins

This edition first issued in 1968 by Fontana,
an imprint of HarperCollins Publishers,
77–85 Fulham Palace Road,
Hammersmith, London W6 8JB

9 8 7 6 5 4

Printed and bound in Great Britain by
HarperCollins Manufacturing, Glasgow

To Innes and George

ONE

The leopard coughed somewhere on the steep slope behind the camp; and Eve Marquis awoke at once. Despite the number of trips she and Jack had made into the wildernesses of the world, she had never been able to take for granted the beasts that might prowl the outskirts of their camps. Each night she went to sleep with one ear still wide awake for any hint of danger; other people's nightmares were supposed to be soundless, but hers were full of lions roaring, elephants trumpeting and gorillas grunting. Lately they had been echoing with the coughing of leopards. English and therefore a supposed animal-lover, a worshipper of the Royal Society for the Prevention of Cruelty to Animals as much as of the Church of England, she had all her life been guilty of what she felt was treason: she hated animals, couldn't bring herself to trust even a day-old puppy. Cruft's dog show was something left over from Dante's *Inferno*; and people who kept more esoteric pets, baby alligators and Siamese fighting fish, were devils she did her best to avoid. Yet year after year she left the comparative safety of Kensington, a region where the wilder poodles were at least kept on a leash, and ventured into these areas where the animals made the beasts of Kensington Gardens look like people-lovers.

Why? she asked herself. And the answer pulled back the flap of the tent and came in, dropping some letters on her as she rolled over on the camp-bed.

'Mail,' Jack said, sitting down on his own bed. 'Chungma just got back from Thimbu. The trucks will be there waiting for us three weeks from to-day. Sleep well?'

She had indeed slept soundly, and that annoyed her. When one was afraid of being torn to pieces, one should not sleep like a new-born baby. But she had always been like that when they were camped at some height. Other people complained of headache, difficulty in getting their breath, even of heart flutters; but it was as if the higher she went, the more relaxed and at home she felt.

7

She remembered how pleased Jack had been when he had first discovered this fact about her. That had been on her first trip with him, their honeymoon trip, to the slopes of Ruwenzori, the Mountains of the Moon, in Uganda.

'I was worried,' he had grinned. 'Someone told me honeymoons should always be taken at sea-level. Shortness of breath in the groom or bride is no foundation for a happy marriage.'

'Ours is going to be a happy one. I don't think either of us is going to suffer from shortness of breath. Not for years, anyway.'

That had been only eight years ago. Their lungs were still good, but she had begun to feel their marriage needed a check-up. She had decided it was suffering from a shortness of compatibility, from a congestion of selfishness; she had had plenty of time in these past seven months to diagnose the reasons. That, of course, was part of the trouble: on these trips she too often had too much time to think. And to feel sorry for herself, something of which she was secretly ashamed. Self-pity was as wasteful as lavishing love on a dog or a cat.

Jack had begun to slit open the letters with the small curved knife he used for prising plants from rock crevices. 'I'm going up to Bayswater Road this morning. There's a patch of *swertia* over there. I want to get some seeds of it.'

All the tracks, streams and ridges in their working area were given familiar names for easier identification; it was an invention that had become a habit with them as they had made these expeditions into regions that were often unmapped. It was better than referring to the ' fourth ridge from the skyline ' or the ' track that branches off at the Kharsu oak '; and at first she had taken it on herself to dream up the names. As it had with soldiers during the war, it evoked a certain nostalgia for home and took away some of the foreignness of an alien land : Piccadilly Circus as a jungle clearing was just as much home as the original. Or almost. But lately, abraded by the moods that had taken hold of her like a girdle that didn't fit, she had begun to look upon the names as an irritating whimsy. But she could say nothing : after all, they had been her idea in the first place. The first Bayswater Road had been a track on Ruwenzori : it was a honeymoon memory.

'Better take your rifle,' she said. 'I heard the leopard again.'

'I'll be loaded down enough, without taking a bloody rifle with me.' He was the animal-lover; he would trust even a starving python. 'I'll be all right, love. Here.'

He handed her the bulk of the letters. She took her arms from under the blankets, felt the chill of the morning air through her pyjama-sleeves, and quickly grabbed at the sweater he tossed her. On their first trip to Ruwenzori she had insisted on taking sheets with them, but it had not taken her long to appreciate that the comfort of them did not compensate for the extra weight and the difficulty of washing them. She had grown accustomed to the roughness of blankets or the constriction of a sleeping-bag, but that did not mean she liked them. Sheets had become a symbol of civilisation for her. Small things assumed a disproportionate importance when one had time, too much time, to think about them. The linen department at Harrods had begun to look like one of the annexes of the Promised Land. She sat up, pulling on the sweater, and began to glance through her letters, the first links for weeks with that Promised Land.

She looked up. 'Anything interesting?'

'Sort of.' He re-read the letter he was holding, then carefully refolded it. She recognised all the signs: he was going to tell her something he guessed she did not want to hear. 'The Bayard Institute wants me to take a party out to New Guinea.'

She put down her own letters: whatever news was in them was unimportant beside what he had just told her. 'What are you going to tell them?'

'Well——'

'Jack, if you go, I'm not going with you. You promised this was our last trip.'

He grinned, as if he did not think she was serious. 'You'd like New Guinea. And we could go down to Sydney for a few weeks. You're always complaining I've never taken you back to my home——'

'We'll go to Sydney. But not to New Guinea. I've had enough——' Suddenly she felt on the verge of tears, but she held them back. She had learned long ago that winning a man over by tears provided only a temporary victory: she was not going to spend her life in a drizzle of weeping.

'We'll talk about it later, on the way back to Thimbu.' He stood up, put a huge rough hand on the back of her head and gently ran it down to stroke her neck.

'Don't start smoodging to me,' she said tartly, her mind made up not to give in to him this time. Then the leopard coughed again, the *ough-ough* sound that told he was angry; and she looked up at her husband with true concern, all her anger at him suddenly gone. 'Darling, please take the rifle.'

He went to say something, then he shrugged, sat down on his bed again and drew out the gun-case from beneath it. She had given him the guns as a wedding present, both from Holland and Holland, a Super .30 Double and a 12-bore Royal ejector self-opener; the type of gun had meant nothing to her, but the salesman had assured her that no sportsman could wish for more. But he hadn't known her Jack. They had cost her nine hundred pounds each and they had almost caused a fierce row between her and Jack; he had rebelled against such extravagance, insisting she was not to buy him gifts he himself could not afford, but she had been just as stubborn as he that she would not take them back. In the end he had accepted them, but they were the last expensive gift she had given him, except for the contributions she always made towards the cost of their expeditions. Being the rich wife of a poor botanist was not an easy occupation.

He took out the Super .30 and wiped the oil from it. 'I haven't had much chance to use it this trip.' His big hands moved caressingly down the barrels and over the stock, the hands of a lover.

'That's your baby, isn't it?'

He looked at her from under his heavy black brows, his dark blue eyes seeming to glaze over as they always did when he wanted to retreat from an argument. It had not escaped her that he only retreated from arguments with her; with everyone else the eyes blazed almost with enjoyment when there was a conflict of opinion. That was the Irish in him: a generation removed from Ireland, the bog-water dried out of him by the Australian sun, he still had the Irishman's belief that an argument was better than a benediction.

'Don't start that again, love.'

'Wouldn't you like a son you could teach to use a gun?'

'With my luck I'd land a daughter.'

'We could keep trying. I'm willing.'

He looked at her for a moment, then again his eyes glazed over. He turned away and began to fill a pouch with cartridges. She looked at his broad back, wanting to apologise, but the words were like stones stuck behind her teeth. It had become like this over the past few months; the old ability to communicate with him with just a look had gone and now there was even difficulty in finding words. She continued to stare at his back, loving him and hating him: once you gave your heart to someone, you could never take it all back. She loved him because physically he had not changed; he was still the man whose touch, sometimes even just the sight of him, could make her tremble with longing. He was big, well over six feet, with the chest and shoulders of a wrestler; she still continued to be amazed at some of the feats of strength she saw him perform on these trips. He was not handsome, with the nose that had been broken in a Rugby scrum and the cheekbones that were too high and too broad: if any Tartar had made it as far west as Connemara and not been talked impotent by the Irish, then Jack could claim him as an ancestor. It was a face which appealed to men as well as to women, one in which strength of character was marked as plainly as the irregular features. She loved the physical side of him, and she loved his warmth, his humour and his tenderness. Lately she had begun to hate him for what she thought of as his selfishness and his total disregard of any of her own ambitions. His strength of character was only a stubbornness to deny his own failings.

'You'd better get up,' he said without turning round. 'Tsering has your breakfast ready.'

'Tsampa cakes and honey?' Their food supplies had begun to run low and for the past month she had been breakfasting on the small unappetising cakes made from roasted ground barley, the tsampa flour that was the staple diet of their Bhutanese porters. 'I can hardly wait!'

But he had already gone out of the tent, leaving her with her sarcasm like alum on her lips. I'm becoming a real shrew, she told herself; and felt disgusted. Naturally good-tempered, she despised bitchery in herself as much as in others.

From outside she heard a few bars of music : Indian music made even more discordant to her ear by static. Nick Wilkins was fiddling with the radio, trying to get the morning news : Delhi spoke in a cracked voice across the mountains. There was a note of excitement in the voice, but she took little notice of it.

She dressed quickly in slacks, woollen shirt and sweater, washed in the basin of now tepid water that Tsering had brought in just before she had wakened, ran a comb through her short dark hair and put on some lipstick. She looked at herself in the cracked mirror that hung from the tent pole; even scarred by that mirror, she thought, I don't look too bad. Her hair had been cut by Jack with blunt scissors a month ago; the effect was only a little worse than the deliberate casualness of some professional hair styles. Her skin was still good, but if she looked closely she could see the faint lines round the corners of her eyes, the result of too many years' exposure to sun and wind. Nick Wilkins had told her that butterflies, at Himalayan heights, underwent a change of melanism, the dark brown pigment in their make-up asserting itself. If she stayed around here long enough she could finish up looking brown and wrinkled like the old women of the Himalayas. In the year of her début, when she had been one of the more energetic of London's butterflies, *Tatler* and *Queen* had described her as beautiful; but in those days in those magazines any daughter of the well-to-do whose eyes were straight and whose teeth had no gaps was described as beautiful. But *Life*, whose standards of beauty were higher and which did not have to depend on the British middle and upper classes for its circulation, had also said she was beautiful. They had done a colour story on Alpine plants and one of the illustrations had featured Jack as a collector. The caption had read : ' In the background is Marquis's beautiful wife, Eve.' She had been half-obscured by a clump of *Megacarpaea polyandra*, but one couldn't have everything; she had accepted the compliment and since then had been a regular subscriber to *Life*.

She guessed she was still beautiful, but the thought did not exercise her; her vanity, as well as her patience, had worn itself out in these remote corners of the world. The good bonework still showed in her face; her lips were still full and had not begun to dry out; her dark eyes still held their promise of passion. Oh, there's plenty of passion there, she told herself; only what the hell do I do with it? Her Cypriot grandmother had died early from too much exposure to the English climate and not enough attention from her phlegmatic English husband. She herself had suffered from a variety of climates and an Australian husband who had lately begun to turn into a stranger.

She turned from the distorted image of herself in the cracked mirror and went out of the tent into the cold sharp air, like a blade laid softly against the cheek, of this narrow valley on the north-eastern border of Bhutan.

Nick Wilkins, crouched by the radio outside his tent, looked up as she passed him on the way to the kitchen tent. 'How do you manage to look so fresh and beautiful first thing in the morning?'

She stopped, pleased at the compliment; it was almost as if Nick knew she needed some reassurance this morning. One did not expect such gratuitous compliments from Englishmen, especially an entomologist from Leeds. 'Nick, you're a continual surprise! Used you to say nice things to the girls back in Leeds first thing in the morning?'

The compliment had slipped out, an exclamation he now regretted. He turned his attention back to the radio, covering his retreat with the blunt awkward remarks that always made him sound surlier than he actually was.

'Never met any girls first thing in the morning back in Leeds. Except my sister and she always looked like the Bride of Frankenstein.' As always when he was embarrassed, the trace of northern accent reappeared in his voice; despite the careful cultivation of the last six years, ever since he had fled Leeds, it was still there wrapped round the root of his tongue. He envied Marquis, the Australian, whose flat vowels would never raise an eyebrow in Knightsbridge. In England, if you were going to be an outsider, it was always better to be a Commonwealth one.

Eve recognised the rebuff, but she tried again: 'Is your sister married?'

'Four kids.'

'That explains it.' But I shouldn't mind looking like the Bride of Frankenstein if I could have four kids. Or even one. She nodded at the radio. 'Any news?'

'The Chinese have crossed the border east of here, over into the North-East Frontier, and in the west, too, in Ladakh. Things look grim.'

He looked up at her, his squarely handsome face sober and worried. He was an entomologist, accustomed to the savagery of the insect world, but he knew little or nothing of what humans could do to each other. Even in Leeds it had been possible to remain innocent; the gangs and the prostitutes had never come to the quiet street on the edge of the city; the chapel singing had been the loudest noise heard at the week-end. He was twenty-eight years old and this was his first field trip to a territory where the amenities and veneer of civilisation were left behind at the border like so much excess baggage.

Eve sat down at the small table outside the kitchen tent. She was protected from the breeze that came down the valley, and the morning sun warmed her and took some of the edge off her mood. Tsering, cheerful as a lottery winner, a prizewinner every day no matter what his health or the weather was like, brought her the tsampa cakes and wild honey.

'Very good breakfast this morning, memsahib.' He said the same thing every morning, never realising the monotony of it; that was one of the advantages of not having a good command of English. 'Cooked special for you.'

Everyone else had had the same breakfast, but Eve kept up the pretence. 'Tsering, you are too good to me. Your wives will become jealous of me.'

'Wives don't know, memsahib.' He grinned and ducked back into the kitchen tent.

Eve looked at Wilkins. 'Jack heard the news?'

'He got the early bulletin. They're broadcasting every hour. Shows how serious it is.' Wilkins switched off the radio and came and sat beside her. He poured some tea into a mug and sat thoughtfully watching the spinning liquid as he stirred it. Eve had the feeling that he looked at everything through a microscope before he offered an opinion on it; he dissected even the most inconsequential happening as if it were some rare entomological discovery. But she knew that the Chinese crossing of the Indian border was more than an inconsequential happening. She had been on enough expeditions with entomologists to think of an analogy : it could be an invasion of Driver ants enlarged to the human level and just as implacably destructive. She said as much, and Wilkins nodded.

' I've never seen Driver ants at work, but I've seen pictures of what they've done. Given time, they can eat their way right through a farm. Crops, livestock and all. These Chinese could do the same to India.'

' What did Jack say?'

' Nothing much. That husband of yours isn't all Irish blarney. He can be as uncommunicative as one of these Himalayan lamas when he wants to be.'

She looked down towards where Marquis squatted on his heels beside Tom and Nancy Breck and the porters. The camp was pitched in a grass plot beneath a tall cliff; a stand of pine trees made an effective wind-break at one end of the camp. A torrent, fifty feet at its widest, split the narrow floor of the valley, tearing its way through a tumble of huge grey-green rocks in flying scarves of white water; a footbridge, which swayed like a banner when the wind was strong, was slung on thin poles across the raging waters just below the camp. Prayer-wheels, long copper cylinders that spun the morning sun into themselves like silken thread, stood at either end of the bridge; each time Eve crossed the precarious gangway she felt she was supported only by prayer, not the most comforting aid to her sceptical mind. Two gardens had been planted on a flat patch above the river, one for growing their own vegetables, the other for keeping alive the plants that had been collected. The porters were now digging up the plants and packing them in polythene bags. The bags were stacked to one side like so many plastic cabbages, and Marquis was checking the labels the Brecks had fixed to each of them.

Eve said, ' I think he'd move us out of here at once if he thought there was any real danger.' But she wondered if what she had said was only a wish and not a conviction.

' I doubt it,' said Wilkins, and looked aggressively at Marquis as the latter stood up, said something to the Brecks that made them laugh, then came up towards the kitchen tent. ' All you're interested in is your bloody rhododendrons. Right?'

Marquis looked at him quizzically, smiling with a good humour that only made Wilkins more annoyed. ' Something worrying you, Nick? Your hair shirt shrunk in the wash? Buck up, sport. You'll be home soon, back there in the Natural History Museum, swapping philosophy and dead flies with the girl students.'

' I'm worried about the Chinese. I think we should pack up and get out while the going's good.'

There was a basin of water on a rough wooden stand outside the kitchen tent; Marquis moved across to it and unhurriedly began to wash his hands. He had large hands, cracked and calloused from working among rocks, and his nails were broken and dirty. Eve had grown accustomed to them, but it had taken her some time to appreciate that the hands of a field botanist had much rougher usage than the gloved hands of her father when the latter had pottered among his roses in his Buckinghamshire garden. It still amazed her, after eight years, that those same coarse hands could be so gentle in their love-making.

' Relax, Nick. We'll be okay.' Marquis began to dry his hands. ' Bhutan is one of the few independent kingdoms left in this part of the world. Any part of the world, for that matter. It took a long distance look at democracy, through a cracked telescope, I reckon, and it turned thumbs down on the idea. I'm a republican up to my dandruff, but if I have to be caught in a kingdom, this is the one I'll vote for.'

' Hates England,' Eve said to Wilkins round a mouthful of cake and honey. ' Always sticks stamps on upside down on his letters. Hopes the Queen will have a rush of blood to the head and abdicate.'

Marquis grinned at her and went on : ' Bhutan is tied up with India for the rather back-handed relations it has with the rest of the world. And the Indians hang out bloody great signs to let everyone know they don't interfere here. For one thing you never see an Indian army man here in Bhutan, not even as an instructor. The Bhutanese were not being just bloody-minded when they took so long to make up their minds whether to give us visas or not. They reckon the less foreigners they allow in here, the more neutral they can claim to be. Neutrality is like chastity, Nick. Once it's gone, it's gone. Right, love?'

'I've never been neutral,' said Eve.

Marquis grinned and winked. Neutrality had once been a private privilege, taken for granted; now one had to produce proof, as if it were a concession given by belligerent outsiders. Civilisation had begun to learn the lesson of barbarism: never trust the silent bystander, give him a clout just for luck.

'I don't blame them,' he went on. 'There are only three-quarters of a million Bhutanese, most of them still living in the sixteenth century, still eating the lotus, unfrozen and not bought at bargain prices in any supermarket. On one side of them they've got seven hundred million Chows, itchy with all the propaganda that's sprinkled on them like lice powder, seven hundred million pairs of legs poised for the Great Leap Forward—and it could be in this direction. On the other side of them they have nearly five hundred million Indians— and if any man can tell what one Indian is going to do from one day to the next, let alone five hundred million of them, he's a better man than me, Gunga Din or Malcolm Muggeridge. The Bhutanese have been sitting on the fence so long they've got crotch-sore. But a sore crotch is preferable to a severed head. Once they start leaning one way, the other side is going to jump in here like a gate-crasher at a party. Only it will be no party for these poor bastards.' He gestured down at the porters. 'In no time at all they'll be like the Tibetans, also-rans in their own country. We had it in Ireland once, till we kicked out the English.'

'You were never in Ireland,' said Eve.

'I inherited the feeling of oppression. It's in my bones.'

'It looks to me as if the Chinese have already begun to gate-crash,' Wilkins said.

Marquis shook his head. 'Not here, Nick. This country is too small. The Chows don't want to lose face with all the uncommitted countries in Asia. I can't understand why they've come across the Indian border, it's not going to win friends and influence anyone for them. But maybe they reckon attacking someone almost as big as themselves won't lose them any popularity. Little blokes get a certain sadistic delight out of seeing big fellers knocking hell out of each other.'

Eve looked up at him and smiled sweetly and innocently, wondering when he had last had hell knocked out of him. She looked around the camp for some Dempsey or Joe Louis, but the camp was barren of heavyweights, and she went back to spreading honey on another tsampa cake.

Marquis cocked an eyebrow at her, wondering at her amusement, then he turned back to Wilkins. 'We're safe enough, Nick. We're a long way from where the fighting is, and in any case we'll be out of here in a fortnight.'

'So you can start preparing, Nick, for the shock of civilisation,' said Eve, wiping honey from her chin with a finger; and Marquis grinned at her.

Wilkins was aware of the undercurrent between the Marquises. He and the Brecks had discussed it once or twice when they had come back here to the main camp for their periodic reports to Marquis. Each scientist took two porters and moved out into an area of his own choosing, staying there for periods varying from two weeks to a month. The Brecks, both botanists, went together and since this was virtually a honeymoon trip did not seem to mind the isolation from the others. But Wilkins, though shy in speech, was naturally gregarious and always looked forward to his return to the main camp. On the last couple of visits he had noticed that the Marquises had become uncertain in their attitudes towards each other; they were like climbers negotiating the slopes in the mountains beyond the camp where new snow lay across old snow and an avalanche could start with one false step. He had an Englishman's distaste for viewing other people's private feelings and he was now wishing urgently for an end to the expedition. He had begun by liking the cheerful, argumentative Marquis, but he had made up his mind now he would not come on another trip with him. For one thing he envied and resented Marquis's ability to deal with almost anything that came up, his gift for leadership. And for another thing, there was Eve.

Then the Brecks came up from the garden, smiling at each other in the open, yet somehow secret way that, Eve had noticed, was international among young lovers. Perhaps she and Jack had once smiled like that at each other; she couldn't remember. Memory, if it hadn't yet turned sour, had begun to fail her when she needed it most. She turned to greet them, looking for herself and Jack in their faces.

'Boy, what a morning!' Tom Breck flung his arms wide, as if trying to split himself apart. All his actions and gestures were exaggerated, like those of a clockwork toy whose engine was too powerful. 'And we're packing up to go home!'

'Another month up here and you'd have your behind frozen off,' Marquis said. 'Ask the porters what it's like up here once the winds turn.'

'I'd like to take a couple of those guys back home with us.' Breck nodded down towards the porters laughing among themselves as they worked in the garden. 'Boy, they're happy!'

'They wouldn't be in Bucks County,' said Nancy Breck, practical as ever. She sat down at the table beside Eve, dipped a tsampa cake in the jar of honey and ate it. 'That's where we're going to live. Lots of tweedy types live there. Bucks County, P.A., is no place for a Bhutanese.'

Tom Breck grinned and sat down opposite his wife, looking at her with undisguised love. He was a tall thin boy who, with his crew-cut and his wispy blond beard, looked even younger than twenty-four. A Quaker from Colorado, he had spent six months in New York where he had met and married Nancy, and in his seven months here on the Indian sub-continent had lost none of his enthusiasm for the world at large. He was a bumbler, forgetful and unmethodical and a poor botanist; and several times Marquis had had to speak bluntly and harshly to him. Always Breck, unresentful of the dressing-down, genuinely apologetic, had gone back to work with the same cheerful enthusiasm. But already in nine months of marriage it had become evident to him that Nancy had come along just in time to save him from disaster. She was and would be his only means of survival; and unlike so many men in the same predicament, he was grateful for and not resentful of the fact. Tom Breck was a pacifist in the battle of the sexes.

'Bucks County sounds just like Bucks, England,' said Marquis. 'Eve's old man was always in tweeds. Even at our wedding. She had me all dolled up in striped pants from Moss

Bros. I looked like a good argument for living in sin, and her old man turned up looking like a second-hand sofa. Twice at the reception I nearly sat down on him.'

Eve smiled sweetly at him, not taking the bait. She had seen the glance pass between Wilkins and the Brecks. She wrapped herself in silence and a smile, aware for the first time that the coolness between Jack and herself was now apparent to the others. Oh, to be back in London, where you had the privacy of congestion! One was too naked here in the mountains. She wondered how the monks in the mountain monasteries, who valued introspection so much, managed to survive the exposure to each other.

Wilkins broke the moment, bluntly, like a man treading too heavily on thin ice. 'I wouldn't mind being tweedy and all in Bucks, England, or Bucks County, P.A., wherever that is. Anywhere, just so long as we're out of here.'

Tom Breck, the morning sun making newly-minted pennies of his dark glasses, looked up towards the mountains north and east of them. The valley ran north-east between tree-cloaked slopes that rose steeply towards the peaks of the Great Himalaya Range. Oak, birch and pine made a varied green pattern against the hillsides; clumps of rhododendrons were turning brown under the autumn chill; gentians that had miraculously survived the frosts lay like fragments of mirror among the rocks, reflecting the blue above. The morning wind, still blowing from the south although it was late October, snatched snow from the high peaks and drew it in skeins, miles long, across the shining sky. He had loved the Rockies in his home state, but they had never prepared him for the grandeur and breath-taking excitement of these mountains on the roof of the world.

'I'd be quite happy to stay here forever.' He looked across at Nancy, grinning boyishly, twisting his beard as if wringing water from it. 'What d'you say, honey?'

Nancy nodded. 'Maybe for a while. Not forever, though. It's too close to China. Sooner or later you'd be wanting to climb the mountains——' She nodded towards the north. 'This is as close as I want us ever to get.'

Breck's face had sobered. The light went out of his dark

glasses as he lowered his head, and a deep frown cut his brows above them. ' You're right, honey. I'd find nothing. Nothing that would help.'

Then he got up, awkwardly, quickly, and went back down to the porters in the garden. There was a moment which, to Eve, was so tangible that she felt she could *see* it; the wrong remark, even the wrong look, could have punctured it as a balloon might have been. She sat waiting for someone to say the wrong thing; but no one did. Marquis and Wilkins turned away from the table as naturally as if they had decided some moments ago to do so, and went down to join Breck and the porters.

Nancy Breck looked after them. ' Tom forgets sometimes. I mean, what happened to his parents. Then when he does remember——' She looked back to the north, to the mountains, with the skeins of wind-blown snow now turning to scimitars, riding like demons out of China. ' I mean, it's almost as if he *wanted* to forget——'

' Wouldn't that be best?'

Nancy shook her head. She was a big girl, strong and well-proportioned; she looked a farm girl from Minnesota rather than a doctor's daughter from Main Line Philadelphia. Later on she would be massive, perhaps even a little frightening; but now she was attractive, if you liked big healthy girls. And Tom Breck obviously did; and what anyone else thought didn't matter at all. She was not wearing her glasses now, and her big short-sighted brown eyes were dark with concentration.

' He *mustn't* forget! I'm not religious, God knows—there, that makes me sound contradictory, doesn't it? Are you religious, Eve? No, I shouldn't ask.' At times Nancy could lose herself and her audience in a flood of words; conversation became a one-way torrent of questions, opinions and *non-sequiturs*. ' Anyhow. Tom's parents died because they *were* religious. Marvellously so—I've read some of the letters they sent him. Every second line read like a prayer.'

I talked like this once, Eve was thinking, listening with only half an ear. I used all those extravagant adjectives; *non-sequiturs* were a regular diet with me. But I never had Nancy's passion, not about the world in general; perhaps that is the

American in her, they make an empire of their conscience. I only had (have?) passion for my husband, a most un-English habit.

She came back to the tail-end of Nancy's monologue: 'Don't you feel that way about Jack? Or shouldn't I ask?'

'No,' said Eve, and left Nancy to wonder if it was meant as an answer to either or both the questions. She turned to the kitchen tent, calling to Tsering to bring her more tea.

'Sorry.' Nancy stood up, mumbled something, then walked away towards her tent, stumbling a little as if embarrassment had only added to her myopia to make her almost blind.

Eve sat alone at the rough table, warming her hands round the fresh mug of tea Tsering had brought her. She wanted to run after Nancy, apologise for the rudeness of her answer; but that would only lead to explanation, and she would never be able to explain to anyone what had gone wrong between herself and Jack. Because she hated scenes, she had done her best to keep their conflict to themselves; they had had one or two fierce rows, but they had always been in their tent and never while Wilkins and the Brecks had been in camp. She knew that Nimchu and the other main camp porters must have heard the rows and discussed them; but she knew also that the Bhutanese would not have gossiped with the Englishman and the Americans. It shocked and embarrassed her to the point of sickness to discover now that Nancy knew that all was not well between her and Jack. To have Nick and Tom know could somehow be ignored. To have another woman, one so newly and happily married, know was almost unbearable.

Tsering hovered behind her, his round fat face split in the perpetual smile that made life seem one huge joke. His name, Tsering Yeshe, meant Long Lived Wisdom; he had never shown any signs of being wise, unless constant cheerfulness showed a wisdom of acceptance of what life offered. He was proud of his attraction for women, and on the trek out he had almost shouted himself hoarse calling to every woman he had passed, even those who were sometimes half a mile away, standing like dark storks in the flooded rice paddies. Eve had no idea how old he was and he himself could only guess; but he had been accompanying expeditions here in the Himalayas, in Nepal, Sikkim and his native Bhutan, every year since the end of World War Two. He had a wife and four children back at Dzongsa Dzong on the Indian border, but he hardly ever saw them; he claimed three other wives in various parts of the country, but Eve suspected these were inventions to bolster his reputation. Eve, a wife driven by her own needs to accompany her husband wherever he went, wondered what Tsering's wife felt about his long absences.

'More cake, memsahib? More tea?' Tsering liked his women fat, and he thought the memsahib much too thin for a really beautiful woman. She had good breasts, but the rest of her was much too flat for a woman who would be really good to make love to. He wondered if that was why the sahib sometimes shouted at the memsahib when they were alone in their tent. 'You do not eat enough, memsahib.'

'You've told me that, Tsering. If I ate as much as you try to push into me, we'd soon run out of food. How are the stores, anyway?' It was her job to supervise the stores. Even on their first expedition she had insisted that she be given a job and as time had gone by she had become an efficient and reliable supply officer.

Tsering made a face and ran a greasy hand over his close-cropped black hair. Men and women here in Bhutan all wore the same close-cropped style, and when Eve had first arrived in the country she had several times been confused as to what sex she was talking to. 'Meat is almost gone, memsahib. Rice, too. Maybe the sahib better shoot something. Yesterday I saw gooral up on hill.' He nodded back at the tangled hills that, like a green waterfall, tumbled down into the pit of the valley.

Eve did not particularly like the meat of the gooral, the Himalayan chamois, but she had tasted worse goats' meat and it was at least better than some of the village sheep they had bought on their way out. 'I'll speak to the sahib. And you'd better check again on the rice. If it's really low, we may have to send Chungma and Tashi back down the valley to buy some at Sham Dzong.'

That was two days' walk: four days there and back. Jack would consider it a waste of time and two men. If she played her stores carefully, she might have them all out of here within a week.

She smiled to herself, like a schoolgirl who was about to bring the holidays forward by burning down the school.

2

Marquis was secretly pleased when Eve told him they needed more meat and would he try for the gooral. There were still some botanical specimens that had to be gathered to make the collection complete, and time was running out; snow was already beginning to fall heavily on the high peaks, and any day now the winds would swing to the north to bring blizzards. On top of that he had been more disturbed than he had shown by this morning's news on the radio. He was not a fool, and he knew that the Chinese Reds had long regarded Ladakh, Nepal, Sikkim, Bhutan and the North-East Frontier Agency as only extensions of Tibet. But he wanted at least another week; he wanted to complete the collection, his best ever. He had fought against the idea, was still fighting it, but this might be his last expedition. He wanted it to be one that botanists at least would remember.

But now only the gooral was on his mind; or so he told himself. He always welcomed the opportunity to hunt game, and it eased his conscience when the hunt was for food and not just for sport. He would go out again this afternoon and collect the *swertia racemosa* he had seen yesterday in the ravine farther up the valley.

He was now a mile above the camp, moving up a narrow track through a stand of evergreen oak. The valley here was almost narrow enough to be called a gorge, a cleft between two steep wooded ridges; the river raced down the floor of the valley, twisting and turning like a rusted knife cutting its way out of the mountains. He knew that the river sped on to join other mountain streams, became a slower-moving river that merged into the Brahmaputra, a procession of waters that wended their majestic way, carrying the prayers, dreams and excreta of men, down to the Bay of Bengal over a thousand miles away. Rivers, as well as mountains, had always fascinated him; he had a voice like a bookmaker's lament, but his heart always rang with a Caruso-note when he came for the

first time on a river. Heaven was a high mountain peak somewhere and he would reach it by way of a river that flowed
uphill. It thrilled him to walk beside such a stream as this
one, to look at the water tearing its way over the rocks and
to see it as the birth pangs of a giant river that, a thousand
miles away, carried ships to the sea. He was passionately
interested in everything that grew in nature: plants, trees,
rivers. And once, in South America, he had seen the birth of
a mountain as a volcano had exploded out of the belly of a
plain.

The opposite ridge was bathed in sunlight, the trees glittering like the plumage of some giant green bird, but this side of
the valley had never seen the sun and was dank and cold.
Strangers to the Himalayas were always surprised at the
difference in temperature between a sunny slope and one
where the sun never reached; he remembered Nancy Breck's
shock when she had taken a sun and shade reading and found
a difference of 30 degrees centigrade. He shivered now as he
trudged up beneath the trees. But this was where he would
find the gooral; it did not like the sun. A Monal pheasant
broke from a clump of rhododendron ahead of him and
flashed like a huge jewel as it crossed to the opposite ridge,
but he resisted the quick impulse to shoot at it. The .30
Double would just blow the bird to pieces, and he had never
been able to bring himself to kill just for killing's sake.

He breathed deeply as he walked, enjoying the thin sharp
air in his nose and throat. Unlike other expedition leaders to
remote places, he had never written a book on his experiences,
had never tried to explain the mystique that brought him to
these high mountains, took him to tropical jungles or, once, had
taken him to the loneliness of the Australian Centre. He was a
botanist by profession and it was his job to collect plant
specimens; it was a job he enjoyed and one in which he knew
he had a high reputation. But deep in his heart, and he was a
man of more secrets than even Eve suspected, he knew that
the botanical searches were now more of an excuse for an
escape from civilisation. Not civilisation, in itself, although
he had no deep love of it; no city could ever bring on the
euphoria that the isolation of those mountains could give him.
He wanted to escape from what civilisation meant: surrender

to Eve and her money, a scarecrow man papered over with his wife's cheques. During their brief engagement he had referred to her as his fiancée; it was a joke that had soon gone sour, like a penny on the tongue. She always contributed a major part of the finance of these expeditions, but he had now convinced himself that this was her money being spent in a good cause, not just in keeping a husband. Which was what would happen to him if he gave in to her and retired to pottering about on the family estate in Buckinghamshire. Civilisation had once meant something else again, a semi-detached morgue in a drab suburb of Sydney where his mother and his two sisters had done their best to lay him out with cold looks of disapproval. Only his father, a rebel who couldn't afford a flag, drunk every Saturday on republicanism and three bottles of Resch's Pilsener, had never complained; but he had never really understood why any man should choose to leave the greatest bloody country in the world, Australia. His parents had worked their fingers bare of prints to put him through university; they had neither understood nor forgiven him when he had changed from law to botany at the end of his first year. In the end he had run away because he knew he was in their debt and he would never be able to repay them. They were dead now, but his conscience would give a free ride to their ghosts for the rest of his life.

Now Eve, not yet a ghost, had swung a leg over his conscience. And he felt the weight of her more than that of his parents. The time had come when he owed her a decision. He could not expect her to go on accompanying him forever to the ends of the earth and comfort; she was a woman who had been brought up in comfort and it had surprised him that she had borne so long the hardships of their trips without complaint. But maybe that was her heritage: English boarding schools, English plumbing, English cooking, bred pioneers. The Stoics of ancient Greece would have tossed in the towel, taken out life subscriptions to hedonism, if they had ever been exposed to life in some of the more benighted ancestral halls of England.

There was also the matter of children.

She had talked about having a family almost from the

moment they had decided to marry. She had then been a girl of impulsive ideas and quick decisions; it had shocked him, a slow starter at romance, to learn how eager she had been, first, to have him make love to her, then, to have him marry her. He had never met anyone like her: she exploded love like a boxful of fireworks. They had met, become lovers, married and she had started talking about a family all within six weeks.

That had been in the autumn of 1954. He had taken a rare holiday and gone to Switzerland for some climbing. He had climbed the Mönch and in the late evening come back to the small hotel where he was staying. In those days English tourists were still limited in their travel allowance and at even the cheapest hotel one met a very mixed bag of visitors. When he had gone into the hotel's small bar the only vacant seat had been beside hers. He had not been then, and still was not, a ladies' man; but his easy-going, casual approach attracted a lot of women. It had attracted Eve and she had attracted him. Within forty-eight hours they had been lovers and were in love: it had been that sort of romance.

It had taken him the same time to discover whose daughter she was and how much money she had. ' Sir Humphrey Aidan —you're *his* daughter? You mean I've been to bed with the Bank of England?'

' Da-ahling, he has nothing to do with the Bank of England.' She sat up in bed and ran a hand through her tousled hair. In those days she wore it long, down to her shoulders. It was the way he still liked it, and he hated it when he had to chop it short for her when they were out on these field trips. ' Da-ahling, we're not going to waste our time talking about money, are we? I hate people who have a *thing* about money.'

' A *thing*? What d'you mean? Oh, if only my dad was here——'

' Thank God he's not. Can I help the bed I was born in? Look at me, stark. Am I any different from the daughter of some man on the dole?'

' Look, love——'

' I absolutely *adore* it when you call me love. It's such a divine change after da-ahling. In my set everyone——'

' Set? You're the sort who belongs to a set?'

'Da-ahling, all right then, my *crowd*. The people I go *around* with.' She shook her head, suddenly sober. 'Somehow I don't think you're going to like them.'

He ignored that and walked to the window to look out at Jungfrau standing out like a mountain of glass against the brilliant sky. A party of four climbers was working its way up the lower slopes of the mountain; that was what he should have done, concentrated on climbing. She lay back on the bed and looked at him, already loving him with a depth of feeling that surprised even herself. 'Have you ever been in love before?'

He looked back at her, then at last nodded. 'Twice. With the same girl.'

'I didn't say how many times have you *made* love——'

'I know you didn't. I fell in love with this girl twice. Once when she was sixteen. Then she went off with another bloke, and I swore off love for life, took the pledge and a double dose of bromide. Then I met her again when she was twenty and by then the bromide had worn off, I fell in love with her again.'

'You were *still* in love with her——'

He shook his head. 'No, it was a new feeling. It can happen. Fall in love all over again, I mean.'

'What was she like? She must have been something special, to make you fall in love with her twice.'

'She was no raving beauty. She had a mouth like an armpit full of loose teeth, and though her eyes weren't exactly crossed they had designs on each other——' She threw a pillow at him. He caught it and came and sat back on the bed beside her. 'Look, love, Aussies have no great reputation as lovers. The only time an Aussie ever compliments a woman, he's asking for a loan or she's got a gun at his head. But one thing we do know—never tell your current girl friend what the last one looked like. Always make out she was about as sexy as a porridge doll. One thing a woman can't stand is to look in a mirror and see another woman's face there.'

'Who told you that?'

He grinned. 'My last girl.'

'I wish Mummy was still alive to meet you. She would

have absolutely *adored* you. But you and Daddy should get on. You have something in common.'

'You mean he has an overdraft, too?'

She laughed. 'I wouldn't know about that, da-ahling. No, he really is like you. He's frightfully interested in flowers. He grows roses.'

He looked as if he was about to swear, then suddenly he laughed and slapped her on the rump. 'Love, the last thing I ever want to do is raise bloody roses. I *collect* plants, not grow them. A lot of botanists do like to grow things, but not me. I'm like the obstetrician who doesn't like to be surrounded by kids.'

'Oh,' she said, linking her hands behind his neck, 'I was hoping we'd have lots of kids. We could start now.'

Two days later he had introduced her to climbing and she took to it as if she had been born on a mountain. He was an expert climber and had been invited to lead several mountaineering expeditions. But always he had found excuses and in the end he had not been asked to join a climbing team even as a member. He knew he had been branded with a reputation for stand-offishness, a climber who considered himself too good to climb with others. He had let the libel stand because it was better than broadcasting the truth. As time had gone on he had wondered if Eve had ever begun to suspect the truth.

He feared leadership. All his life, even as a boy at school, he had been big and confident-looking : a born leader, everyone had said. He had been captain of the school cricket and rugger teams in his last year and they had been the most disastrous seasons in the school's history; but no one had blamed him and instead had commiserated with him on the poor material he had been given. At university he had been elected captain of the rugger team and the only two matches the team had won had been when he was out of action through injury. Again no one had blamed him, but by then he had come to know the truth about himself.

Still he had been plagued by people wanting to elect him a leader. Or, what was just as bad, wanting to dispute his title to leadership. It never seemed to matter to them that he had never been known to nominate himself for any leader's job :

they took it for granted that he was in the running and began attacking him sometimes even before his name was mentioned. They were invariably small men : the Big Bastard, as he knew he was called, was always fair game for small men. Sometimes he had wished a big man would dispute his title to leader : he couldn't bring himself to throw a punch or two at the small men, even if they had attacked him in pairs. So he had retreated farther and farther, never committing himself to any expedition larger than this current one, comfortable in the thought that in such circumstances he was not called upon to be responsible for any man's life. In small groups such as this each man was accountable for himself and indeed resented that it should be otherwise. Leadership of such an expedition often entailed no more than being responsible for the cost and the day-to-day running of the camp.

But he had regretted missing the opportunity to climb with some of the top mountaineering teams. Hunt had passed him over for the Everest ascent the year before, and his omission from other teams had been conspicuous to those who knew of his ability. He regretted the reputation he had and it worried him. He did not like arrogance in others and it disturbed him to know he was branded with the same sin.

He had also been worried when Eve had insisted she was going to accompany him on the trip to Ruwenzori, wondering if he would have the patience to tolerate her when he was immersed in his work; but she had proved more help than hindrance, and from then on he had never thought of making a trip without her. Her father had died a year after their marriage, leaving her without any close relatives and a fortune that came from shipping and mining. The first fact had bound her closer to him, the second was a barrier that kept pushing itself between them. He was depressed, weighed down by his wife's wealth, a form of slavery dreamed of by most men who don't know the value of their freedom.

But now, as it so often did, his depression suddenly lifted. Up ahead he saw the gooral working its way along the steep slope above him. Everything else now dropped out of his mind. He stopped, turning slowly as the gooral, still unaware of him, moved with unhurried and uncanny agility among the rocks and trees on the precipitous slope of the hill. It was no use going up there after it : the gooral would stop, look at him curiously, then be gone out of sight while he was still trying to find a foothold on the hillside. He had learned long ago never act like a goat to catch a goat. He would have to be patient, hope that the animal would come down closer within range. He started up the hill, all his concentration focused on the grey moving shape above him, his ears only half-hearing the other sounds here in the gorge : the hissing rumble of the racing river, the soft explosion of a pheasant taking off from a bush close by, the rattle of falling stones disturbed by the gooral as it bounded from one spot to another.

It worked its way above and past him, began moving back down the gorge towards the camp. He turned and began to follow it, keeping to the track and the cover of the trees. Sometimes it would disappear behind a screen of trees or bushes, and a moment later it would come into view again, still moving down towards the camp. It was lower down the hill now and he could see that it was a male and a big one. Both male and female gooral had horns and often it was difficult to tell which was which. But Marquis had remarkably good eyesight and on this beast he could see the thicker horns and the way they diverged outwards, the mark of the male.

The breeze had freshened and was now coming down the gorge, putting him at a disadvantage. He glanced up anxiously when he saw the gooral stop and look down towards him ; he froze, wondering if it had caught his scent and was about to take off farther up the hill. He kept absolutely still, remembering the cardinal rule that even some experienced hunters often forgot in their excitement : that a wild animal, having no education in such things, was more times than not unable to distinguish a man at a glance unless the latter betrayed himself by some movement. To the gooral he could be no more than another object among the trees and rocks which surrounded him. Only his scent, if it got to the gooral, would give him away. The gooral would not recognise the scent, but it would be a strange one and he would be warned.

Then the animal bent down, wrenched at a shrub and a moment later, still chewing, moved on. Marquis relaxed, then he too began to move on. He knew now that the gooral could not smell him, despite the fact that the breeze was blowing from behind him. This often happened in these narrow valleys of the Himalayas : the breeze created its own cross-currents by bouncing off the steep hills and a scent could be lost within a hundred yards.

The gooral was moving slowly down the hillside, and Marquis quickened his pace. The camp would soon be in sight, round the next bend in the valley, and he wanted to get his shot in before the gooral sighted the camp and was possibly frightened by some of the moving figures it would see down there. He was sweating a little with excitement, but his hands were cold from the breeze, which had a rumour of snow on it, and he kept blowing on his right hand, trying to get some flexibility into his trigger finger. The breeze was quickening by the minute, and once he turned his head it caught at his eye, making it water. Autumn was not the best time for hunting in these mountains : the cold fingers, the chill of the metal against the cheek, the wind that watered the eyes, none of it made for easy marksmanship.

The gooral stopped again, its head raised; it gave a hissing whistle, a sign that it was frightened. Then suddenly it bounded down the hill, racing with incredible swiftness ahead of the stones and small rocks disturbed by its progress. The hillside was open here and Marquis had a clear view of the animal as it raced down at right angles to him. Something had frightened the gooral, but there was no time to look for what it was; he raised his gun, tracking a little ahead of the flying gooral, then let go. The shot reverberated around the narrow valley, its echoes dying away quickly as the breeze caught them; the gooral missed its step, then turned a somersault and went plunging down to finish up against a rock just above the path. Marquis felt the thrill that a good shot always gave him. He moved down the path towards the dead gooral, the gun held loosely in one hand, relaxed and happy and forgetful of everything but what he had just done. He would not boast of his shot, but he never denied to himself the pride that he felt. He might have seemed less self-confident if he had talked more about his accomplishments, but at thirty-six a man found it difficult to change the habits and faults of a lifetime. A leopard couldn't change his spots. . . .

The leopard! He knew now what had frightened the

gooral. He turned his head quickly, and the breeze, now a rising wind, sliced at his eyes. His gaze dimmed with tears, but not before he recognised the leopard coming down the hillside in smooth bounding strides that he knew would culminate in a great leap to bring the beast crashing down on him. He whipped up the gun, but even as he did he knew the shot would be useless : he could not see a thing.

Then he felt the bullets rip the air inches above his head and he ducked. The short burst of automatic fire started the valley thundering; again the echoes were snatched away by the wind. But he heard nothing, only felt the thud on the ground as the leopard landed less than a yard from him; his eyes suddenly cleared, and he stepped back as the dying beast reached out for him with a weakly savage paw. He stood on shivering legs, staring down at the leopard as it snarled up at him, coughing angrily in its throat, its jaws working to get at him, its eyes yellow with a fierceness about which its body could do nothing. Then the head dropped and it was dead.

'Jolly lucky shot, that. I almost blew your head off, instead of hitting him. Just as well you ducked, old man.'

Marquis turned, in control of himself again. On the other side of the river stood an Indian soldier, a Sten gun held loosely in the crook of his arm. Beside him, his hands bound together, was a second soldier, a Chinese.

TWO

'Is there any way of crossing this river?' the Indian asked.

Marquis nodded downstream. 'There's a bridge down opposite our camp.'

'Jolly good.' They had to shout to make themselves heard above the hiss of the water as it boiled past the rocks that tried to block its path. 'Are you going back there now?'

Marquis looked down at the dead leopard, then at the gooral still wedged in above the rock. He would send Nimchu and a couple of the other porters back for them. The shots would have frightened off any other game that might be about, and the carcasses would be safe for some time. In any case he had to find out what the Indian and the Chinese were doing here.

He walked back along the bank of the river, watching the other two men as they picked their way along the narrow track on the other side. The Chinese walked with his head bent; with his hands tied in front of him he looked like a man deep in meditative prayer. The Indian kept glancing across at Marquis, smiling and nodding like a man throwing silent greetings across a crowded room. Occasionally he prodded the man in front of him with the barrel of his Sten gun, but the Chinese either ignored it or did not feel it. Captor and captive, it was obvious to Marquis even at this distance that they hated each other's guts.

Before they reached the camp, Eve, Nimchu and three of the porters had come up the track to meet them. 'What's the matter? I heard the shots——' Then Eve looked across the river and saw the two strangers as they came round an outcrop of rock. She saw the Sten gun carried by the Indian, and she looked quickly at Marquis to see if he had been wounded. 'Did he shoot at you?'

He shook his head, warmed by her concern for him. He took the hand she had put out to him, and quickly told her what had happened. He spoke to the porters, telling them to collect the dead beasts; then, still hand in hand with Eve, he continued on towards the camp. She kept glancing across towards the two men opposite, and Marquis saw the Indian smile at her and incline his head in a slight bow. The Chinese remained uninterested.

'Who are they?' He could feel the tightness of her fingers on his. 'The shorter one's Chinese, isn't he?'

'I think so. He's too big for a Bhutanese or a Sherpa.' He looked across at the baggy grey uniform and the cap with earflaps that the man wore. 'I've never seen a Chinese uniform before. If he's a Red, he's out of his territory. So's the Indian, for that matter.'

'What about the Indian? He looks pretty pleased with himself.'

'Maybe he's just glad to see us.'

'Are you glad to see him?'

He didn't answer that, just pressed her fingers. They came into the camp and walked down to the end of the bridge to wait for the two strangers as they crossed it. The Chinese slipped once or twice as the narrow catwalk swayed beneath him and, with his hands tied together, had trouble in keeping his balance; but the Indian made no attempt to help him, just paused and watched as if he would be pleased to see the Chinese topple over on to the rocks and be swept away by the rushing cataract. Then, wet from the spray flung up from below the bridge, they were clambering up the bank and Marquis and Eve advanced to meet them. The Indian slung his Sten gun over one shoulder, saluted Eve and put out his hand to Marquis.

'Awfully pleased to meet you.' His accent was high and fluting, a northern Indian provinces accent overlaid with an Oxford exaggeration that was now out of date. It suggested a languid world that was also gone : tea at four, Ascot hats in a Delhi garden, polo, gossip, and a shoving match among the rajahs to see who could stand closest to the British Raj. But the hand the Indian put out was not languid : the fingers were almost as strong as Marquis's own. 'I am Lieutenant-Colonel Dalpat Singh, Indian Army. This is General Li Bu-fang, Chinese Army.' His black eyes gleamed with amusement. 'The wrong Chinese Army, I'm afraid. He's not one of Chiang Kai-shek's chaps, are you, old man?' He looked at the Chinese, who turned his head away and stared down the valley. Singh looked back at Marquis and Eve. 'Chinese politeness died out with Communism. It's always the way when one allows the masses to take over.'

Marquis, a paid-up member of the masses, ignored the Indian's remark and introduced himself and Eve. 'You're out of your territory, aren't you, Colonel?'

'Oh, indeed we are. Both of us.' He looked at the Chinese again, but the latter still remained detached from them, continuing to stare down the valley as if waiting patiently for someone to come. For a moment a flush of temper stained the Indian's face, then he shrugged and smiled. He was a handsome man, tall and well-built, his jowls and waist perhaps a little soft and thick for a soldier in the field. He wore thick woollen khaki battle-dress with his badges of rank woven on the shoulder-straps, and a chocolate-brown turban that was stained with blood from a dried cut above his right eye. The eyes themselves were black and amused, almost mocking: they would have seen the human in Indra, the god who drank ambrosia for no other reason but to get drunk. But now, too, they were tired eyes: the Indian had almost reached the point of exhaustion where he would begin to mock himself. 'I wonder if we might have a cup of tea? We haven't had a bite to eat since yesterday at noon.'

Marquis led them up to the camp, and soon Tsering brought them tea, tsampa cakes, honey and fruit. At first it looked as if the Chinese would refuse to eat; then he seemed to make up his mind that it was pointless to starve himself to death. He sat down at the rough table opposite Singh and awkwardly, with his hands still bound, began to eat. The Indian himself was obviously famished and had begun to eat as soon as the food was put in front of him.

While they ate, Marquis and Eve left them alone. Nimchu and the other porters had now returned to camp with the leopard and the gooral. Tsering came out of his kitchen tent with a long knife that he sharpened on a stone. He stopped once, to look up at the Chinese general; he ran the blade along his thumb, then looked at Nimchu. The latter shook his head; and Tsering shrugged like a disappointed man. Then he set to work on the two carcasses, skinning them with the practised hand of a man who had been doing this since he was a child.

As he slit the throat of the leopard, he glanced once more up at the Chinese; he grinned and committed murder by proxy. Nimchu and the other porters had cast curious, hostile glances up at the two strangers outside the kitchen tent, but then they had gone back to work digging up plants from the garden. Marquis, who hadn't seen Tsering's gestures, looked down at Nimchu and the others, wondering what they thought of these invaders.

'I'd like to keep the leopard skin,' Eve said. 'It would make a nice handbag.'

'Too many holes in it. He put about five bullets into it. He's a handy man with that Sten gun. It wasn't an easy shot. I mean, if he wanted to miss me.'

'You're lucky he is handy with it.' She looked down at the leopard, now almost divested of its skin, and shuddered. The bloody carcass could have been Jack's. 'He could have killed you, darling.'

He nodded, not wanting to disturb her further by telling her how close he had come to death. He had not yet thanked the Indian for saving his life, but he wanted to do it when and if he had a moment alone with him. For some reason he could not name, he did not want to thank Singh in front of the Chinese. He remembered something he had read : that the victors should never acknowledge their indebtedness to each other in front of the defeated enemy : it was a sign of weakness and at once gave the enemy hope for revenge. It was probably a Roman or a Chinese or a Frenchman who had written it; the English and the Americans were too sentimental about their enemies once they were defeated; and it could not have been a Russian or a German, he found them unreadable. And it could not have been an Irishman or an Australian : whenever they won anything, they then started a fight amongst themselves.

He looked up towards the kitchen tent at the two men, the tall Indian and the thickset Chinese each ignoring the other as he ate, each self-contained in a sort of national arrogance.

Then he looked down at the leopard, grudgingly admiring the dead beast. Its long tail, so beautiful when the animal was alive, now lay like a coil of frayed rope on the grass; the skin, no longer living, already looked as if it had lost its sheen. The head was still attached to the body and now the skin had been peeled away he could see the amazing muscular development of the neck, thick as that of some tigresses he had seen, even though the tigresses must have been at least twice the weight of this graceful beast. The leopard would have torn him to pieces before he could have cleared his eyes of the tears that had blinded him.

'What actually happened?' Eve asked; and when he told her she said, 'That wouldn't happen back in Kensington.'

'Oh, I don't know. The Jaguars on Cromwell Road are just as lethal.'

He's dodging the argument again, she thought; but before she could say anything Wilkins and the Brecks were coming across the bridge.

'We heard some shots. Didn't sound like rifle shots——' Then they all looked across at the kitchen tent and saw the two strangers. It was Tom Breck who said, 'Soldiers? Up here?'

'Whatever happened to Bhutan's neutrality?' said Wilkins, slipping his sarcasm out of its sheath for a moment.

Marquis glanced at him, and Eve prepared herself for a sharp exchange between the two men. She saw Jack's eyes darken as they always did when temper gripped him; he had the Irish weakness of wearing his emotions on his face. Then he turned away, casually, and said, 'Let's find out.'

He led the way up to the kitchen tent. He introduced Wilkins and the Brecks, then he sat down at the head of the table and looked at the Indian. 'Now maybe you'd better put us in the picture, Colonel.' He kept the note of worry out of his voice and hoped that his expression was equally bland. 'If our camp is going to be turned into a battleground, we'd like to get to hell out of it.'

'Of course.' Singh leaned back in his chair, crossing his legs; unshaven, unwashed, he still carried an air of authority with him. And an air of something else, Marquis thought. An out-of-date peacock pride? A demolished splendour? Marquis couldn't quite put his finger on it. He had the feeling that he was looking at a ghost that was only too substantial, that mocked its own grave. The Taj Mahal could have been turned into a bowling alley, but this man would still go there.

Singh took the cigarette Wilkins offered him, lit it and drew on it with relish. Wilkins offered the packet to the Chinese, but the latter shook his head. Singh blew out smoke, then looked at the cigarette between his long elegant fingers. ' Ah, Benson and Hedges. Jolly good.'

' My last packet.' They were Wilkins's one snob symbol : he couldn't afford the Savile Row suit, the Aston Martin. He had bought a dozen cartons just before leaving London and had severely rationed himself to a certain number of cigarettes a day. It was the story of his life : even his snobbery had to be on the bargain-rate level.

' I used to smoke them when I was at Oxford. Before the war they used to make a special cigarette for my father. He was very particular about his pleasures. Pleasure, he used to say, was the foretaste of Heaven. He had sixty wives, including my dear mother. He expected a very special Heaven, too, I'm afraid.' Singh looked at Marquis. ' You don't smoke, old chap?'

' My husband is afraid of lung cancer,' said Eve, drawing on her own cigarette. ' He doesn't believe in hastening towards Heaven.'

' It is a pity all pleasures have their price. Or don't you agree, Mr. Marquis?'

Marquis saw the Chinese flick a quick glance at the Indian, then the almond eyes were still again, staring down at the bound hands resting on the table in front of him. The inscrutable bloody Orient was not as inscrutable as it thought : behind the impassive face Marquis had glimpsed a mind that was lively and (or was he wrong?) even optimistic. He jerked a thumb at the Chinese. ' Does he speak English?'

' I don't know, old chap. I've been chatting to him for almost eighteen hours now, but I haven't got a word out of him. Later on, when I feel a little stronger, I'll have a real chin-wag with him.' There was no mistaking his meaning. He stared at the Chinese, his dark face turning to wood; for all his educated accent and his out-of-date schoolboy slang, Singh looked to Marquis as if he could be as cruel and direct as any wild tribesman of the Indian hills. He had been brought up on pig-sticking; he could turn the lance to other uses. Then abruptly Singh seemed to remember the others, and he looked back at them and smiled. 'But to put you in the picture. I'm afraid it is not a jolly one.'

'I knew it,' said Wilkins, but he might just as well have not spoken for all the notice the others took of him. They all leaned forward, concerned with what Singh might have to tell them. Marquis saw the eyes of the Chinese shine for a moment, but the muscles of the face remained fixed. But the eyes had given Li Bu-fang away: he was laughing at them.

'These chaps,' Singh nodded at Li Bu-fang, 'have set up some posts right across the border here in Bhutan. At least three, possibly more. Border posts with quite a large number of men manning them. Fifty or sixty men to a post. They're building up for something.'

'Invasion,' said Nancy, and put on her glasses to look at the Chinese with an expression that startled Eve with its intensity.

'That doesn't explain what you're doing here,' said Marquis.

The Indian's face stiffened again, as it had when he had looked at the Chinese a moment ago. He looked obliquely at Marquis, seeming to recognise for the first time that he was not really wanted here. At the same time it became obvious to Marquis that Singh was a man who expected to be welcomed wherever he went. Not the expectation of a man looking for popularity, like a politician or pop singer on the make, but that of a man *accustomed* to being welcomed. You're not only in the wrong country, Marquis thought, you're in the wrong century.

'No, it doesn't, does it? Do I have to explain to you, Mr. Marquis?'

Everyone looked at Marquis, embarrassed by the sudden tension between the two men. Even the Chinese looked up for a moment, then his gaze quickly slid back to his hands. Marquis knew then that Li Bu-fang could speak English and he wondered for a moment if he should continue this discussion, which could become an argument, in front of the Chinese. Then he mentally shrugged: the man was the Indian's prisoner and the latter's concern.

'You are in *my* camp, Colonel. Foreign military men in uniform are prohibited visitors to this country—I'm sure you know that as well as I do, and that it applies to Indians as much as Chinese. I could get it in the neck for harbouring you. That's why I think I'm entitled to an explanation.'

Eve hesitated, then she said, 'I think my husband is right.'

Singh looked about the table, at Wilkins and the Brecks, who nodded their agreement; then he looked back at Marquis. 'I was—I *am* the commander of a battalion that has been doing border duty in the North-East Frontier Agency for the past two months. A week ago we were overrun by a brigade of Chinese. I escaped with some of my men, eighteen to be exact——' He spoke directly to Marquis, as if the latter was the one he felt might judge him too harshly : cowardice was a disease of lesser men. 'I did not run away, Mr. Marquis. It was the circumstances of the fighting in the mountains that I was one of those who were cut off.'

'I'm not criticising you, Colonel,' Marquis said quietly. 'Go on.'

Singh hesitated, then he went on : 'Our only way of escape was west over the mountains into Bhutan. Yesterday morning we came upon the first of the Chinese border posts, well inside the border. We managed to avoid them, but unfortunately we then ran into a second post. We had quite a scrap, didn't we, old chap?'

Li Bu-fang took no notice. He could have been a man waiting on a railway station for a train that he knew was bound to come; Singh and the others were passengers without tickets, strangers who didn't interest him. There was a monotony about his indifference that was beginning to irritate Marquis : the latter looked back at Singh with a little more sympathy.

'All my men were killed, but we managed to kill most of the enemy—those we didn't kill took to the hills, as the saying has it.' He glanced up at the towering mountains to the north. 'That left my friend and me facing each other, the two most senior men of the little battle. A survival of the most fitting, as you might say. I took him prisoner. I'm beginning to wish he had volunteered for suicide. He is a damn' nuisance, you know.'

'Why didn't you let *him* make for the hills?' Breck asked.

' He is a general, Mr.—Breck? How often does one capture a general? Especially a Chinese general.'

' How do you know he's a general?' Wilkins said. ' He has no badges of rank.'

Singh smiled and looked at Li Bu-fang. ' I asked him his rank. Didn't I, old chap?' The Chinese lifted his head a little and Marquis saw the mark on his throat, as if a cord or something had been tightened round it. ' I told you I wished he had preferred suicide. But he didn't. The Chinese are supposed to be awfully fatalistic about dying, but not this chappie. I think the Communists are much more realistic and practical. Since they don't believe in Heaven, a dead comrade is a—shall we say a dead loss?' He smiled around at them; he was proud of his English colloquialisms; the years at Oxford hadn't been wasted. ' When I tried a little persuasion, he told me what I wanted to know. Then I found some papers——' He stopped as Nancy leaned forward.

' Did he tell you in English?' Nancy looked at the Chinese with new interest.

' No, Hindi. He doesn't speak it awfully well, but he does speak it. A good general should always have at least one other language, eh, old chap? Comes in handy for surrendering.'

' He speaks English, too, I'll bet,' said Marquis.

' I'm sure he does.' The Chinese remained staring down at his hands. He was not sullen; he looked more like a man who felt he was alone. Singh shook his head, then turned back to Marquis and the others. ' I am taking him back to India, to my headquarters. He is all I have to offer in return for the men I have lost this past week.' He paused for a moment and his face clouded. He put his fingers to his forehead and bowed his head slightly as if in prayer. Then he went on : ' The battalion was not at full strength up there on the border, but I have lost something like three hundred men. Men who were my children. Some of them were descendants of families who have worked for *my* family for generations. My batman, for instance. His father had been personal servant to my father, and *his* father served my grandfather.' He noticed their polite looks of curiosity. ' I am the Kumar Sawai Dalpat Singh. My father was the Maharajah of Samarand. It means nothing to you gentlemen? Ladies?' He looked disappointed, then he shrugged. 'Samarand was a princedom that no longer exists. When India became independent, my father's state was absorbed. A democracy cannot afford princes. A pity, don't you think?'

'I think so,' said Eve.

'You would,' said Marquis without rancour.

'My husband is a socialist and a republican.' Then Eve looked with surprise at the Chinese, who had grinned suddenly. 'What's so funny?'

Li Bu-fang bowed his head slightly to Marquis. He had an attractive smile, one that completely changed his face. 'I am pleased to meet a fellow socialist.' He had a soft pleasant voice, the sibilants hissing a little.

'Up the workers!' said Tom Breck, grinning.

'I'm not your sort,' Marquis said to Li Bu-fang. 'Alongside you, I'm a right-wing reactionary, a joker who wouldn't shake hands with a left-handed archbishop. I'm not a canvasser in your cause, mate.' He looked back at Singh. 'But I don't vote for princes, either. Now where do you go from here?'

Singh seemed to be considering the remark about princes. Then once again he shrugged: even in the days of princes, no one had ever voted for them. 'The easiest course would be to head for Thimbu, the capital, and hope the authorities there would allow me to smuggle him out over the new motor road. But they may not allow that——'

'I wouldn't blame them.'

Singh nodded. 'Neither should I. No one can blame them if they don't want to antagonise the Chinese, give them an excuse for invasion. One man, even a general, may seem an insignificant excuse for an invasion, but I don't think the Chinese want much more. They could soon twist it into something that made very good propaganda. No, I think I shall have to by-pass Thimbu.' He turned round in his chair and looked over his shoulder at the steep hill that blocked out the view to the south-east. 'That's the way I'll have to go.'

'Take him all that way on your own?' Nancy's voice cracked with incredulity. 'It must be nearly a hundred miles into India—as the crow flies, that is. And you won't be following the crow. You'll be climbing up and down mountains all the way.'

Singh nodded and looked at Li Bu-fang. 'Do you think we'll make it, old chap?'

Li Bu-fang grinned, suddenly enjoying himself : the battle hadn't finished back there in the mountains, it was only just beginning. 'I assure you *you* won't, Colonel.'

2

Late that afternoon Singh came to see Marquis. All through the day there had been a growing air of tension throughout the camp : the Indian and the Chinese were the eye of a storm that had yet to break. The Bhutanese porters had stopped their laughter and their games; as they worked they stared up at the camp where Singh and Li Bu-fang sat outside the kitchen tent, all their innocence now gone behind a mask that was frightening because it was unreadable. Even the Brecks had fallen silent; Nancy, uncertain of herself, now looked as vulnerable as Tom. Wilkins made no attempt to disguise what he felt : once, as he passed Singh, he called out, 'When are you leaving, Colonel?' and passed on before the Indian could answer : it was not a question but a suggestion, as frank and blunt as a Yorkshire question could be. Eve busied herself about the camp, trying to hide the elation she felt : she knew with the newcomers' advent, Jack would have to think seriously about breaking camp and beginning the journey home.

As Singh came down towards him, Marquis looked up from the note-book in which he was entering the particulars of the plants now being readied to be taken back to England. Half the garden had been dug up and the stack of polythene bags had already reached a formidable size; Marquis had begun to wonder if he would need to hire more porters to carry out the collection. That would mean asking Eve for more money. He had already exceeded the budget he had been allowed by the Royal Horticultural Society, the co-backers of his part of the expedition. But he knew he would force himself to ask Eve : this was the greatest collection of plants he had ever achieved, and he would be damned if he'd leave any of it behind.

'Marquis, I want a word with you.'

Marquis closed his note-book, stood up slowly, dismissed

Nimchu and the other porters who had been working in the garden, then turned to Singh. He did it all unhurriedly and deliberately, and when he at last looked at the Indian, the latter's face was flushed. 'What can I do for you?'

Singh contained his anger and forced a smile, a polite grimace that looked as if it might tear a muscle or two. 'I'm not accustomed to being kept waiting, old chap. But then you are probably aware of that.'

'I'd guessed it,' said Marquis and smiled broadly. 'But then I'm not accustomed to jumping to attention when spoken to.'

'You'd have made a poor soldier.'

Marquis nodded good-humouredly, determined not to let the other man upset him. 'I'd have made a poor lot of things. A poor politician, a poor diplomat'—he grinned—'a poor prince, too, eh?'

Singh suddenly smiled; he was not going to stoke up an antagonism that was pointless. Occasionally, very occasionally, he regretted the arrogance he had inherited: it was a birth-mark that was not always acceptable in all circles. 'Forgive my myopia, old chap, but I've never been able to see Australians as princes. You might have made the grade in medieval times, but you were a little late for that.'

Marquis shook his head in wonder. 'You must have been a pain in the neck to the British Raj, Colonel. Did they ever gaol you princes?'

'Hardly, old chap,' said Singh, and looked horrified at the thought.

'A pity,' said Marquis. 'Well, what can I do for you?'

'I shall be on my way first thing in the morning with our friend.' He nodded up towards the kitchen tent where Li Bu-fang, his hands still bound, sat at the table surveying the camp activity like an early spectator waiting for the main event to begin. Tsering came out of the tent and appeared to snarl at him; but the Chinese turned away with all the disdain of an old mandarin. 'Could you give me enough food for five days for the two of us?'

'Five days?'

Singh smiled without opening his lips, another grimace, but this time not caused by any attitude of Marquis. 'If we are not over the mountains in five days, old chap, then we'll be dead somewhere up there in the snow.'

The Indian's fatalism took what remained of the antagonism out of Marquis. He had never feared death, but he had never had to contemplate it as coldly as Singh was now doing. Suddenly he was aware of it; the air for a moment was chillingly still. He looked up towards the mountains. The last of the westering sun, already gone from this narrow valley, caught the high peaks, turning them to jagged burnished shields against the darkening eastern sky. The wind had begun to turn from the south even since this morning: a mile of wind-torn snow lay like a brass sword across the sunlit sky, stretching due west from the highest peak. 'I don't fancy your chances, Colonel.'

Singh shrugged. 'What other way is there? If I went the easy way, down to Thimbu, the Bhutanese *might* let me go on through to India. Then again they might not. They might just throw me into prison and forget all about me. They certainly wouldn't allow me to take my prisoner with me. The last thing they want at this moment is to be accused by the Chinese of taking sides.'

Marquis nodded. 'I guess you're right. But I don't know if I can give you all the food you're asking for. We're short as it is——'

'You can't refuse Colonel Singh.' Eve, unobserved by either man, had come down from her tent. 'He needs the food more than we do, Jack.'

Marquis wondered if Indian princes hit their wives when the latter interfered in their husbands' affairs; but that would be a full-time job, with sixty spouses all lined up for a marital clout. He didn't voice the question. It was obvious that Singh was as much on Eve's side as she was on his. I'm up against the British Raj, Marquis thought; now I know how Gandhi felt. 'Love, I don't dispute his need. But that will cut our own stay short——'

'You could send Chungma and Tashi back to get supplies for us.'

He grinned, admiring her strategy: the war colleges of the world had never known what they had missed when they refused to admit women. 'It would take too long. And I'd be without two men just when I need them most. My wife is in a hurry to leave here, Colonel.'

' I don't blame her, old man. It must be a lonely life up here for a woman. And uncomfortable.'

' I don't blame her, either,' said Marquis, suddenly trapped into admitting what he had felt for some weeks. But he felt more than just concern for her discomfort. All at once he knew she was in danger; everyone in camp was in danger, but all his concern at this moment was for her. He looked at her and, not wanting to frighten her, disguised his anxiety with a wink. She smiled at him, a little puzzled by his sudden change of attitude, but said nothing.

Marquis turned back to Singh. ' I'll give you the food, Colonel. And some blankets and a pup tent.'

Singh bowed his head slightly. His look of arrogant amusement suddenly went and at once he seemed to take on a new dignity. ' There is something I did not tell you before—a reason why I *must* get back to India——' He hesitated, as if wondering whether he should go ahead; then he reached into his battle tunic and took out some papers. ' I found these in the post where '—he faltered a moment—' where I lost the last of my men. A dying Chinese was trying to burn them. I killed him and took them from him. Then the general appeared out of nowhere and we had quite a bash, just the two of us.' He touched the dried cut above his eye. ' He seemed terribly keen that I should not read these papers. Do you read Chinese?' Marquis and Eve shook their heads. ' Neither do I. At Oxford I read English History. Not an awfully useful subject for this part of the world. I should have taken languages.'

' What do you reckon they are?' Marquis nodded at the papers.

' I don't know. But if the general thought they were so important, they could be battle orders or something along those lines. Whatever they are, he thought them important enough to try and kill me for them.'

' I'm no soldier, as I told you, but why should valuable papers be kept in a forward post? Aren't those sort of things kept well behind the lines?'

' That's the idea, old chap. But somehow it never seems

to work. You would be surprised at the number of mistakes our side made in World War Two. And don't forget, our friend up there is a general—it was probably one of his staff whom I caught trying to burn them. If these papers *are* important, I'm very happy to know that the Chinese can be just as incompetent as we. It gives one hope.'

Marquis looked up towards Li Bu-fang, who was staring down at them, his face as blank as one of the rocks that studded the bank behind him. He had the look of a man who possessed more than hope; he was a man who had faith : he wore it like another badge of rank. He turned his head and looked down the valley again. The bastard is so confident, Marquis thought; and looked down the valley himself, but saw nothing to shake his own confidence. But I'm *not* confident, he told himself, I'm worried; and tried to borrow some of the Chinese inscrutability.

' If those papers are important,' he said, ' the Chow hasn't yet finished with trying to kill you.'

' No,' said Singh. ' But I haven't given up the idea of killing him, either.'

' Just don't do it in my camp,' said Marquis, and left Eve and Singh and went up to the porters' tents. Nimchu saw him coming and came a few steps to met him. ' Nimchu, I want Chungma to leave now for Sham Dzong. He's to buy enough rice and tsampa to last us for a week, and get back here as soon as he can.'

' Chungma is only one man, sahib. He will not be able to carry so much food himself.'

' I know that!' Marquis snapped, and was at once regretful of his sharpness; there was no need to work off his worry on Nimchu. He smiled, trying to take the edge off his voice : ' Get him to hire two more porters, Nimchu, bring them back with him. We'll need them anyway, to help us carry out the collection. Tell him to get moving at once. If he takes his finger out, he can make four or five miles before dark. I want him back in three days at the outside.'

Nimchu nodded, then shouted orders in his own language. Chungma, the youngest of the porters, short, squat, moving always in quick jerky movements like a boxer waiting for an opponent to make a move, showed no surprise at the sudden journey he had to make. He grinned cheerfully and ducked into his tent to collect what he would take with him. Marquis knew that most Bhutanese, for all their country's isolation, were gregarious and he had noticed that over the past few weeks the porters had begun to ask when they would be returning to Thimbu. He was sure that Chungma would find a diversion or two in the three days that he would be gone.

Nimchu watched Chungma disappear into the tent, then he turned back to Marquis. He was the oldest of the porters, somewhere in his early forties, and the most travelled. The leader of a previous expedition had taken him to London as a bonus; it had been such a shock to his system that he had almost died of lack of oxygen climbing Highgate Hill. He had returned to Bhutan after only a month, shaking his head at the devastation that could be caused by civilisation. There had been similar reactions to other trips he had made, to Delhi, Calcutta, Rangoon, Singapore. An itching curiosity had drawn him to the wider world, but always he came back to this land where the mountains and the gods were one and the same. Marquis had first met him in Burma in 1950 and had used him as a porter on an expedition to the headwaters of the Irrawaddy. He had used him again in 1956 on a trip through Assam, and an affection and respect for each other had developed and still survived despite the six years' separation between that last trip and this one. Sometimes, feeling traitorous towards Eve, Marquis felt that Nimchu was the only one with whom he had real affinity on these journeys into the wild and lonely mountains.

'The strangers, sahib.' Nimchu ran a finger up and down the side of his long well-shaped nose. He was a handsome man, spoiled only by his wall eye and the long scar on the cheek below it, a legacy of an encounter with a leopard. His voice was soft, that of a man used to the silences of nature; but Marquis knew that it could erupt in terrible storms of temper, and there were several lesser porters who had made the mistake of thinking Nimchu's soft voice was a sign of weakness. 'Are they staying with us?'

'They are leaving in the morning, Nimchu. What do you think of them?'

Nimchu knew Marquis well enough to know that the latter

wanted a frank answer; the sahib didn't ask idle questions of his porters. 'I do not like them in my country, sahib. I heard the news on the wireless, that China and India are fighting. We do not want them to bring the fight into our country.'

'How do the other porters feel?'

'The same as I, sahib.'

'I know you will not touch them here in my camp——' Marquis hoped he spoke the truth, but he gave Nimchu no chance to deny it. 'But if you met them somewhere in the mountains, alone, what would you do?'

Nimchu stroked his nose again while he considered, then he looked up at Marquis. 'Kill them, sahib. It would be the simplest thing to do.'

Marquis knew that the Bhutanese religion, a mixture of Buddhism, Hinduism and, the country's original cult of sorcery and animism, Bon, all meant a great deal to Nimchu. 'You're a Buddhist, Nimchu. Killing is against your principles.'

'I am a practical man, sahib. I can only *try* to be a religious one.' He smiled up at Marquis, not impudently but with the smile of a man who had recognised the need of compromise. The path to Heaven was narrow, but the gods had never taught that one had to walk on the precipice edge. He put a finger to the scar on his cheek, ran it up to the eye that could see only with memory. 'I killed the leopard that did this. A man should not lie down and die if he is not ready for Heaven.'

Marquis grinned. 'When *will* you be ready?' His own religion was a frayed and tattered thing, taken out, mended and worn like an old garment that didn't fit but could not be thrown away. Eve, a non-Catholic, never laughed at his occasional bursts of piety, but he knew she would never understand them. The Catholic could never really rid himself of his Catholicism: his own father's atheism had been more an act of defiance than an act of belief. The message was engraved on your soul, even if you bellowed to Heaven that you didn't have a soul: Rome never took no for an answer. He never decried another man's compromises with his religion: he knew how far short most of us fell of being a saint.

Nimchu shook his head, enjoying his own good humour and that of the sahib. 'Not for a long time, sahib.' Then, still smiling, he looked across at the Indian and the Chinese, the invaders, and said, 'That is why I should kill the strangers if I met them in the mountains. Our only way to stay alive is to have no masters but ourselves. Kill them both and drop their bodies in the river. That way nobody would know and nobody could say we were taking sides.'

So Singh had accurately guessed the Bhutanese reaction to his and his prisoner's presence. 'I'm not taking sides, either, Nimchu. That's why the colonel and his prisoner are leaving the camp first thing in the morning.'

'You are a wise man, sahib.'

'Not always, Nimchu.' Wisdom was often a question of luck : if he had been wise in the past, it was because he had been lucky. He hoped his luck would hold.

He went up towards his tent, past the kitchen tent, where Li Bu-fang sat staring impassively at Nancy Breck while she abused him. 'You're a menace! I could kill you and all your kind, you know that? You've got no——' Nancy's anger made her almost incoherent; her eyes shone with tears, she looked blindly at her enemy, sometimes talking right past him. When Marquis spoke to her, she looked around, trying to find him in the fog of tears. 'Jack? I——' She rubbed her eyes, fumbled in a pocket for her glasses, put them on; they began to mist up at once and she snatched them off again, wore them like glass knuckledusters on her fingers. 'Jack, why do you let him stay? Why don't you——'

'He's not my prisoner, Nancy. Colonel Singh is taking him out first thing to-morrow morning.' He looked down at Li Bu-fang. 'You people killed the parents of Mrs. Breck's husband.'

Li bowed his head to Nancy. 'I am sorry.'

'Sorry? How could you be sorry——'

'Nancy——' But she took no notice of Marquis, and he had to bark at her: 'Nancy!' She stopped with her mouth open, peered at him as if he were a stranger she was trying to identify. 'Forget it. Abusing him isn't going to bring back Tom's mother and father.'

'I could kill him!' Her voice hissed with hate. Even Li Bu-fang looked up disturbed; for a moment there was a flash of something that could have been fear in the dark blank eyes.

'Not in my camp,' said Marquis gently but firmly. 'There are seven hundred million of them. Killing one gets you nowhere. Killing a million would get you nowhere. You've got to think of some other way of beating them. Don't ask me how——' He looked down at Li. 'Do you think we shall ever beat you?'

'No,' said Li, and looked after Nancy as she turned quickly, her voice catching in a sob of anger, and ran across the camp to her own tent. Then he looked back at Marquis. 'I am truly sorry if Mr. Breck's parents were killed. What were they?'

'Missionaries.' Marquis looked across towards the Brecks' tent. 'Mr. Breck is a Quaker. So were his parents. I feel sorry for Mrs. Breck—she has to dig up enough anger and hatred of you bastards for all of them.'

'We have made mistakes, killing the missionaries. We have only made martyrs of them, and they were not worth it. Christianity is not a threat, not in China. Even in the capitalist world, who pays much attention to it? The emptiest places in England are the churches.'

'You're well informed. Where did you get that—in the *People's Daily*?'

'In *The Times*. I go to Peking occasionally. At the British Legation you can read the English newspapers. Democracy is stupid—it advertises its mistakes.'

'Stupid but honest. Or anyway we try to be—honest, I mean.'

Li laughed. He had a not unpleasant face, especially when he smiled; the three scars on his cheeks melted then into the laughter lines. He looked the sort of man born to laugh, but the circumstances had never presented themselves; even now the laugh broke off short, as if he had had a sudden sense of guilt. 'You are stupid if you believe that the men who run your capitalist world are honest.'

In five minutes he had been called both wise and stupid. It was a fair assessment of him in general, he guessed. Marquis shrugged: he had never aspired to perfection. He left Li and went on over to his own tent. He would not ask Eve what she thought of him: a wife's truth had a more cutting edge than that of a stranger.

Eve was immersed in steaming hot water in the collapsible rubber-and-canvas bath. It was a tight fit even for someone her size; when he got into it, he always felt like a five-fingered hand in a three-fingered glove. He sat down on the edge of his camp-bed and looked appreciatively at her. 'This is the only time I ever see you without your clothes.'

'Whose fault is that?' Then she looked down at the sponge in her hand and squeezed the water slowly from it. 'I'm sorry. I've been pretty bitchy to-day, haven't I?'

He leaned towards her, savouring the warm smell of her, and kissed the hollow between her shoulder and throat. 'It won't be long now. I'm ready for home myself.'

She lay back as far as she could in the short bath and looked at him carefully. 'Would you care to make me pregnant?'

'Not under water.'

'Not here, silly.' She laughed, and raised a dripping hand to stroke his cheek. He shaved only once a week, on their rest day, and he now had four days' growth of stubble; but she didn't mind that, she knew that beards protected the men's faces from sunburn in the high thin air. She had never been a woman who wanted her man sculptured out of soap and shaving cream. The weatherbeaten skin, the calloused hands, the bone and muscle, all made up part of what she loved in this man. She, too, had never asked for perfection in him. 'No, when we get back home. Because you know, don't you, that I'm not coming on any more trips with you?'

He hesitated before he nodded. 'Will that keep us together —a child?'

'It will help.'

He stared at her for a while, then he lay back on his bed. They lay side by side, she in the bath, he on his bed. 'It's so bloody cold-blooded. Let's have a baby, just like that. It's like deciding to take out an insurance policy.'

'It wouldn't be cold-blooded once we got down to it.'

'Don't be sexy, love. I'm not in the mood for it.'

'All right, I'll be sensible, then. It's not being cold-blooded, darling. People plan to have children, just as they plan not to have them. We decided not to have any——'

'You mean I decided.'

'All right. But I agreed. Now I'm the one who's doing the deciding——'

'Decide, decide! God Almighty, what's decision got to do with love-making?'

'That's a man's outlook, darling. When a woman makes love, there's always some decision about it.'

'Even with her husband?'

'Not always, but sometimes. Like now. Hand me my towel.'

'You still look as good as you ever did. Will you look as good as that after you've had a baby?'

'Better.'

'I'm a lucky bastard.'

'So am I, darling. Don't ever let our luck run out.'

She bent and kissed him. He held her to him, his rough hands scratching like bark on the silk of her body. Outside the radio was switched on: Wilkins, the other pessimist, searched for Delhi on the dial. Then the voice came over the mountains, lugubrious and hopeless: 'The Chinese continue to advance . . .'

THREE

Marquis came awake with a start, the shot ringing in his ears like an echo from a dream. Then he heard the shout, and he knew he hadn't been dreaming. Eve sat up in her bed, her voice cracking with sleep and shock. 'What's that?'

Marquis tumbled out of bed, pulled on trousers and sweater over his pyjamas, slid his feet into the old desert boots he wore around camp; then just before he stepped out of the tent he dragged on his anorak and zipped it up to the neck. He was glad that he did: as soon as he came out into the dark morning the cold attacked him. The wind had swung right round to the north, was blowing out of Tibet with all the chill of approaching winter. Marquis shivered, chilled by omen as much as by the wind.

His eyes watered as the wind cut at them, but he saw the dim figure running away from the kitchen tent. It ran towards the stores' tent; Marquis shut his eyes to blink away the tears; when he opened them, the figure had gone. He wiped his eyes and looked back at the kitchen tent.

Singh had come out of the kitchen tent, a pistol in his hand. As Marquis crossed to him, Tom Breck and Wilkins came out of their tents. 'What's going on? What the hell——?'

Singh said, 'Someone tried to kill my prisoner.'

Marquis flung back the flap of the kitchen tent. Two rough beds had been made for Singh and Li Bu-fang on the floor of the kitchen; Li lay flat on his back on one of them, his hands still bound. Pots and pans lay about him like discarded helmets; whoever had tried to kill him had been clumsy. A sack of flour had burst: Li was white as far up as his waist, like a man half-way to being embalmed.

'You all right?' Marquis said, and the Chinese nodded. He was no inscrutable Oriental now: he was as frightened as the most emotional Occidental. Marquis turned back to Singh. 'Who was it?'

'I didn't see. I heard Li cry out, I saw this shape, I fired at him, but he got away——'

The whole camp was astir now. Eve and Nancy stood in the doorways of their respective tents, each wrapped in an anorak and a blanket. The porters had come out of their tents, but had not moved up towards Marquis and the others; they stood in a broken line, watching carefully like spectators at a political rally they resented. Marquis could not see their faces, they were just black shapes against the lamps in their tents; but he recognised the stiffness of their attitude, he had seen it in Africa and other parts of Asia when trouble occurred. He, Eve, the Brecks, Wilkins were now one with Singh and Li Bu-fang: they were all foreigners.

'We'd better ask some questions, then,' said Wilkins. 'It must have been one of the porters.'

'Get them up here at once,' Singh said.

Marquis turned his head slowly. 'Colonel, this isn't Poona, or wherever your barracks are. This is my camp—*mine*, not yours. Don't start chucking orders around here, or you're likely to be cut down to lance-corporal. Don't forget, no one invited you in here.'

The two men stared at each other in the dim glow from the lamp in the kitchen tent. Singh still held his pistol; the barrel of it came up. Marquis tensed, waiting for the bullet; he found it incredible that the Indian should shoot him, but he knew it was going to happen. Singh's face was distorted with an anger that made him ugly. I was right, Marquis thought, he does belong to another century. And waited for the bullet.

Then down by their tents the porters turned all at once, as if turning away to avoid seeing the murder. Or perhaps they were going to break and run. That thought seemed to strike Singh; the pistol swung away from Marquis in the direction of the porters. And without quite knowing why, Marquis stepped in front of the pistol again, keeping it aimed at himself, but at his back this time as he turned towards the porters. He shouted, 'Nimchu!', but the wind snatched away his voice and the shout sounded more like a bleat. Then Nimchu came towards him, another porter with him. It was Chungma, breathing heavily, trembling with exhaustion.

'What the hell brought you back, Chungma?'

'Chinese, sahib.' The boy had only a few words of English; he hissed them into the wind. 'Down valley.'

' There are forty or fifty of them, sahib.' Nimchu had been
speaking to Chungma as he had brought the young porter up
to Marquis. ' Camped where this river joins the river from
the east. Chungma was camped there himself when they
arrived. He was very lucky to escape.'

' Did they see you, Chungma?'

' Not know, sahib.' His teeth glimmered in the lightening
darkness; he was still young and innocent enough to joke
about disaster. ' Ran too fast.'

Marquis also grinned, although he was in no mood for
joking. He glanced over his shoulder at Singh; the latter had
put away his pistol. Then he looked back at Chungma.
' Which way were they heading?'

Nimchu spoke to Chungma, then turned back to Marquis.
The older Bhutanese knew this was no time for joking; his
voice had a nervous edge to it. ' Chungma thinks they are
coming this way, sahib. They were coming *up* the valley, he
is sure of that.'

Marquis remarked the nervousness in Nimchu's voice and at
once his own apprehension increased. He cursed, and stood
thinking while the wind whetted its blade against his cheek.
He could hear it coming down the narrow valley, its sound
drowning the hiss and rumble of the river; the trees creaked
and keened under its scything, leaves whipping through the
darkness like bats. Up in the high peaks he knew that a
blizzard must be blowing, the snow whirling through the passes
in thick blinding clouds. He wondered why the Chinese
should be down the valley, *below* the camp; then guessed
they might be from another post farther west, who had got the
word that one of their generals had been captured and had
come down one of the side valleys. It didn't matter where
they had come from. What mattered was where they *were*,
down there at the bottom of the valley, oiling the bolts on their
rifles, chanting some Red propaganda to keep themselves warm,
just waiting for daylight to come marching up the valley.

' Could it have been one of the Chinese who tried to kill
the general?' Tom Breck said.

' Why would they want to do that?' Marquis turned away
for a moment, told Nimchu to have Tsering come up to the
kitchen tent and start preparing breakfast; then he turned back

to Breck and the other men. 'They wouldn't travel at night in
one of these valleys. Too easy to get lost——'

'Then it must have been one of the porters,' said Wilkins.

'Could be.' Marquis glanced across at Nancy Breck, still
standing in the doorway of her tent. The morning had light-
ened enough now for him to see more clearly; beneath the
blanket she had wrapped round her he could see she was
wearing trousers and boots. She was fully dressed and her boots
were laced up. He looked at Tom Breck, but the latter looked
as innocent as ever. Then he turned to Singh. 'But I'm not
going to start questioning the porters, Colonel. I've got
other things on my mind right now.'

'Such as?'

I'm going to give myself a hernia, trying to control my
temper with this bastard. 'Such as trying to work out what
we can do to get out of this spot we're in. You look after
your prisoner, Colonel. We'll look after ourselves. If we don't,
we might all be dead by to-night.' He heard Tom Breck gasp;
Wilkins made a noise that sounded like a snort. 'Better start
packing, Tom. You too, Nick.' He looked at Singh again,
felt suddenly too tired to be angry at the man; the danger of
a hernia passed. 'All these bloody mountains to get lost in,
and you had to choose this valley!'

'It'll work out all right, Jack.' Tom Breck rubbed his
beard. 'Nick and I have got confidence in you, haven't we,
Nick? Whatever you say, we're right with you, aren't we,
Nick?'

That's what's going to give me the hernia: Tom is going
to overload me with trust. He looked at Breck, who nodded
his head in encouragement: one almost expected him to shout
rah, rah, rah. Then Marquis looked at Wilkins, who grimaced
sourly. And at that moment he felt more affection for Wilkins
than he did for Breck.

'Whatever you say, Jack,' said Tom Breck. 'Anything
you decide, we're with you all the way.'

'Thanks, Tom,' said Marquis, and wondered how many
men had killed their friends for burdening them with too much
devotion.

Then he walked on towards his own tent, looking up towards

the east. It would be full light in another hour, a cold dawn that would show new snow on the peaks and perhaps even on the lower slopes. Something cold brushed against his cheek, a leaf, a snowflake: whatever it was, it was cold, chill as the finger of fate. He felt suddenly depressed; the fire in him was beginning to turn to ashes; if they cut him open now they would find he had a clinker for a heart. Eve had been right: they should have left for home a week ago.

She was waiting for him in the tent, still wrapped in her anorak and blanket. 'Was that Chungma I saw?'

'Get dressed, love. Properly dressed, put on your warmest things. Looks like we're in for a long hike over the hills.' He took off his outer clothing, slid out of his pyjamas, then dressed again, substituting a wool shirt for his pyjama-top and walking boots for the old desert boots. 'There are fifty or so Chows camped down the valley. Chungma ran into them, thinks they are coming this way.'

She shivered, as much with shock as with cold. Half-dressed, she looked up at him. 'Are we in any danger?'

'I don't know,' he said, but he knew he was not being honest with her. 'I'm not going to take any risks, though.'

She recognised his restraint towards her, that he was trying not to frighten her. She was not given easily to panic, but because it had never really been severely tested she was not sure of the extent of her own courage. There had been moments of danger on expeditions in the past, but she had survived them; mainly, she thought, because they had only been moments and she had reacted by instinct. Real courage, she knew, was more than a matter of reflexes.

'What are you going to do?'

'We're getting out of here as fast as we can.'

Five minutes later he was telling the rest of the camp the same thing. 'I could tell Colonel Singh to get out of here with his prisoner, but I don't for a moment think that would give us any guarantee of being left alone if the Chinese come up this way. The mere fact that they've come this far down into Bhutan shows they're either desperate or they don't care. Either way I wouldn't like to have five bob on our chances.'

'What's your plan, then?' Wilkins asked.

'We'll have breakfast, then as soon as it's daylight we'll be on our way.'

'Where?' Eve said.

To New Guinea, to Kensington, anywhere at all; even the rose garden in Buckinghamshire looked an attractive destination now. He sipped from the hot mug of tea he held. He stared down into the fire round which they all stood; then looked up at the faces all turned towards him. This was different from anything that had ever confronted him before : the problems of a cricket or a rugger captain suddenly became a joke. People stood waiting on him to be responsible for them : he looked at Tom Breck, who gave him the old nod of encouragement.

'We'll go over the mountains,' he said at last, and tried to sound decisive. 'We'll go with Colonel Singh and his prisoner.'

There was silence for a moment, broken only by the moan of the wind. Then Wilkins said, 'What if some of us think that isn't a good idea? It could be damned rough, trying to get over those peaks in this weather. What about Eve and Nancy?'

Marquis looked at Nancy, but she just stared at him as if she didn't see him. Then he looked at Eve. He felt a weakness run through him when at last she said, 'I'll depend on Jack.'

Then Nancy fumbled in the pocket of her anorak, put on her glasses as if she were going to read some proposition before she agreed to it. Then : 'I'll go with Jack.'

'So will I,' said Tom Breck, tugging on his beard as if to give emphasis to what he said.

Wilkins hesitated. The seven months here in the mountains had almost exhausted him mentally and physically; he had not even been looking forward to the comparatively easy walk out down the long valley to Thimbu. At last he shrugged. 'Majority rules, I guess.'

Singh had said nothing during this short debate. Li Bu-fang stood beside him, silent, contemptuous in his lack of interest. Singh glanced at him, as if wanting to goad him into some remark; then he looked back at the others, knowing now that he was as involved with them as much as with his prisoner.

For all his outward self-assurance he had not felt comfortable
since entering the camp; not because he felt unwelcome,
although that had disturbed him, too, but because he knew
that his and Li's presence had at once placed a premium on the
safety of Marquis and the others. But apology, even diffidence,
came hard to him; he still lived in the memory of a day when
such an attitude, on the part of a prince, had been a sign of
weakness. In certain ways he was still tongue-tied by inheritance; Oxford had educated him in Western ways, but it had
not entirely eradicated the East from him. He looked at
Marquis as the latter spoke to him.

'You and I had better have a look at my map, Colonel.'

Singh hesitated, then with difficulty that none of the others
recognised he said, 'I am sorry this has happened. The
Chinese would not be coming up this valley if it were not for
me and my prisoner. I shall make it up to you. I shall
guarantee to get you and your party safely into India.'

'Thank you,' said Marquis, and only Eve noticed the harsh
dry note in his voice.

While the others set about packing their gear, Singh and
Marquis consulted the latter's map. 'It's an old one, Colonel,
and it's not too accurate. But it'll give us some idea where to
head. Nimchu tells me there was an old trade route farther
east from here, one that the Tibetans used to take when they
brought their wool out. We'll try and find that.'

Singh was looking at the map. 'The ridges run north and
south. If we head south down one of the valleys, that might
bring us into more settled country and we could be picked up
by the Bhutanese. I must avoid that if I can.' He looked
at Marquis. 'But you and your friends could split up and
leave us when we come to a valley that runs in the right
direction.'

'We'll do that if we get the chance. Otherwise——'
Marquis examined the map carefully. 'We've got about five
days' heavy slogging ahead of us. That trade route isn't marked
on here, but I guess it finished up down in Assam. We'll head
that way——' He ran a finger across the map. 'Five days,
and as you said, Colonel—if we haven't made it by then, we'll
never make it.'

Singh looked across to where Li Bu-fang sat. 'I know that

every inch of the way, I'm going to want to kill that chap. But I have to get him out into India.' He looked back at Marquis. 'Do you understand what face means in Asia?'

'I've come up against it once or twice.'

'If I can get him out to my country, it won't only be the positive propaganda we can make of it. There will be the other effect—the loss of face for China.'

'What about his own loss of face? Won't he try to do something about that?'

'You mean perhaps commit suicide? I think not. Not at first. He'll stay alive so long as I still have these papers.' He tapped his pocket.

'Then you're going to be stuck with him all the way.'

Singh looked back at the map, then up at the distant peaks. 'All the way.'

It took them half an hour to break camp. There was so much to be left behind, so little to pack. Enough food for five days, tents, rope and climbing gear, blankets and sleeping-bags and cooking utensils : survival, not comfort, became the yardstick of choice. Li Bu-fang, the veteran of several such hurried flights but now the only one unconcerned with this one, sat in a canvas chair, his hands and feet bound, and watched with silent amusement.

'What are you grinning at?' Marquis, coming up from the garden with a polythene bag in his hand, stopped beside the Chinese.

Li Bu-fang looked up. Sitting in his chair, his bound hands in his lap, the only man not on his feet working, he could have been a general idly watching his staff dismantle their field headquarters after manœuvres.

'All this hustle and bustle. You will all be dead in twenty-four hours. Why bother?'

'Maybe it's because I've never taken anything for granted, Chow.'

'Chow. Is that a term of insult, like Chink? You whites never grow up, do you? Always sounding like schoolboys abusing the lesser races. Why do you bother to insult me like that? It's a sign of a small mind.'

Marquis stared down at him, then he nodded. 'I'd never

thought of it. You're right. You're pretty smart, aren't you?'

'For a Chow?'

'You're insulting yourself now.'

'You're smart, too.'

'Where did you learn to speak English?'

'Various places. Certain of our schools and universities teach it.'

'Part of your preparation for taking over the world, eh?'

Li Bu-fang grinned. 'If you like.'

'They teach you pretty well.'

'Oh, I have had practice. I started learning very early. I was in Chungking during the war. The one you imperialists call World War Two. Such a conceit. Less than half the world fought in it, but you still called it a world war.'

'I wouldn't let it worry you. A war by any name is still a war. You're talking to a pacifist, sport. What were you doing in Chungking?'

'Working as house-boy for an American major.'

'That made you a Communist?'

'No. He hated Chiang Kai-shek, too. In those days it was safe for an American to feel that way. We Communists were not the main enemy then.'

'You were a Communist then? You must have started young.'

'I was born one. I was twelve years old when I accompanied my father on the Long March. You've heard of the Long March?'

'I've heard of it,' Marquis said, and wondered if he himself could have survived such a journey when he had been twelve years old. At twelve, a day on the beach at Coogee had tired him out. But then, as a child, survival had not been a driving force: the ice-cream cone, the meat-pie and the saveloy had not been meant to fight off starvation. 'It was back in 1934 and 35, wasn't it?'

'You seem to know something of China.'

'I always wanted to collect there.' His voice was wistful, but somehow it didn't seem ridiculous in such a big rough man; the tone of regret and disappointment was too genuine. 'I used to read all about the French missionaries, blokes like David and Delavay and Soulié. People pottering about in their gardens in England and America and Australia, anywhere at all, most of them don't know where their plants originated. They came from China and most of them were found by those French missionaries. Then blokes like Wilson, Forrest, Kingdon Ward. I read all about them and I wanted to follow them. No, I wanted to go one step further, bring back something they'd never discovered. I wanted to go up into northern Yunnan, all my rainbows seemed to end there in Yunnan. Then you bastards came along and put the kybosh on the idea.' He looked back at Li. I'd have walked all the way into Yunnan if your government would have given me permission. It would have been some hike, but I don't suppose you'd have thought it much beside the Long March?'

'Hardly, Mr. Marquis. Six thousand miles, across twelve provinces, for three hundred and sixty-eight days. We fought fifteen major battles and I've forgotten how many skirmishes. We climbed eighteen mountain ranges and crossed six rivers. A hundred thousand of us.'

'You know your facts.'

'We were not looking for plants, Mr. Marquis. We were looking for the survival of an ideal. The facts were beaten into my brain, my heart and my body. I lost my father and my two elder brothers on the march. I have not forgotten a day nor a mile of it.'

'I guess you wouldn't,' Marquis said ungrudgingly. He admired courage and endurance; he had never been the sort to withhold his respect for a man as a man because of the latter's politics. 'Then you won't think much of this little walk we're going to do in the next few days, eh?'

'It will stretch my legs, that's all.'

'Well, behave yourself or you might get your neck stretched, too. Someone tried to do you in a while ago.'

Li nodded. He was more composed now, there was no sign of the fear that had gripped him immediately after the attempt on his life. 'My comrades will still kill you.'

The dialogue had gone full circle; the Chinese had even gone back to his same grin of amusement at what was going on in the camp. Marquis, suddenly frustrated and angry, bounced the polythene bag in his hand, wanting to throw it at Li Bu-fang's head.

'What is that?' The Chinese nodded at the bag.

'A plant. It's called *Meconopsis regia*, one of the poppy family.'

'You admire flowers?'

'When I see them growing wild, yes. But not in drawing-rooms. Or in neat little gardens.'

'You are like the man who cannot bear to see wild animals in a zoo?'

'If you like.'

'But flowers are beauty. Don't you like to see beauty indoors?'

'Maybe it's just that I don't like indoors. Are you an admirer of beauty?'

'Why not? If you had lived the life I have, you might find need of it. Indoors and outdoors, wherever you can find it. What are you going to do with it?' He nodded at the polythene bag. 'Take it with you?'

Marquis glanced down towards the garden. The polythene bags glistened in the early morning light, a clump of artificial blooms that seemed to mock him. 'There's seven months' work there. The best collection I've ever made. When you come to think of it, there's no more peaceable work than that of a botanist. Beside us, Bertrand Russell and his mob are cannibals with a tapeworm. And now I've got to throw away seven months' work because of you bastards.' He bounced the bag in his hand. 'I'll take this back and name it after you. It's bright red in colour, very appropriate.'

'I'll be honoured.'

'No, you won't. I'll explain the reason I named it after you, and then every botanist in the world will hate your guts.'

'The prospect frightens me.'

Marquis suddenly grinned. 'I could almost like you, you bastard.'

'Bastard? You are insulting me again?'

'No. Australians use bastard as a term of affection.'

'An odd people. Is illegitimacy encouraged in Australia?'

'It's an old capitalist sport.'

Li Bu-fang smiled. 'I'm going to enjoy this little walk, Mr. Marquis. For as long as it lasts.'

Marquis left him at that and went up to his tent. Nimchu and Eve were there packing the last of the Marquises' belongings. Eve, as if with the coming of daylight she could already see the Chinese down the valley, was now working with nervous speed, fingers fumbling as she tried to tighten a strap on a pack. Marquis knelt down beside her, gently pushing her aside, and tightened the strap. 'I'm sorry about this, love.'

'Sorry about what?' She looked at him in surprise.

'That I've got you into this. If I'd known this was on the cards, I wouldn't have brought you.'

The wind whipped across her cheeks; her eyes glistened with tears. 'Darling, this isn't *your* fault! Please don't start thinking like that.'

He realised he was too much on the defensive. The atmosphere between them over the past few months had worked on him to the extent where he would have blamed himself if she had got toothache. He put his hand on hers, as cold as his own; at once he felt the warmth start between them and he said, 'At least we can keep each other warm.'

No matter how tangential his remarks, she had always been able to follow them if they were an expression of love between them. Then over the past few months that perception had begun to escape her : but now it came back to her as strong as ever. She fitted her hand into the glove of his, moving her knuckles against the callouses of his palms. 'That's all I want, darling. To be kept warm.'

It was only a truce, he knew that; but it was enough for the time being. The argument of their future was now out of context in their present predicament : half-way between an airplane and the ground was no time to be worrying about your vertigo. He stood up, drawing her up with him.

'Are we ready, Nimchu?'

The Bhutanese looked about the camp, then back at Marquis. 'Yes, sahib. Do we burn what we leave behind?'

'Do you think we should?'

'One should never give gifts to the enemy.'

'A sound philosophy.' He looked across at the enemy's representative, sitting in his chair with all the smug complacency of a man who expected gifts. He went to ask Nimchu about the attempt on Li's life; then he changed his mind. Li's life was no longer important; there were too many others to consider. ' Okay, have a bonfire.'

Nimchu grinned like a small boy, spun on his heel and raced across to the kitchen tent and the fire burning there, shouting to the other porters. They responded like pupils invited to burn down the school: in a moment the whole camp was ablaze. Flames leapt up like giant flowers, a sudden summer of fire; a tent bloomed like a giant red bush, then fell in on itself, dying as if under a swift killing frost. The porters raced around, yelling gleefully, collecting chairs, tables and beds, throwing them into the fire with the reckless abandon of men disposing of other people's property : they laid waste to the camp without regret, acting like looting invaders even as they prepared to flee. Tsering and Lombi, another of the porters, ran up towards Li Bu-fang, grabbed the legs of his canvas chair and emptied him head over heels backwards out of it. They stood above him for a moment, laughing and gesturing obscenely, then they raced down and threw the chair on to the fire.

Wilkins stood by the fire, throwing his boxes into the flames. They were small square cardboard boxes and they burned brilliantly, mockingly : no butterflies or beetles had ever had colours as bright as these. He was smiling wryly to himself, at a joke he could never tell to the others. He had discovered, as had so many other entomologists before him, that working with botanists who specialised in flowering plants was not an ideal arrangement. The botanists always wanted to be on the move, whereas an entomologist liked to stay in the one place : the botanist's field could cover an entire valley or range of mountains, the entomologist needed only a few trees or a straggle of rocks. Well, they were certainly going to be on the move from now on.

Wilkins opened a box, took out a half-dozen galls from the polythene bag in which they were wrapped. He rolled the small nut-like growths around in the palm of his hand; then one by one, like marbles, he fired them into the flames. He opened another box, took out a butterfly pinned to a card. He pulled back the cellulose wool that covered it and looked at the beautiful green and yellow creature. *Teinopalpus imperialis*, said the note on the card; and imperial it was, a king of butterflies. Butterflies had prompted the first desire to escape from Leeds, the first hint that a world of beauty lay beyond the grimy horizon. Nothing like this one had ever fluttered down on to the gritty bushes in the tiny back garden; if it had he would not have believed it, would have thought he was suffering from hallucinations and gone to work beside his father at the dye works, where a fit of hallucination would have been a help towards survival. He put *Teinopalpus imperialis* back in its box. He had seen too much ugliness to want to destroy beauty. He would take this one back with him.

Marquis and the others had now moved up the path. Eve stood looking back at the burning camp; woman-like, she hated to see anything destroyed. Marquis, not lamenting the burning of the tents and other camp equipment, never having had any love of possessions, turned away for only one reason: he had seen Chungma run down to the garden and begin to jump up and down on the stacked polythene bags. Seven months' work, the best collection he had ever made, exploded with soft pops; it was too much to bear watching. He opened his gun-case and took out the two rifles. He looked at Tom Breck.

The latter shook his head. 'I'm sorry, Jack. You're going to have to do my shooting for me.'

'You don't have to apologise, Tom.' Marquis slung the .30 Double over his shoulder and handed the 12-bore to Wilkins.

'I'm the world's worst shot,' said Wilkins.

'Let's hope you don't have a chance to prove it. But if you have to, just see it's pointed in the direction of the Chinese. I don't want one of my own bullets up my behind.'

'That would be getting your own back with a vengeance,' said Eve.

'Don't be vulgar, love. Not in company.' But Marquis grinned at her, recognising that her small joke was a cover for her nervousness: she and Nancy had now begun to look anxiously down the valley. He looked at Singh. 'How are we for ammo? I've got about seventy-five rounds for each of these.'

'Perhaps a hundred rounds for my Sten gun, a dozen rounds for my pistol. Not enough for a pitched battle, I'm afraid.'

'Let's hope we don't have one. I think that should be our motto : run like hell all the way. Cowardice is better than discretion or valour. We're going to get nowhere if we stand and fight.'

'You are going to get nowhere, anyway,' said Li Bu-fang.

'No one asked you!' Wilkins raised his gun threateningly, then blinked, as if surprised at his own belligerency. He lowered the gun, looking a little foolish, and turned back on Li. 'Sorry. I got a bit carried away. Is this what a gun does to a man?'

'You're just a killer at heart,' said Nancy, joking nervously as Eve had done; then looked as if she were going to be sick. She turned away, trying to smile, but she was retching on the taste of her words.

'It would be terrible if I were, wouldn't it?' Wilkins's own smile hung precariously on his lips, a cobweb of amusement that could be brushed away by the wind. He had frightened himself more than he had frightened Li Bu-fang; he glanced at the Chinese and hated the latter for his composure. He had long suspected the excitement that had gripped him when he had first seen insects attacking each other; he was sick now at the proof he had just experienced. Even his hands betrayed him : almost as if they did not belong to him, they were clutching the gun hungrily. He loosened the sling and slung the gun on his shoulder, tucking his treacherous hands into his pockets. There his right hand, the one that would have rested on the trigger, clutched the box that contained the butterfly.

'You're not, Nick.' Eve turned back from watching the burning camp. 'Killers aren't as kind as you are.'

He smiled gratefully at her, only regretting that she had mistaken the reason for his past attention to her. His friendships with people had always been ramshackle affairs, built more on distrust of himself than on trust in others. It had been that way with Eve. He had fallen in love with her on their first meeting in London when this expedition had been discussed, but only delirium would have made him give voice to his love. Even though he knew that Marquis and Eve were somehow not as close to each other as they had been at the beginning of this trip, he still did not give himself any hope. He was a man for whom fulfilment of love was not even an ambition : his whole attitude towards other people, men or women, was defeatist. And so people disliked him, only confirming his lack of faith in himself.

'I hope none of us has to do any killing,' Marquis said.

Then Singh said, 'We had better get started at once. Call up your porters, Marquis, and we'll get under way. I'll lead and you had better bring up the rear.'

Marquis resisted the impulse to spring to attention and throw a mock salute. But before he could say anything, Tom Breck, the bones seeming to protrude from his thin body in his angry excitement, had stepped forward.

'You take the medal, Colonel! You come in here, uninvited, unwelcome, bring the Chinese in on us like flies, make me and Mr. Marquis and Mr. Wilkins throw away seven months' work, face me and my wife and the rest of us with a trek over the mountains that none of us is going to like, and then you have the gall to assume command as if we were just a lot of new recruits called up from the slums of Calcutta or wherever, glad to have you with us and us in a hurry to salute you! Well, I'm one who's not going to salute you, Colonel. Mr. Marquis is the boss of our party!'

Drop dead, Tom, thought Marquis; or at least fall unconscious.

'My dear chap'—Singh's incredulity seemed to match that of Tom Breck—'I am an experienced commander. This is a military action——'

'I don't care if it's the Second Punic War or the Battle of the Bulge,' Breck snapped, his beard bobbing. 'We're just a bunch of civilians trying to get away from a military action. Isn't that right, Jack?'

'Yes,' said Marquis. 'But, Tom——'

'But nothing!' The others had never seen Tom Breck so angry and obstinate. 'I know you're just trying to be modest,

Jack. But I've got confidence in you and so have the others. Right, Nancy? Nick? Eve?'

Nancy nodded at once: she really didn't give a thought to whether she had confidence in Jack Marquis or not: she was just thrilled to see Tom being so forthright. Wilkins hesitated a moment, then he too nodded his agreement. Eve looked at Marquis, sensing his lack of enthusiasm and puzzled by it. But she could not let him down when the others were so obviously for him. She smiled encouragingly at him and nodded.

Singh looked about the group. 'Perhaps we should take a vote?'

The fires in the camp had now begun to die down: there had not been much to burn. Nimchu shouted to the other porters and they all came running up the path to where the packs were stacked waiting for them. They were all laughing, chattering to each other like children who had just left a successful birthday party: the host's house had been burnt down and whose birthday was next? Then abruptly they became aware of the tension among the others, and the laughter and chatter died in their open mouths. They stood watching Marquis and Singh, their smooth brown faces suddenly as devoid of expression as polished wooden masks, sixteen small men who said nothing but all at once decided the issue. Singh looked at them, saw where their devotion lay, and knew they would never obey any order he gave them.

He did not bother to canvass the whites any further. He looked back at Marquis and said, 'You are in charge, my dear chap. Shall I take up the rear?'

Marquis held back the sigh of despair that bubbled in his chest. Stone the bloody crows, why wasn't I born small, skinny and sheepish? He wanted desperately to turn over command of the party to Singh, recognising the other man was trained to do the job, was used to and welcomed authority. But one look at Eve, Tom Breck and the others told him they would not accept such a suggestion without argument, if they would accept it at all. It would do nothing for morale if Singh was forced on them as a leader they all resented. Reluctant though he was, almost afraid of the responsibility they were pushing on him, Marquis knew there was no way out: he was stuck with the task of leading them all to safety.

He nodded at last, trying to make his voice sound as friendly as possible towards Singh: he was going to need the Indian's help and co-operation all the way. 'Righto, Colonel. Nick will walk with you, just in case you need a hand with your prisoner.'

'Glad to,' said Wilkins, recognising that Marquis was now trying to smooth out the ill-will that had almost erupted, and doing his best to help. He was not sure that Singh would not have made a better leader, but he knew he would have been in a minority of one if he had said so. He looked with mock affability at Li. 'Are you going to give us any trouble, chum?'

Li Bu-fang shrugged and smiled. 'Who knows?'

Eve looked at the stocky man in his grey quilted tunic, wondering how one could like an enemy as much as she was coming to like this man. In another hour or two they might all be dead, and all because of this man; yet she felt no hatred towards him, indeed she preferred him to the arrogant Indian who was his captor and their ally. She had spoken to him once or twice while she had been moving about the camp during the packing, and even the few words they had exchanged had impressed upon her that he was a man of humour, politeness and, she suspected, a good deal of humanity. Why she should think he had the latter quality, she did not know. It was one of her virtues, and at the same time a weakness, that she always thought too well of strangers: a friendly smile could be projected, in her estimation of a person, into a depth of charity that not even the stranger, no matter how conceited, would have claimed for himself. She was not naïve, only too charitable herself.

Then she felt Marquis's hand on her arm. 'We'd better get moving, love. How do you feel?'

She looked up at him. 'Scared, you mean?' He hesitated, then nodded. 'I'm scared, darling. But that will make me walk faster and longer. That's what you want, isn't it?'

'I want more than that,' he said quietly. 'I want you safely back home.'

She couldn't resist it: 'Never to come away again like this?'

He hedged. 'We can pick our places to go to.'

'Like New Guinea?' Then she shook her head, not wanting to argue with him at a time like this. 'Let's get out of here first, darling.'

'I'll do my best,' he said, and even to his own doubting ears sounded full of confidence.

Then he turned away, shouting to the porters to take up their packs, and a moment later they were heading up the path. The wind had dropped and the sun, exploding out of the ranges like a ball of lava, blazed in their faces as they headed east up the narrow valley. The sky was clear of clouds, a phenomenon that Marquis, a slightly superstitious man, took as a good omen. He mentioned it to Nimchu walking beside him, and the Bhutanese nodded cheerfully in agreement.

'Perhaps the gods will be with us, sahib. They are smiling at us now.' He nodded up towards the high peaks ahead, standing out like a fleet of wind-creased sails against the blue. The sky itself glittered, as if fragments of ice spun like motes in its immensity, the clean shifting debris of the blizzard that had blown itself out at dawn.

'We'll spin the first prayer-wheel we come to,' Eve said, and Nimchu nodded again. 'You say your Hail Marys, darling, and Nimchu and I will spin prayer-wheels to his gods. I must say, they are beautiful gods this morning.'

'If you have to have an earthly god, you can't choose better than a mountain,' Marquis said. 'What do you reckon, Tom?'

Breck grinned. 'So long as the mountain isn't spoiled, I don't care. But I don't think I'd deify a Swiss Alp, not with all those amateur mountaineers scrambling all over it.'

'Maybe they're more religious than you think,' said Marquis, a dedicated mountaineer. 'Climbers are pilgrims in a way.'

Nancy looked at the mountains up ahead of them. 'This is one pilgrimage I wish I didn't have to make.' She smiled at Tom and put her hand in his. 'But it'll be something to tell them back in Bucks County.'

They moved up through the stand of evergreen oak, disturbing a pair of ibexes that went scampering up through the trees, their curved horns still glistening with morning dampness. The porters shouted at them, the voices echoing back from the sides of the gorge, and the ibexes increased their speed, flying up the steep hillside as if drawn on swiftly-running ropes. They came out into the open above the trees, paused for a moment, then disappeared round a buttress of rock.

Half an hour later the party reached a steep col that cut across the end of the valley. They toiled up it, following the rough path, and at the top Marquis called a halt. He took his binoculars from their case and looked through them down the long narrow corridor of the valley. The air, polished by the dawn wind, was so clear as to be hallucinatory: everything seemed so much nearer than it was. The camp, a black smudge of ash beside the bridge over the river, looked no more than ten minutes' walk behind them. Beyond it the valley sloped down, a vent in the wall of mountains. At the far end a line of ants was moving east up towards the burnt-out camp.

'There they are,' said Marquis. 'We've got a couple of hours on them, no more.'

2

Marquis looked at Singh, who had come up beside him. 'Looks as if they're after your mate.'

'Or those papers.' Singh took his binoculars away from his eyes and turned to Marquis. 'What do you want me to do? I can sit here and wait for them with Li, while you and the others go on. They won't chase you then.'

'What's going on? What papers?' Wilkins and the Brecks had come up to stand with Marquis, Eve and Singh. They were grouped together, all staring down the valley, their backs to the wind that had sprung up again and sliced down over the edge of the col. They could have been admiring the view, except that none of them could see the view: they were all myopic with worry. 'What papers?'

Singh said nothing. Marquis recognised that the other was handing him the initiative, was testing him; he had been elected leader and now Singh was leaving the decisions to him. Once again he had no enthusiasm for it; but it was too late to back out now. He quickly told Wilkins and the Brecks of the papers that Singh carried on him. 'They may be important—we just don't know. But those blokes down there aren't chasing him——' He nodded at Li Bu-fang, who stood apart from them, the prisoner and yet the only calm and confident one of the whole party; behind him even the normally ebullient porters were now silent and morose, staring down the valley with long-sighted eyes that saw not only the pursuing Chinese soldiers but the invisible hordes who waited behind them. 'He's a general, but is he important enough for sixty or seventy men to go hunting through these mountains to try and rescue him? But him and the papers, together they might be important enough.'

'Why don't we just burn the papers?' Nancy asked.

Singh shook his head. 'That would achieve nothing, Mrs. Breck. I'm afraid I feel it's my duty to learn what's in them.' He looked at Li. 'You're not going to tell us, old chap?'

Li smiled. 'You don't really expect me to tell you, do you—old chap?'

The two men stared at each other, smiles fixed on their faces like errors of make-up. It was Wilkins who growled, 'Keep being funny, cock, and something's going to happen to you.'

'Let's keep the papers and let's get moving again.' Eve looked anxiously down the valley. The line of ants hadn't had to stop for any discussion : they knew what they wanted.

Marquis glanced at her, grateful again : twice this morning she had made a decision for him. He shouted to the porters, they picked up their packs and once more the small caravan got under way. Marquis looked up ahead, as if he might glimpse some hint of safety, but the mountains offered no comfort; they reared against the morning sky, cold and implacable. Gods had never looked less forbidding.

The march now led down at a slant across the south face of the col. The track was clearly defined, but the travellers of centuries, their own boots and the hooves of their yaks and mules, had not managed to make it any easier to negotiate. Traps of loose stones were scattered all down the path, ready to snatch the unwary foot from beneath its owner; once Nancy slipped and Tom had to grab her to stop her falling headlong down the steep slope. Several times they passed the bones of animals, yaks and mules that had not completed their journeys.

Marquis looked for the bones of men, but there was none: they had either survived or their companions had given them decent burial. He looked at the earth beside the track and wondered how anyone could have dug even the shallowest grave in it: the skin of the mountain looked like iron.

No trees grew here on this slope; the winds had seen to that. A few shrubs were scattered among the rocks, but they looked black and dead; not even the most curious botanist would stop to look at them. Far below, the river ripped its way down through a narrow gorge; one could imagine the water eating its way through the mountain like a dark drill. The party was below the worst of the wind now, but gusts of it occasionally swept down on them and one always had to be careful: it needed only a push from the wind for a man to be sent sprawling down the slope. A sense of isolation began to grip Marquis, but this time it was a depressing feeling, not the euphoria he usually experienced. If the Chinese caught them and killed them here in these high valleys, no one would ever know. He had no ambition for an obituary, but he did not want to disappear from this life like a forgotten promise. Even a grave in a cemetery was some sort of destination, a recognition, no matter how late, of a man's meaning. The thought of eternity did not worry him unduly, but before he opened the gate and went in, he would like to scrawl on the wall outside: Marquis, like Kilroy, was here.

Each of the others had his own thoughts, but all of them were focused on the Chinese two hours behind them. Eve walked without much thought of where she put her feet; she had the natural grace of a dancer and her feet had their own sensitivity to danger: it was a sensitivity that natural climbers also had. Goats also had it, as Jack had so insensitively told her. So she had little or no distraction from thoughts of what lay behind her and the others. She was afraid, but it was a fear that had not yet settled fully on her; it hung over her, like some dark bird; she had a moment of fancy and wondered if fear was a vulture that feasted on dead spirit. Her own spirit was not entirely dead yet. She looked at her husband two paces ahead of her; Jack, the insensitive spouse. He seemed to feel her look on the back of his neck and he turned and smiled encouragingly at her. So long as he remained alive, so would her spirit.

The party was now coming down towards a forest of pine trees. In the morning sunlight that struck at an angle across the forest, the dark green of the pines had a soft brilliance after the dull iron colour of the bare upper slopes. There was a movement just above the line of trees, and Marquis said, 'Thar!'; but no one stopped to watch the swift movement of the goat as it leapt down the slope and disappeared into the trees. Such small excitements meant nothing to them now that they themselves had become quarry. An eagle planed down across the narrow valley they were entering, dragging the eye with it; suddenly it dived, but the pheasant it had been stalking moved too quickly, the flash of its plumes exploding in a burst of colour as it vanished into the trees. The eagle soared off, began to climb again, patient as death itself.

'I used to go shooting eagles when we lived in Sinkiang,' Tom Breck said to Nancy. 'I was never very good.'

'They are not easy birds to shoot.' Singh, with Li Bu-fang beside him, was walking just behind the Brecks. 'I prefer to shoot grouse myself. I used to go up to Scotland when I was at Oxford. Jolly good fun. Are you fond of shooting?' He looked at Li.

'How can you ask him such a question?' Nancy flared. 'Of course he's fond of shooting! How many people have you shot?'

'Honey——' Tom said, but Li shook his head at him.

'Your wife may ask such a question, Mr. Breck. I have shot men—I have had to, to go on living. Where Mrs. Breck comes from, maybe they do not have to shoot men to remain alive themselves.'

'She comes from Philadelphia, the City of Brotherly Love.' Tom Breck smiled, then regretted it; Nancy looked at him angrily, as if he had betrayed her. He wished she would forget how his parents had died; he knew her anger at the way they had died was born out of love for him, but it didn't console him. In his heart he sometimes wondered if his parents would not have welcomed the manner of their death : martyrdom was preferable to a tiny pension and retirement in some small

Colorado town. He had met other retired missionaries, dying on the vine, their fervour squeezed out of them by the indifference surrounding them. At least among the unconverted one had the hope of saving a soul.

'When were you in Sinkiang, Mr. Breck?' Li asked.

'Years ago. I left there when I was thirteen to go back to the States to school.'

'The year his parents were murdered,' said Nancy.

Singh was growing tired of Mrs. Breck; one would think that her in-laws were the only people who had ever been killed by the Chinese. He thought of his own men dead in the snow in the pass to the north; none of them was his kin, but at least he had known them. Mrs. Breck was mourning the death of strangers. She should come to India, where strangers died every day by the thousand, murdered by neglect. He had never agreed with the point of Donne's sermon : any man's death did not diminish him at all. You could not mourn the world, the weight of such sorrow would only lead to suicide. Mourn those whose death you saw and forget the rest : that was the only way to go on enjoying what was left of life. His father had been right : pleasure was the reason for existence. He wondered what his father would think of India to-day.

'Can you read Chinese, Mr. Breck?' he asked, thinking of the papers in his pocket.

Breck shook his head. 'I could speak the dialect, that was all. And I've forgotten most of that.'

Singh looked at Li, but the Chinese had turned his face away, hiding the look of satisfaction that had creased it for a moment. The papers were still a mystery; they rested in Singh's pocket, a secret he could not unravel. What if they proved to be nothing more than routine orders, no more than bumf? Would he have endangered the lives of these people, perhaps (the thought suddenly chilled him) have had them killed, for nothing at all? Then he looked back at Li and shook the thought from his mind. The Chinese looked too smug, too secretive, for the papers to have no importance.

They were down among the trees now. The exertion of their walking had warmed Marquis and the others, and the morning sun had helped; but now here beneath the trees it was cold, it was like walking through a dark ice chamber. In the sudden silence that fell on the party as they entered the forest they heard the distant tinkle of bells, a sound so light that at first Marquis thought it was only a trick of hearing. Then he felt Nimchu's hand on his arm.

'Someone coming, sahib. Big party.'

Marquis held up his hand and the rest of the party came to a halt. He moved on ahead, his gun now held at the ready. He heard Eve whisper behind him, 'Be careful, darling'; and he nodded. He had no desire to play the hero, but he was stuck with it. He wondered how many of the world's heroes had been reluctant to begin with. He shied away from cowardice, but that didn't mean you had to go galloping off full tilt in the other direction. He remembered his father, the Friday night orator who could rub two fools together and start a riot and be gone when the police were still two blocks away. He wondered if Tim Marquis, in the special Heaven reserved for Irishmen, was looking down now with a quizzical eye on his son as, gun in hand, he advanced slowly down the path.

He came round a bend in the track and saw the long line of monks heading up towards him. He stopped and blew out in a sigh of relief. There were almost two hundred of the monks, their faded magenta robes showing beneath the tattered brown cloaks they wore for extra warmth. Mules and yaks carried their belongings; it was the harness bells that had made the music Marquis had heard. The whole caravan moved with the slow steady march of a funeral; some of the monks carried prayer-flags, others spun small prayer-wheels; and all of them were murmuring a chant that was led by a tall elderly lama at the head of the procession. The dark forest was no longer an ice chamber. It was still cold and dark, but now it had become a huge chapel, brought to life by the long line of holy men as they wound their way up its single aisle of path.

Marquis stood unmoving for a moment. It was a long time since he had been a regular churchgoer, but religion was a long way from being dead in him; he could not but be impressed as the long caravan of monks, carrying their air of piety with them like an invisible prayer-flag, came up towards him. These men of the mountains were the truly religious; these were not the politicians or the social arbiters of a church. He all at once envied them their faith.

He turned and waved, and Eve and the others came down the path. He remarked at once that Singh and Li Bu-fang had disappeared, but there was no time for questions; the head of the procession of monks was now only yards from them. The leader turned and said something to the monks behind him, and the word went swiftly down the caravan. The long line of men and animals came to a halt in a jingle of bells. The music echoed and re-echoed in the vaults of the forest; the woods were alive for a moment with a shimmer of sound. Then one of the monks, on a word from the lama, came forward and said something to Marquis. The latter turned to Nimchu, who translated.

'He asks where we are going, sahib.'

'A good question,' said Marquis wryly. 'Tell him what's happened, Nimchu, but leave out anything about Colonel Singh and his prisoner.'

Nimchu seemed to hesitate, and for a moment Marquis thought he was going to rebel at being told what to do in his own country where invaders were involved. Then Nimchu turned back to the monk. The latter was a small man with a thin drooping grey moustache and sad disappointed eyes; Marquis had a moment of doubt, wondering if all the holy men found what they wanted here in the isolation of the mountains. Perhaps isolation wasn't the answer, after all. The monk sucked in his breath past toothless gums when Nimchu told him about the Chinese soldiers; when he spoke to the lama, the latter shook his head and behind him other monks muttered in concern. The spokesman looked at Marquis and said something, a look of disbelief on his face: behind him the bells tinkled, like the sound of innocence.

'He says he cannot understand why the Chinese come into our country, sahib.' The rebellious look was there again in Nimchu's face. 'Shall I tell him about the Indian and the Chinese?'

'Why not?' Wilkins said. 'Who the hell are you supposed to be looking after, Jack? Us? These monks? Or those two bastards up in the trees?'

'I don't see why we have to protect them,' Nancy said. 'If these monks run into trouble with the soldiers, don't you think they should know why?'

Tom Breck nodded, and Eve said, 'They're right, Jack.' It hurt her to go against him, but she knew he was wrong. 'You'll have to tell them.'

He had made his first mistake as leader. Abruptly he turned and bellowed up into the trees, 'Singh! Come on down and bring your mate with you!'

His voice bounced back and forth among the trees, then died away and was gone finally as a whimper. To Marquis's ears the last faint sound had a note of desperation to it; only two hours before people had placed their faith in him and now already they were beginning to doubt him. Then he saw Singh and Li Bu-fang coming down out of the trees, sliding a little on the damp needles on the ground. The monks all turned and gazed up towards the newcomers, two hundred faces wide open with surprise and, a moment later, the first hint of fear. It suddenly struck Marquis then that it was as if these men had suddenly been dragged forward several centuries. These two men, the Indian and the Chinese, coming down through the trees towards them were Asia of the twentieth century, with its rivalries, its conflicts, and its blind groping struggle to catch up with the rest of the world. The monks wanted none of it.

An angry mutter ran down the long line. The monks' temper communicated itself to the mules and yaks; the animals began to move restlessly. Marquis felt his own party bunch up behind him, as if they expected the monks to attack them. Involuntarily he brought his gun up again and held it across his body.

Singh and Li Bu-fang slid down on to the path and came to a halt beside Marquis. 'Why did you bring us out in the open?' Singh asked.

It had not been his decision, but he took the blame for it. 'These monks are entitled to know what they're in for. Now they've seen you and the general, they can make up their minds whether to keep on going or turn back.'

Singh hesitated, then he spoke to the lama in Hindi. The latter understood the language and he listened patiently while Singh spoke to him. Li Bu-fang meanwhile stood looking down the long caravan, speculatively, like an invader wondering if these gentle withdrawn men were worth conquering. They in turn stared back at him, seeming to Marquis to become more worldly and challenging by the minute.

Singh turned back to Marquis. 'I have apologised for coming into their country—I regret I can do no more than that. The lama seems to accept my story. He says they will go on. They have closed their *dzong* in the mountains—they always come down to the valleys for the winter.'

'Tell him I hope he has a good winter and a long one,' said Marquis. 'The longer the winter, the less chance of more Chinese coming over the mountains into his country. Oh, and ask him not to tell the Chinese, if they meet up with them, that they've seen us.'

Singh spoke again to the lama, who nodded. He was a tall thin old man, with dark eyes hidden in a cat's cradle of wrinkles. The wrinkles gave a suggestion of laughter, yet the eyes themselves were calm, almost dull; the effect was of a face that was a mixture of impishness and serenity. It was Marquis's idea of the face of a saint; he had never understood the artists of his own church who had always depicted saints as men of anguish, contorted piety and heartburn. The lama spoke in a surprisingly young voice, light as a boy's. He spoke directly to both Marquis and Singh, and the latter translated: 'He says he'll tell the Chinese nothing of what they've seen on their march. If they have to lie, it is better to lie than to help a man towards his death. They won't give us away.'

Marquis bowed his head in thanks to the lama, then looked at Li Bu-fang. 'And you bastards still want to come in here and take over a people like these?'

Li Bu-fang didn't answer, but turned away and stared up at the trees. But not before Marquis had seen the flicker of doubt on his face.

The monks' caravan began to move on up the path. Nimchu and the porters had already begun to move on down along the edge of the path. The monks went past, staring resentfully at the turned back of Li, then smiling and jerking their heads in little polite bows to the others. It seemed to Eve that the prayer-wheels they carried where being spun more quickly, but that might have been her imagination or her own sceptical faith: did a holy man pray twice as hard when his life was in danger? As the last of them, a young boy who looked no more than fourteen, went by he turned and waved his prayer-flag at them. The inference was plain: he would pray for them.

'And we'll pray for you,' said Tom Breck, and the young monk bowed his head as if he understood.

The tinkling of bells died away slowly among the trees. Marquis and the others trudged on down the path, and the cold of the forest came down again, rusting their blood and thickening their joints so that they stumbled like elderly cripples.

'They will all probably be massacred,' said Singh, as if talking to himself. 'Will your chums kill them, old chap?'

'Why should they?' Li said.

'Why shouldn't they? Your chappies don't want to advertise they're here in Bhutan, so why not kill the witnesses?'

Eve and the others listening to the Indian and the Chinese, were aware of the division that separated themselves from the two soldiers: they were listening to the East talking to the East. Their two nations between them made up one-third of the world's population: a few lives here or there were never missed.

'How can you be so casual about it?' Eve missed her footing as she snapped the question back over her shoulder at Singh; Marquis had to grab her to prevent her from falling. She felt him squeeze her arm in warning: don't interfere, let them argue between themselves. She looked up at him, dropped her voice: 'How can *you* be so casual about it?'

'I'm not,' he said, and she saw the look of pain on his face. 'But do you think our arguing about it is going to save them? They had enough prayer-wheels and prayer-flags to save an army. If those things don't save them, no amount of talking from us will help them.'

'You believe in prayer, don't you?' It struck her that she had never asked him that question before.

He walked in silence for a few steps, then he nodded. 'At least it's worth a try.' And despised himself for the hedging note in his voice. It was as if he were afraid that she would laugh at him; he kept his gaze averted, like a man who had just confessed to sin. He had not been home to Australia for years, so he did not know what it was like there; but in England the act of prayer had become a social error, something one didn't do in polite society. Something you didn't do in front of your wife.

'I'd better start learning then,' she said, and once again he looked gratefully at her. I'm like Tom Breck, he thought with surprise. I need my wife to keep me going.

3

They came out of the pine forest and found themselves on a long open scree that sloped down to a narrow gorge through which the river raced with a thunder that came up to them on the now-still air. The wind had dropped and here on the open mountainside, in the blaze of the morning sun, the warmth soon crept back into their chilled bones. The track zigzagged its way down the scree, and Marquis at once saw their danger. It was a gauntlet path, one where they would be as exposed as if stood against a wall. The river was no more than five or six hundred yards below them, but the twisting, turning track was over a mile.

Marquis stopped for a moment and looked back, but the trees hid the upper slopes of the mountain from his view. He had no idea where the Chinese soldiers might be; meeting the procession of monks, they might even have turned back. But he held no hope of that; he had to act on the assumption that the Chinese were still chasing them. He looked down at the river again, saw the fragile bridge across it, and suddenly hope blazed in him. If they could cross the river, chop down the bridge. . . .

'I'm hungry,' Nancy Breck said.

'We'll eat when we cross the river,' Marquis said.

'You're pushing it a bit hard, aren't you?' Wilkins sat down on a rock. He looked to the north-west with the eyes of a man made long-sighted by memory. The enemy was there, hidden somewhere beyond the trees, but beyond them, beyond Tibet, beyond Europe, was England and Leeds: home. He felt suddenly angry, his grip tightened on the gun in his hand. 'Christ, why do *we* have to run from them? Let the colonel and this bastard go on——' He had always been careful of his language in front of Eve and Nancy; now anger made him deaf to his own words. 'Why don't we bloody stay here? The Chinks don't want *us*.'

'You want to take your chances on that?' Marquis said quietly.

Wilkins stared at him, looked back up at the trees, then shook his head and stood up. The anger drained out of him. I'm a coward, he thought, a miserable lily-livered mucker who won't take his chances on anything. He looked at Eve, expecting to see contempt in her face; it hurt him even more to see that she pitied him. Suddenly he *wanted* the Chinese to come, he wanted to prove himself to her. He looked up the mountainside again, but the trees showed nothing: his bravado was a hollow blast on a tin trumpet.

'Watch your step,' Marquis said, and Wilkins looked back at him quickly. But the remark was addressed to everyone, and Marquis had already begun to lead the way down the steep rocky path.

At every bend in the path there was a prayer-wheel; the porters spun each wheel as they passed it. The thunder of the river increased as they got closer down to the gorge through which it hurtled; it came up at them like a threat, a bombardment warning them to turn back. Mist hung in the air like cannon smoke; sun blazed for a moment on a streak of water like a flash of flame. Above the pounding tearing waters they could see the bridge, a narrow catwalk that shivered like a loose cable in the disturbed air in which it hung. At either end stood a prayer-flag and a prayer-wheel, the flags limp and sodden, the wheels motionless. One would have to pray hard crossing this bridge.

The last fifty yards of the path was a mud slide, tricky and treacherous, marked with long scars where the monks and their mules and yaks had slipped and slid coming up it. Marquis went down first, clutching for hand-holds on the wet glistening rocks on the upper side of the track. He shouted a word of warning to Eve only a yard behind him, but she might just as well have been a mile away; his shout was only a silent movement of his mouth in the roar that engulfed them. The short narrow gorge was a cauldron of sound that punched at every nerve. And it was cold: Marquis felt his fingers freezing on the wet rocks. Already ice had formed in the pools below the huge boulders past which the river raced; in another week or two this wild torrent would be tamed, would be frozen still.

Suddenly Marquis's feet went from beneath him and he went sliding down on his back towards the bridge and the river. He grabbed desperately at the base of one of the thin poles that held a prayer-flag. He felt it give in the cleft of the rock in which it was stuck; the pole leant towards him, the sodden flag drooping mockingly down on to his face. Then he felt the base of the pole grip and hold. His legs hung over the edge of the bridge; he could feel it trembling beneath him like a living thing. Slowly he dragged himself back. Stretched full length, he looked up and saw Eve and Nimchu reaching out to help him; but he shook his head and went on hauling himself over the slippery logs and up on to the ice and mud of the approach. Then he was safe, flat on his back like a drunk, breathless, shivering with both cold and relief, his hand still tight like a madman's grip round the pole of the prayer-flag. He looked up at Eve, shook the flag and grinned. She nodded, smiling back at him, dumb with the shock that she had almost lost him.

It took twenty minutes for all of them to negotiate the last treacherous yards of the path and the short rickety span of the bridge. Marquis, the last to cross, kept glancing at his watch and then looking back up the path to the lip of the gorge. Then it was his turn to cross and it looked at last as if they might have beaten the pursuing Chinese.

Marquis was half-way across the narrow swaying gangway, balancing himself against the movement of it, when he saw Chungma fling up an arm and point up towards the mountain-side. He didn't endanger himself by trying to turn round and look back; he saw everything reflected in the urgent faces of the others waiting for him at the end of the bridge. He kept treading deliberately, putting his feet down carefully on the slippery trembling logs beneath him. Then he was across, had turned and looked up past the lip of the gorge and saw the Chinese coming down out of the trees on the run.

Seen through the mist above the gorge, the Chinese soldiers

assumed strange shapes and movements; they seemed to dance on the mountainside, grotesque misshapen figures out of some nightmare. The first shots they fired were like shots out of some terrifying dream: no sound at all, only the chips flying off the rocks as the bullets hit them.

Marquis leaned close to Singh, shouted in his ear, 'Get Li and the women up round that bend out of the way!' He nodded towards a large outcrop of rock. 'I'm going to chop down the bridge!'

Singh nodded and moved on up the track, pushing Li, Nancy and Eve ahead of him. Eve hesitated for a moment, looking at Marquis; but he nodded and gestured for her to go with Singh. Then he took an axe from one of the porter's packs, brandished it to show what he wanted done, then went to work on the bridge.

There were two other axes in the packs; Nimchu and Tom Breck seized them and joined Marquis as he hacked at the supports of the bridge. But the bridge, despite its look of fragility, had been built to stand. It had withstood years of high winds, floods and heavy snowfalls; it would not fall easily under the onslaught of three small axes. Marquis found it difficult to keep his footing, so that he could not put his full weight behind each blow of his axe. Breck and Nimchu were having the same trouble; they appeared to be no more than chipping at the bridge. Desperation took hold of the three men.

Marquis was blinded by sweat and mist; he felt he was working under water. When he breathed he seemed to take in mouthfuls of liquid; he had the crazy feeling that his lungs were sloshing inside him like half-filled waterbags. A beer drinker all his life, he was going to die from a surfeit of water. He swung the axe with a savage desperation, but it was almost as if he were trying to hack through thick rubber; the supports bounced under the impact of the axe, seemed even to dodge the blows. He remembered the Australian axemen he had seen at contests back home; men brought up on the hardest of timbers, they claimed themselves as the world's best; they would have laughed like tickled kookaburras to see him now. He swung again, saw the axe-head bounce, felt the handle,

slippery with water, slide li! : an eel out of his hands, saw the
axe sail gracefully through the mist and disappear into the
stream below. His own rage exploding within him was no
less than that of the torrent below. He grabbed at the supports,
tried to demolish the bridge with brute strength. He might as
well have tried to move one of the surrounding mountains.

He stopped, panting to force some air into his lungs; looked
up and saw the Chinese soldiers through a break in the mist.
Some were kneeling on the track high up on the slope, taking
deliberate aim and firing down at the bridge. But the angle of
fire was too acute; the bullets were still hitting the rocks a
yard or two above the heads of Marquis and the others.
Wilkins and the rest of the porters had taken refuge behind
some rocks below the track; they were being drenched by spray
from the river as it tore past them, but they were safe from the
Chinese fire. Marquis looked towards them and saw Wilkins
coming along the rocky bank, two tomahawks clutched in his
hands.

He shook his head: what good would a tomahawk do where
an axe had failed? But Wilkins, the impractical man, had
grasped the practical fact of the bridge's construction. Its
strength lay in the fact that every support complemented
another; the mountain men who had built this bridge had
been engineers who had acquired their skill the practical way.
The bridge would not collapse if only one or two supports were
torn down; they would have to rip away more than half of
the long poles. Wilkins handed Marquis one of the tomahawks and with the other began to hack away at the ropes
that bound the supports to the bridge.

Marquis grasped the tomahawk and the idea at the same
moment. He was not slow to act on the suggestion; but once
again he had failed as a leader. Time had been lost while he,
Breck and Nimchu had chopped futilely at the support poles.
He looked up through the mist again, saw some of the soldiers
now coming full pelt down the slope, doing a sort of glissade
down the scree of loose stones. It would be only a matter of
minutes before the Chinese were at the top of the shallow
gorge, could pick them off like sitting ducks. He began to
chop furiously at the ropes.

Breck and Nimchu had each caught the idea; with their axes

they too began to attack the ropes. Marquis worked like a man in a frenzy, one word burned in his brain: destroy, destroy, destroy. He swung the tomahawk like a madman; in desperation and yet with a sort of wild crazy humour; Lizzie Borden had never worked harder. The ropes gave, curled back like severed snakes; he leapt across the bridge to attack the ropes on that side. Something flew off the timber near him; he glanced down and saw the new scar where the bullet had hit the log. He looked up, saw the first of the Chinese already at the top of the gorge, his rifle at his shoulder for a second shot. Marquis swung down beneath the bridge just as the soldier staggered, let his rifle drop, then came plunging down into the white boil of water at the bottom of the gorge. Singh stepped out from behind the outcrop of rock farther up the path and waved his Sten gun at Marquis. The message was clear: get on with the job, I'll look after the Chinese.

Marquis went back to work on the bridge. He was knee deep in water now, leaning upstream against the tearing force of the river as it curled up against him in a biting wave. He could feel the cold of it eating its way into his very bones; any moment his legs would freeze, snap off like brittle branches from a frost-killed tree. He swung the tomahawk, saw more ropes snap apart; moved on, began the attack on another binding of ropes. Here beneath the bridge he could barely see. He was working in a deluge; he had to turn his face down-stream to catch his breath. The roar of the river deafened him as it bounced back from the walls of the gorge; his ears were clogged with water and thunder. His legs were now numb; only instinct told him where to put his dead feet. His pelvis felt like a block of ice; good-bye fatherhood, he thought. He slipped on the rocks, smashed his knee against the jagged edge of a boulder; but the cold had anæsthetised him against pain, he might even be shot and not know it. This was what the last moment of life must be like: the body already dead, but the mind still struggling for survival. He kept his arms going, hacking away at the ropes, hacking at death now, trying to drive it back.

Farther up the track Singh was using his ammunition care-fully, only shooting at the Chinese when he thought the fire would be most effective. Li Bu-fang sat on his haunches behind a rock, flinching occasionally when a Chinese bullet came too close, but otherwise calm and patient : the end of the game was in sight. Farther along, behind another tumble of rocks, Eve, Nancy and the porter Lombi were crouched in the mud. Lombi, a thin nervous little man with a gap-toothed smile and half of one ear missing, had taken Wilkins's gun when the latter had gone to help Marquis on the bridge. He would peer up through the mist at the soldiers on the high side of the gorge, mutter to himself, then look down at the gun in his hands. He would dearly love to kill the Chinese, but he had never even held a gun before and he had only a hazy idea how one used it. He kept glancing at Singh as the latter took an occasional shot at the men up on the rim of the gorge, but he couldn't bring himself to try to do the same with Sahib Wilkins's gun.

Suddenly Nancy, squatting beside him, snatched the gun from him. She had been peering up at the gorge rim, then down towards the bridge, seeing everything only through a haze of mist and myopia. She had been putting on her glasses and almost at once snatching them off; she could hardly see without them, yet as soon as she put them on they clouded up with mist. But she had to do *something* : she couldn't sit here while Tom possibly died from the same bullets as had killed his parents. She pointed the gun up at the dim figures she could see beyond the top of the gorge and pulled the trigger. Nothing happened; the safety catch was on. She grappled blindly and furiously with the gun, managed to snap off the safety-catch and raised the gun again. It kicked in her loose grip and she sat back in the mud, crying with pain and frustration.

Eve, intent only on the safety of Marquis, staring down at the bridge to the exclusion of everything else, had been taken unawares by Nancy's action. But now she turned back and grabbed the gun from the sobbing girl. She handed the gun back to Lombi, then pulled Nancy to her as a mother might comfort a distraught daughter. She said nothing : in the roar from the river and deafened by her own volcanic emotion, Nancy would have heard nothing. The two women sat there in the mud, one holding the other; and Singh, glancing at them, was reminded of the misery of women in his own country. He had seen them by the roadside after riots, outside homes destroyed by floods: their misery always silent and somehow more terrible than that of men. In those moments something in him had always rebelled against his father, the man who had believed women were only for pleasure. He looked at these two white women now and regretted that there was no woman in the world who would pray for him as these two were praying for their husbands. He had had three wives and he knew he had meant nothing to any of them, as they had meant nothing to him. He turned back and fired a burst up at the rim of the gorge, shooting blindly and extravagantly, shooting at a wasted life.

Down at the bridge Wilkins was signalling frantically to Marquis. The last of the ropes had gone; now the support poles had to be pushed out from under the gangway. Breck and Nimchu came running back from the far side of the bridge; the narrow gangway bounced and swayed under the pounding feet. Somehow or other neither of them slipped and fell; Nimchu had given the far prayer-wheel a violent spin before he ran after Breck. The two of them reached the end of the bridge, knelt down and took the tomahawks that Marquis and Wilkins passed up to them. Then Marquis and Wilkins took hold of the first of the support poles and leant their weight against it.

On the slippery rocks, off-balance against the racing current, it was almost impossible to get any purchase; all their strength had to come from their shoulders and arms. They heaved against the pole, felt it resist their efforts as if it were a living mocking thing; then the top of it slid slowly out from under the gangway and a moment later the complementary support suddenly snapped in half as the bridge tilted. For a moment Marquis thought the whole gangway would come crashing down on them; Wilkins ducked instinctively, slipped on the rocks and would have fallen into the torrent if Marquis had not grabbed him. But the gangway held: at an angle but still crossable.

Marquis looked up and saw Tom Breck gesticulating, urging him to hurry. The last of the porters was now scrambling up the path, heading for the protection of the outcrop of rock.

Marquis couldn't see Singh, nor could he see the Chinese
soldiers; he could only guess that they were now trying to come
down the path, but were being held back by Singh's fire. He
nodded at Tom, then turned and stepped out into the middle
of the river towards the one pole that now seemed to be
holding up the bridge. The water tore at him, numbing him
with its cold, trying to force him off balance and go plunging
with it down through the long wound it had gouged out of
the mountain. He was at the end of his endurance; he survived only on the memory of strength. He stood with his feet
anchored in crevices among the rocks, grasped the support pole
and heaved. The top half of his body was still unfrozen: he
could feel pain there, the torture of muscles being exerted to
their utmost. There was no air left in his lungs; he was
slowly drowning in the mist and spray that enveloped him.
The pole stood firm, solid and unyielding as a pillar of rock.
He might just as well let it go and give himself up to the
plundering river. He was going to die anyway, and it would
be a better death than at the hands of the Chinese.

Then the pole gave, suddenly and without warning. He
saw the gangway sway above him like a long brown pennant
that threatened to wrap itself round him before it fell into the
torrent and was swept away; he had destroyed it and now it
would destroy him, be both his killer and his shroud. He flung
himself backwards, clawing at the rocks, feeling his hands slide
off them as if they were oiled. He turned, on his knees, the
water crashing right over him in a bruising lung-crushing
assault; a rock was behind him, holding him against the brutal
rape of the water, forcing its own jagged blades into his spine.
He tried to open his mouth to scream (farewell? defiance?),
but you couldn't scream under water: it even made you die
in silence.

Then he felt the hands clutching at him, saw dimly through
the water the two shapes above him, Wilkins and Nimchu. He
couldn't help them, his legs were already dead. He shook his
head, trying to tell them to leave him, not to die with him; but
if they understood what he was trying to say, they gave no
heed to it. He felt them lift him, dragging him across the
rocks; then Tom Breck and Chungma were leaning down from

the bank, were hauling him up as if he were a carcass. Then he was lying in the mud and ice on the track behind a rock, only half-alive but not yet a carcass.

He turned his head, shaking the water from his eyes, and saw the bridge go hurtling down the river, plunging and whipping in the savage waters like the frenzied tail of a dying dragon.

FOUR

'That might hold 'em back half an hour or half a day. You never know with those bastards.' Marquis looked at Li Bu-fang. 'I'm not being affectionate this time, calling them bastards.'

'In the ultimate society, Mr. Marquis, there will be no bastards.'

'There'll always be bastards of some sort,' said Marquis. 'I expect to meet them even in Heaven.'

'Are you going there?' Eve lifted her eyebrows in mock surprise.

Marquis grinned and kissed her cheek, something he had never done in public before. 'I nearly made it just then, love.'

'Nearly,' she said, and blinked. She still felt hollow with relief; she would crumble in his arms if he embraced her. But he didn't have time for that; he had already turned away, was no longer a husband but a leader again.

'There's no time to stop and eat now.' Marquis grinned at Nancy. 'Sorry Nance. We'll just have to chew on a tsampa cake as we go along.'

Nancy made a face, but no complaint. Tom was safe and that was all that mattered right now. Tom put his arm about her and said, 'I'd sooner die of starvation than a bullet. It's more saintly.'

Singh and Wilkins came stumbling up the path to where Marquis and the rest of the party stood in what could have been a small fort of huge rocks. The river and the gorge lay nearly four hundred yards below them; they were safe from any fire from the Chinese. The party had moved up here as soon as Marquis had recovered enough to be able to walk; then Singh and Wilkins had gone back down the track to have a closer look at the Chinese. They came in now behind the ring of rocks, panting a little from their exertion.

'There are about sixty of them, give or take one or two.'

'You took one at least,' said Marquis. Twice now the Indian had saved his life; he was building up a debt to Singh that he could never hope to repay. 'Thanks.'

Singh nodded in satisfaction, seeming to miss the point that he had saved Marquis's life. 'A pity it wasn't more, but I had to conserve my ammunition.' He looked down the slope: worry lay like an expression of pain on his face. 'I think we are going to need all the ammunition we have. They are well equipped. This isn't some rag-tag peasant brigade.'

'The revolution is over.' Li lounged against a rock. He showed no disappointment that the Chinese pursuit had been foiled; it was only a question of time, the end had just been delayed. He looked around at them almost pleasantly, a little grieved by their ignorance. 'You imperialists forget that. We are now equipped to fight *anyone*. And beat them.'

Everybody stared at him, but nobody answered him: it was as if no one had an answer, as if they had suddenly been faced with a fact that they had suspected for a long time. Then Marquis dismissed Li the only way he knew how: he turned his back on him and looked at Singh and Wilkins: 'What have they got?'

'Rifles, Sten guns or something like them, machine guns, even a couple of mortars. And perhaps a couple of dozen mules.'

'They look a self-contained little commando,' Wilkins said.

'Well, if they haven't got any portable bridges with them, we're okay for a while.' Marquis looked through a gap in the rocks down towards the gorge. His boots squelched as he moved, and his clothes were still dark and heavy with water; if he had to climb any higher and the wind sprang up again, he knew he would freeze solid. Caravans in years to come would find him posed by the side of the track, acting as his own statue: you couldn't give the old ego much freer rein than that. But there was no time to change into dry clothes now; he would have to risk turning into a quick-frozen memorial to himself. Like Tom Breck, while there was still life he preferred a slow death to a quick one; though he had no ambitions towards sainthood, such as Tom had expressed. All he wanted, while there was still hope, was to live. He looked back at Eve and for no reason at all—he saw the puzzled but pleased look in her eyes—he winked. Then he looked down towards the gorge again. 'They're moving upstream. They're not going to give up—they'll find *some* way of getting across——'

'Naturally,' said Li Bu-fang. 'Those men down there are not only Communists, they are Chinese. We invented the virtues of patience and persistence.'

'We invented a thing or two in the West,' said Wilkins, who was surprising even himself at the belligerence he was finding every minute. 'A punch up the snout, for instance, for blokes who can't keep their traps shut.'

'Not enough.' Li shook his head, pityingly. 'A punch up the—snout? Against a machine gun? Who is the primitive peasant now?'

Singh was looking steadily at Li. 'We Indians have one or two inventions to our credit. Rather jolly ones—ghoulish, you might say. If you feel you must go on talking, General, I think it would be better if you said something constructive. Such as telling us what is in these papers '—he touched his pocket—' I could help you talk, help the old memory, with an old Indian invention.'

'Which one is that?' asked Nancy innocently.

'Strangling,' said Singh; and Marquis thought : Oxford never touched the heart of this man. Culture and sophistication had a hundred forms; a man could graduate in savagery. This was no gentle Indian; Gandhi would never have recognised him.

Nancy shook her head in disbelief. You could read her thoughts : Colonel Singh was one of us, people on our side didn't murder other people, not even the enemy.

Then the party had begun to move on, and the conversation died. Eve had noticed how during the march inconsequential talk filled an incongruous moment, as if everyone was working consciously to distract himself from what their fate might be. But the talk always died suddenly, like a birthday candle in a dark gale. No amount of talk, inconsequential or otherwise, would affect their fate. Only action, the simple action of keeping moving, could do that.

Marquis looked back, but the Chinese soldiers were out of sight, looking for some way to cross the river. He and Nimchu led the party, with everyone else strung out in single file down the track. Tsering had produced tsampa cakes and everyone ate as he walked. It was almost midday and the sun blazed down on this southern slope out of a sky whose brilliance was both pain and pleasure against the eyes. Everyone but the porters had now put on dark glasses, including Singh and Li Bu-fang; it was not the first time that Marquis had had the fanciful thought that mountains made a family of strangers. He looked back down the line and half a dozen anonymous faces, but all with the same blank dark eyes, like holes in a family of skulls, returned his look. He turned back, plodding on beside Nimchu, feeling his clothes drying on him, till they came up into a pass and stood below the tall sheer cliffs on either side.

A cairn of stones, supporting a bunch of prayer-flags like a faded bouquet, stood to one side of the track. Nimchu moved across to the cairn and added a stone to it; he bowed his head to each of the other porters to signify he had acted on their behalf. Then he touched the prayer-flags, separating the thin faded pennants as he might have separated the fragile petals of a dead rose.

' Why did he do that?' Nancy asked.

' On all these old trade routes, at the tops of passes, they have these cairns of stones,' Marquis said. ' I think the Tibetans started it. When you've reached the top of a pass, you've reached the end of one stage of your journey and you begin another. You say a prayer, of thanks and hope, and add another stone.' He looked across at the cairn, the petrified prayers of a thousand caravans. ' My old man once helped build a cairn, but every stone was an Irish republican's curse. It was a memorial to King George the Fifth.'

' Why did he build it then?' Wilkins said.

' It was the Depression, sport. In those days he'd have put the hinges on the gates of hell if they'd paid him.'

' I thought you told me he was an atheist,' said Eve, smiling.

' Atheists believe in hell. They just don't believe in God and Heaven, that's all. You believe in hell, don't you, General?'

' Of course,' said Li. ' I've experienced it. Under the Kuomintang.'

Marquis grinned. He was coming to like the bastard more and more. Love thine enemy : was it possible? Then Singh,

Г

whom he knew he would never love even if he became his
dearest ally, said, 'Shall we move on, old chap? We really
don't have time for philosophising.'

Marquis grinned again. 'It's when you think you have no
time, that's just when you need a little philosophy.'

'I think we had better get moving,' said Eve diplomatically,
and began to move down through the pass with Nimchu beside
her. If there was to be five more days of this before they
reached safety, she wondered who, indeed, would reach safety
at all. She put the thought out of her mind by asking Nimchu,
'Where does this path lead to?'

Nimchu shrugged, the pack on his back bouncing a little.
Each pack weighed close to eighty pounds, and Eve never got
over her admiration for the way in which the porters plodded
on mile after mile under a weight which would have forced
most white men to their knees after half a mile.

'Not sure, memsahib. It is a very old road, many many
years old. It was used a lot before the Chinese conquered
Tibet.' He glanced back at Li Bu-fang at the rear of the line
and spat. He made no apology to Eve for the rude gesture;
he was innocent enough to believe that a man's feelings
towards an enemy did not have to be excused. 'But since
then——' He shrugged again: the pack bounced on his back
like the hump of a philosophic cripple. 'I think the road
leads down into Assam, but I am not sure.'

Eve tried to lay out in her mind the map of this part of
the world. She knew that the eastern section of Bhutan had
never been mapped properly; indeed there were parts of it
where no Westerners had ever penetrated; but she had a rough
idea of the country's boundaries and its relation to the countries
around it. 'If it doesn't lead down into Assam, it could
swing east and we'd wind up in Tibet!'

Nimchu nodded. 'The sahib will find a way,' he said, and
Eve for the first time felt the burden that her husband had had
to carry as leader. She had remarked the mistakes he had
made this morning, and they had surprised and hurt her.
Surprised her because they had shown weaknesses in him that
she had never suspected; and hurt her because she had seen at
once that at least two of the others, Singh and Li Bu-fang,
had noticed the same weaknesses. She looked back up the

line, wondering how many of the others still depended on Jack. Only the two men at the end of the line, the two doubters, were independent.

By midafternoon they were well down below the tree-line again, in a descending valley with a narrow but flat floor. Mountains rose steeply on all sides but the south; there the valley ascended through a series of hills to another range of mountains that were lost in a thick pelmet of clouds. All the hills were cloaked with forest, and down on the valley floor the forest began to thicken into what was almost jungle. The path began to twist and turn like the track of a demented serpent.

With the thought of the pursuing Chinese constantly on his mind, it was some time before Marquis noticed the lack of wind down here in the valley. They were passing through a thick stand of trees and he looked up; the tops of the trees were as still as the crests of totem poles. The stillness of the forest was eerie.

'No wind,' said Tom Breck. 'Notice something else? The vegetation, it's almost sub-tropical. I noticed some *Cymbidium* back along the track.'

Marquis looked about him, at the almost solid walls of forest that bordered the track. This was almost a monsoon forest. He had no idea of their altitude; the altimeter was stowed away in one of the porters' packs and there was no time to stop and search for it. He could tell by the ease of his breathing that they had descended quite a way; but he could not believe that they had dropped to sub-tropical level in such a short time. This valley, protected from the north winds by its high battlements of mountains, must be a freak of nature. Rhododendrons, brown with autumn, hung down in great trusses; the wilting flowers, faded now, were the deep red type, which normally did not grow above 9000 feet. Orchids, *Cymbidium* and Vanda, and magnolia grew in profusion among the thick stand of evergreen Kharsu oak, and vines hung down like the shredded skins of a thousand snakes. Water dripped constantly, and the path itself was a mire of mud and leaves. And something else. . . .

'Hold it!' Marquis bent down and pulled his trousers out of his sock tops. He stretched his socks away from his

ankles and saw the leeches, already thick with blood, clinging
to his skin. He stood up and looked back at the others, who
had now come to a halt behind him. 'Anyone else carrying
any leeches?'

Everyone else was. The leeches had attacked with the quiet
stealth of some insidious disease. Eve discovered one between
her breasts, hanging there like some dark obscene pendant;
two had got inside Nancy's belt and were fastened to her
belly; both Tom Breck and Wilkins had them in their groins.
And everyone had them clinging to their legs and ankles. The
worms, needle-thin, had insinuated themselves through every
entrance that offered, the double thickness of socks, bootlace
holes, the warp and weft of woollen garments, even through
the occasional worn patch of an anorak. And now they clung
to everyone, feasting on the human blood that made them as
thick and as long as cigarillos.

Eve and Marquis had experienced leeches before in other
wet forests, but this was the first time the Brecks and Wilkins
had been attacked by them. Nancy was almost hysterical. She
tore at her clothes, trying to get at the loathsome creatures;
Eve would not have been surprised if Nancy had tried to strip
herself naked. She moved to the sobbing girl, gesturing to
Tsering at the same time. 'Bring some salt, Tsering.'

'What good will salt do?' Nancy's glasses were misted;
she could hardly see Eve. She had turned away from the men
and opened her trousers; the leeches clung to her like cancerous
growths. She was pulling at them with nervous fingers, but
the leeches would not let go, only discharged blood as her
fingers pressed into them.

'They don't like salt. The only other way to get them off
is to burn them. Do you want me to try that?' Nancy shook
her head, shuddering; and Eve began to sprinkle the salt. Even
as she did so, another leech dropped silently on to Nancy's
shoulder and began to slide down the faded green slope of
her anorak; Eve saw it and brushed it off and trod on it. 'A
lot of the early explorers used to stick tobacco leaves in the
tops of their boots. That is supposed to be pretty effective,
too.'

Nancy had quietened down under Eve's matter-of-fact
approach. She looked along the line of men, most of whom

were now in some state of undress, sprinkling salt on the leeches that clung to them or trying to burn them off with lighted cigarettes. Everyone was spattered with blood : this might have been the aftermath of an ambush. ' I can't stand the sight of blood, Eve, not even my own. I think that's why I get so upset when I think about Tom's parents—I mean, they must have died in a lot of blood.'

Eve had opened her shirt, was rubbing salt on the leech, thick and black, that hung between her breasts. It had begun to disgorge blood : her skin glistened with it. ' You don't know that, Nancy. Why do you torture yourself with the thought of it?'

' I don't know.' One of the leeches let go of Nancy's flesh; she brushed it off and shivered with revulsion. ' Perhaps it's because Tom is so—I don't know, *unvengeful*, is that the word? I sort of feel I have to have enough anger for both of us. And so I think about them dying like that.' She looked back along the line of men. ' I wonder how much blood the general has lost?'

Li Bu-fang sat on a log beside Wilkins. Both men had freed themselves of leeches and now were wiping the blood from their legs and ankles. ' You are an entomologist, Mr. Wilkins. Do these little creatures interest you?'

Wilkins shook his head. ' I'm a hymenoptorist. I specialise in four-winged insects. Bees, wasps, things like that.'

' What about butterflies?' Singh, sitting on another log on the other side of the track, nodded up at a horde of butterflies that floated among the upper branches like a gentle storm of petals.

' I collect those, but more as a sideline.' Wilkins went to say that he loved them for their beauty, not for their entomo-logical interest; but the old shyness held him back, he had come from a home where any talk of beauty would have had his father querying his maleness. He looked down at the twitching, sated worm on his palm. He lifted up his hand, then with finger and thumb of the other hand flicked the leech away into the bushes. ' But I don't collect these.'

Singh began to pull on his boots again, smiling affably at Li. ' I suppose in China leeches are a symbol of imperialism, eh, old chap?'

'The analogy is too obvious, Colonel.' Li had not had his hands untied and he was finding it difficult to lace up his boots again. Wilkins went to help him, then drew back. Singh, his own boots now laced up, was smiling with what Wilkins could only think of as sympathetic sadism at the fumbling efforts of the Chinese. Wilkins knew if he knelt down to help Li he would be told by Singh to mind his own business. He was not going to be told by anyone to mind his own business, least of all by a bloody Indian, even a prince : there was more of his father, the working-class bigot, the worst bigot of all, still in him than he cared to admit. But he took the easy way out, as he knew he would : he sat back and did nothing.

'I thought all your propaganda was obvious, General.' Singh was enjoying himself, smiling broadly. He stood up, and Wilkins almost expected him to stand on Li's clumsy fingers.

Li didn't look up, went on working patiently to thread the stiff wet laces through the eyelets. Damn the man, Wilkins thought. He had noticed how Marquis, Eve and even Tom Breck seemed to respond sympathetically to the Chinese. Without appearing to try, the man was gradually winning everyone's goodwill. Everyone's, that is, but that of Colonel Singh.

'I spoke to you, General!'

Li straightened up, leaning backwards on the log to take the stiffness out of his back. Then he looked up at Singh. 'I am your prisoner, Colonel. But that doesn't mean I have to indulge in elementary polemical arguments with you. In politics, Colonel, I think you would be no more than a school-boy. Despite your jolly years at Oxford.' The voice was soft and gentle : the sarcasm had the needle point of a bamboo spear.

For a moment Wilkins thought more blood was going to be spilled; Li Bu-fang was going to be spread all over the path as a feast for the leeches that hadn't yet fed. Singh's hand went to his belt; for the first time Wilkins saw the silver-handled knife stuck there in a sheath. Singh's hand quivered on the handle; the blade came an inch or two out of the sheath. A leech fell from a branch and wriggled through the mud towards Li, eager for the feast that must come.

The Indian and the Chinese stared at each other, the silence between them having its own edge. As if from far away, Wilkins heard the murmur of the other members of the party, heard a bird cry and another sound that could have been the sawing of a leopard : none of it meant anything to Wilkins sitting on a log waiting for one man to kill another. He had watched a spider kill a fly the same way, with clinical detachment and yet at the same time a fascinated horror : a twin being, the scientist who could never lose his wonder as a man.

Then Wilkins stood up, stepped between the two men. 'I wouldn't draw your knife, Colonel.'

'Get out of the way, Mr. Wilkins.' Singh's voice sounded higher than usual; his anger was verging on hysteria. 'This has nothing to do with you!'

'Don't talk cock.' Wilkins kept his voice low; for some reason he could not name, he did not want Marquis or Breck or the women interfering in this clash between himself and Singh. He had been surprised to find himself on his feet in front of the Indian; he was not even sure if he was doing the right moral thing in protecting Li Bu-fang. But once he had challenged Singh, he had to go through with it; too often he had turned aside, or had allowed others to divert him, from finding out the truth about himself. He had no desire to be heroic : all he wanted to know was how much strength he possessed. 'When you joined our party, your little war stopped being a private one.'

Singh stared at him, fury threatening to split him apart as lightning splits a tree. Then his hand came slowly away from his knife; it slid silently back into its sheath. The flush of anger drained out of his face; the black eyes lost their flash, became once more tired and jaded. Wilkins had a moment of insight, as if Singh had suddenly been laid bare to him under a microscope. The Indian was kept alive only by these clashes : anger was the only fire he had left.

Singh looked past Wilkins and down at Li Bu-fang. 'You'll find, General,' he said quietly, 'I have only one real argument. That is to see that my country never loses its independence again. We didn't get rid of the British Raj to make way for you Chinese Communists.'

Li said nothing, but just looked down at the leech he had brushed away from his boot. Then he lifted his foot and trod on the leech; the gesture could have meant anything or nothing. But Wilkins was looking at Singh, trying to contain the surprise he had felt at what Singh had said. Another facet of him had shown up under the microscope: he was an Indian first, and only then a prince. You could never tell what the patriot looked like till he declared himself; Wilkins supposed a rallying cry, a shout of defiance, was not less sincere for being uttered in an obsolete Oxford accent. All the sneers at democracy, the regrets for a lost life of luxury, didn't come from the heart of the man. India was his heart.

Then Singh looked back at Wilkins. 'If you are going to join our war, Mr. Wilkins, think carefully where your sympathy lies.'

He turned away and walked on down the track to where Marquis stood talking to Tom Breck. Wilkins glared after him, an angry retort bubbling on his lips; but he knew if he said anything, that was all it would be: a bubble. The Indian had left him without words.

Li Bu-fang said quietly, 'Thank you, Mr. Wilkins.'

Wilkins turned back, angry now at the Chinese; but again he had nothing to say. He stood there, as inarticulate as he had been in his childhood anger: he could even taste the grit of Leeds in his open mouth. Then suddenly he dropped on one knee and clumsily, angrily, began to lace up Li's boots.

He was aware of Li looking down at him, but he did not dare look up. He was not sure what he would find in the Chinese face: friendship, contempt or pity. He was afraid of them all.

2

They camped that night farther down the valley, in a ravine that cut into the mountainside. Marquis and Singh agreed upon the choice of site: they could light a fire for cooking without its being seen farther back up the valley, and the narrow entrance to the ravine meant they were open to attack only from the one side. Marquis was pleased that he had chosen the site first before he had consulted Singh; when the latter nodded in agreement, he knew then that his mistakes were over for this day at least. It brought back some of his confidence in himself, and he began to wonder if that was all that good leadership was: an accumulation of correct small decisions. Great decisions needed a great leader, and he would never aspire that high.

Tsering cooked the gooral Marquis had killed yesterday and the hot meal revived everyone's strength and part of their morale. Marquis, anxious to retain Singh's goodwill, recognising now that he might need it more than he had suspected, consulted the Indian army man on a picket roster. Only one man at a time would be needed, since from the ravine entrance he could command all the valley. It was unlikely that the Chinese would keep moving during the night, but if they did they would need at least one flare or torch to show them the path through the forest which could be seen from the ravine. Marquis did not expect his party to be attacked during the night, but he was not going to take the risk of posting no guard at all. Exhausted as they were by to-day's prolonged march, they could oversleep and be attacked in broad daylight in the morning.

He divided up the shifts, with himself taking the first two hours and Singh the last two hours and Tom Breck, Wilkins and several of the porters taking an hour each of the intervening time.

He crawled into the pup tent where Eve was already in her sleeping-bag. 'Good night, love. It's been a rough day.'

'I'll stay awake for you.'

He bent and kissed her. 'Care to bet on it?'

'Well, I'll try,' she said, but not very confidently: even love could lose out to weariness. She wanted to stay awake, wanted to be near him; she felt his need of her, though she was not even sure that he felt it himself. She took a hand out of the sleeping-bag, warm from the heat of her body, and put it against his cold cheek. The bearded skin felt as if it were cracking: she had a frightening image of him coming apart under her touch, cracking like a plaster saint. He was no saint, but she had always attributed to him a core of strength that to-day had somehow been only intermittent. She did not blame him for having disappointed her: even as a girl, she had not married a hero. 'Watch yourself, darling,' she said, and meant it not only for the hours of his guard shift but for the rest of the march.

'There's nothing to worry about,' he said, misunderstanding her; and went out into the cold black night and down to the ravine entrance.

He pulled up the hood of his anorak, wrapped two blankets about himself and sat down to wait out his two hours. The moon had been blacked out by dark cloud and the valley at which he stared was only a suggestion in his mind rather than a shape in his gaze. He could feel the cold beginning to prick at the end of his nose like a needle, so he wrapped his scarf round the lower half of his face, then put on his snow-goggles, so that no part of his flesh was exposed to the risk of frost-bite. In the darkness of the night and his snow-goggles he was now almost blind; but he didn't mind. Blindness, he had often pondered, should help a man to think.

He had been shaken to find the cracks in himself that had been exposed to-day. They were larger than he had anticipated, perhaps large enough to have been seen by the others. And if they had been seen, then not only was his own confidence gone, but theirs too. Eve, the Brecks, Wilkins, the porters, all of them to-morrow would show their doubt of him. For a moment he caved in; despair and the cold made him long for sleep, sleep from which he would not want to wake. Then the will to survive, the ember that never died till death itself had blacked out the spirit, flared again: if he had to die he would do so on the move, walking, climbing, fighting: not crouched here like a mindless embryo. He straightened up, his bones creaking. To-morrow he would try again: he would be cheating, brandishing a counterfeit confidence, but maybe it would be enough. He would not be the first leader who had resorted to fraud.

After two hours, cold as the rocks against which he had leant, he roused himself and went and woke Chungma. Then he crawled into the tent beside Eve, to tell her he loved her and to find some strength in her that would keep him going through to-morrow and the other days to come. He was frozen in mind, spirit and body, but her instinctive tenderness would soon warm him into life again. She might suspect the reason why he needed her comfort, but he would take that risk.

But she was asleep. He had enough spirit left in him to grin at the humour of his disappointment. No matter what his confidence was like, there were no cracks in his love. There couldn't be, not if it could survive the snoring indifference of a sleeping wife. If the altitude is right, he thought, she'll sleep through Judgment Day. He leant over and kissed her hair, then settled down in his sleeping-bag. A few minutes later, worn out by the long day and his own doubts, he too was fast asleep.

They were on the move again first thing in the morning. There was no sign of the Chinese, but they could be camped up in the forest and Marquis was taking no chances. It was another fine day but cold. By mid-morning they were climbing the hills to the south; then at noon the track abruptly swung east. They were moving down into a second valley, long and narrow, a roofless corridor that stretched ahead of them to a distant escarpment. Beyond the escarpment they could see the peaks, thick with snow now, a jagged-topped wall over which they had to find a way.

Marquis's heart sank at the sight of them, but he said nothing. Though this was only a day and a half's march from their main camp, he had never been this far east before. The authorities at Thimbu had laid down precise boundaries in which he and the others could gather specimens, and mindful of the Bhutanese suspicion of outsiders, he had kept rigidly within those boundaries. As far as he was concerned this was an exploration of virgin territory. The distant mountains looked even more formidable than he had expected.

The valley was bare of trees, but stunted grass grew in the hard rocky earth. It was some time before Marquis was struck by the absence of any life. This was a valley that should have been terraced with fields growing rice or grain; houses should have dotted the landscape; the still air should have carried the bark of dogs and the grunt of yaks. In a land of mountains, this was a valley that should have been settled.

Marquis felt the uneasiness of the porters long before Nimchu spoke to him. The party was walking in the open, still warmed by the afternoon sun, but the porters had now begun glancing all around them with the nervous eyes of superstitious men walking through a cemetery at dead of night.

'I think I have heard of this place, sahib,' Nimchu said. 'This is the Valley of the Spirit. The *sounday* lives here.'

Marquis had learned long ago not to laugh at the superstitions of another man. The Kukukuku tribesman of the New Guinea highlands smoking the bodies of his dead, the Kachin peasant of the Burma hills revering the tops of trees where the spirits of his ancestors lived : he had not found those men any more ridiculous than the Roman priest who flung holy water about in a wet blessing or the London alderman acting out all the mumbo-jumbo of Masonic rites. Nimchu was entitled to his belief in the *sounday*, the spirit that, in the shape of a dog, a leopard or even a beautiful woman, could lead a man to his death.

'I have heard people talk of it, sahib.' It was strange to see Nimchu so nervous; somehow Marquis had never connected fear with the little man. But he wasn't the first brave man made nervous by the unknown. 'I have met a man who was almost strangled by it.'

'Strangled?'

'It turned into the shape of a mosquito net, attacked him while he slept. I saw the marks on his throat.'

You couldn't laugh, couldn't explain that mosquito nets had a habit of trying to smother or strangle people, even in lands where the *sounday* didn't exist. You didn't laugh at real fear, the sort that now shone on Nimchu's face as sweat.

'We'll just be careful,' Marquis said gently, and tried not to sound as if he were talking to a frightened child. He had to protect Nimchu's dignity. That was something else he had learned long ago : that the best way to retain the respect of even the most primitive savage was to protect that man's dignity. That had been the difference between the successful and the unsuccessful colonialist.

The whole valley was a giant trough of silence; the mountain seemed to shut out the thunder of the world. Marquis had met these silences in high places before; it was one of the attractions of mountain country. But what disturbed him, as it had yesterday in the other valley, was the complete absence of wind. This was the time of the year when the winds began to blow, whirling in the fields of sky, scratching their signature with slashes of cloud; when they attacked the mountains to rip the snow from them as rapists might tear a gown from a woman; when they tore down the gorges into the valleys, flattening the crops, slicing at men with invisible knives. The winds should have been hissing and moaning through this valley, bending the grass, whipping up the dust into swirling shapes that ran before it as fugitives before a marauding army. The whole air of the valley should have been a chaos of currents: instead it was as still as death. And the silence was the quiet of the grave.

Then they heard the sound: far away, a deep cry that chilled them all, even the sceptics. Though it was only midafternoon, the sun dropped suddenly behind a high western peak; shadows raced like black ice across the valley. The air turned cold in a moment; Marquis took a deep breath and felt it burn his lungs. The party had stopped abruptly, as if on some silent given signal; everyone stood frozen in an attitude of concentrated listening. The cry came again, a hoarse strangled moan.

Marquis unslung his gun. 'It came from that gully up ahead.' He nodded towards where the path disappeared down into a broken fold in the valley floor. 'I'll go along and have a squint what's there.'

The cry came again, and Tom Breck shivered. 'Gives you the creeps.'

Marquis looked at Singh. 'What do you reckon it is, Colonel?'

The Indian shrugged. 'It could be what the porters say, a *sounday*. But do Australians believe in spirits?'

'I'm half-Irish. I believe in anything.'

'Want me to come with you?' Wilkins said.

Marquis went to say no, then changed his mind. He recognised the look on Wilkins's face: the man was trying to prove something to himself. Marquis knew that the same look must have been on his own face numerous times in the past; for the first time he felt drawn to the blunt-mannered awkward Yorkshireman. He nodded and moved off down the path towards the gully. Wilkins hesitated, looking for a moment as if he regretted his volunteering, then he unslung the 12-bore Royal and, holding it almost gingerly in front of him like a raw recruit suddenly ordered into battle, he fell in behind Marquis.

The rest of the party moved up to stand in a tight group. The porters clustered together, as if lassoed together by their fear; Breck put his arm about Nancy, holding her tightly to him; Eve moved in front of Singh, looking anxiously down the path after the disappearing Marquis and Wilkins. Only Li Bu-fang seemed unmoved; he gazed around him like a property investor deciding if the valley was worth taking over. And that's what he and his government would like to do, Eve thought, stealing a glance at the impassive Chinese. For the investment of some ammunition and a few men, they would dearly love to take over not only this valley, but the whole country, even all the Himalayas. Perhaps the *sounday* had recognised him: its cry could be one of despair, not a threat.

Marquis and Wilkins were on the point of disappearing from the view of the others. The track wound round a small hump-backed hill bearded with spiky shrubs, then dropped suddenly down into a long gully. It was dry now after the long summer, but in spring, after the thaw, it would be a raging torrent. The rocks that littered the bottom of the gully showed that: they had been smoothed and polished like dark helmets by centuries of spring floods. A few pools of dead water lay in basins in the gully floor, black and silent; they looked bottomless, the sort of pool where spirits traditionally dwelt. Marquis and Wilkins slid down the path into the gully, at once aware that down here they were even colder than they had been up on the valley floor.

The stillness and silence above had been almost a turmoil compared to the atmosphere here in the gully. Nothing moved; it was as if nothing had ever moved down here. Two minutes of this, Marquis thought, and my old man would have gone off his head. Another minute and I'll do the same myself. Brought up in a house of windy talk, he had come to appreciate silence; but this stillness was an earache, it made an ice-bucket of the skull. He and Wilkins, some eight feet apart, began to walk cautiously along the track that twisted, like a lure that warned them yet which they could not resist, through the frozen convulsion of rocks. Their boots grated on the gravel of the track; the sound was like the crunching of bones in the dead atmosphere. Marquis came round a rock and stopped:

a prayer-wheel stood beside the track, its pole stuck in a crack in a rock. Its copper cylinder was dark green with age but for one bright streak at the top where nervous fingers had grasped it to spin it furiously. Marquis touched the wheel, looked at Wilkins, then spun it gently.

'In lieu of rosary beads,' he said, and his voice came back from the high banks of the gully as a mocking whisper.

Then they heard the *sounday* again, not a moaning cry this time but a threatening growl. Both men looked quickly about them; the growl and its echo mingled, coming at them from all sides. Marquis gripped his gun harder; he felt the skin tighten on the back of his neck. This is crazy, he thought. I'm believing in spirits, too.

Then the growl was immediately above them. Marquis swung round, looking up at the huge rock by which he stood. He was too late to dodge the giant dog as it hurtled down on him, its jaws agape and aimed at his throat.

3

Marquis had been attacked before: by a drink-crazed native in Uganda, by an old man kangaroo in Queensland, by a crocodile in the upper reaches of the Amazon. He had had to come all the way to the Himalayas to be attacked by a dog, the bane of postmen and delivery boys. The thought flashed across his mind even as he went down beneath the weight of the dog. But this was no joke: the dog was going to kill him. He could feel its breath against his jaw as the dog tried to get at his throat; its slobber ran down over his hands as he tried to thrust the huge snarling head away from him. After the savage joke had stabbed home as he went down, his mind had stopped working: everything he did now was a reflex action.

He was flat on his back on the rough gravel of the track, struggling desperately to roll out from beneath the weight of the dog. He could feel its paws digging into him, the nails ripping at his clothes; behind the snapping teeth, so close to his face, he could see the wild eyes of the animal. Its smell sickened him; his hands slipped on the thick greasy coat. Man and dog rolled over and over on the rough track, locked together as a twin beast: man and dog had the same savage animal sound as they tried to kill each other.

They rolled down off the path into the rock-warted bed of the dry stream. Marquis's head bumped against a rock, but he hardly felt it; sharp stones stabbed at his cheeks as he struggled to keep his throat away from the jaws of the dog. Then Marquis was on top of the dog.

His fingers tightened on the greasy fur at the dog's throat. He looked down at the slobbering jaws and the mad white eyes; he hated the struggling animal as if it were a man. The deepest hate was that which you felt for your own kind; but you could hate anything that tried to kill you. The dog knew the fight had turned against it; it threshed beneath Marquis as it tried to escape. But all Marquis's great strength was now in his fingers; he began to swear in a low savage mutter. His fingers tightened, he pressed down with all his weight and strength. Then suddenly the huge body of the dog stiffened and it lay still. It was dead.

Marquis sat back, straddling the dog. Then slowly he stood up and looked at Wilkins. 'Some bloody spirit.'

'I'm sorry.' Wilkins felt he had somehow failed Marquis. 'I couldn't get near to help you. If I'd tried to shoot——'

'I'm glad you didn't.' Marquis felt no anger towards Wilkins; he wondered what he himself would have done if the dog had attacked Wilkins. The fight had been fierce and short; trying to stop it would have been like trying to break up the elements of a storm. He looked down at the dog, prodding it with his boot. He recognised the breed, a dog that made lions look like overgrown domestic pets. 'It's a Tibetan mastiff. I should have just knocked the bastard out. Then I could have taken him back to London, let him loose at Cruft's Dog Show. He'd eat half the Pekinese in London for lunch.'

'Where did it come from?'

Then they heard the sound of bells, of dogs barking and yaks grunting. Round a bend in the gully came a caravan of animals, men, women and children. The procession pulled up sharply; people and animals jostled together. But half a dozen dogs, all of them as big as the one Marquis had killed, came racing towards the two white men, barking furiously and their teeth bared. Someone shouted, but the dogs paid no heed, all hellbent for supper; Marquis and Wilkins put their guns to their shoulders, slid back the bolts. But they didn't have to fire. The leading dog suddenly skidded to a stop as it saw the dead animal at Marquis's feet. The other dogs crashed into it; the six of them went down in a snarling, snapping riot. By the time they were on their feet again, three men had come running up, shouting at the dogs and hitting about them with whips. The dogs, growling and snarling at Marquis and Wilkins, retreated a few yards, but still remained within attacking distance. They would look at the dead dog, then at the two white men and growl, as if threatening revenge for the fate that had befallen their mate.

Marquis lowered his gun, but before he could speak to the three men who stood regarding him curiously and with some antagonism, he heard Eve and the others coming down into the gully behind them. The dogs whirled, barking and snarling, but one of the men shouted to them and they subsided again.

Eve came stumbling along the path, grabbed Marquis by the arm. 'Darling, you've been hurt!'

Marquis put his hand to his cut cheek, felt the blood running there. For the first time he was aware of the bruising his body had suffered as he had rolled among the rocks with the dog; it seemed that every bone and muscle had been met by a sharp-edged rock. He squeezed Eve's hand, then turned as Nimchu came up beside him. 'Better find out who these people are.'

The rest of the caravan had moved up the gully; the two groups were separated by no more than a few yards. The caravan was not a large one: fifty or sixty men, women and children, and about the same number of yaks.

'They are Tibetans, sahib,' said Nimchu, and spoke to the apparent leader of the caravan, a man slightly taller than his companions. All the men were dressed alike, in tattered trousers tucked into thick-soled boots whose uppers reached as far up as the knees, like crude copies of a wellington boot; the men's upper garments were a one-piece fur cloak over rough woollen shirts. All the men but the leader wore rough turbans; the leader stared at Nimchu from beneath a greasy but magnificent fur hat. He had a cruel face and sly eyes: one could imagine his achieving leadership of his small band by a combination of threats and cheating. To Marquis's sensitive nose, he smelt as rank and sour as the dead dog.

The leader said something to Nimchu, spitting out the words through broken teeth as if spitting out bile. He nodded down at the dead dog, then held out his hand : the gesture was unmistakable. Nimchu looked at Marquis. 'They are traders, sahib. He wants money for the dog you killed.'

Marquis looked at the Tibetan and made a rude remark. Eve pressed his arm. 'I don't think he speaks Anglo-Saxon, darling.'

'The bastard got the point,' said Marquis; and indeed the Tibetan had. He growled something to the men around him, and for a moment Marquis thought the dogs were going to be let loose on them all. The dogs were poised ready to attack : huge brutes with thick rough hair and bushy tails that curled over their backs, bigger than an Alsatian and too vicious really to be called domesticated. Three of the dogs wore big woollen ruffs as collars and these only added to their frightening appearance. One of the Tibetans opened his mouth as if to shout a command to the dogs; then he saw Wilkins and Singh bring up their guns. It was enough. The man looked at his leader, and the latter turned back to face Marquis, his face made more evil-looking by his anger and frustration.

Marquis said to Nimchu, 'Tell him the dog attacked me and I had to kill it to save myself.'

Nimchu relayed the message, and he and the leader of the caravan talked angrily at each other for several minutes. Meanwhile, Eve and Nancy were exchanging curious glances with the women and children of the party. The women were a little more brightly dressed than the men; some of them wore aprons that had once been gay but were now dirty and torn; all of them were cloaked in thick padded jackets beneath which Eve and Nancy could see shirts that, like the aprons, had seen better and cleaner days. None of the women wore a hat, and their thick black greasy hair was pulled back in a tight bun. Their only make-up was a pat of yak dung on each cheek.

'You couldn't get more basic make-up than that,' said Eve.

Nancy giggled. She was scared, and the long walk throughout the day with little food had tired her. She had come on this expedition expecting and hoping for adventure; she had had the romantic's idea that adventure would be an uplifting experience. Instead the experiences on this march so far had been frightening, exhausting and something she hoped would end soon. Now Eve's small joke was enough to provide a safety valve. She giggled again and said, 'Aren't the kids filthy but cute?'

The children, a dozen of them, from babies in packs on their mother's backs to one or two teenagers, stared at the two white women with bright mischievous eyes. They were covered in a second skin of dirt and already the youngest seemed to smell as badly as their parents. They were dressed in tattered cast offs, and despite the cold and the rough path over which they had to walk, they were barefoot. Oh God, Eve thought, how terrible to be without hope at this age! The children stared back at her, innocent of their tragedy.

The conversation between Nimchu and the Tibetan leader suddenly stopped. The Tibetans, even the children, seemed to become one with the rocks around them; only their eyes moved, like brown beetles in the dark yellow plates of their faces. Everyone looked at Li Bu-fang, aware of him for the first time; evidently no one had recognised the uniform of the Chinese till Nimchu had mentioned him. Two of the dogs growled in the sudden silence; none of the Tibetans told them to be quiet. To Eve, the gully all at once turned into a pit in which they were all going to be massacred. The men of the caravan had begun to slide their hands beneath their cloaks, as if to clutch the weapons hidden there. The dogs growled again, seeming to congeal together into the one thick threatening mass of fur and snarling jaws. A baby whimpered and its mother put a dirty hand over its mouth, gagging it. The yaks sensed the atmosphere and began to back up, grunting and snuffling. Somewhere far off there was a loud crack, like a gunshot, then a thundering rumble; it was the first natural sound Eve and the others had heard since entering the valley, the birth and death of an avalanche. Then the distant thunder of it died away and the silence came back into the gully, seemingly more oppressive.

Singh stepped forward to stand beside Marquis. The dogs

snarled at him, inching forward, but he ignored them. Without looking at Marquis he said, ' We can't afford to waste time, old chap. These blighters have to get out of the way or else.'

Disturbed though he was, Marquis remarked the words Singh used : the out of date schoolboy slang and the movie gangster's ultimatum only increased the unreality of the situation. Yet the threatening attitude of the Tibetans was only too real; no dialogue could alter that. The leader of the caravan, without turning round, muttered something; the men behind him began to move away from each other, giving each other room to move. It was the centuries-old guerilla tactic : never offer the enemy a concentrated target. The women and children began to back up along the path, pushing the yaks back behind them. Only the Tibetan leader stood firm, staring at Li Bu-fang and muttering in a fierce undertone.

' What's he saying, Nimchu?'

' He is going to kill the Chinese, sahib. They will kill us if we try to stop them.'

Marquis looked back over his shoulder. Li Bu-fang stood with his head bent, resigned, like a man with his back already against the firing wall; but the bound hands were clutching at each other, nails digging into fingers, the man's fear trapped there in his hands by the tourniquet of the rope. Marquis looked despairingly at Li, pitying him and hating him; hating him not for being what he was, but because involuntarily, even unknowingly, he had committed his life to Marquis's care. No man had the right to lay his life on another man's shoulders. If Confucius hadn't said that, he'd been loafing on the job as a philosopher.

Marquis turned back to face the caravan leader. Outwardly he looked calm and determined; nobody, not even Eve now, could guess at the turmoil going on inside him. The storms of a man can sometimes be clearly seen : rage, passion, laughter can break out of a man like hurricanes out of a paper bag; but the storm that does the most damage, the tempest of doubt, often shows as no more than a frown on the brow or the teeth chewing on the bottom lip. Marquis did not show even these : the Occidental had become even more inscrutable than the Oriental.

' Tell him,' he said to Nimchu, ' that if he or his men touch

General Li, I'll knock his bloody block right off his shoulders.'

'Better still,' said Singh, more sophisticated in the art of the threat, 'tell him that I shall shoot all the women and children.'

There was a gasp from Eve and Nancy as Singh raised his Sten gun and aimed it at the group of women and children now some twenty yards back along the track, stopped from going farther by the wall of yaks banked up behind them.

'You can't!' Eve went to move forward, but Marquis looked at her and shook his head. 'Jack, don't let him do it!'

'Let them kill the Chinese, sahib,' Nimchu said; and for a moment Marquis thought how simple it would be. The peasant mind often had the knack of getting to the logic of a problem while the sophisticated mind was still troubling itself with moralities.

'Kill? Kill?' Tom Breck shook his head from side to side like a man trying to clear his ears of words that made no sense to him. 'These people are supposed to be Buddhists— why are they talking about killing?'

'These jokers have only survived by killing, I guess.' Marquis nodded at the Tibetans, now spread across the gully, each with a hand hidden beneath his cloak; the cloaks gave them the appearance of huge birds of prey ready to plunge. 'Isn't that right, Nimchu? They're like you, they've made their bargain with Buddha.'

Nimchu said nothing, not wanting to repeat in front of the others what he had told Marquis two days ago. Oh Christ, I've made another stupid bloody mistake, Marquis thought: you could ask a man to affirm or deny his faith, but you couldn't ask him to declare that he had compromised. He stared at Nimchu, silently asking for the little man's forgiveness.

Nimchu's face was saved by Singh. He had inherited through several generations the ability to recognise the uses of compromise; it had been part of the education under the British Raj. 'These chappies will let their dogs kill the general. That will satisfy their principles, and yours, too, eh, Nimchu? But I'm not going to let them do it, Marquis.'

'I'm not going to let you kill the women and children!' Eve suddenly ran towards the women and children, to stand there facing Singh and his gun. Then Tom Breck followed her, stood beside her with his thin young face suddenly aged with determination. The dogs bunched together, snarling; they looked for a moment as if they were about to hurl themselves at Eve and Tom Breck. But one of the Tibetans spoke to them, and they remained where they were, still snarling.

Breck was looking directly at Singh. 'You'll have to shoot me, too, Colonel.'

'Tom——' Nancy had advanced till she was half-way between the two groups.

'I'm sorry, honey, but I don't want anyone killed. Not even the general. But certainly not these women and kids!'

'If you want to save your prisoner, Colonel,' said Eve, 'you'd better think of another way!'

'This is bloody ridiculous!' Marquis slapped his hand against his thigh in exasperation. The whole situation was becoming comic; even the Tibetans had turned to look at Eve and Tom Breck in puzzlement. Marquis was nonplussed for a moment; what would a real leader do in a situation like this? Then abruptly he turned, reached back and dragged Li Bu-fang forward. He stood with his arm about the Chinese, like a father protecting his boy; he couldn't stand off to see himself, but later he would recognise that he must have only added to the comic appearance of the scene.

'This man is our prisoner. Tell them that, Nimchu.' Nimchu hesitated, and for a moment Marquis thought the rebellion started by Eve and Tom was going to widen. Then the porter relayed the message to the caravan leader. 'To kill him you will have to kill all of us first. And that won't be easy.'

He had made another decision, another one forced on him by Eve and, to a lesser extent, Tom Breck. He had committed himself to Singh and the safe delivery of the latter's prisoner over the mountains into India. Neutrality was like chastity, the world no longer believed in it; men were flat out trying to turn all the virtues into myths. He had conducted his own assaults on chastity, but he had always respected another man's neutrality. And now suddenly he had had to commit himself.

'Not easy at all, old man,' said Singh, recognising Marquis's dilemma and at the same time recognising Marquis's commitment to him. He turned the Sten gun on the caravan leader, then glanced at Li Bu-fang. 'This is all for your benefit, General. I hope you're appreciative.'

Li said nothing, stood silently in the crook of Marquis's arm.

The Tibetan leader stared at them for a moment, then he snapped something to the other men of the caravan. They came in beside him, taking their hands from beneath their cloaks; they spoke to the dogs, telling them to be quiet. The tension abruptly relaxed. No one was going to be killed.

Marquis, all at once embarrassed by his embrace of Li, let the Chinese go. 'It would have saved a lot of trouble, mate, if I'd let the dogs have you for supper.'

'They would not have liked me. No flavour.' The Chinese smiled fleetingly, then looked soberly up at Marquis. 'Thank you, Mr. Marquis. I shall not forget that I owe you my life.'

'Not just me,' said Marquis, more embarrassed than ever. 'All of us. Including Colonel Singh.'

Li Bu-fang hesitated, then he nodded. 'I hope I can do the same for all of you when the time comes.'

One of the children had put out a tentative hand to Eve; she looked down, smiled and took the grubby hand. She brought her forward, a girl of eight or nine coated with eight or nine years' dirt: Eve felt you could peel the years off the child as you would peel bark off a tree. The girl looked up at Marquis, squinting over the yak-dung that daubed her cheeks like scraps of peeling paint. But then she smiled and innocence came through as clean as the flash of water on a river rock.

'You wouldn't have shot her, would you, Colonel?'

Singh looked down at the child with distaste; children, even clean ones, ranked with other domestic animals till they were sixteen. He had children of his own, but he had never really recognised any of them till they were grown up. 'Probably not, Mrs. Marquis.'

Eve studied him, then she said with quiet amazement, 'I think you might have, you know.'

Singh shrugged, not denying it. 'One has to make one's point. Pussyfooting was all right for the Oxford Union, but this chappie doesn't understand the merits of debate. Do you, old chap?'

He looked at the caravan leader, who stared back, slightly bewildered by the behaviour of these foreigners. He cast one more look at Li Bu-fang, a savage glance of hate that should have disembowelled, castrated and quartered the Chinese in an instant; but Li, safe now, stared back at the Tibetan, impervious to hate. Their looks locked; each killed the other in his mind. Then the Tibetan turned away, shouting to his party, and the caravan began to move on up the gully, leaving the dead dog where it lay.

Marquis and the others stood aside to let the caravan pass. The yaks went by, taller than the Bhutanese porters, huge beasts that smelt of the sweat and dirt of a thousand caravan routes; on their backs they carried boxes of tea, bolts of cotton, sacks that contained a hundred mysteries. These caravans had been tramping this road, carrying these goods, for centuries. Ancestors of these animals might have carried gifts from the Shans of Assam to the great Kublai Khan. Marquis, a man with a sense of history, watched them go by, aware that here in these mountains history was a tapestry whose design sometimes did not change for generations. Then he looked at Li Bu-fang, stepping back quickly as a yak lurched towards him. The tapestry was being torn apart by Li and his countrymen; history was no longer moving at the slow pace of these huge lumbering beasts. The caravan went on up the gully, a relic of a time already gone.

Marquis looked at Nimchu. 'Did you tell them about the Chinese being after us?'

Nimchu nodded. 'They will take a side path, sahib.'

'Are they going right through to Tibet?'

'No, sahib. They are going west, into Sikkim. They have left Tibet forever, they say. That is why they wanted to kill the Chinese.' He looked at Li Bu-fang, then back at Marquis. 'You should have let them kill him, sahib.'

Marquis shook his head. 'If we get out of this alive, Nimchu, I want to be able to sleep peacefully each night for the rest of my life. I couldn't do that if I'd let them kill the general to save ourselves.'

Nimchu shook his own head, but in wonder. 'I do not understand you, sahib. You make life so complicated for yourself.'

The last yak of the caravan went by; it and its owner looked at Marquis and the others with the same dull animal stare.

'They're a happy lot,' said Wilkins.

'What have they got to laugh about?' asked Marquis.

And after a moment Wilkins nodded. On the dole in Leeds on a rainy January day would be a lotus existence compared to this. Suddenly he felt homesick, sniffed hard and smelt the smog and the dye-works, wanted to weep for the brassy taste of grit on his lips.

They moved on, came up out of the gully and began to cross the valley, climbing again. The sun had disappeared completely from the valley; the landscape had turned blue. But shafts of sun, coming from between the western peaks, still lay across the sky; a scarf of snow blowing from a distant peak turned into a golden banner, the last challenge to night before the latter's invasion. The air had sharpened, turning the cheeks to bone.

'We'll have to stop before dark,' Eve said.

Marquis looked up ahead. The hills had risen out of the valley, turning into escarpment. The path had become a series of steps hacked out of the rock of the cliffs, a long twisting staircase that led up to a monastery that clung to the cliff like the giant nest of some legendary bird.

'We'll camp there,' Marquis said.

FIVE

It was almost dark when they reached the gates of the monastery. The long walk during the day, culminating in the climb up the hundreds of rough steps, had exhausted even the porters; everyone slumped down, falling into graceless heaps. Marquis almost staggered across to thump on the tall closed gates in the towering white wall.

'It reminds me of a Howard Johnsons.' Tom Breck, lying flat on his back, looked up at the coloured gabled roofs of the several monastery buildings.

'What's a Howard Johnsons?' Wilkins sucked in the thin cold air, feeling it going down his throat like a glassful of chopped razor blades.

'A chain of roadside restaurants back home. Sort of modern coaching inns. Pilgrims in their air-conditioned Cadillacs pull in there for sustenance.'

'I'd settle for a Lyons Corner House. Steak and kidney pie and two veg. And a double helping of trifle to follow. And a pint of black-and-tan.' He grinned at himself, accentuating his accent. 'Ah'm a real bloody gourmet.'

'I'll join you, Nick.' Eve had noticed the change in Wilkins over the past twenty-four hours. From the first day of their meeting months ago she had seen behind his façade: the careful accent, the reluctance to discuss his background. It was a form of snobbery, but it was something that in its context she understood; she was as aware as Wilkins himself of the defects of the English social system, where an accent could be as damaging as a ghastly birthmark. But over the last twenty-four hours Wilkins had given up impersonating a class he didn't belong to, and he was a much nicer person because of it.

Wilkins looked at her, dreaming his dream; but his face didn't give him away, he just smiled and said, 'I'll book the table.'

'You can all have your high living,' said Nancy. 'I'll

settle for a nice soft bed, a couple of tsampa cakes and a cup of tea. All I want is a good night's sleep.'

Then the gates were being opened. Nimchu had got up and crossed to stand beside Marquis. The gates swung back and a young monk stood there. No surprise showed on the bland young face: the strangers had been observed an hour ago coming up the valley.

'Tell him we want shelter for the night,' Marquis said to Nimchu. 'Don't tell him about the Chinese being after us— not yet, anyway. And you'd better not mention the general.'

Nimchu nodded and spoke to the young monk. The latter said nothing, but abruptly stepped back and closed the gates in their faces. They heard a heavy bolt slide home.

'Welcome to the Himalayan Hilton,' said Marquis.

'They will not refuse us, sahib,' said Nimchu, and with the patience of a man accustomed to being kept waiting, sat down with his back against the monastery wall.

In the last of the fading light Marquis looked up at the monastery above him. It was perched on a series of ledges, at broken levels, above the cliff that Marquis estimated dropped sheer for almost a thousand feet. The main wall, thirty or more feet high, surrounded half a dozen houses, the tiled roofs of which were loaded down with rocks; without them, Marquis could see the tiles flying off like so many birds in the winds that must buffet this cliff-face in the winter. The roof of each house bristled with prayer-flags, and at each corner of the monastery, suggesting there was a raised walk behind the parapet of the wall, a large prayer-wheel spun lazily, their polished copper surfaces the only colourful note in the dying day. The wall of the monastery had once been bright white, with a deep reddish-brown band running round the upper edge; but the paint had faded, and the wall in the dusk looked like a lighter face of the cliff. From inside the wall came the murmur of voices, the chant of men at prayer.

The gates swung back and the young monk beckoned them in. The party got to its feet and began to follow Marquis and Nimchu into the monastery. But as Eve and Nancy reached the gates, the monk stepped forward and shook his head.

'What goes on?' Tom Breck demanded, and took Nancy's

arm; but the young monk stood in front of them, shaking his head and waving a hand in a gesture of dismissal.

Eve looked at Nimchu and for the first time saw that the latter was embarrassed. The little man was looking down at his boots, rubbing the back of his neck with a nervous hand. At last he looked up. 'I am sorry, memsahib. This monastery has a high lama living here. That means a woman may not enter.'

'Oh, for Pete's sake!' Nancy's exhaustion made her cry of exasperation sound like the slubber of a mare. Marquis, equally tired, grinned idiotically, expecting her to stamp a hoof. 'What the hell are you grinning at, Jack?'

'The Daughters of the Revolution won't like that.' Then Marquis looked at Li Bu-fang. He was still grinning, weak from exhaustion, wringing out a joke like a drunk. 'The American revolution, not yours.'

'They're letting him go inside!' Nancy, too, looked at Li; her indignation almost over-reached itself into horror.

The Chinese bowed mockingly. 'I apologise for being honoured, Mrs. Breck. But you cannot blame me if women have not been emancipated in these mountains. We'll remedy that soon, I promise you.'

Nancy straightened up. 'Don't bother. Your sort of emancipation doesn't appeal to me.'

'What's the idea of all this?' Eve demanded of Marquis.

'I'll go in and see if the lama will change his rule for the night.' He looked at her in the last wash of light: she was exhausted, older-looking than he had ever seen her before. He put his arm about her, drew her to him and put his cold fingers against her equally cold cheek. His breath blew as a small mist across her face. 'It's been a hell of a day, love.'

She nodded, wanting to be angry at being kept here outside the gates, but knowing that her anger would look unreasonable and petulant. He had kept his hand against her cheek, and she leaned her face into it: some warmth began to flow between them. 'Tell the lama I'll act like a nun if he'll let me in.'

He kissed her, the second time in one day that he had done it in public; he's becoming positively Gallic, she thought, and was glad. Then he left her and went into the monastery.

The yard of the monastery was tiny, crowded in upon by the

half a dozen houses surrounding it. The houses themselves appeared to grow out of each other, and a succession of balconies ran from house to house, linking them all. There were no doors at ground level in the yard, but rickety ladders led up to the balconies. Leaving Li Bu-fang with Wilkins and the porters, Marquis, Singh and Nimchu followed the young monk up one of the ladders to the balcony that ran round the largest building.

An elderly monk stood waiting for them, the gullied yellow mask of his face lit from the side by a lamp hanging above a decorated doorway. He stared at them unblinking, and at first Marquis thought the old man was blind. Nimchu squatted down, took off his boots and dropped to his knees. He bowed three times with his head touching the floor. At last he stood up and looked at Marquis and Singh. 'This is the lama, sahib.'

'Tell him——' Marquis began.

'You may tell me yourself, sir.' The old man moved forward and put his hand, soft and cold as a leaf, on the forehead of each man in turn. He did it first to Nimchu, then to Singh; but when he came to Marquis, he hesitated. Marquis bent down, offering his forehead for the lama's blessing. The old man put his fingers gently on the tall white man's brow. Then he stood back and the mask of his face broke into a smile. 'Welcome. I learned English many years ago in Darjeeling. I worked as a clerk for a British magistrate. My tongue is rusty, but my ears will know your words.'

Marquis introduced himself and Singh and explained the circumstances of their being there. 'But we have two women outside, my wife and the wife of another colleague.'

The lama inclined his head. 'I am sorry, sir. It is not permitted. Your presence has caused a disturbance as it is——'

He looked around at the surrounding balconies. Monks had come out on to them and stood in their rust-red robes beneath the yellow fans of light from the lamps hung above the doors behind them. The monks stood unmoving, clustering together on the balconies, like the one long russet tapestry hung round the courtyard. Again Marquis had the feeling that he was looking at a fading picture of history: these monks and their ancestors had been here for centuries, but time was

catching up with them. He, Singh and the others were the
first of the dry rot that would crumble this life. Shame
pricked at him like a nervous disease.

'You are the first white man most of them have seen, Mr.
Marquis. We are very isolated here. To allow a woman—*two*
women and both white——' He shook his head, smiling
gently; he had seen something of the outside world. 'Our
religion is a contemplative one. No disrespect to your spouse,
sir, but women do not encourage contemplation.'

I should have discovered this religion sooner, Marquis
thought; and mentally felt the clout on the head that Eve
would have given him if she had known of his treachery.
Singh, a man with three wives and no marital conscience,
nodded sagely. 'Absolutely the truth, my dear sir. We would
not think of disturbing your serenity.' He looked at Marquis
and smiled. 'But there will be no serenity outside the gates
when you tell your wife and Mrs. Breck the news.'

Nor was there. Eve and Nancy, cold, hungry and tired,
having had ten uncomfortable minutes for their own particular
contemplation, fell on Marquis as he emerged from the gates.
'Well, what did he say? Is he as wise as he's supposed to be?
Did you tell him we'd act like a couple of nuns? Look at us
—Mother Eve and Mother Nancy——'

'You're not going to like this——' said Marquis; and
they didn't. Eve's language would have rubbed the rust off
the lama's English, and Nancy's remarks must have spun her
missionary in-laws in their graves. The two women marched
up and down in front of the monastery gates like a couple of
militant pickets, while Tom Breck chased them, trying to
placate them. He was not helped by Marquis, who leaned
against the wall and laughed till he was weeping.

Then he was hit a resounding blow across the ear by Eve.
'It's not that funny, Jack!'

He wiped his eyes, put his arms round her and drew her,
struggling, into him. 'It is, love. You'll laugh about it
later on.'

'Not to-night, Jack. I'm worn *out*——'

They never call you *darling* when they're angry. They call
you by name, they get almost formal; oh, there's so much you
could contemplate about women, they're a religion in them-

selves. 'I'll have Chungma put up a pup tent for us. And I'll try and get us a hot meal.'

She relaxed against him, trembling with exhaustion. 'Oh darling, do you think we're going to make it?'

He was facing north, straight into the face of China. 'We'll make it, love,' he said, but hope tasted like a lie on his tongue.

Chungma came out of the monastery to erect two pup tents. While they were being put up, Tom Breck came across to Marquis. It was now dark, and the only light came from a lamp which one of the monks had brought out and hung on a hook beside the gate. The wind had not yet come round the angle of the cliff, but here on the small ledge outside the monastery it was already cold enough to deaden the flesh on one's face.

Breck's breath hung before his face, making his approach even more tentative: 'Jack, I'm—uh—sorry about to-day. I mean, back there with those Tibetans. I don't want you to think—well, I wasn't sort of going against *you*——'

'Tom.' The cold, exhaustion, or perhaps it was a sudden affection for the young American: something robbed Marquis of further words. He put out a gloved hand, pressed the young man's arm through the thickness of a padded sleeve, a sweater, a woollen shirt: in these bitter mountains it was even physically difficult to touch a friend.

'Good night, Jack,' said Tom Breck, and understood.

Each man went to his tent, crawled into his sleeping-bag beside his wife.

'Now I'd like some Chicken Marengo,' said Eve to Marquis, 'followed by a huge slice of Walnut Torte with, as you would describe it in your crude Colonial way, a dirty great dollop of whipped cream.'

Instead of which Tsering brought them hard-boiled eggs, so small that at first Eve thought they were white pebbles; hot tsampa cakes; tea; and some Lachen apples, the flavour of which compensated for the rest of the meal. They ate by the light of an oil lamp Tsering brought out from the monastery, wolfing the food down as if it were ambrosia.

Eve waited till Tsering had taken away the tin mugs and plates; then she took off her anorak and snuggled down into her sleeping-bag. She ran a finger down the side of her nose, streaking the dust there. Tsering had forgotten to bring her hot water to wash in, and she had been too tired to care. ' A few more days of this and I'm going to stink like those Tibetans we met to-day.'

Marquis put out the lamp and lay looking up at the darkness above him. The tent roof was only a few inches from his face and he could feel it billowing in towards him under the gusts of the rising wind. The tents had been put up in an angle between the monastery wall and the cliff, but the wind could still snatch in at them. It had begun to moan along the cliff-face, assuming sounds that the winds of cities and plains never achieved. Mountain winds, to Marquis's Celtic mind, were always ridden by spirits and he could imagine how the peasants of Bhutan could hear quite distinctly the cry of the *sounday* in the night.

' Darling, I love you.' Eve's voice came from beside him, the voice that could exorcise all the spirits that might attack him; all but one, the doubt of himself. Their sleeping-bags were close together in the narrow confines of the tiny tent; they lay together like two mummies, each embracing the other mentally; it was enough sometimes when you were truly in love. He turned his face towards her, feeling for the warm breath of her.

' Remember in that Hemingway book, how they made love in a sleeping-bag?'

' Impossible,' she said, and giggled in the darkness. ' Unless it was a communal sleeping-bag.'

' Or a Hollywood king-size.'

She was silent for a while, then she said, ' Darling, I'm sorry you've lost your collection. We'll never come back here again, will we?'

He shook his head, then remembered the darkness. ' No,' he said, and wondered if she meant they would never go any-where at all again. But was afraid to ask her if that was what she had meant : he was tired enough, without taking argu-ment into sleep with him.

' But first, we have to get out of here,' he said, and remembered all the mistakes he had made so far : they came howling back at him, spirits on the wind.

'You'll get us out,' she said, and tried to keep the doubt
from her own voice. She had recognised the subsidence within
him, the collapse of confidence : it shook her, as if she had
seen a fort or a cathedral fall down before her eyes. That,
of course, was the trouble : he had all the pretensions of a fort.
Big, strong, challenging, you did not look for the sand on
which he might be built. Perhaps, after all, it was easier for
the small man to be a leader; had Napoleon found it easier
because not so much had been expected of him? She did not
blame Jack for where he had failed. Instead she blamed
herself and the others for having expected so much of him.
Yet she did not want him to fail, not in the end. She knew
that only he could keep her going. He was both her strength
and her weakness.

'You'll get us out,' she said again; and ten minutes later
he fell asleep, carrying the whole party with him on his back
throughout the night and forever, over mountains that rose
and fell like the waves of a giant sea.

Eve, too, fell asleep; but dreamlessly. Altitude was her
Ovaltine, her nip of brandy, her sleeping-pill; despite her
earlier plea for a bed, she fell asleep on the rock of the ledge
as if on a mattress of feathers. The wind beat at the tent,
infiltrating spirits into Marquis's sleeping skull. But Eve,
dreamless, heard none of it.

In their tent the Brecks, too, slept, each of them troubled
and frightened. But they had not confessed their fears to
each other; neither heard the cry of the other in his sleep.
Each of them dreamed of childhood, the haven we can never
go back to. The wind moaned in the sleep of each of them,
an echo of long ago : Tom heard it coming down out of the
pass above Steamboat Springs in the Rockies, Nancy heard
it sighing down the valley of the Susquehanna. Their sleeping minds tried to deny the reality, that it was blowing out of
China, had blown across the graves of another couple named
Breck.

In the monastery itself, Wilkins, Singh and Li Bu-fang,
unencumbered by women, were just getting up from the meal
they had eaten with the monks. They had eaten in a side room
off the main temple, a room bare of furniture but for a large
coarse mat on which they had all sat. The walls were covered

with stylised portraits of the Buddha in a variety of attitudes; everywhere one looked the plump impassive face stared back. Wilkins, brought up in a chapel that would have fallen down if anyone had decorated its walls, had been uncomfortable throughout the meal; even more uncomfortable than Li, the one among the three of them who was not at all welcome. The lama had said nothing that was even impolite to the Chinese, but it was his silences in between that had made clear his concern at the general's presence in the monastery. He was not an enemy, since their religion demanded of them that no creature should be recognised as an enemy. But the lama had obviously balked at the alternative of recognising the Chinese as a friend.

The meal had, to Wilkins's unaccustomed eye, seemed full of ritual. They had begun by drinking millet beer out of small earthenware cups. The lama had led the ceremony, doing everything with a slow, almost mesmeric grace. Wilkins had watched every movement carefully from the corner of his eye; as it had been all day, the past came back to him and he was reminded of his first formal dinner in London, when he had been faced with more knives, forks and spoons than had seemed necessary for one meal. But there was more meaning to the ritual of this simple meal than there had been to the elaborate banquet in London.

Yak butter was smeared delicately on the edge of each cup to bring luck. 'I am sure all of us can find need for luck,' said the lama.

'Oh, indeed,' said Singh, a man more accustomed to ceremony than the other two visitors.

'Luck is an illusion,' said Li Bu-fang, traitor to a race of gamblers. Wilkins looked at him and wondered: had fan-tan and other gambling games been eliminated like the household fly in Communist China?

'You're wrong, dear chap. Even your most regimented society will never be able to stamp out luck. If it were an illusion, my father would never have allowed me to believe in it. He warned me often—princes can never afford illusions. Practically anything else, old chap, but never illusions. Believe me, luck is very much a reality.'

'Then it had better start manifesting itself pretty soon,' said Wilkins.

'An offering to the demons of earth,' said the lama, sucking up beer through a straw and spitting it out on the floor. Then he dipped a finger in his cup and flicked it towards each wall of the room. 'And one for the spirits of hell.'

'Your friends,' said Singh to Li Bu-fang, and the latter smiled thinly.

Then they had eaten bamboo shoots, beans, tomatoes, red peppers and rice. The final course had been yak cheese that was strung in small cubes on a cord, like a necklace of soft pieces of amber. After the initial exchanges between the lama and the three outsiders, the meal had been eaten in virtual silence, broken only by the sound of smacking lips from the dozens of monks. Wilkins, exhausted and hungry, had concentrated on eating, glad to be rid of the irritant of meal-time small talk. This was how it had been back home in Leeds: at the dinner-table mouths were for eating.

'You will want to retire early,' the lama said to Singh. 'Especially if you are leaving early.'

His tone and manner were meticulously polite, but there was no mistaking his meaning; his remark had been punctuated by a quick glance at Li Bu-fang. Singh was equally polite. 'We shall leave at first light. We have a long journey ahead of us to-morrow.' He looked at Li. 'Haven't we, old chap?'

Li shrugged. 'Depends how fast you move, Colonel.' He bowed to the lama. 'Thank you for your hospitality.'

'You are welcome to it, poor as it was.'

Wilkins watched the ritual of politeness with a sceptical North of England eye, and tried to imagine a Yorkshireman and a Lancastrian bowing to each other like this while hating each other's guts. His acceptance of what he thought of as Eastern hypocrisy was not helped by his tiredness and his queasy stomach. The meal had been finished off with cups of Tibetan tea. Thirsty and unable to see properly in the gloom of the room in which they had eaten, Wilkins had taken a scalding mouthful before he had discovered what he was drinking. He had seen it made by the porters in camp— brick tea with yak butter, salt and soda added—but he had always managed to avoid it. Now half a cupful of the rancid oily mess was lying in the bottom of his stomach, just waiting to be regurgitated.

The young monk who had opened the gates came forward to lead the three outsiders away to their beds. But Singh, as if coming to a decision he had deferred all through the meal, turned back to the lama. 'Do you, or anyone else here in the monastery, read Chinese?'

Wilkins was standing beside Li Bu-fang. He felt the Chinese stiffen and heard the sharp intake of breath. 'I am afraid not, Colonel. You see——' The lama looked at Li. 'Our interests do not lie towards China.'

Li Bu-fang relaxed, letting out his breath in a soft hiss. He bowed once more to the lama. 'This is one occasion when your lack of interest in my country is not resented.'

Singh, disappointed, dug the Chinese angrily in the ribs. Wilkins hesitated, wondering how he should take his leave of the lama, then he nodded briskly and turned and followed the Indian and the Chinese out of the room after the young monk.

They were led along the balcony and into one of the smaller houses. From behind each closed door they passed, Wilkins could hear the murmur of prayer, a sound as melancholy as that of the wind ghosting through the yard. Then they were shown into a room where Wilkins's sleeping-bag and some blankets for Singh and Li Bu-fang had been laid out by the porters. It was the coldest room Wilkins had ever been in in all his life; he put out a hand to trace the pattern of the ice that he knew must be papering the walls. But the room was panelled in wood, and in the feeble glow of the lamp set in the middle of the floor he could see that the walls were covered with paintings of fearsome monsters. Mad eyes and sabre teeth hemmed him in; a ghoul and a dragon fought for possession of him. He looked about him and shivered.

'Leeds was never like this.'

'What, old chap?'

But Wilkins shrugged and turned away. He and the others, according to custom, had taken off their boots as soon as they had entered the buildings of the monastery. In his socks now, he felt his toes curl up with the cold and something that he would not admit was fear. He turned his back on the walls and walked to the narrow window. One panel of glass had been broken and replaced by two timber planks; the other panel, unwashed in only Buddha knew how many years, was almost as opaque as the timber. Wilkins scrubbed at the dirty glass with the sleeve of his anorak and peered out.

' Come to bed, old chap,' said Singh. ' There'll be plenty of time to look at the scenery to-morrow.'

Wilkins turned back and got into his sleeping-bag. He looked up at the ghouls and dragons above him, then he blew out the lamp and turned over. What he had seen through the dirty glass of the window would disturb his sleep more than the fearsome faces on the wall.

Far down in the valley he had seen the camp fires that he knew were those of the Chinese.

2

When Marquis clambered out of the pup tent in the morning he found it had snowed during the night. Not heavily, but enough to have sprinkled the valley below with white lace. Higher up, on the mountains around the valley, the fall had been heavier; the trees stood out more clearly than yesterday, dark stains in the white fabric of the steep slopes. Here on the ledge it had been blown into pockets in the cliff face and was banked up against one side of the tent. His view obstructed by the cliff above him, Marquis could only guess at the depth of snow that lay on the mountains they would have to climb to-day.

The wind had dropped and the morning air was so thin and clear as to bring the valley up to only a goat's leap below the ledge. So that when he walked to the top of the steps up which they had climbed yesterday he saw the Chinese camp at once, as clearly as if he had been looking at it through binoculars. But he went back for his binoculars anyway : Irish as ever, he liked confirmation of bad news.

While he was in the tent on his knees, searching through his pack for his binoculars, Eve woke. ' What's the matter?'

He hesitated a moment; but what was the point of trying to cover up the inevitable? ' The Chinese are down in the valley.' He found the binoculars in their case, separate from his pack and where he had placed them last night. He wasn't thinking very clearly this morning; he would have to watch himself. He hadn't slept well and he had the first touch of nausea he had had for months.

Eve had slept soundly, would be sleeping still if Marquis hadn't disturbed her. She was refreshed and ready for another day, even a day that already seemed to have got off to a bad start. She pulled on her boots and anorak and followed Marquis out to the top of the steps. He took the glasses from his own eyes and handed them to her. She raised them, focused them and at once the distant Chinese were personal and threatening. They were moving about their camp, loading their gear on to the mules that stood in a line as if waiting to move off as soon as the command was given. Two of the soldiers stopped and looked towards the monastery. One of them raised an arm and pointed directly at Eve, and she involuntarily took a step back. She lowered the binoculars and looked at Marquis.

'Can they see us?'

'I doubt it. We're against this cliff, we wouldn't be so easy to pick out.' He looked down into the valley again. 'A couple of hours, that's all we've got on them.'

'That's all we had the day before yesterday. And they nearly caught us.'

He seemed to flinch, as if she had blamed him for what had happened. But before she could tell him that that was not what she had meant, he turned away. 'Wake Tom and Nancy. I'll get the others.'

Ten minutes later the whole party stood outside the monastery gates, packed and ready to move. All the monks had come out to bid them farewell, standing in a tight bunch in the gateway and staring with frank, unmonastic eyes at the two white women. Only when Nancy, in a fit of pique at having to spend the night out here on the ledge, stared back at them did they drop their eyes. Then they giggled among themselves like schoolboys caught making eyes at the new mistress. Eve saw their embarrassment and smiled. She had never understood the celibate and monastic life, the vocation that took priests, monks and nuns out of the stream of life. She never sneered, because she was free of the conceit that would have her judge other people's lives; but she could not comprehend the retreat from all that life meant to her, the sensuality of the flesh, the joy of close companionship, the giving and taking of love. Sometimes she could envy the innocence of children, but nothing could make her begrudge these men and boys their innocence. Children, by her standards, had something to look forward to; these monks had nothing but the hope of Heaven. Then she turned and looked down into the valley, at the Chinese, their camp now broken, ready to move off; and she wondered how these monks would survive in the face of torture, whether their religion had prepared them for the possibility of a violent death. This was one of the most remote valleys in one of the most remote countries in the world, yet even here isolation was now vulnerable. The world was turning inside out : the day might come when the only real hermitages would be found in the heartless centre of a city.

The old lama, the wrinkles of his face smoothed out in the morning light, as if his skin began each day anew and only aged as the day itself aged, came forward to Singh, bringing with him the young monk who seemed to be the general factotum of the monastery.

' Colonel, you asked last night if anyone here could read Chinese. I have learned that our brother here can read the Chinese script. What did you want to show him?'

Singh's face lit up; he looked at Li Bu-fang with triumph. Then he took the papers from the pocket of his battle tunic. ' These——'

But he got no further. Suddenly Li Bu-fang lunged at him; when the Chinese stepped back he had the Indian's silver-handled knife in his hand. And his hands were free; somehow he had managed to wriggle them out of the ropes that had bound them. Marquis, standing by, had a moment of cheap elation for which he felt ashamed : it was not he who had made the mistake this morning, it was not he who should have checked Li's bonds.

Li moved with incredible swiftness. Everyone stood flat-footed, caught off-guard. By the time they had collected themselves Li was backed up against the monastery wall, the young monk held in front of him, the knife at the boy's back.

'Throw the papers on the fire, Colonel.' Li nodded to a fire nearby, where Tsering had made tea for the party. 'Or this young man dies.'

There was a hiss, a moan, from everyone, an echo of last night's spirit-ridden wind. Singh stood with his hand still held out, as if he expected the young monk to come forward to take them. 'Let the boy go, General. He has nothing to do with the war between you and me.'

'You know that isn't so, Colonel.' Li's voice was soft, toneless. 'You recruited him, Colonel. Not me.'

Marquis took a pace forward. 'Let the boy go, General——'

Li shook his head. 'I wish I could, Mr. Marquis.' There was genuine regret in his voice. 'But I can't. Not unless Colonel Singh throws those papers into the fire.'

'Burn them!' Eve grabbed Singh's arm, but he shook her free without looking at her. 'Colonel, the boy's life is in your hands—you can't let him die!'

'I'm sorry.' Singh's voice had the same regretful note as Li's had had. 'This is not your war. If these papers are so important to the general, then they are important to me. To my government. I'm taking them back to India with me.'

Wilkins, Tom and Nancy Breck stood to one side; out of the corner of his eye Marquis could see the one expression of disbelief that they all wore. Behind them the porters were staring at Li Bu-fang with a fierce concentration of hatred; they killed him in their minds, just as the Tibetan leader had done yesterday. The look on the faces of the monks grouped by the gate surprised Marquis: it was a look of sadness, as if they had already accepted the death of their brother. The young monk himself stood paralysed in front of Li Bu-fang, the bones jutting through the flesh of his face as fear took the substance out of him.

Marquis went to reach down for his gun lying on his pack, but Li Bu-fang saw the movement. 'Leave it there, Mr. Marquis. You may kill me, but the boy will die with me.' Marquis straightened up, and Li looked back at Singh. 'This is your last chance to save the boy, Colonel. Throw the papers on the fire.'

'Burn them, Colonel!'

It was a chorus; but Singh shook his head. He looked at the lama, his dark handsome face as old as that of the aged monk. 'I am sorry, sir. But these papers are worth more than one life.'

'This isn't an Indian life you're sacrificing!' Tom Breck looked as if he was about to weep; he put out a hand, pleading as if for his own life.

Singh shook his head again, pain making him almost blind. Then he looked back at Li Bu-fang. 'I am not going to burn the papers, General.'

Li said nothing for a moment. All the pain that had been in the Indian face was mirrored in the Chinese face : war made brothers of enemies. There was a moment of stillness on the ledge, in which tiny sounds became magnified : water dripped somewhere, a prayer-wheel on the wall above rasped as if some invisible hand had spun it. Then Li drove the knife into the back of the young monk.

The boy died without a sound; everyone else gasped his last breath for him. He slid slowly down in front of Li Bu-fang, his robe turning crimson as the blood gushed out of him. The knife was exposed, still in Li's hand, its blade bright red with the life it had just taken. Then Marquis saw the knife turned upwards.

He had never moved so quickly in his life. He was on Li when the knife was still several inches from the latter's breast. He grabbed the wrist, twisting the arm sideways; the knife fell to the ground, and Li went down with something like a cry of disappointment. Marquis sprawled on top of him, easily overpowering him.

But then hands were pulling at Marquis himself, trying to drag him off the Chinese. He saw Nimchu, Tsering and Lombi wrestling to pull the Chinese out from under him. He let out a roar, trying to hold on to Li Bu-fang and fight off the porters at the same time. He could hear yelling and a woman, Nancy or Eve, he wasn't sure which, screaming. Then there was a blast of gunfire, and the porters abruptly fell away from him : for a moment he thought they had all been shot. He stood up, gasping for breath, dragging Li up with him. He looked at the monastery wall, saw the line of bullet marks, then he turned and faced Singh, who stood in the same attitude as three days ago, when he had shot the leopard, the Sten gun held loosely in front of him.

Marquis thrust Li in front of him. 'Okay, he's your prisoner. Do you want to kill the bastard?'

The look of pain was still on Singh's face. He looked down at the dead monk as four other monks came forward, picked up the body and carried it over to lay it just outside the gates. 'How can I kill the General? I'm as much to blame as he is. Should I let your porters kill us both?'

Marquis looked at Nimchu. 'Is that what you want, Nimchu?'

Tsering and Lombi nodded emphatically, but Nimchu hesitated. He looked at the Chinese and the Indian, hating them both for bringing their war into his life; then he looked back at Marquis and shook his head. 'I think it is too late now, sahib. We should have killed them three days ago.'

There was an angry murmur of dissent from Tsering and the other porters. Lombi took a step forward, but Marquis put out an arm and pushed him back. Lombi pressed with his chest against Marquis's hand; he stared at the white man with the same hatred as he had shown towards Li. Then Nimchu said something in the native tongue, and Lombi stepped back, muttered something that was repeated by one or two of the other porters.

Li stood listlessly, his jacket collar still gripped by Marquis's hand. Marquis jerked him around and snarled at him, 'Are you worth keeping alive?' But it was an angry fruitless question and both of them knew it. Marquis shoved the Chinese at Wilkins and Tom Breck. 'Tie him up again.'

'Are we still taking him with us?' Nancy said.

Marquis looked at Singh, and after a moment the latter said, 'I'll leave the decision to you, Marquis.'

'You bastard,' said Marquis.

But once again someone made a decision for him. He caught a movement out of the corner of his eye and swung round. Lombi was taking his pack from the heap of packs stacked by the gate.

'Where are you going, Lombi?'

The porter straightened up. 'I stop, sahib. Not go any more.'

The man's face was stiff and sullen; he was beyond argument. Marquis looked around at the other porters. There were sixteen of them altogether, men whom up till now he had trusted completely. He had had trouble with porters in other lands, but these sturdy little men had given him so little concern that he had taken their loyalty for granted. But now, he realised, he was no longer their boss. They looked woodenly at him for a moment, then slowly, without fuss, they began to cross to stand beside Lombi. All but three: Nimchu, Tsering and the young Chungma. And the latter two seemed to be waiting on Nimchu to make up their minds for them.

Marquis looked at Nimchu. 'I shan't blame you, Nimchu, if you want to go back.'

Nimchu bit his lip, wiped the back of his hand across his nose, fingered the scar on his cheek. His one good eye seemed to water; he stared glassily at Marquis with the wall eye. He turned and looked at Tsering and Chungma, and after a moment they both nodded almost imperceptibly. He turned back to Marquis. 'We shall go with you, sahib.'

Marquis could find no words to express his gratitude for Nimchu's loyalty. He just inclined his head, put out a hand and pressed the little man's shoulder. Then he turned quickly, leaving Nimchu to arrange the sorting of the packs.

'We're all going to have to hump a pack,' he told the others; and looked at Eve and Nancy: 'Sorry, girls. I'll get you a light one each.'

Eve nodded, but Nancy was turned away, was staring out across the valley. Eve moved to her and put a hand on her arm. She asked nothing, but she knew how the other girl felt. It would be exactly as she herself felt: her scream of horror when the young monk had been killed had been echoed by Nancy. She was still sick inside, still quivering with the shock of what she had witnessed; when she put her hand on Nancy's arm, she could feel the trembling in the other girl. When the young monk's blood had gushed out to stain his robe, it was as if her own blood had run out of her. And now she remembered how Nancy had said she could not stand the sight of blood, even her own: part of the girl must have died, never to be revived, as the young monk had died.

She squeezed Nancy's arm again, getting no response. Then

she looked back at Li Bu-fang and, as if in some tiny act of vengeance, said, 'I think the General should be made to carry something.'

'Oh, he bloody will,' said Marquis with quiet savagery. 'I ought to make him hump the lot.'

Li Bu-fang, his hands now retied, said nothing, but stood gazing across at the body of the young monk. Singh, beside him, picked up his knife from where it lay in the snow and wiped the blood from it. He slid it back into the sheath at his belt, then he too looked across at the dead boy.

Lombi and the other porters, as if to make up for their desertion of Marquis, worked speedily to put into ten packs all that would be needed for the rest of the trip. Nimchu supervised them, making sure that Marquis's poppy and Wilkins's butterfly were not left behind.

Then it was time to go. Marquis put out a hand to the old lama. 'I am sorry we ever knocked at your gate.'

The old man looked down towards the distant bowl in which the Chinese ants were already on the move. 'I do not blame you, sir. Nor even these men.' He nodded at Singh and Li Bu-fang. 'All of us are only instruments of fate, not the manipulators. We can only await the will of the gods.'

Marquis had no answer to such acceptance of tragedy. Instead he looked quickly at Li Bu-fang. 'General, can you leave an order for your men not to touch these monks and my porters?'

Li looked up in surprise. 'An order?'

'You couldn't trust him,' said Wilkins.

'Get me a brush and paper,' Marquis said to the lama. The latter said something to those behind him, and one of the younger monks, a boy of twelve or so, went running back into the monastery, his robe flapping as he skipped gingerly around the body lying outside the gates. In half a minute he was back, and Marquis handed the paper, brush and ink to Li Bu-fang. 'Tell them not to touch the monks or the porters or the monastery itself. Tell them anything else you like—it doesn't really matter, I guess. But tell them *that*! They've got to leave these people alone!'

Li stood unmoving for a moment, looking at the monks and porters with an expression that was unreadable: it could have been contempt, pity or indifference. Oh God, thought Marquis, praying in his own vernacular, squeeze a little compassion into the bastard. The heretical bastard would never admit it, but You made him : add a few late drops of pity. Then Li looked again at the body of the young monk, then turned and held out his hands to Marquis. The latter quickly undid the ropes.

The Chinese brushed some characters on the paper and handed the incomprehensible note to Marquis. 'It will worry you, won't it, what I have said? I could have told my men to massacre them all and burn down the monastery.'

'I don't think you have,' said Marquis.

Li looked up at him quizzically. 'No, I haven't. But why are you so sure?'

'Because I trust you,' said Marquis, and saw the worm of indecision in the Chinese's eye : no man likes his enemy to trust him, it is not one of the rules of war.

Li's hands were rebound by Singh. 'Unlike my friend Marquis, I don't trust you.'

'We understand each other, Colonel. If our two countries got together, in time we could rule the world.'

'I don't share your ambition, General. The happiest prince is the one with the smallest domain. I never wanted a kingdom.'

'I wasn't talking about kingdoms. Ours would be a republic.'

'Then you'd better talk to my husband,' Eve said, and looked down into the valley : the ants were now recognisable even with the human eye as men and mules. 'But while we're on the move, not now.'

Good-byes were said and the party, much smaller now, began to move on up the rough steps that still formed the path above the monastery. The porters who had elected to stay behind stood in a tight group about Lombi, their leader; all their exuberance had disappeared and they stood in a sort of silent shame, struck dumb by their own disloyalty. But Marquis could not bring himself to blame them : this was their land and they had to go on living in it. In a way they were showing more courage than he or the others who had chosen to try and escape over the mountains.

The monks stood by the gates, the dead boy still lying in the snow at their feet. They looked shy and a little afraid of demonstration; a thousand caravans had passed these gates, but they had never been comfortable with farewells. Marquis, looking back, understood: only those who needed company had to make an exercise out of parting. The monks stared silently up, rusted statues in the niche of the gateway; the dead boy lay at their feet, a man who had unwittingly sacrificed his neutrality by learning a foreign language.

Then a bend in the stepped path wiped them all from view. But not from memory: Marquis would remember them for as long as his mind lived, wondering at their fate. The old lama had held Li's order in his hand, but it was a mystery; he could have been a blind man holding a loaded gun at his own heart. But there had been no concern on the ancient face, the twig-like fingers hadn't trembled as they had taken the paper. The lama, Marquis knew, suffered from the same weakness that had overtaken himself: trust.

But sometimes it was the only weapon.

SIX

It took them almost half an hour to complete the steps, climbing up the face of the cliff, treading carefully where the snow had already turned to ice. The path was not wide, and Tom Breck, pausing once for breath, asked, 'How do they get yaks and mules up and down here without losing them over there?' He nodded down, feeling a touch of vertigo as he did so: it was like clinging to the edge of the world, he was no more than four or five feet from spinning into orbit.

'They lose them, sahib,' said Tsering, grinning hugely and making catherine-wheel motions with his hands. 'They fall over—whoom, whoom, whoom, bang! I have seen it on other paths.'

Breck spat in the snow. 'I don't think even mules should die like that.'

'No, sahib,' said Tsering, and the grin stiffened on his face as he looked up ahead at the back of Li Bu-fang. 'But Chinese, yes. Very quick death, nothing to clean up.'

Breck spat again, angrily this time. 'Okay, you've said enough, Tsering. Let's forget it.'

'Not easy to forget, sahib.'

The porter swallowed his grin, turned abruptly away and went plodding on up the last of the steps. Tom Breck wanted to call out to him, but his voice was stuck in his throat. Perhaps he was breathless, perhaps he knew in his heart it was useless: whatever the reason, he shut his mouth and said nothing. He had no enemies, but he had come to learn, gradually and painfully, that the alternative was not a world of friends. Nothing he could ever say to Tsering would bring the Bhutanese round to his way of thinking.

He climbed the last few steps, came up round a buttress of rock and saw what lay ahead of them. They had climbed out of the last of the big valleys; they had heard the last whisper of wind-disturbed trees. The mountains had now taken over, rising one upon another like a broken statuary of fighting beasts; the last peaks challenged the sky itself, glittering pinnacles of ice and rock that looked timeless and indestructible. It seemed to Tom Breck that the end of their journey already stared them in the face.

Marquis had called a five-minute halt, and Breck slumped down with the rest of the party. Marquis came and sat beside him, and Breck said in a low voice, ' Is it worth it, Jack?' He nodded up towards the towering peaks. 'I mean, going on.'

' I'm surprised at you, Tom. I always thought you'd be the last one to want to call it quits.' Marquis's own voice was low. He was not sure that Breck was not right, but till he had made up his mind he did not want his doubts spreading like measles among the rest of the party.

Breck was dejected, at the sight of what lay ahead of them and at his own sudden collapse of confidence. He was a bumbler, destined always to trip over his own feet; but he had always had the bumbler's confidence, the optimism of a man blind to details. ' I'm sorry, Jack. I guess it's what happened back down at the monastery '—he shook his head, trying to clear his mind of a memory he didn't want—'killing that young guy. That's the most senseless piece of butchery I've ever seen.'

' How much senseless butchery have you seen?' Marquis tried to keep any sarcasm or unkindness out of his voice.

Breck admitted his ignorance; he shrugged and shook his head. 'Okay. But *why*, Jack? Why?'

' Do you want to ask the general? Or the colonel? They're soldiers, Tom, and this is a war they're in. I hated their guts, both of 'em, back down there. If anyone had suggested a little mayhem on either of them, I'd have bought a ticket. But climbing up those stairs, I must have got a bit lightheaded with charity and lack of breath. I began to get a hint of what makes the general and the Indian tick.'

' I'll never understand them.'

' You ought to give it a go, Tom. Don't think Quaker. Don't even think American. Try and think Chinese and Indian.'

' Is that possible?'

' Tell you the truth, I don't bloody well know. But until we all start to think Asian, I mean us whites in the West, I don't think we're in the race to come to terms with Asia. That goes for China, India, Vietnam or anywhere else. It goes for those two bastards up there.' He nodded up towards where Singh and Li Bu-fang sat side by side, each locked in an armour of thought. 'We're stuck with them, Tom, till this little hike is over. Whichever way it ends.'

Breck looked at the big Australian. '*You* surprise *me*, Jack. You've got more tolerance than I ever gave you credit for.'

'Not tolerance.' Marquis stood up and hoisted on his pack. 'I'm looking for a way out. Not just out of these mountains, but out of a lot of things. In the end it might only be cowardice.'

He called to the party to be on the move and went on up the track, leaving Breck wondering what troubled the big confident Australian. He also left Breck further depressed: the young American had invested his only hope in Marquis.

They were climbing through open country now, moving up a great scree slope on which the snow lay in intermittent drifts. The day was bright and clear, but the sun had not yet come over the eastern peaks and they were still walking in shadow here. The higher they climbed, the more they saw of what lay ahead of them and the more depressed they became. But no one voiced his despair. Climbing through the thinning air took all their breath: each was saved from being a doubt-monger only by his own exhaustion.

It had taken Wilkins months to adapt himself to even the comparatively low altitudes in which he had done his collecting. Now, burdened by his pack, he felt the effect of every step he took. Till he had come here to the Himalayas he had never climbed anything higher than Snowdon. Those sorties into Wales had made him a competent rock-climber and improved his hymn-singing, but they had not prepared him for the effect of high altitude on his system. He had never suffered there as he was suffering now from headache, nausea and a starving desire for something sweet to eat. He stopped once, retching with nausea, then began to cough, feeling his chest tearing apart as the spasms shook him.

Eve stopped beside him. She helped him slide out of his pack straps, then let him lean on her while the coughing continued to rip its way out of him. At last he looked up, gasping for breath, tears running down his cheeks from his watering eyes. He sucked in: the air made a rattling sound in his throat, like that of a dying man. He croaked, 'Why do you bother with me, Eve?'

'It's no bother, Nick.'

Wilkins reached for her hand, kissed it through her glove; his lips smacked loudly on the nylon fabric. Then the light-headedness which had attacked him went as suddenly as it had come. He stood holding her hand in his, staring at it as if she had pressed on him a grenade with the pin drawn. He flung it away from him, rude and awkward again in his embarrassment.

'Sorry, lass.' His voice thickened a little with accent. 'You must think something's wrong with me.'

Eve tried to hide her puzzlement. 'It's the altitude, Nick,' she said lightly. 'We're all feeling it.'

'Aye, it's the altitude.' He struggled into his pack straps again, turned away from her with the same old rude abrupt-ness and went stumbling on up the track.

Eve stared after him, then she hitched up her own pack and moved on after the others. Marquis was waiting for her. 'What was that all about?'

'What?'

'The hand-kissing. Who does Nick think he is—York-shire's answer to Charles Boyer?'

Unaccountably she felt she had to defend Wilkins. 'There's never any danger of an Aussie getting that way.'

'I kissed an Aussie girl's hand once and she thought I was up to something dirty. She broke my nose.'

'You told me you broke it playing Rugger.'

'That was the second time,' he said, lying like an Irishman.

'Well, anyway, Nick was just thanking me, that was all. I helped him catch his breath.'

'And he kissed your hand for *that*? Leeds must have a more gracious atmosphere than I suspected.'

The exchange was stupid; words had the knife-edge of a cutting wind. The mood between them had been tranquil and warm; suddenly now they were slashing at each other again. Is Jack, too, becoming affected by the altitude? she wondered. 'Darling.'

'I'm listening.'

It was a snarl, but she was patient. 'Don't bite my head off, darling. What's the matter with you? We're not high enough yet for you to need oxygen.'

He bit his lip, then he grinned. 'Which hand did he kiss?'

'The left one.'

He took her right hand, raised it to his mouth and bit one of her fingers, the sort of lover's gesture she understood. 'I'm a stupid bastard. Forgive me?'

She said nothing, just pressed her gloved hand hard against his bearded chin. They stood like that for a moment, alone on the vast mountainside, in a world of their own, then they turned and began to trudge up the track after the others.

A hundred yards ahead of them Wilkins had stopped and looked back. Jealousy burned him, catching at his chest worse than had the thin air : he almost cried out with the pain of it. Nimchu spoke to him and he looked at the porter with blind eyes. He blinked, found his sight again and saw that Nimchu was offering him some chocolate. He took it, muttering his thanks, and devoured it like a man on the verge of starvation. He was starving for love, but he would never have expressed the thought. Poets had been no more welcome in the house in Leeds than butterfly hunters.

They moved on, stopping at frequent intervals to get their breath and rest their quivering legs. The worst affected were Wilkins and the Brecks. Nancy's pack had already had to be split up between Tsering and Chungma, but neither of the porters complained. At each rest Tsering hovered solicitously about Nancy, as if he felt that Tom could not look after her. She had bled once from the nose, but Tsering had come to her with a handful of snow and told her to sniff it up her nostrils. This she had done and at once the bleeding had stopped. But the cold snow up her nose had only increased the headache she already had, and each time she stopped for a rest she looked more distressed.

'Mrs. Breck looks very bad,' Singh said.

Marquis nodded, then looked up at the mountains that still lay ahead. 'She's never going to make it. We're only about twelve thousand feet now. We're going to have to go up to sixteen thousand at least. Maybe higher.'

Singh pondered for a moment, then he suggested without much enthusiasm, 'We could split up, old chap.'

'How?'

'The general and I could continue on up the main path. It's us they want, not you. The rest of you could make for one of those side ravines, hide up there till the Chinese had gone by. Then you could go back the way we have come.'

'Do you think they'd let us get away? Colonel, up here on these bare slopes we stand out like shags on a rock. With glasses they could pick out you and the general from five miles away. As soon as they saw you were on your own, they'd branch out looking for us.'

'Why should they?' Singh was not arguing strongly.

'I think the altitude is getting to you, Colonel. You're not thinking very clearly. They don't want you. I don't think they even want the general that much. They want those papers you're carrying. Do you think they're going to take the risk of letting us get away? Why shouldn't you have given the papers to me?'

'So you think we all have to stick together?' Marquis nodded; and Singh then looked back at Nancy sitting bent over in the crook of her husband's arm, miserable to the point of looking sub-human. 'Some of us may not make it, as you say.'

Li Bu-fang had been sitting listening to the conversation. He had been very quiet and preoccupied since they had left the monastery. It was impossible to read the scarred yellow face; it was as illegible to Marquis as the papers in Singh's pocket. But Marquis, watching the Chinese even more carefully than Singh had been, had detected a certain hesitancy in the man. Some of the young monk's blood had stained the cuff of Li's tunic, and during one of their halts Marquis had seen him trying to scrub away the stain with some snow. It was not a gesture of fastidiousness; Li had obviously seen too much blood to be repelled by it. It was the act of a man who had committed his first murder and regretted it.

'Why do you have to sacrifice all these people?' Li said now.

'You know why,' Singh said wearily, and tapped his pocket.

Then he took out the papers and opened them. There were four sheets of them, neatly covered in script. But the pages might just as well have been blank.

Li saw the frustration on the faces of the two men and smiled. 'It is a pity we did not conquer the world sooner. Say several thousand years ago. Then Ts'ang Kie could have invented the one script for us all and you would be able to read those papers.'

'Who's Ts'ang Kie?'

'In my country he is the legendary inventor of writing.'

'He could have done a better job.' Marquis looked at the papers again, wishing for some neat Roman script; even if the language was still unintelligible, the characters would have been recognisable to the eye. It was a shock to discover at thirty-six that, in the most important circumstance of your life, you were illiterate. 'How many keys are there to your characters? Two hundred? Three hundred?'

'We have simplified it, Mr. Marquis. Under the reform of 1956 we reduced the keys to only 187. There are no illiterates now in our country.'

'There are a couple here,' said Marquis. 'And one of them feels like——'

He glared at Li, and the latter smiled and said, 'Punching me up the snout? That's no way to literacy, Mr. Marquis.' Then he looked back at Singh. 'Are the papers worth the lives of all these people, Colonel?'

'I don't know, General. You tell me.'

But at that Li remained silent, and Singh had his answer. And so did Marquis. He hoisted his pack on again and picked up his gun. Then he looked back down the long slope and saw the Chinese soldiers come up over the edge of the distant escarpment.

He shouted to the others to get started, then ran back down to Tom and Nancy Breck. He grabbed Nancy and lifted her to her feet. She was wearing her anorak hood and dark glasses, but even so Marquis could see the pain in the little of her face that was exposed. And he could see the hopeless resignation.

'Get going, Tom!'

Breck hesitated, then he shook his head. 'We'll stay here, Jack. Go on without us.'

Marquis swore at him, then looked at Nancy. 'Lean on me. And start walking!'

She tried to struggle out of his arms, but he held her tightly; they wrestled like quarrelling lovers. She was crying with pain and despair, but he was brutal with her. He grabbed one of her arms and put it round his neck. Then half-carrying, half-dragging her, he began to move on up the track, stumbling on the loose stones. After a few yards, still crying, still pleading with him to leave her behind, she began to stagger along, taking some of her weight on her own legs. Tom Breck took one quick look back down the long slope, then he turned and followed them.

They came up over the crest of the slope and another, steeper slope fell away below them down to a long narrow lake that ran up into what looked like the end of a dead glacier. There was little snow on this slope, and the barren scree stretching down to the lake shore gave Marquis an idea.

'We'll lose too much time sticking to the track.' The path zigzagged its way down the bare slope; they would still be within rifle shot by the time the Chinese reached the spot where they now stood. 'We'll risk sliding down. We'll go two at a time, fifty yards apart, so we don't start any avalanche. Righto, Colonel, you and the general go first.'

But Li Bu-fang shook his head. 'This is as far as I go.' Singh raised his Sten gun, but Li just smiled. 'That doesn't frighten me, Colonel.'

Marquis swore angrily and stepped between the Chinese and the Indian. 'We haven't got time to wait on you two! Righto, the rest of you start down! Show 'em how, love!'

He slapped Eve on the rump and without argument she took off. She did not want to leave him, but she knew he was depending on her to get at least some of them moving. She went down the long slope of small stones, trailing a plume of dust behind her, glissading with almost as much grace as if she were ski-ing down the snow slopes of Klosters or Chamonix. Then Tsering and Chungma took off after her, going down with great shouts of glee, their natural exuberance breaking out of them for the first time since they had left the monastery; their yells of delight came up out of the great bowl in which the lake lay, echoing from the surrounding mountains and filling the air with a merriment that no one else shared. Wilkins was next and despite his weakened condition he looked as if he was going to make it without mishap.

Then it was the turn of the Brecks. Nancy looked ready to collapse, but Marquis took her by the shoulders and spoke to her gently but firmly. 'I know how you feel, Nan. Bloody awful, as if a couple of motor-bike boys are doing a Wall of Death inside your skull. But I reckon that lake must be fifteen hundred feet below us. If you can get down there, you should be all right. Want to give it a go?'

Nancy looked down the slope, just wanting to plunge over and down it to her death. But she nodded. 'I'll——' she tried to smile, but couldn't manage it. 'I'll give it a go.'

'Let's go, honey,' said Tom Breck, and they started off, slowly at first, then gathering speed as they gained confidence.

Marquis looked at Singh. 'Okay, Colonel, now it's our turn.'

'I don't want to have to shoot the general,' said Singh. 'But I'm afraid I'm going to have to.'

Marquis slipped off his pack. 'Think you could take this down for me, Nimchu?' The porter nodded and picked up the heavy pack, holding it by its straps over one arm. 'Okay, see you at the bottom.'

Nimchu asked no questions. He looked at the Chinese and the Indian, spat deliberately, then turned and went plunging down the slope. Marquis turned back to Singh, handing him his gun. 'Look after that, Colonel. It was a wedding present from my wife.'

'How appropriate,' said Singh, then smiled. 'Sorry. I was thinking about my own first marriage. But now what, old chap?'

'We're taking the general with us.' Marquis looked at Li Bu-fang. 'This is your last chance. You want to come quietly?'

Li Bu-fang shook his head. 'The only way I shall come quietly will be as a corpse.'

'That's what you think, mate,' said Marquis. 'I hate to do this, but as my old man always said—the best time to hit another bloke is when his hands are tied.'

Then he bunched his fist and hit Li Bu-fang hard on the jaw. He caught the Chinese as he fell, undid his hands and slipped the pack off his back. He looked at Singh, gesturing at the gear. 'Think you can carry that, too?'

Singh wasted no time. He picked up the pack, hoisting his own round so that he could sling Li's over one shoulder. Only the three porters were carrying full packs, but the two on Singh's back must have weighed at least eighty pounds. To add to his difficulties he was encumbered with his own and Marquis's guns. He staggered a little and smiled at Marquis. 'Oxford was no training for this sort of thing. And to think that *my*—er—old man once had seven hundred servants. The good old days, eh?'

'Good luck, Colonel,' said Marquis, suddenly liking the Indian. 'Watch you don't go over arse over tit.'

'Princes never assume that position, old chap. Not even when they're deposed. Cheerio.'

He started off, more slowly and cautiously than any of the others. Twice he seemed on the point of losing his balance, but each time he recovered, letting out a shout of triumph as he did so. Marquis watched him for a moment, then he bent and picked up Li Bu-fang. He was surprised at the weight of the Chinese, but it was too late now to have second thoughts. He knew there had been some famine in China over the past few years, but Li Bu-fang felt as if he had been on full rations; come to think of it, Mao Tse-tung never looked as if he'd gone short a few calories. I want my head read for thinking up this, he thought; as Nick said about Bhutan, whatever happened to my neutrality? He had a moment of temptation when he almost slid the Chinese off his shoulder. Then right at the bottom of the slope, a distant tiny figure but still recognisable, he saw Eve waving to him. And a third of the way down the slope Singh had stopped and looked up at him. Neither Eve nor Singh were accusing him, but suddenly he knew he could not take the easy way out. He hitched Li over his shoulder and started down.

Long scars had been cut in the scree by the boots of those

who had gone down before him. The slope was now much rougher and more treacherous; several times he was caught in ruts in the loose stones and slipped and fell. Fortunately each time he fell backwards and was able to prevent himself from plunging headlong down the slope. With Li over one shoulder he could not twist and turn as most of the others had been able to do; he had to go down with one shoulder turned into the slope, taking all his and Li's weight on the one leg. Stones broke away beneath him, whole sections of the scree sliding down ahead of him, sending up great clouds of dust that hung like yellow mist in the still air. But the slope above him held, did not suddenly gather itself into one huge moving crust and come sweeping down after him. The thigh muscles of the leg taking all the weight began to burn; the knee-cap began to feel as if it were about to burst through the skin. Tiny pebbles had got into the tops of his boots, biting at his ankles like scorpions. And all the time the dead weight of the unconscious Li hung across the back of his neck.

He was a hundred yards from the bottom of the slope when he felt his leg giving way on him. He tried to pull up, to swing round on to the other leg, but he was too late. He went down in a heap, falling forward this time and pitching Li over his head. He saw the Chinese hit the slope; then he was plunging after him. He went over and over, sometimes rolling, sometimes sliding, hitting rocks, deafened by the rattle of stones as they followed him down. Something smacked him in the side of the head and suddenly everything went black.

When he came to he was lying in a heap of stones at the bottom of the slope and Eve was washing dust and blood from his face with a wet cloth. His body felt as if it had been the target of a dozen jack-hammers; every bone seemed embedded in the underside of his flesh. His head ached and he could taste blood in his mouth. He wanted to lie down and die; but he had always known he would never find dying easy. And it was not so now.

He sat up, retching a little with the taste of blood and dust in his mouth. He raised one hand and saw that his glove had no fingers; his own fingers were raw and bloody. His anorak was torn and frayed and one knee had come through a trouser-leg. Only his boots seemed to have withstood any damage, but down around his ankles the scorpion stones were still biting at him.

'How's the general?' His voice was thick with what was in his mouth. He spat out: blood, dust and a piece of tooth. He put one of the raw fingers to his mouth and was pleased to find that it was not one of the front teeth that had gone. He grinned to himself and felt better: if a man had some vanity left, then he was still a long way from being dead.

'He's all right, darling.' Eve had begun to unlace his boots, emptying them of the pebbles. 'A bit scratched, but not as badly as you.'

Marquis looked up at the others standing around him. They were concerned for him, but they were also concerned for themselves: they kept glancing up towards the distant top of the slope. 'Get them moving, Colonel. Eve and I will catch up with you.'

'Do you want a hand, Jack?' Wilkins addressed the question to Eve as much as to Marquis: he didn't want her staying behind, sacrificing herself for her husband.

Marquis stood up, testing his legs and ankles: nothing appeared to be broken. He had missed Wilkins's look at Eve, had had the memory of a little while ago jolted out of him by his fall down the slope. 'I'll be okay, Nick. Don't hang around here. The Chows should be over the top of that hill pretty soon.'

Wilkins, still unobserved by Marquis, looked once more at Eve. She was about to smile, but something warned her to turn away: he was attaching himself to her, trying to marry her mood to his. Wilkins hesitated, then he started off after the others who had already begun to hurry along the lake shore.

Marquis began to draw on his boots again, but his fingers were too sore for him to tie the laces. Eve, still disturbed by Wilkins's scrutiny of her, squatted down and tied the laces. Then she stood up and said worriedly, 'Are you sure you're all right?'

God Almighty, he thought, how could I ever go anywhere without her? But the question might never need to be answered; not unless they got on the move again in a hurry.

He picked up his pack and took his gun from Singh. Then he looked at Li Bu-fang.

The Chinese was as dusty as Marquis, but he seemed to have suffered less damage. There was a red gash on his cheek and he was feeling his hip tenderly, but otherwise he seemed to be unharmed. His pack had been put on his back again and his hands had been re-tied. He stared at Marquis for a moment, then he smiled and lifted his hands to his chin.

'Was that a punch up the snout?'

Marquis grinned, still finding himself liking the Chinese. 'Not quite. Sorry about it, General. But I had no other argument.'

'The practical argument is often the best. Dialectics only waste time.'

'That's what you're trying to make us do now,' said Eve.

Li bowed. 'One can never fool a woman.'

'Did Confucius say that?'

'Women had proved their practicality long before the time of Confucius, Mrs. Marquis.' Li glanced up the bare slope, shrugged, then looked at Singh. 'I suppose you want to push on, Colonel? I am a very reluctant runner in this race.'

'Don't let it worry you,' said Marquis. 'No one's having any bets on you.'

They set off quickly, skirting the lake. There was less than a hundred yards of flat shore between the lake and the slope down which they had come. The ground was hard and bare of rocks, trees or promise; nothing had ever grown here from the beginning of time; a blade of grass would have been a desecration. This was the truly naked earth, dead and stripped for Judgment Day.

The sky had darkened quickly, as it so often did in these mountains. Clouds were racing in a wild tumult, like riderless horses, over the hurdles of the peaks. Once again the temperature had dropped suddenly; the cold air rasped in their throats, threatening to tear away the lining. Marquis cast an anxious glance up to the north behind them, where purple-black clouds boiled down out of the gaps between the peaks. The wind now came ahead of the storm, finding dust in the rocky frozen earth that Marquis would never have suspected, whipping it up into battalions that blew right across the lake; out on the lake the dust unaccountably seemed to thicken, as if the water itself was yielding up reinforcements. A flight of ducks, the only wild life they had seen during the day, suddenly took off from the lake, rising like brilliantly-coloured arrowheads before the bowstrings of the wind.

The lake, green-black and corrugated now under the assault of the wind, lay in a deep bowl. The long scree slope down which the party had come formed one side of the bowl; the other three sides were jagged peaks. Rising almost sheer out of the lake shore, their ridges saw-toothed and unscalable, they were stacked one upon another like an emplacement of giant broken tank-traps. A wrath of cloud whirled between the peaks, seeming to tear away the fabric of the mountains in their fury. There was no sky now, only a louring roof of dark turmoil that destroyed all perspective : the mountains closed in, became unreal and threatening, seemed to advance till they stood on the lake itself. It was easy to understand how the Bhutanese took their mountains for gods.

The track followed the edge of the lake till it came to the dead glacier at the southern end. Here it broke away from the lake and led up beside the long grey tumble of ice and rock, through a pass banked on either side by sheer, brutal-looking cliffs. Snow was now mixed with dust on the wind and visibility had dropped to less than fifty yards.

Marquis and the others caught up with the rest of the party as the track swung up beside the glacier. The wind roared up between the cliffs, snatching words from the mouth before they had any sound; Wilkins turned to say something, then shrugged and gave up. They moved on up through the gap between the cliffs, pushed along by the wind. The track veered to the left and suddenly they were in a long narrow gorge, the wind cut off by the angle of the cliffs. The dust and snow had been left behind and now they could see what lay ahead of them.

The glacier sloped up gently, a frozen cataract that had been born out of a crumbled wall of mountain dead ahead, the top of which was lost in a wild tangle of cloud. The track seemed to follow the glacier all the way up the gorge, only cutting sharply to the right out of sight at the base of the wall. Once up round that bend they would be less exposed than here in the long open funnel of the gorge.

'How's everyone feeling?' Marquis was still stiff and sore from his fall, but he knew that would wear off; years of hard living had given him an animal's power of recuperation. 'Nancy?'

'Much better.' The strain had gone from her face and she even managed to smile. Then she looked at the mountain ahead of them and the smile became a nervous tic. 'But if we have to climb again——'

Marquis cut her short, not wanting her to surrender again so soon. 'Nick?'

Wilkins, too, managed a grin. 'I'd rather be in Leeds.'

Marquis wrinkled his nose. 'Give me another choice.'

He was about to joke with Wilkins, when he saw the latter staring at Eve. Something he had never experienced before bit at him like the scorpion stones, but this time in the breast. He knew all the symptoms of mountain sickness; but was jealousy another of them? Then Wilkins had turned away and was walking on. Marquis looked at Eve for reassurance, bewildered by his own reaction to Wilkins's attitude towards her.

Eve had seen Wilkins's stare, franker than any he had yet given her, and it had shocked her. As a beautiful woman she had become accustomed to looks of admiration, of flirtation; they had been part of the social currency of her world. But no man, other than her husband, had looked at her with love in the past eight years; or if he had, he had kept it well hidden. She wondered how many times Nick Wilkins had looked at her like this in the past seven months, and was disturbed at all the pain she might have caused him. Then she looked across at her husband and saw on his bearded, scabbed face that other look, that of the enemy of love, jealousy.

She moved to him, put her gloved hand in his. They were alone, all the others had gone on ahead, and she looked up at him, stripping her face of any mask. 'Want to bite it?'

He understood then that she was telling him he had nothing to worry about. He lifted her hand and bit her finger again. 'I'm sorry he feels like that.'

'So am I. Let's hope it's just the altitude.'

'A man could fall in love with you at sea-level.'

'You're becoming absolutely Gallic!'

'I was brought up on French beans.'

She nodded. 'It is the altitude. The higher you climb, the worse your jokes are.'

Still in love, they had fallen in love again : it was the sort of renewal that had kept their marriage alive. It had been missing over the past few months, but now it had suddenly come back. They exchanged the ridiculous words that lovers do, the idiocies that are not idiocies because the words are not uttered for their meaning but only as the sound of love.

Then something flew off the ground beside them, they heard the whine of the ricochetting bullet and a split second later the crack of the rifle. Marquis grabbed Eve's hand and, packs bouncing on their backs, club-footed in their heavy boots, they ran stumbling up the track and fell in behind a straggle of big boulders. The rest of the party was already there, Singh and Wilkins unslinging their guns and taking aim down the gorge.

Marquis slipped out of his pack, then rolled over and peered down through a vent in the rocks towards the bottom of the gorge. He could see several Chinese soldiers spreading out to take cover behind the rocks that lay at the foot of the tall cliffs. There were no more than half a dozen of them, and at once he guessed that this was a forward party that had been sent on at full speed to catch up with the fugitives before the storm closed down on them. He looked up at the sky : it had darkened still further as avalanches of cloud came tumbling down off the mountains. Then he looked at Singh.

'What do you reckon, Colonel?'

'I can't do any damage with this.' Singh patted his Sten gun. 'They're too far away at present.'

'You're still thinking in terms of a fight. I'm thinking about running away.' He looked over his shoulder up the gorge. 'What do you reckon are our chances?'

'We shan't get far if we all try to run at the same time. They could then just come out in the open and pick us off like ducks.' Then Singh looked back up the gorge. 'But there are enough rocks there to give cover, if one or two of us stays behind to keep those chappies down there pinned down.'

'I'll stay. I could do with the rest.' Wilkins blushed as soon as he had spoken. He hadn't meant to sound so laconically heroic, like those stiff upper lip heroes in war films; but no one seemed to notice, he was now accepted as one who could be relied upon to do his part. The others were beginning to have more confidence in him than he had himself. He went to say something else, but he abruptly shut his mouth. He was learning, perhaps a little late, not to spoil the image of himself.

'You and me, then, Nick,' said Marquis, and remarked to himself upon the irony of it. 'We've got the guns with the distance. Righto, Eve, you take off first.'

'I'd rather stay here with you.'

'Don't argue, love.' He winked at her, deliberately not looking towards Wilkins. 'I'll catch you up in no time at all.'

She hesitated, then she turned away to slip her arms back into her pack straps. And in that moment Li Bu-fang suddenly left them. He rolled out from behind the rocks, was on his back, he kept slipping and falling, but all the time he was getting farther and farther away from them.

Tom Breck had slipped out of his pack and had gone sprinting after the lumbering Chinese.

'Let the bastard go!' Marquis yelled. 'Tom, come back!'

But Breck didn't hear, went running on. He was fifteen yards across the rutted ice of the glacier before he fell the first time; he went down in a wild whirl of arms and legs. But he was up at once, stumbling on after the fleeing Chinese. Chips of ice flew up around him, but then as he got closer to Li Bu-fang the firing in his direction stopped. The Chinese soldiers evidently didn't want to run the risk of shooting their own general.

Breck closed on Li, slipped and fell as he made a lunge at the Chinese; but his outstretched hands caught at the bouncing pack and the two men went down, sliding down into a trough in the ice. Li rolled over, kicking furiously, trying to club Breck with his bound hands. But Breck, who had never fought a man in all his life, had an instinct for survival. He swung his fist desperately while he tried to dodge the savage kicks of the Chinese.

The clouds were rolling down the gorge, coming down from the wall of mountain like the birth of another glacier. The gorge was lost in an angry twilight that almost at once became a grey silent fog. The clouds rolled on down the gorge, blinding every man to everything more than a few feet from him.

The world was reduced to nothing, a couple of yards' circumference of thick grey mist.

Marquis scrambled to his feet, leaving his gun against his pack. 'Be ready to move as soon as I get back!'

Then he began stumbling off into the rolling, wreathing cloud, shouting to Tom Breck and hearing his voice dying quickly in the fog. He fell as soon as he put his feet on the glacier, going down with a bone-jarring thump. He scrambled to his feet and began to move more cautiously, still yelling for Breck. He heard two shots ricochet off the ice near him; a rifleman had chanced his aim; but there was no more firing. He fell several more times, feeling the ridges of ice chop at him as he landed on them. But he stumbled on, still yelling for Breck.

Then he stepped off into nothingness. Panic rippled through him as he fell into what seemed a pit of cloud; then he landed with a terrible thump at the bottom of a trough. He slid along the ice and bumped hard against a rock. He lay for a moment getting his breath, then he stood up and shouted again, roaring with all his power.

And almost at his feet he heard Tom Breck gasp, 'Jack!'

He fell on his knees and groped towards the voice; then he saw the two figures, locked in a weak but still desperate struggle. He grabbed the figure with the pack on its back, pulled it off the panting, threshing Breck.

He put his arm round Li Bu-fang's neck and grunted, 'I'll break your bloody neck this time, General!' The darkening face was bent back close to his own; he could see the staring eyes, the teeth in the gasping open mouth. 'Don't make me kill you!'

Li stared at him. Cloud wreathed about them in thin veils; even Tom Breck seemed to be cut off from them. They glared at each other like animals, but they were enemies who had no real hate for each other. Yet Marquis found his grip tightening on the other man's throat. Anger pumped through him: all at once he *did* hate the Chinese, not for being his enemy, not for any clash of ideologies, but because the latter was inviting him to kill him. Was this how murder sometimes happened, because the victim insisted on being killed? He kept pleading with Li, even as his grip tightened.

'Don't make me kill you, you bastard!'

Then abruptly Li went limp. For a moment Marquis thought the Chinese was dead; then he saw Li nodding his head. He relaxed his grip.

'You win, Mr. Marquis.' Li's voice was strangled, as if Marquis's arm was still round his neck. 'I can't burden you with my death.'

Marquis sucked in a mouthful of cloud. 'Thanks,' he said, and meant it. Then he looked at Tom Breck. 'You okay, Tom?'

Breck stood up, wavering in the shifting tide of cloud like a man under water. He looked as if he was about to fall, but he seemed to find some unexpected strength in his legs and straightened up. 'Let's go.'

They both helped Li Bu-fang, still with his hands tied and still hampered by his pack, up out of the trough. All three of them slipped and fell on the ice; then they were stumbling back through the grey blindness in the direction of the track. The ruts in the glacier ran downhill, parallel to the track; if they kept crossing the ruts, they must come to the track eventually. But in the chase after Li Bu-fang, how far had they come *down* the glacier? In the dead blind world of cloud it was impossible to tell.

Marquis pulled up. 'We should have reached the track by now!'

'We must be way down the gorge!' Tom Breck looked wildly about him; his voice involuntarily dropped to a hoarse whisper. 'I noticed when we first came into the gorge, the glacier was much wider at the bottom end.'

Marquis turned to Li Bu-fang just as the latter opened his mouth. But Marquis was too quick: his big gloved hand was clapped over Li's mouth before the latter could bring out his yell. 'Tom, your scarf! Gag him with it!'

Breck whipped off his scarf and tied it round the lower half of Li's face. Marquis slid his hand out and Breck pulled the scarf tight. It was an effective enough gag; Li would need to make much more noise than the strangled grunts he was managing. Marquis clipped him lightly on his ear-flap. 'You're a bloody nuisance, General. Now shut your gob and behave yourself.'

'Which way, Jack?' Breck whispered.

Then they heard the voices, soft and urgent, dead ahead of them. A moment later there was the rattle of stones and the clink of metal against rock. Marquis strained his ears, trying to count the number of men by the sound of their footsteps; but it was impossible, there could have been six or a dozen. All he knew was that they were moving up the track, and the track was no more than twenty yards away. If the cloud suddenly cleared, he and Tom Breck might just as well walk across and hand over Li Bu-fang without fuss.

He leaned close to the shadowy figure of Breck and whispered, 'We'll head up the glacier. Make it as soft-footed as you can.' Breck nodded, and Marquis turned to Li Bu-fang, putting his hands on the latter's shoulders and pressing him down. Li stared at him in puzzlement, but sat down without a struggle. Marquis at once dropped on his knees, untied the Chinese's boots and pulled them off. He felt Li's feet: the latter's socks were thick. 'Sorry, General. But I can't have you giving us away by thumping about in your boots.'

Li nodded, smiling with his eyes. With his own men so close, he knew this farce would soon be over. He could afford to admire the ingenuity of Marquis, even though it was only delaying the inevitable.

Marquis slung the boots over his shoulder by their laces and yanked Li to his feet. He jerked his head at Tom Breck, then the three of them began to move quietly up the glacier, following the line of the ruts.

The cloud was still rolling down the gorge, sometimes so thick they could barely see each other at a couple of paces, other times thinning out so they could see clearly for twenty yards or so. All sound seemed to have been killed in the thick mist; they were both blind and deaf. Once Marquis stopped, listening for the movement of the Chinese soldiers over to their right; but the sound of his own heavy breathing was enough to prevent him from hearing anything else. They were moving slowly, putting their feet down cautiously in the ruts so that they wouldn't stumble and fall; once Li tried to fall, but Marquis grabbed him by his pack straps and held him up. He pressed his mouth against Li's ear-flap, like a lover.

'Do you *want* me to kill you?'

Again Li stared at him, then again he shook his head.

They moved on, their legs beginning to ache with the exaggerated caution with which they were putting down their feet. The cloud continued to roll down on them; it was like walking into a towering grey surf in a dream; they were engulfed but they felt nothing and they didn't drown. Then suddenly the mist cleared. Fifteen yards away, his back to them, was a Chinese soldier.

Marquis froze, grabbing at Li Bu-fang and holding the Chinese still. Tom Breck paused in mid-stride, his head turned towards the soldier; he looked like a man caught in a badly-focused photograph. Despite the cold Marquis could feel the sweat breaking on him; every nerve-end was suddenly raw. He held his breath, staring with eyes that had begun to burn at the back of the soldier. Unconsciously his arm began to tighten on Li's throat; the latter's stockinged feet scraped noiselessly on the ice. The soldier looked to his right, down the track, then he turned and began to move on, glancing to his left.

But in the moment he turned his head the cloud thickened again, blinding him to the three men who stood only yards from him.

Farther up the gorge Eve and the others had begun to worry as the cloud thickened and there was no sign of the return of Marquis, Breck and Li Bu-fang.

'What's happened to them? Have they got lost?' Nancy stood up, peering into the fog. Her myopia didn't matter in the dense cloud; everyone suffered from the same shortness of sight. Whether it was because of the drop in altitude they had undergone in the last half-hour or because in her concern for Tom she had forgotten all about herself, her headache and nausea had gone. Her only sickness now was her worry over Tom, and she shouted desperately for him into the fog.

'I'd go after them——' Wilkins gestured at the grey nothingness: insanity could not have had less dimension.

'You could get lost, too, Nick.' Eve had stared into the shifting cloud until her eyes hurt. She closed them for a moment to ease them, then she opened them and looked at Singh. 'I'm beginning to wish I'd never seen you, Colonel.'

Singh nodded; he had the same grey look as the fog. 'I am frightfully sorry, Mrs. Marquis——'

'You should never have come into our camp, Colonel,' said Nancy sharply. She turned round to glare at Singh, and almost stumbled over Marquis's pack at her feet. His gun rolled off the pack and she bent down to pick it up. As she straightened up with the gun in her hands she saw the figure coming up the track out of the cloud. 'Tom?'

Eve and the others turned quickly as the figure stopped. Singh's Sten gun was held loosely in the crook of his arm, Wilkins had his slung over his shoulder; neither of them had time to shoot as the Chinese soldier brought up his rifle. Nancy's hands moved independently of her mind, a reflex action; it was as if the hands themselves remembered everything they had seen Marquis's hands do with the gun. They snapped off the safety catch, pulled the trigger. The gun bounced off her hip with the recoil, but she didn't feel it. She saw the Chinese soldier stiffen, sit down with a bump and roll over, quietly and without any exaggerated theatrical gestures. It was not the way she had expected a man to die and at first she didn't believe she had hit him.

The Eve had dragged her down behind a rock as Singh and Wilkins began firing at the other dim figures that had now materialised out of the cloud. The Chinese seemed taken by surprise, as if they had expected the fugitives to have retreated farther up the gorge in the fog. Singh and Wilkins kept firing, while Eve, Nancy and the three porters huddled behind the rocks. The soldiers stumbled around, looking for cover; one man turned and went running back into the mist. Wilkins followed Singh's example: their shooting was systematic. Four more of the Chinese went down, dying without a sound; one of them must have been on the edge of a bank because he slid away into the fog like a man disappearing into a grey spectral sea. The remaining two soldiers fired wild bursts in the general direction of Singh and the others, then they turned and fled back down the gorge, the cloud swallowing them in a moment.

Singh and Wilkins stopped firing. In the thick silence that followed, a silence that to Eve seemed to be the fog itself, all sounds were magnified: the ejection of the shells from the guns, Tsering's hissing as he sucked in his breath. Then they heard the stumbling footsteps and they all swung round, Singh and Wilkins bringing up their guns again.

'Nancy?'

Nancy sprang to her feet, flung herself at Tom Breck as he, Marquis and Li Bu-fang appeared out of a thick swirl of cloud. She was crying and moaning, like an animal in pain. Breck wrapped his arms round her and looked distractedly at Eve. 'Has she been hit?'

Nancy herself answered him, shaking her head violently. 'I killed him! I shot him!'

'Good on you, Nan,' said Marquis, and looked down at the dead soldiers, lying like rocks on the mist-shrouded path. 'A pity we haven't got another gun for you——'

Nancy shuddered, whimpering with her teeth tight together. Then she struggled out of Breck's arms, leant over and was violently ill. Breck stood behind her, holding her by the waist, his voice thin with anguish. 'What's the matter, honey? Nancy——?'

Eve, shaking her head at him, pushed him aside and put her arm round Nancy's heaving shoulders. There was nothing left in Nancy for her to bring up; she was only retching now. Eve looked around, then bent down and picked up a handful of snow. 'Here, rinse your mouth with this.' Nancy took the snow, and Eve looked back at the men who stood in a tight embarrassed circle about the two women. 'She'll be all right. Hadn't we better get moving?'

Marquis went to say something, then just nodded. He picked up his pack and gun, then looked at Li Bu-fang, dangling the latter's boots in front of him. 'You'll have to do without these for a while, General. We haven't got time to put them on you now.'

Li Bu-fang might not have heard what Marquis had said. He had looked down through the fog at the dead soldiers, then turned quickly away. His eyes had dulled, as if the fog itself had got into them. His face was as impassive as ever, but something had gone out of it. Impassiveness suggested confidence; but Li Bu-fang's confidence had begun to run out of him. His face had inherited the Oriental trick of masking the emotions; but his body had given him away. The slumped shoulders were an expression in themselves.

Marquis gazed at the Chinese for a moment, then he turned away and jerked his head at Nimchu and the other two porters. 'You lead the way, Nimchu. You've got a better sense of direction than I have in these sort of conditions.'

Nimchu started off at once, followed by Tsering and Chungma. Unarmed except for their knives, they had been almost terrified as the bullets had ripped into the rocks around them; once Chungma had been about to stand up and flee, but Nimchu had grabbed him and pulled him down again. The porters were not cowards, but they were sensible. You did not stop to fight rifles with knives.

Wilkins looked at Tom and Nancy Breck, both standing with their backs to the others; then he nodded at Marquis and he, too, walked off into the fog. Singh knelt down, pulled on Li Bu-fang's boots but didn't lace them, then he stood up, jerked his head at Li and the two of them started off up the track.

'Better get started,' Marquis said to Tom Breck. 'We don't know how long it'll be before the rest of the Chows catch us up.'

Breck nodded, picked up his pack, took Nancy by the hand and led her, as if she were his young daughter instead of his wife, up the track and into the fog. Their roles had been reversed: suddenly it was she who needed him.

Eve picked up her pack, settling her shoulders into the straps. She looked down at the dead soldiers, then back at Marquis. 'I don't think she'll want to kill any more Chinese.'

'I could have bitten my tongue off.'

'You weren't to know, darling. At heart she's really as gentle as Tom. She just had to find out—the hard way.'

She put her hand in his and they began to walk quickly up the track; the cloud had begun to thin a little and it was possible now to discern the path. Ghosts scurried past them, shapes of men, animals, trees: Eve remembered a poem of her childhood, that clouds were the souls of all past life. How soon would the clouds of herself and Jack go blowing through these lonely mountains? She squeezed his hand in fear; but he mistook it for a gesture of love and lifted her hand and bit her finger. Tears sprang to her eyes, but he didn't see them.

'Darling,' she said, 'if we get out of this——'

'Don't talk like that.' He tried to remember how a confident voice sounded; it was almost a ventriloquial trick, using a voice that didn't belong to him. 'Our luck hasn't run out yet.'

She hadn't meant to sound so despairing. When he had interrupted her she had been about to say that if they got out of this alive she would not think of settling down in England: she would continue to go with him on his trips to no matter where, she would never be able to bear the waiting at home for him. But now she recognised that he was the one who was despairing: the ventriloquial trick hadn't come off, she had recognised the false voice.

'I always did believe in luck,' she said. 'I was a great gambler in my girlhood. I was the most successful bookmaker my finishing school ever turned out——'

'Bookmaking isn't gambling. Bookies never trust to luck.'

'This one will,' she said.

2

They climbed out of the gorge and the cloud at the same time. The track swung up through a deep defile at the base of the wall of mountain and came out on a long broad ridge. Ahead of them rose the main massif that blocked their way to the south. These were sharp-ridged peaks and to Wilkins, his moments of light-headedness now more frequent, they were another memory of home. He remembered a camp on the cliffs at Whitby, the rows of white tents stacked close together like these peaks, their canvas stretched by the wind blowing in off the North Sea, just as the steep white slopes of these mountains seemed to billow in under the wind that blew out of the north. The umbilical cord was never entirely severed, not till the skull was empty of mind and memory.

His lips had taken on a purplish tinge and once when he took off a glove he saw that the veins on the back of his hand had turned deep blue. He knew that this was the result of lack of oxygen and he was ashamed of the fact that he should have been affected at this comparatively low altitude. He tried to disguise his laboured breathing, but it was useless; he only distressed himself further, then had to take in the air in great gasping lungfuls. He knew that the heart enlarged as one climbed into more rarefied air, and he began to imagine that he could feel it growing inside him, a white-hot balloon that would soon burst its way out of his chest. He was coughing more frequently as the day wore on, hacking the strength out of himself and watching it drift away as thin mist on the cold blue air.

None of the others was as bad as Wilkins, but Nancy still had a headache. They were climbing through a thin layer of snow that flung back the bright sunshine as another assault on their endurance. They were all wearing sun-glasses and every-one was smeared with anti-sunburn cream. Marquis stopped once and waited for Wilkins as the latter, mouth gaping, came labouring up the track.

'Try and keep your mouth shut, Nick.'

Wilkins looked up, his mind as blank as the sun-glasses he wore. He was too exhausted to be surprised or indignant : mouth still open, he just gave Marquis an idiot stare. 'What?'

'You'll get the roof of your mouth sunburned. I'm not pulling your leg, Nick——' Wilkins shook his head in dis-belief, mouth still agape. 'The reflection from the snow will burn the inside of your mouth in no time. You're feeling pretty crook now. You'll feel a bloody sight worse with a mouthful of sunburn.'

Wilkins took a moment to understand this, then at last he nodded. 'Thanks, Jack. You're not a bad bastard.'

'I know,' said Marquis, grinning. 'You want me to carry some of your gear? I'll take the gun.'

'No!' The moment of comradeship for Marquis went out of him as a sharp gasp. Suddenly he was jealous and resentful again of the big man; not of his possession of Eve but of his strength. He would die before he would surrender any more of himself to Marquis. The Australian already owned his dream; he could not allow him to take over the means of his survival. A man had to retain some illusions about himself, especially that he had the strength to hold back his own death. In one bright frighteningly lucid moment Wilkins knew that if he gave up and let himself depend upon Marquis or any of the others, he was finished. Without knowing it, he was akin to Marquis : he was not going to find dying easy. All his adult life he had tried to be a rationalist, had turned his back on the lessons of the chapel; but now suddenly the wind of eternity blew through his bones, and he was frightened for the soul he had so long denied. But he would fight the battle alone. 'No, I'm all right, I tell you!'

Marquis said nothing, a little taken back by the sudden change of mood. He stared at Wilkins for a moment, a breath of anger coming out of him like an explosion of steam on the cold air; then he turned away and went on up the track, walking too fast in his temper. Ten yards away he stopped and looked back at Wilkins, who stood gazing after him, his mouth open as he sucked in air.

'Keep your mouth shut,' Marquis said, then turned and went on.

Nobody but Eve had taken any notice of Marquis stopping to talk to Wilkins. When her husband caught up with her, Eve recognised the old signs, that he was splitting apart with anger. But she knew enough not to ask any questions, was inarticulate when it came to explaining his anger. She would have to be patient if she wanted to know what had passed between the two men. Apprehension forced her to make no guesses.

They saw no signs of the pursuing Chinese during the rest of the day. Everyone occasionally looked back, Li Bu-fang with hope, Marquis and the others with despondency. All knew that the Chinese soldiers had not given up the chase. They were as relentless as the mountains.

They ate in the middle of the day, tsampa mixed with condensed milk, then a spoonful of honey all around : everyone was now feeling the craving for something sweet to eat. They sat in the snow and ate in silence, surrounded by silence : the world had all at once become dumb. When the stillness was broken, by the cracking birth of an ice-fall somewhere up ahead, the sound disturbed no one; it was as if they didn't hear, didn't want to hear it, but had become impregnated by silence. Despondency and exhaustion withered the roots of their tongues, driving each of them into an isolation that he both welcomed and regretted. Only Li Bu-fang looked as if he might reply if anyone spoke to him, but no one even looked at him. Mocking confidence was no answer to the sort of question that lay on their dead tongues. The sickly sweetness of the condensed milk and honey was mixed with the sour taste of despair.

By early afternoon they had completed the climb up the long broad ridge and were traversing another wide open slope. The snow here was a little more than ankle deep, not difficult to plod through but it hid the loose stones that strewed the path and all of them, at one time or another, slipped and fell. Each time they went down, it seemed harder to get up; even Marquis and the porters were beginning to feel the effects of the long hard day. The path was easy to follow despite the fall of snow : it wound between rocks on which the occasional prayer-flag hung limply like a relic of a long gone carnival procession. Marquis touched one flag and it crumbled like charred paper in his hand. He looked quickly ahead to see if the porters had noticed what he had done : not guiltily but because he feared they would see the crumbled flag as some sort of omen and perhaps decide to turn back. But Nimchu and the other porters now had eyes only for the track and mountains ahead. They had committed themselves to not looking back, except during the rest halts when there was nothing to distract them from their fears.

It was Nimchu who first saw the bright stain of colour on the snow up ahead. The slope here was barren of rocks and the snow lay in one bright vast carpet for perhaps half a mile or more. Right at the end of the open space, just before the rocks began again below a steep cliff, a pool of colour glittered amidst the shining glare. Everyone stopped and stared at it, thinking it was some hallucination. The colours seemed to change even as they looked at it : from yellow to green to blue to black, and all the time there was the same shifting metallic glint. With the snow surrounding it, the image that sprang to Eve's mind was that of a huge sheet of Christmas tinsel.

Wilkins let out a shout that was unintelligible to the others. He dropped Marquis's gun and slipped off his pack and started

stumbling through the snow towards the patch of colour.
Marquis shouted after him, but Wilkins was deaf to everything.

'I'll go after him——' Tom Breck said.

'Let him go, he'll be all right.' Marquis looked at Breck,
who stood gasping in the thin air, his cheeks collapsed below
his dark glasses : Marquis had the sudden chilling feeling that
he was looking at Tom Breck's skull. 'There's no point in
you busting a gut. We'll catch him up.'

'But what *is* it?' Nancy asked.

'Beetles, memsahib,' said Nimchu. 'Come up from forests.'

Eve then remembered Wilkins telling her of the summit
haunting habits of certain insects. No entomologist had discovered the reason for the insects' behaviour, yet every year
they rose from the forests and plains and sought the summits
of mountains; they reversed the migration habits of lemmings,
climbed towards the peaks instead of descending to the sea.
Thousands of the insects might die in the mass flights to
regions that were unnatural to them, but entomologists had
established that it was no suicide urge that drove the tiny
creatures to the high places of storm and snow. It happened
not only here in the Himalayas but in Europe, Central Asia and
North America. The type of insect might be different, but the
habit was the same. They flocked to their summit rendezvous
as humans flocked to Blackpool or Coney Island. Eve wondered
if they fled there for the same reason : escape from everyday.

Marquis picked up Wilkins's pack and Singh took his gun,
and the party plodded on, taking its time. Wilkins fell several
times before he reached his target, but each time he struggled
up without resting and stumbled on. They all watched him
with concern and once Nimchu looked at Marquis as if to
suggest that he should hurry on after the demented man; but
Marquis shook his head and indicated that Wilkins was safe
as long as they kept him in view. It would show a certain
craziness on their own part to go chasing a crazy man across
a mountain slope at this height. None of them, not even
Marquis, had that much strength to squander.

By the time they reached the vast flock of beetles Wilkins
was in the middle of it, stamping around like a child wading
delightedly in a multi-coloured pool. He was picking up the
beetles in great handfuls and throwing them up in the air; he

was covered in a confetti of glittering insects. He was gasping
and crying incoherently, a man who had discovered gold when
the world had just gone off the gold standard. He stamped
around, making no effort to be careful where he trod. He
would pick up a handful of insects and stare at them as if he
held a handful of treasure; then he would throw it in the air
and stumble on under a glittering rain to scoop up another
batch. Marquis and the others stood on the edge of the bright
shifting mass and looked with pity on the drunken, reeling
Wilkins.

Nancy dropped on her knees in the snow. 'Look at them!
There must be millions and millions of them!'

The pool of beetles must have been twenty yards square.
Its outer edges providing the shifting pattern of colour as the
insects, green, blue, brown, black, struggled over each other
towards the reddish-yellow centre of the pool. The effect was
of a slow vortex, a creeping whirlpool that would inexorably
swallow its own bright centre. And Wilkins was now on his
knees in that centre, scooping up the beetles and showering
himself in a yellow rain, chanting aloud like a man caught up
in some religious ecstasy.

'I'd better get him out of there.'

Marquis stepped on to the mass of beetles, hearing them
crunch beneath his boots as he made his way towards Wilkins.
It was like walking on coloured ice that splintered beneath
his weight; for a moment he had the terrible fancy that he
was going to go right through the dark pool under him, that
the beetles would close over his head and devour him. Death
had become a constant image now, too constant for comfort.
Which was why all his anger at Wilkins had now gone and he
felt only concern for the deranged man.

He stood behind the still-chanting Wilkins and said gently,
'Nick, time we got moving again.'

Wilkins didn't hear him. '*Carabidae, Coccinellidae——*'
His voice droned on, chanting the words of his own religion;
he ran the beetles through his fingers as if they were the loose
beads of a thousand broken rosaries. His breath was coming
in great hoarse gasps and he was rocking his head from side to
side.

Marquis knelt down beside him. He, too, was in the centre

of the pool and he saw now that they were surrounded by millions of ladybird beetles; all at once he remembered the entomological term for them, *Coccinellidae*. Then he saw the reason for the vortex effect. The larger, darker beetles on the edges of the pool, those with the other names that Wilkins was chanting, were converging on the ladybird beetles to eat them. He looked down, for the first time aware of the sickening smell, and saw the wholesale slaughter going on. The ladybird beetles hardly stirred, just lay sluggishly in their millions while the carnivorous beetles, in their greater millions, pressed in on them to devour them. This was the insect world at its most savage. Marquis was suddenly taken by an insane urge to stamp out the predators. He stood up, ready to run riot with his boots among the shifting glittering mass. Then he looked about him and sanity came back. It would take hours to kill all the carnivorous beetles and the ladybird beetles still wouldn't be safe. They would lie here in the snow, unable to come fully to life again till the spring, waiting for the heavy snowfalls to cover them and keep them alive during the winter. Till they were covered they would be at the mercy of any sort of predator.

Marquis bent down, shook Wilkins by the shoulder. 'Nick, we've got to get moving!'

Wilkins continued to mumble his chant, still rocking his head from side to side. The beetles had begun to crawl up his legs in a thick rising tide; they were covering him with their own glittering armour. Again Marquis had a moment of frightening fancy: if Wilkins were left here, the beetles would devour *him*. Angrily, almost in a panic, Marquis slapped Wilkins's face, shook him fiercely by the shoulder.

'Nick, for Christ's sake get up! Get up, blast you, get up!'

Wilkins stopped his chanting and looked up. He stared at Marquis as if the latter were a stranger, then he looked down and around himself in bewilderment. He stood up quickly, brushing the beetles off himself in panicky desperate sweeps: it was as if he, too, saw himself being devoured by them. Marquis grabbed him by the arm and they stumbled back across the dark shifting mass to the snow, the smell of the beetles crushed by their boots rising about them like the stink of some evil pit.

Wilkins seemed to be trying to find some way to express himself, but the words were locked inside him; he opened his mouth, but all that came out was the hacking crippling cough. Marquis picked up Wilkins's pack, heaved it up to rest on his own on the back of his neck; he staggered for a moment, then steadied himself. Breck hesitated, looking at Wilkins still bent over coughing; then he bent down and picked up Wilkins's gun and slung it over his shoulder. He looked at Nancy, but she turned away, shutting her mind against the gun and what it had done in her hands. Without a word the party got under way again.

Wilkins stumbled along at the rear, burdened with shame heavier than the pack and gun he had surrendered, but unable to do anything about it. He was only glad that Eve walked at the head of the party, her back to him.

It was an hour later when they sighted the monastery. The huge walled complex of buildings, more like a fort, suddenly came into view as they toiled up over a rise. From their first distant sight of it it looked like a squared-off mass of rock that had fallen from the mountain behind it. It stood at the end of a long open ridge, seeming to dance in the thin blue air against the glare of snow and ice behind it. But rock or monastery, it was something to aim for. They struggled towards it with gasping impatience, punishing their lungs and their limbs like drowning swimmers who have just caught sight of a faraway shore. The snow on this ridge was thicker and this only heightened in Marquis's mind the impression of swimmers: they stumbled through a white frozen surf that did its best to pull them down. No one spoke, as if each of them harboured in his own mind the doubt of what he saw: it could be an illusion, a mountain mirage that would keep them stumbling on till they collapsed from exhaustion and lay down ready to die. In the thin bright air it at first seemed to get no closer; they could see it clearly, but with every step they took it seemed to retreat. Then at last they were gaining on it: it became real, stood waiting for them.

'I don't care if there are a dozen lamas in residence,' Eve gasped, 'I'm sleeping in that place to-night!'

Nancy giggled hysterically and nodded. Now they were so close to the monastery everyone seemed on the verge of hysteria; simple excitement ran through them like a fever. They made a brave but futile effort to increase their pace, came up before the big wooden gates on shuddering legs that would not have carried them another quarter of a mile. The thick walls of the monastery towered above them, stretching on either side of the gates for sixty or seventy yards. They leaned in exhaustion against the walls and gates while Marquis raised his gun butt and hit it against the big brass gong that hung in a wooden frame beside the entrance. The sound boomed out, splintering the silence; but its own note was hollow and the silence soon conquered it. Marquis, hearing the sound die away across the snow-blanketed ridge like the echo of a dead voice, had the feeling of a man who shouts with all his lungs but silently into the face of thunder. He knew, without the gates being opened, that the monastery was empty and the gong would summon no one.

The gates swung open when they pushed hard on them, and in another ten minutes they had assured themselves that the monastery was empty. It was the biggest monastery they had so far seen in Bhutan, and its emptiness was like a concentration of all the loneliness of these high mountains. The series of temples and the long high-roofed galleries that connected them were sinister with silence and shadow; Eve and Nancy, less in control of their imagination than the men, shivered with something more than cold. Footsteps echoed like the bones of strolling skeletons and the wind coming through the unshuttered windows had the plaintive sound of the cry of dead men. But if it should haunt the party, it was still preferable to spending the night on the open slope.

All the temples were subdivided into chapels, dark rooms whose tall ceilings were lost in shadow; giant gilded deities sat about the walls, their heads lost in the mist of darkness beneath the ceilings. Bats flew about the upper galleries like lost souls, and in the gallery of one bare chapel they found a hawk had nested: it attacked Marquis and Nimchu and they soon retreated, leaving it whistling and beating its wings in anger. The party had split up, moving in groups through the empty chambers, but their presence brought no warmth or life to the monastery. Yet they found signs that it had been recently occupied.

'It must be the home of the monks we met the first day, sahib,' said Nimchu, turning over some mats they found stacked in one corner of a chapel. 'Sometimes, when winter comes, they come down from these high places to other monasteries in the valleys.'

Marquis nodded, prepared to accept any explanation for the deserted place. It was a roof over their heads; and Tsering had found some firewood to start a fire and cook them a hot meal. After the last few days the monastery was as welcome as a Himalayan Savoy. He felt certain that the Chinese would not travel during darkness, so the party could rest without worry to-night and recoup their strength for what remained of their journey.

Everyone's spirits and physical condition had been revived with their arrival here. Even Wilkins seemed to have found a new strength; he busied himself starting fires to warm up the rooms where they had chosen to sleep. Being busy slowly melted the shame he had felt; he worked harder than anyone else as he carried great armfuls of wood round to the various fires. It was as if he were climbing hand over hand back into their acceptance of him, never realising that not one of them had given a thought to deserting him. If they had turned their backs on him it had been out of sympathy, not callous indifference.

Eve had found some big copper pots and while she was heating water in which to wash herself, Marquis went out on to the long balcony that ran along the western wall of the monastery. Singh and Li Bu-fang were there, standing at the balcony rail and admiring the view like fellow tourists.

'We have discovered we have something in common. We both like sunsets.' Singh had taken off his sun-glasses, but his face was still streaked with anti-sunburn cream. His beard was now a thick stubble and he looked more like a beggar than a prince. Except, Marquis noted, for the arrogance: that would always show through, no matter how Singh looked.

'Sunsets are a-political,' said Li, smiling. He, too, was streaked with cream; and his light beard was darkened with dirt. If there were now no Chinese beggars, then he was a peasant: he certainly did not look like a general. Except,

Marquis again noted, for the confidence: no peasant had ever had the confidence that Li showed.

Marquis looked back along the ridge, half-expecting to see the Chinese soldiers advancing at full speed towards the monastery. But the ridge was bare, and he turned back to look at the view.

The ridge at the western end dropped away sharply into a cloud-filled gorge; the monastery looked like a ship about to be launched on a golden sea. The sun was caught for a moment in the cup between two peaks; the whole scene below all at once blazed with colour. The sea of cloud turned pink, then red; mountains in the distance became reefs of amethyst. A peak of ice suddenly caught fire, reflected its colour in the long scarves of cloud that rode the wind above it. Marquis nodded at the clouds.

'There's the Princess of Streaked Clouds,' he said to Li. 'Do you blokes still bend the knee to her or has she been booted out with the rest of tradition?'

'What do you know of our mythology?' Li looked with interest at Marquis, and so did Singh.

'A little. You forget I'm a Celt—once removed, but the bogwater is still there in my veins. I was fed myths with my mother's milk. I grew up with a taste for them. When I got my ambition to go collecting in Yunnan, I began to learn everything I could about you Chinese.'

'Everything except the language, old chap,' said Singh. 'I must say that might have been of more use than a few old legends.'

Marquis nodded glumly. 'I tried, but I gave it up. I was never a man for nuances, and Chinese is all that.'

'It is only an expression of our character,' said Li. 'We were a subtle people when you barbarians of the West were still debating with stone axes.'

'Don't knock the West too much, General.' Marquis looked at Singh, who seemed amused by the good-tempered exchange between the Australian and the Chinese. The bastard, Marquis thought: I keep forgetting that he's an Asian, that he's half on Li's side when it comes to questions of East and West. But he kept his observation to himself. It had taken

him some time to accept the Indian and what his entry into
their camp had brought on them. But now, committed as they
were, he knew they needed Singh perhaps even more than
Singh needed them. He could not afford to let the Indian think
too much of being an Asian. Even if it meant putting up with
Singh's unwitting caricature of an Englishman.

'Did you know their heaven is in the west, Colonel?'
He gestured towards the distant peaks. 'The Land of Extreme
Felicity is as far west in the universe as you can imagine. It
must gripe the guts of the general's bosses to know that, as
the compass points, America is closer to the Chinese heaven
than China itself. How have you got over that one, General?'

'We turn our faces to the east, and there is America.
Farther from heaven than anyone.'

'A real Chinese answer.'

'What did you expect,' said Li, a spark of bitterness coming
through again, 'from a Chow?'

Marquis was surprised at the taunt, but he ignored it. 'So
you still believe in your myths?'

'I don't. Nor, I think, do my—er—bosses.' Li's voice
had lost its momentary sharpness; he seemed to regret now
that he had spoken to Marquis as he had. 'But you don't take
everything away from the masses, Mr. Marquis. Tradition has
its uses at times.'

'Your pantheon would have its uses for you Reds.' Marquis
looked at Singh, who was showing silent but polite curiosity.
'It's arranged just like one bloody great bureaucracy, Colonel.
A sort of civil service of gods. Right at the top there's the
August Personage of Jade, and all the other gods have to
furnish him with annual reports.'

'In triplicate?'

Marquis grinned. 'I don't know. Maybe that's only a
pantheon—the Reds could use it any day as a model.'

Li smiled. 'A good idea, Mr. Marquis, but not very
practical in our society. We could never afford to have a
Minister who might come to look upon himself as a god.'

'Not even Mao Tse-tung? Your propaganda boys try to
build him up as one.'

'You're wrong, Mr. Marquis. They are only trying to
keep alive the old revolutionary spirit.'

'Trying?' Marquis said, and saw the swift shadow of chagrin that had crossed Li's face: the Chinese had made a slip of the tongue. 'Who wants to let it die, General?'

'Perhaps it is the old revolutionaries themselves,' said Singh. 'They become tired when the battle is won. It was that way in India.'

Marquis looked at Li Bu-fang. 'Are you tired, General?'

'The battle isn't won yet, Mr. Marquis.'

'It's a different battle. You're not a revolutionary any more, you're trying to be a conqueror.'

'There's need for revolution everywhere.'

'You're just re-adjusting your thinking, General,' said Marquis with a flash of clear insight.

Li stared at him, then he shrugged. The political officers, the eager young men with their parrot phrases and their busy concern for everyone's conscience, were not here: all at once Peking was another world, as distant as the Land of Extreme Felicity. 'It is a Chinese talent, Mr. Marquis. We have had to do it for thousands of years. But I am no less a Communist because of it.'

'But the good days are over, eh?'

'The good days are over for so many of us.' Singh was looking at Li Bu-fang with none of his old suspicion and antagonism: they could have been comrades in arms. 'I enjoyed being a prince, the general enjoyed being a revolutionary. But things are not personal for us any more, are they, General?'

Li hesitated, then nodded. 'I would only admit here'— he looked around at the silent loneliness surrounding them— 'that a prince and I might have something in common.' He smiled. 'But you have adjusted, Colonel, haven't you?'

'One has to, old chap. A measure of happiness is better than none at all.'

A measure of happiness, Marquis thought; was that all one was entitled to? These two men had accepted it; what right had he to expect more? The good days are over for many of us, Singh had said; and perhaps that went as much for him, the roving botanist, as for the ex-prince and the ex-revolutionary. If he kept on, insisted on going to New Guinea, when would he ever reach the time for re-adjustment? Would he leave it too late to expect even a small measure of happiness?

'Quick, sahib!' Chungma burst out on to the balcony from a nearby doorway. 'Sahib Breck want you!'

Marquis dropped the questions from his mind at once. Choked with sudden dread, conditioned now to expecting the worst, he spun round and followed the running Chungma. They clattered down a flight of steps and along a long dark gallery. It seemed to Marquis that they ran for miles through one gallery after another; his lungs began to burn and his legs to ache. Then at last he stumbled after Chungma into a chapel lit only by the flickering oil lamp held by Tom Breck.

The young American turned slowly, his thin gaunt face with its shredded beard crumbling like burnt paper in the quivering light that played on it.

'I've just gone out of my head, Jack,' he said. 'I've just discovered a fortune.'

He raised the oil lamp, let its yellow light play on the wooden crates stacked against the walls of the small chapel. Their lids had all been prised off, showing an inner wrapping of tinfoil which had also been opened. Marquis moved from case to case, shaking his head at what he saw, wanting to peel the film of illusion from his eyes but knowing that if he did the truth would still be there. He was staring at a myth that no leprechaun could ever have conjured up out of a Celtic bog.

The crates were packed tight with American dollar bills.

SEVEN

'There's millions of bucks there,' said Tom Breck. 'I feel like I've just been made Treasurer of the United States. Alexander Hamilton Breck.'

'I think you might have more in the kitty here than old Alex had.'

Marquis moved to one of the cases and picked up a bundle of notes. It was wrapped in a brown paper band and on the band was stamped: $1–$100. He fitted the bundle neatly back into its layer, as if he were re-laying a brick; moved on to another case and took out another bundle. This one had the same brown paper wrapper but it was stamped: $5–$500. He replaced this bundle with the same care; moved on to a third case and took out a third bundle. Its wrapper was stamped: $10–$1000. All the time a disbelief and a kind of anger was growing in him, as if he felt he was being made the victim of some huge tasteless joke.

He put the last bundle back, then turned to Breck and Chungma. 'They must be forgeries.' His voice was too argumentative, too aggressive. But whom was he arguing with—fate, the biggest practical joker of them all? He retreated, forcing a smile. 'But how did the monks get hold of them? Unless they do this instead of saying prayers.'

Tom Breck shook his head. 'I had a good look at one of the notes, Jack. I'm no expert, but I'd swear it's not a forgery. Those are for real, Jack. Every million of 'em.'

Marquis looked around the chapel. The cases had been pushed into the recesses between the huge statues of the gods; he had the feeling that the deities were looking at the offerings out of the corners of their eyes. He didn't blame them: even gods had cause to be suspicious of such unexpected treasure.

Then he heard the light barrage of approaching footsteps and a moment later the rest of the party had come crowding into the chapel, bringing it alive with their shock, excitement and their movements as they swooped from case to case, running their unbelieving hands over the tightly packed notes. No one looked greedy; that, perhaps, would come later. The tall narrow room hummed with their intoxication as they reeled around it; even the three porters, who did not understand the value of the currency and had lived most of their lives by bartering, were affected by the discovery. Li Bu-fang stood in one corner, like the forgotten relative at the reading of a will, but his usually impassive face was alive with thought and speculation.

' Just ten per cent of this and I could be the Sultan of Leeds!'

' You could turn the mills into harems. Have there ever been any concubines with Yorkshire accents?'

' Tom, we could buy up *all* of Bucks County!'

' I'll buy back Northern Ireland from England. That'll make my old man comfortable in his grave.'

Only Eve and Singh, the two who had had money all their lives, could think of nothing they could do with the fortune before them. Eve was infected with the excitement of the others and she laughed at their proposals on how to spend it; but, never having had to count her pounds, let alone her pennies, she could look at the stacks of money almost with indifference. She knew that, as with the saint who strives to be more saintly, there were rich men who dreamed of being richer; but her own ambitions had never lain in the direction of wealth, her money was something she took for granted like her looks. But she did not feel superior towards the others because of their excitement.

Singh picked up one or two of the bundles of notes, then dropped them carelessly back into the cases; his reaction was so casual it could have been a pretence, but for once the Oxford nonchalance was real. Only later would Eve and Singh begin to see the possibilities in the fortune.

' But how did it get here?' Eve asked.

Singh had been examining some markings on the sides of the cases. ' Here's a United States Air Force stencil.' He straightened up, his brows creased in concentration. ' I remember something—it was while I was in Calcutta—early 1945, I think it was. Yes. There was a rumour, some talk in the officers' clubs—you know what it's like——'

'We don't know at all what it's like,' said Marquis impatiently. 'Get on with it!'

Singh smiled. 'Patience, old chap. Well, the rumour was that the American government had sent money, a loan, to the Chinese Nationalists in Chungking. The plane carrying the money ran into some sort of trouble over the mountains, began to ice up or something like that, and had to throw out everything. Including the money.'

'How much money was supposed to have been lost?'

Singh shrugged. 'No one really believed the story, of course. It just made another good rumour to fill in the time.'

'Forty million dollars,' said Li Bu-fang quietly from his corner.

They all turned quickly, surprised to hear from him at all, even more surprised at what he said. He had suddenly become the important one in the chapel : knowledge promotes a man, more so when it is unexpected. Li was human enough to be pleased by their sudden attention and he smiled with a satisfaction that only irritated Singh, who had up till now held the centre of the stage. They all stared at the Chinese and he leaned back against the huge thigh of one of the gods, smug and amused, as if their positions had all at once become reversed and now they were his prisoners. Even the way he held his bound hands in front of him somehow gave him an appearance of arrogant confidence.

'We knew about it—we Communists, I mean.' He smiled at Marquis, then did something Marquis had never seen a Chinese do : he winked. There was no reason in the world why a Chinese should not wink, but Marquis could not remember ever having seen it before. It was only a tiny thing, but somehow it seemed to increase the bond growing between the two men. I hate the bastard, Marquis thought; but why do I like him so much? Li had gone on talking: 'The major I worked for in Chungking, Mr. Marquis, was in American Intelligence. I didn't go to work for him just to wash his dishes and sweep his floors. I kept my eyes and ears open——'

'You mean you were spying,' said Marquis.

Li shrugged. 'If you like. We knew we would eventually take over our country and we wanted to make sure all that money was not dissipated by the Kuomintang. Corruption was one of the major talents of those reactionaries. I can remember even the Americans used to complain about it.'

'Were you going to hi-jack the money or something?' Tom Breck asked.

'Hi-jack? You mean rob?' Li smiled. 'I don't know, Mr. Breck. There were plans, but I didn't know them. I was only a major then—in the wrong army, too, at that time. Majors are never taken into confidence, are they, Colonel?'

Singh grunted, and Marquis said, 'Then how did you get anything out of the American major?'

'I got nothing from him. But the senior men who came to his house—they were often indiscreet. It is never the ordinary soldier who gives away secrets. It is their commanders who are most careless. The more you know, the more silent you should be.' He smiled again, enjoying himself. 'Old Chinese proverb. By Charlie Chan.'

Singh gestured at the cases. 'Then this is what your men are after? They know it's here?'

Li shrugged again. 'You guess, Colonel. I'm no longer a major, I'm a senior officer now. The more I know, the more silent I should be.'

'He's bluffing!' Wilkins leaned on one of the cases as on a counter and thumped a fist on the tightly packed notes. He coughed and wiped his hand across his mouth, shivering a little and swaying on his feet. He had been staring at the money as Li had been talking and now suddenly he was drunk on it. 'It's just sheer bloody coincidence!'

'Coincidences like this should happen to all of us,' said Tom Breck, recognising that Wilkins was once again on the point of collapse and trying to speak soothingly.

'He's just trying to rub our nerves! The money's ours!'

'Okay, Nick, it's ours.' Marquis had difficulty in making his voice sound placatory: he had more on his mind than the task of keeping Wilkins happy. 'But if his blokes find this——' He banged the side of one of the cases with his open palm; the sound was like that of a pistol shot in the tall narrow room. 'No Chinese lottery ever had a prize like this one. No opium dream ever had one like it, either.'

'Forty million dollars!' Tom Breck suddenly saw the

implications. 'They could buy trouble in any country in Asia with that!'

'We mustn't let them get it!' Nancy threw out a challenge; then collapsed under her own echo. 'But how? How do we stop them?'

'We could burn it,' said Eve quietly.

Marquis grinned wryly: she had always been extravagant, but now she was being ridiculously prodigal. He remarked with even more wryness that she was probably the only one in the room who could afford to be that way. He did not know how much Singh was worth, but the days of the fabulously rich Indian princes were over.

Then he noticed that Chungma was grinning and nodding. 'What's wrong with you, Chungma?'

'Burn it, sahib. Make big fire, keep warm.' This was Chungma's first expedition and so far he had received no money; a signed note from Marquis, promising to pay him and all the other porters, was held back in Thimbu by a government official. Like Eve he had been infected by the others' excitement but he could not comprehend what the dollars meant. To a boy who had seen his father buy tools and pay taxes with dried yak meat and bags of rice, the cases of money were just so much paper that could be put to a useful purpose, such as stoking up a fire. His only wealth was his innocence and Marquis, thinking of children in the outside world, wondered how soon the young Bhutanese would be struck poor.

'You can't burn it!' Wilkins glared at Chungma, his eyes hot and wild. 'That'd be criminal! You can't!'

'It would be a shame, old chap,' Singh said to Marquis, and Tom and Nancy Breck nodded in agreement. 'But it's your decision.'

It would be, thought Marquis; and looked up at the deities that sat about the room. He recognised one or two of them: Demchhok, in his tiger skin and with the chain of human skulls round his neck, and his wife Dorje-Phangmo: these were the gods of these mountains, this neutral land. They stared down at him, frozen-eyed, cruelly indifferent: he was a foreigner, an invader of their domain. He wondered how the invaders had felt when they had first entered Christian churches. Had Mehmet had moments of doubt in

the Church of Santa Sophia when he had sacked Constantin-
ople, had he looked at the images of the saints for guidance
and been met only with marble stares?

Then high in the purple gloom, on a balcony that he hadn't
noticed before, he saw eyes that were alive. They stared down
at him, animal eyes that were filled with an animal's fear.
Marquis, without a word, put out a hand, took the oil lamp
from the puzzled Tom Breck, leapt up on to the lap of one
of the gilded gods and held the lamp high. Its flickering glow
washed a little higher in the dark chapel, rinsed out the
shadows, threw into relief the dark shapeless figure leaning
over the rail of the balcony. But even as the light reached it
the figure was already on the move, had turned and disappeared into a doorway behind it.

Marquis thrust the lamp at Breck and went out of the chapel
on the run, calling to the porters to follow him. Which they
did, sprinting after him with great shouts: any sort of chase
appealed to them. The long chamber outside the chapel was
not so dark; Marquis saw the steep flight of wooden stairs and
stumbled up them in his heavy boots. As he came up on to
the long balcony that ran the entire length of the chamber he
saw the man, creature, whatever it was, disappearing round
the far corner. He shouted to Nimchu and the other porters
and went galloping along the balcony, feeling the timbers
bouncing under his heavy steps. I want my bloody head read,
he thought: I've done more galloping since I've been in this
monastery than at any time since I gave up playing Rugby.
He reached the corner and looked back for the porters; then
he pulled up short and shouted at them again. But Nimchu,
Tsering and Chungma, stood at the top of the stairs, shaking
their heads.

'No, sahib!' Nimchu's voice was a hollow echo in the
long dark gallery. 'It is a spirit, maybe a yeti! Listen!'

Marquis swore angrily, but he cocked an ear and listened:
there *was* a sound, eerie and terrifying. A high-pitched
whistling scream, that cry that Sherpas had described to him
as the voice of the yeti, the Abominable Snowman: it pierced
the ear like a cold needle, numbed the brain and turned the
blood to ice. Despite his scepticism Marquis shivered; civilisa-

tion after all was only a thin armour. Then, angry at himself now and not at the porters, he turned and blundered on through the gloom. He came to another flight of stairs, went down them too fast, fell and picked himself up. And saw the creature standing with its back to a wall between two giant statues, its eyes wide with terror, its arms spread out in the attitude of crucifixion, its fear whistling out of its gaping mouth and magnified by the hollow chamber.

'Now take it easy, feller.' Marquis spoke to the figure in front of him as if he were talking to some animal, a dog or a horse; the words meant nothing, only the tone in which they were uttered. 'I'm not going to hurt you——'

He advanced on heavy but cautious feet, one hand held out in a gesture of friendship. The man, wrapped in rags, still looking more animal than human, tried to press himself into the wall; he shrank with terror, trying to dissolve himself in his own too-solid shadow that wouldn't accept him. His fear increased his smell: vile and nostril-shrinking, it hit Marquis when he was still feet away from the man. Marquis stopped, halted by the stink and by his sudden concern that the stranger would collapse from fear if he got any closer.

Then Eve and the others, the porters hiding at the rear, came running along the chamber and pulled up behind Marquis. They stared at the man and he stared back at them; he looked wildly for escape but he was trapped by the gods between which he stood. The fire Tsering had lit to cook the evening meal blazed in a nearby room; its glow through the open doorway lit the dark chill gallery. Shadows worked grotesquely on the walls, threatening to demolish them; the deities came alive without moving as the fire's glow bounced off them. Tom Breck raised his oil lamp and the man stood pinned against the wall by spears of light.

Marquis spoke to him again, squeezing friendliness into his voice as he might have pressed a gift into the man's hands; and cautiously, so slowly that it was barely noticeable, the stranger relaxed. He came no closer, still stood hard against the wall, but he lowered his arms, was no longer crucified by his own terror.

'Better say something to him, Nimchu,' Marquis said, and

Nimchu, overcoming his own fear now that he saw he was not faced by a *sounday* or a yeti, came forward. 'Tell him we shan't hurt him.'

Nimchu spoke to the man, but the latter looked at him blankly. Slowly now, as his fear melted, he was taking on dignity. He straightened up, drew his rags about him as if they were an expensive cloak. The rags were thin, looking almost like a coil of dirty tattered bandages; beneath them the man wore only a frayed sweater, a faded football jersey that he had found only his gods knew where. His head was wrapped in a purple turban, the one bright clean note about him; he wore it like a crown, a reminder of other days or perhaps a symbol of aspiration, it was hard to tell. His feet and hands were bare, blackened and cut by the cold but showing no signs of ever having been ravaged by frost-bite. He stared at Nimchu as the porter spoke to him, his dark Mongol face stiff as that of the deities high above him in the shadows.

Nimchu turned back to Marquis. 'He does not speak our language, sahib.'

'Who is he?' Nancy asked.

'He could be from farther east than here, memsahib,' Nimchu said. 'The people in the east of our country are darker and shorter than we people in the west. This man is like that.'

'I'm guessing,' said Marquis, scrutinising the man carefully: his rags, his bare stone-like feet, his indifference to the cold, 'but I think he's probably a hermit. There are plenty of them in these mountains.'

'Is that why he's so dumb?' Wilkins coughed, swayed on his feet and looked belligerently at the stranger: it seemed that he hated everyone now.

Marquis glanced at Wilkins, kept his voice gentle. 'I'm not familiar with hermits, Nick.'

'We've never seen any before.' Wilkins seemed to be having difficulty in focusing his eyes. 'Never seen any at all.'

'Down where we were camped, we wouldn't. These blokes like the high places, as close to Nirvana as they can get.'

'You mean he manages to survive up here in the winter dressed like that?' Nancy shook her head in disbelief. 'What do they do, go into trances or something?'

'Maybe. Maybe they've just trained themselves not to notice the things that worry us. Comfort's only relative, Nan. The colonel will tell you that. Tie a knot in the digestive tract and the poor convince themselves they're not hungry. That's how it is in India, eh, Colonel?' Suffer, you bastard, like I am. Have an attack of conscience. But Singh just looked blankly at him; and Marquis turned back to look at the hermit. 'If he doesn't understand the local language, Colonel, you might have a go at him with Hindi.'

'He doesn't *look* Indian.' Singh spoke to the stranger in Hindi, but he was met by the same blank stare as had greeted Nimchu.

Then Marquis, almost apprehensively, looked at Li Bu-fang. 'You try him, General.'

Li had been looking at the hermit with amused curiosity, a sort of tolerant contempt for a man who chose to live this life of retreat and self-discipline, almost masochism. Marquis noticed the look on Li's face and guessed that the general had long ago lost patience with the old Chinese custom of contemplation. Action and service were everything now; the mystic in the People's Republic was no more than an egoist. So much for the Great Leap Forward: self-denial was now a crime unless done in the service of the State.

Li turned his gaze away from the hermit and smiled at Marquis. 'What if he does speak my language?'

'I told you once before, General—I trust you,' said Marquis, and once again saw the momentary flinch in the other's stare. 'Just ask him who he is and what he's doing here.'

Li spoke to the stranger in Chinese, softly and quickly; and at once the dark grimy face came alive. The mouth opened, showing black broken teeth, and words hissed out; language warmed him and at the same time made him aware of the cold; he shivered and drew his rags closer about him. Li turned back to Marquis and the others, composing his face again, disguising the excitement that had lit him for a moment. But not before Marquis had noticed it and begun to worry about it.

'He says he does not have a name, that he left that behind in the outside world with all his other possessions. He comes from much farther east than here, from the borders of Sikang.'

'So he is Chinese!' Tom Breck pulled distractedly on his beard, dragging open his jaw.

'He doesn't admit to it,' said Li. 'He says he belongs to no country.'

'What the hell does he expect to find in these bloody mountains?' Wilkins was all belligerence now, trembling on the verge of hysteria again, coughing like a dying man as the night air hacked at his throat. 'What's he looking for?'

'Peace,' said Li Bu-fang, and smiled.

'Who isn't?' said Eve.

Li looked as if he was about to say something to her; instead he turned and spoke once more to the hermit. The man hesitated, then nodded. Li seemed satisfied; he leaned back against the thigh of the god behind him.

Singh slapped his sides in a sudden fury of exasperation. 'What did you say to him then?'

Li took his time about answering. 'I asked him how long he had been here in the mountains.'

'You're lying!'

'How would you know, Colonel?'

Singh let out a curious bark of anger. He suddenly switched his fury from Li to the hermit, advancing on the man and snarling at him in Hindi; the stranger backed up into his shadow again, once more cringing with fear. Singh raised his arm as if about to strike him, but Marquis, moving quickly, grabbed the fist and pulled it down. Singh's whole body quivered as he strained against Marquis's grasp, but his strength wasn't equal to that of the bigger man. All at once he relaxed and stepped back.

'What the hell's the matter with you, Colonel? What was that all about?'

Singh was breathing heavily, struggling to regain control of himself, aware that his fury had reduced his intelligence to that of one of the porters. He glared at Li Bu-fang, the other man who really understood the meaning of face. His anger was not diminished by the smile on Li's face.

'Don't you see? Here is someone who can read the papers for us——?'

'Read them, sure,' said Marquis. 'But who'd translate them? The general?'

Singh stood with his mouth open, knowing how stupid he had been. Then control came back, he donned the air of nonchalance again and smiled. 'Awfully stupid of me. But damned frustrating, don't you think?'

'What did you read at Oxford, Colonel?' asked Li.

Singh stared at him curiously. 'English History.'

Li shook his head. 'Now *that* was stupid, Colonel. You had no anticipation of history. You must have known even then that the British were finished in your country. But that has always been the failing of kings and princes, hasn't it? They have never anticipated history.'

'Don't lecture me, General.' Singh dropped his air of nonchalance; his voice was as cold as the room. 'You're still my prisoner. Perhaps you should start anticipating your own personal history.'

The tension, forgotten during the last few hours, came back. Despite their isolation from the rest of the world, these two men were at war: they could not forget their identities as soldiers.

Marquis looked at them, recognising their commitment, then he looked back at the mystic, still staring with frightened eyes at Singh. How did I ever think I could stay neutral? he wondered. How does Nehru, the professional neutral, feel now? Here is the real neutral, the mystic hermit, and even he has been trapped.

'Let's eat,' said Eve, the practical woman, and turned and led the way into the side room where the last of the gooral meat was stewing in a pot. 'All I want to anticipate is a full stomach.'

Eat, drink and be wary, thought Marquis. And holding his nose, he pushed the stinking hermit ahead of him into the other room.

2

Eve lay in her sleeping-bag and watched the glow from the fire bring the deities out from the walls, making them even larger and bring them leaning over her. Yet she was not frightened, because she had never been able to bring herself to believe in the images of gods and saints; she had wandered through cathedrals with Jack, her reaction to the stone figures as cold as theirs to her. But the darkness itself frightened her; the devil in the shadows behind the gods had nothing to do with religion. She shivered despite the warmth of the sleeping-bag and turned towards Jack for comfort. But he, the protective spouse, was asleep.

She could hear the wind rising outside, moaning like wolves at the shuttered windows. The bats moved restlessly in the high corners, sketching nervous traceries as they whipped across the flickering ceiling. She closed her eyes, but the atmosphere of this dead room still intruded on her: on the red ceiling of her eyelids the bats still scratched their meaningless warning, in her shuttered ears the wind still demanded to be heard. The storm was increasing by the minute and she knew before the night was out the monastery would be shaken by its savage assault. She wondered if any of them would have survived to-night if they had not come upon the monastery.

The bats scratched a question: who would survive anyway? There had been further discussion while they had eaten on what should be done with the fortune in dollar bills; but the talk had all been academic and everyone seemed to know it. There had been no excitement, that had all soon gone; they had all talked with the bland boredom of people who had more money than they could use. A million dollars might have been comprehensible; forty million was zero to the umpteenth degree. They had talked of the money as if it were a hypothesis rather than a fact. Survival, too, she knew now, was no more than a hypothesis.

She turned her thoughts away from what to-morrow might mean and deliberately began to think of the money. She knew that in the inner mind of all of them, even herself, the money *had* been a fact. She had seen the thought of it in the eyes of Jack; and recognised the danger of it. She had never considered her own money as being a chain on him, indeed after their initial row over the wedding present of the guns she had done everything she could to dispel that impression; but in these past seven months she had become more aware of her money than ever before, had begun to curse it for its taking away of Jack's independence. She had often heard the canard that money was of no importance except to those who did not have it; but did a poor woman have to worry about her husband's independence? Jack had never mentioned her money since that day she had given him the Holland and Holland guns, but she had known all these years that it was always in his mind. She did not know all of his thoughts, but she knew the way of his thinking. She had read once, a German poet if she remembered correctly, that we never really know anything about anyone else. But she had never believed that; the Germans had always been the most pessimistic about human relations. She knew Jack, not all of him but enough. He would be sleeping now with the money cached in his mind, buying an escape she hoped he would not want when he woke.

Oh darling, she cried silently, while the wind tried to bend in the gates and the gilded gods laughed silently in the flickering glow. Above them the bats squeaked evilly in the black evil of the shadows, and she heard Jack moan like a man in despair. She dropped off to sleep, the fire on her eyelids turning to ashes.

In another room the Brecks lay side by side, dying without knowing it : each had given up hope, but would not confess it to the other. Nancy had felt the strength leaving her all day, taking with it her life by degrees. She had never known a day's serious illness and so she was unprepared to fight death. Always an optimist about living, she had never thought about dying; so now pessimism took the strength out of her as much as the long hard day had done. She coughed, dried out like a husk : the thin air had begun to dehydrate her. She was desperately thirsty, but she did not complain, not wanting to worry Tom.

'Darling.' Her voice was a croak : it made a mockery of the endearment. 'Can we go straight home to Bucks County?'

Tom Breck grunted and shrugged, not wanting to discuss the dream that was already dead. Exhaustion gave them the appearance of an old married couple; gestures sufficed instead of words. Nancy looked at him with loving sympathy, marvelling at her luck. Cautious about affection all through her childhood and adolescence, daughter of a mother whose love of her God took precedence in the house, she had fallen in love with Tom an hour after meeting him. Marriage had been a heaven she had not been taught to expect on this earth. She had all the small perquisites : the waking in the morning without guilt beside the body of her lover, the responsibility of caring for someone else other than herself, the subtle yet noticeable added status of being a married woman instead of a hopeful girl : all these had given her a happiness she had only dreamed of and never really expected. But marriage was also something else : it was Tom. And she had become Tom. Everything that he felt, she felt : every ache, every disappointment, every regret. It was the only way she knew how to love.

'Darling, what do you think Jack will do with the money?'

'I don't know, honey. I'm just glad it's not my decision.' He was glad that none of the journey's decisions had been his. He had come almost to worship Marquis, seeing in the big man's strength and competence everything in which he himself had failed; he felt no resentment, as weak men often do, but instead borrowed some of Marquis's strength and prayed for some of his competence. But without any real hope, because he knew he was doomed all his life to be a bumbler, a man whose feet wove their own traps. All his life : he closed his eyes in pain, knowing his life was over.

Nancy coughed, dying of thirst. 'Do you think we could hide the money and come back for it?'

He looked at her, not hiding the pain in his eyes. 'Do you think we're ever likely to come back?' Meaning : do you think we are going to live long enough for the money to mean anything to us?

She recognised the real meaning of his question, but she knew that neither of them could have stood a true answer. Oh God, she thought, we'll both be dead soon, yet we still can't speak to each other. We're wasting our last hours together because we are still strangers, we don't know each other well enough to talk of death.

'We might come back,' she said, more dry-throated now than thirst could ever make her. 'You never know.'

' No, you never know,' he said, and thought how true, in another context, the banality was.

Fires burned in other rooms, the glow on the walls a reflection of the magenta robes of the departed monks : the monastery was populated by ghosts. The porters shared a room with the hermit, settling down to sleep on the opposite side of the room from him; his smell did not drive them away, but his mysticism. They envied him his holiness, but at the same time it frightened them. He was too close to their gods.

Singh and Li Bu-fang slept in another room, lying side by side like friends, bound together by their distrust of each other. Li Bu-fang, of whom less trust was needed, had already gone to sleep, the only one of them all who did not fear to-morrow. Singh lay on his back, the Sten gun by his side beneath the blankets, his pistol still in its holster, the bed comforters of the cautious soldier. He dreamed in the half-world between waking and sleeping, a young man again : the bats above him turned to wood-pigeons, the wind was the echo of a peacock's cry, a woman materialised out of his own flesh and lay with him. Selfishness took hold of him, as it does when there is no one else to pass judgment : he began to dream of being a prince again. Ah, what he could do with all that American money ! He slept in the luxury of the past while the present began to gnaw at his bones.

In a fourth room Wilkins slept alone. Or rather did not sleep, but lay in his sleeping-bag wishing for the last sleep of all, dying by self-compulsion. He coughed now only spasmodically, scoured out. He was not cold in his sleeping-bag, but he shivered continuously as his bones turned to ice inside him. His heart had grown to an enormous size; he could feel it trying to burst its way out of his chest. Thirst had dried him out till his skin felt like tissue-paper, but he resisted the urge to get up and go looking for water. But he could not fight the craving for something sweet to suck.

He sat up, searched in his pack and found some boiled sweets. And found the box containing *Teinopalpus imperialis*. He leant back against the base of one of the statues, opened the box and took out the butterfly. He sat there, sucking on sweets and gazing at the butterfly, a boy again in the tiny garden in Leeds. His dry fingers ran lovingly over the equally dry wings of the insect. The glow of the nearby fire touched the colours on the wings and for a moment Wilkins held a jewel in his hand. He began to cry with the beauty of it; tears were the only moisture he had left in him. He lifted his arm, holding the butterfly flat on his palm.

'Fly away, Emperor!' he implored, and a breath of wind, coming from somewhere, stirred the wings.

Then he looked up and saw the figure, trailing feathers of rags, flit by the doorway to the room. He blinked back the tears, tried hard to remember where he was and who was with him. But he was alone, as he had been all his life. He got up, swaying on legs that were no more than dried sticks and, still carrying the butterfly, he lurched across the room and out into the long gallery outside. He caught a glimpse of movement to his right, and he turned that way, stumbling along in his stockinged feet. But he had gone no more than a few yards before he forgot why he was out here in the gallery. He staggered on, as lost as if out on the open mountain; he saw a doorway ahead of him and he plunged towards it. He fell up some steps and sprawled into a dark room that was as cold as a tomb. He was coughing again, his whole body shuddering as if being beaten. He crawled towards the rear of the room, deeper and deeper into the darkness, looking for the warmth and security where he had begun so long ago. The butterfly was crushed in his hand, but he had forgotten that too. His head bumped into wood; he put out a hand and pulled himself up. Then he was sprawled over what seemed like an altar, his cheek laid against bricks of paper. He opened his hand, letting go of the pulped butterfly, and ran it over the surface on which he lay. Paper?

Suddenly his mind cleared. He began to giggle, weeping without tears. He *was* on an altar, a communion table of money. Too late he had been smiled upon by the most unchari- table god of all, Mammon. He turned his head, peering into the darkness; but all the other gods had disappeared, they had no use for him. Who cares? he wept; and began to take apart the altar brick by brick. Ah, what beauty I could buy with this! In the darkness he could see nothing, but his mind was now ablaze with dreams. He began to tear at the bricks, ripping off the paper bands; dollar bills began to drift down about him in the blackness. He could not see them but he could feel them building up about his stockinged feet; he began to move about the room to the other cases, stumbling through a fortune. He was weeping and laughing and coughing, dying by the minute, the richest man ever to have come out of Leeds. He did not hear the shouts from the other room along the gallery.

Marquis heard them. He came awake in an instant, despite the depths of the sleep of exhaustion in which he had been sunk. He lay only a moment getting his bearings, then he struggled out of his sleeping-bag, dragged on his boots and, not waiting to lace them, stumbled out of the room and along to Singh's room. As he reached the door Li Bu-fang came out on the run. He caught Marquis off-balance and sent him crashing back against a wall. Before the big man could pick himself up Li had recovered his own balance and gone sprinting off down a side gallery.

Marquis got to his feet as Singh, blood streaming from the old wound above his eye, came out of the room. 'Someone cut him free!'

Marquis hastily laced up his boots, his fingers already numbed by the cold. 'Did he get your gun?'

Singh held up his Sten gun. 'No——' Then he put a hand to his open holster and cursed. 'He's taken my pistol!'

Without a word Marquis went back to his room and shook Eve awake. 'Get into the next room with the Brecks, love. Come on, get weaving!'

'What's the matter?' Eve tried to fight her way out of the nets of sleep.

'Li's on the warpath. Stay with Tom and Nancy and don't move out of that room!' He loaded his gun, put a box of ammunition in the pocket of his anorak and took his torch from his pack. By that time Eve had scrambled out of her sleeping-bag and dragged on her anorak and boots. 'I'll get Nick in with you, too. And none of you come out of the room or you're likely to get shot at!'

'Darling!' She caught at his arm. 'Do you have to go chasing the general? He's not your prisoner!'

He stopped and looked at her. In the dim glow from the dying fire in the centre of the room his bearded weatherbeaten

face was that of an old man's : the skull had already begun to
assert itself. When he moved he seemed to creak with age;
the hand that touched hers had no strength in it. Even his
voice had nothing left of the old fire of argument.

'I'm sorry, love. He *is* my prisoner. Just as much mine
as Singh's. I'm in this war with them—at least till we get out
of the mountains. There's nothing else I can do.'

She stood staring at him for a moment, then she stood on
her toes, kissed him on his dry cracked lips and pressed her
body against his. They stood like that for a moment, bound
by a cold passion that never touched their blood. Then she
turned and went out into the gallery and along to the room
where the Brecks had already been awakened by Singh.

Marquis stood at the door and bellowed for the porters and
in a moment they came running, their eyes still clogged with
sleep. Singh had gone along to Wilkins's room and he came
back just as Nimchu and the other two porters arrived with a
slap-slap of unlaced boots.

'I can't find Wilkins!'

'The hermit's gone, too!' Marquis snapped, and felt a
sudden weight of doubt. Why not go back to his room with
Eve, why not let Singh search alone for his prisoner? But he
knew he would not be able to sleep if he did. He might as well
join in the search, he told himself; but he knew there was a
deeper reason that drove him to it. 'It must have been him
who slipped the ropes off the general. If I catch the holy
bastard I'll squeeze some prayers out of him!'

'But where's Nick?' Eve felt responsibility for Wilkins
and was angry at herself for doing so : she was becoming
involved with him against her will. And was ashamed of
herself for her lack of charity.

'I don't know, but I hope he doesn't run into the general.'
Marquis looked at Tom Breck. 'Look after the women and
the porters, Tom. If the general comes back this way and you
have to use that gun '—he nodded at the 12-bore that Breck
held reluctantly, like a man with sin in his hand—' for Christ's
sake use it!'

He turned on his heels at once, not wanting to have to argue
further with Tom Breck's principles, taking the coward's way
out and leaving the younger man to fight with his conscience.

He shouted to Singh to take one direction and he set off the opposite way. He had no idea where Li Bu-fang might hide himself in the huge monastery, but the howling brawling wind outside gave him some hope. Li Bu-fang, unless he became desperate or suicidal, would not try to leave the monastery while the storm lasted.

There was no point in running : this might be a long night of searching and hunting. It struck him then that he had never hunted a man before. This was going to be more difficult and dangerous than stalking a gooral or even a leopard; he was stalking one of his own kind, a man who knew the habits of man. If he were caught in an open space it would be fatal to freeze and trust not to be recognised; four days ago the trick had worked with the gooral, but it would not with Li. And Li had a pistol : unlike the leopard he would not have to get close to kill Marquis.

And how would he feel himself, when he raised his own gun and had Li in his sights? He put the thought out of his mind before it stopped him dead and sent him back to the room with Eve and the Brecks.

He moved at a cautious walk down the long galleries, stopping outside each chapel and flashing his torch into it, careful to keep his body shielded by the wall in case Li fired at him. Each time he switched on the torch he could feel his skin tighten on the back of his neck; he began to ache at the base of his skull. He held his breath all the time the torch was on, breathing out with a loud sigh of relief as he retreated into darkness. He began to wonder if he really wanted to find Li Bu-fang.

The bats were on the loose, swirling through the upper reaches of the tall galleries and chambers like black smoke. Shutters were hammering at the walls, hammering at the nerves too : Marquis's head began to ache even more. The wind had now found an entrance into the monastery; it howled and trumpeted through the galleries with the fury of an invading horde.

He turned a corner into the face of it; ducked just in time as a bat was hurled at him like a dark stone. He bent into the wind, feeling the freezing lances of it driving through him. What the bloody hell am I doing here? he thought. But knew :

he was here, as were all the others, because like climbers on a rope they were bound together. Even Li Bu-fang, the man he hunted, was bound to them.

He turned another corner, out of the wind, and saw Li running ahead of him down the largest gallery in the monastery. He broke into a run at once, galloping on heavy feet down between the long lines of indifferent gods. The gallery was dark, but there were big open windows high up in the walls through which enough light, reflected from the snow outside, came to turn the blackness into a smoky gloom. Marquis, switching his torch on and off as he ran, managed to keep the fleeing figure of Li in sight. The Chinese was running with desperate speed. Each of them was wearing heavy boots, but their footsteps were silent in the howl of the wind through the high windows. They raced down the dark corridors of a nightmare, past the blank golden eyes of the gods, beneath the weaving thunder-heads of bats. This is worse than a dream, thought Marquis, because there isn't even the escape of waking up.

He saw the bobbing lights ahead of him at the far end of the gallery just as Li cut sharply to the right. The lights came towards Marquis as he kept running; he pulled up panting and trembling as Nimchu, Tsering and Chungma came up to him. Each of them held a burning brand in one hand and a long machete in the other. And in the eye of each was murder.

'I told you to stay with Sahib Breck!'

Nimchu shook his head. 'Am going to kill Chinese, sahib!'

He snapped something to the other two porters and the three of them went running down the side gallery into which Li had turned. Marquis leaned against the tree-sized leg of a god, struggling to get his breath, staring after the disappearing porters. Nimchu led the way, followed by Chungma, with Tsering bringing up the rear. The last two were silhouetted against the glow of Nimchu's torch, and all at once Marquis knew who it was who had tried to kill Li Bu-fang back at the base camp. The squat rolling figure of Tsering was the same as that he had seen that night running across the camp towards the stores' tent. The cheerful cook, who loved his life and all he found in it, had been the first to take measures to see that it was not destroyed by the invader. Once again Marquis envied the simplicity of the peasant mind.

He leaned against the peeling golden leg, exhausted as much by responsibility as by running. Why not let the porters kill Li? Whose country had he invaded? Who stood to lose the most? Be neutral, Marquis, you mug. Buy a ticket and stand on the sidelines. Be like the Swiss : they have substituted a clock's tick for the heart beat, locked their conscience away in the vaults of their banks; but they have survived, mate, they have survived. One dead Chow in seven hundred million : who'll miss him? Not you, Marquis.

What was it his old man had said? Fight only the English Protestants, Jack, me boy; just abuse will do for the rest of the world. But Tim Marquis had never really had to fight. He had left Ireland before The Troubles and all his life he had had nothing to expend but abuse. And that was easy. You could be as abusive as hell and still claim to be neutral. Politicians in the newly emerging nations the world over were proving that every day. But when you had to fight . . .

'No!' he shouted, and took off after the porters.

But they were already far ahead of him, their torches slashing the gods and the walls with great strokes of red light. Panting, dry-throated, he stumbled after them, yelling to them not to kill Li. He ran down the long gallery, pursued by the wind and the bats. Nimchu and the others turned a corner, still far ahead of him. With their torches gone he was faced with darkness; he pulled up exhausted. He switched on his torch, looking for something to lean against; and saw Li staring at him from between two seated gods. Behind him dragons writhed on the wall, snarling their defiance at Marquis. Three bats streaked across the beam of the torch, followed by three more : it was as if the creatures were spinning an evil circle about Li into which Marquis must not enter. And as the final deterrent Li held Singh's pistol pointed directly at Marquis's chest.

'Don't make me shoot you, Mr. Marquis.'

The plea echoed in Marquis's ears : *don't make me kill you, General*. He stood helpless, his gun held loosely by the barrel. 'You can't get away, General. Listen!'

The storm outside was at its height. The mountains them-

selves seemed to be exploding, adding to the blast of the wind.
The walls of the monastery trembled under the onslaught; one
expected them to bend in like cardboard. Shutters banged with
the sharpness of small-arms fire, and the wind that had got
into the galleries moaned and shrieked like a hell of furies. It
seemed that nothing, not even the mountains, could survive the
violence of the night.

'It won't last forever,' said Li.

'No,' said Marquis, and began to walk slowly towards
the Chinese.

The pistol came up, steady as if held in a vice. 'I'll kill
you if I have to.'

Marquis stopped. 'You still won't get away. The others
will kill you, even Colonel Singh. I'm your only insurance,
General.'

The pistol remained steady, but the eyes wavered for a
moment. 'Why do you bother, Mr. Marquis? I don't want
to be your friend.'

'I don't know that I want to be yours. I hate your Chinese
guts for what you've done to us. But you're a man, a human
being. That's what keeps getting in my way all the time.
You're wearing a uniform, but I can't see you as a soldier. Not
up here, not when you haven't got an army behind you.'

'There are my men—they'll eventually catch up with you.'

'That's when I'll see you as a soldier and that's when I'll
probably want to kill you. But not now. Don't ask me why,
but not now.'

'I hate your guts, too,' said Li. 'For being a man and
not a soldier.'

Then he turned and disappeared quickly into a narrow
doorway behind one of the gods. Marquis hesitated, then he
moved swiftly round the squat painted figure of the god and
stepped through the doorway. He flicked on his torch and saw
that he was in a long narrow tunnel. The noise of the storm
was shut out from here and he could hear the running footsteps of Li somewhere up ahead. He began running, praying
that he would get to Li again before the others did.

He turned a corner and was half-way down a second tunnel
when he felt the wind blast at him as if a door had been
opened up ahead. He was running with his mouth open and

the first punch of the wind went down his throat like a fist.
He staggered, coughing, and dropped the torch, which went
out. He went down on his hands and knees, searching frantically in the howling bruising blackness for the torch. For the
first time he was really afraid, terrified of the darkness as a
child might be : he had stepped alive into death. He began to
gibber, bereft of language. Panic numbed his fingers more
than the cold had ; twice he touched the torch without recognising what it was. Then his hand closed over it and he flicked
the switch : it worked. He sat back on his heels, breathing
hard, staring at the yellow beam of light as if it contained the
sanity that had left him for the moment.

He stood up, fighting the wind as if it were a gang of
thugs, and battled his way up along the tunnel. The wind got
stronger all the way, tearing into the tunnel with all the force
and roar of an express train. He fell to his knees, couldn't rise,
and continued on, crawling crab-like as if up a steep icy slope.
He came to an open doorway, its door blown back in off its
hinges, and the storm hit him with all its fury.

If he had not been lying flat on the tunnel floor the wind
would have killed him, would have hurled him back and
broken every bone in his body. He held his arms across his
face and narrowed his eyes and looked out on the white
maelstrom of the main courtyard. Sleet slashed into his face
and he ducked his head, looking under his arm this time. Snow
had been whipped up and flung in waves against the walls ;
broken shutters stuck out from the drifts like the flotsam of a
wrecked ship. Prayer-flags were being snapped off the walls and
hurled like spears across the yard. In the centre of the yard a
huge prayer-wheel, twelve or fifteen feet high, leaned drunkenly, spinning furiously and shrieking as the wind beat at it.

Li Bu-fang lay beneath the leaning wheel, a prayer-flag
caught round his head and pressed against his face by the wind
as if to smother him. Marquis left his gun and torch and began
to edge his way out into the yard. He crawled through the
snow, burrowing into it as the wind tore at him, trying to
pick him up and take him with it out of the yard and into
the oblivion of the mountains. He could feel the sleet ripping
the skin from his face and his hands had turned to lumps of
ice. He tried to turn his face away from the wind, but it

seemed to come at him from all angles, brutal and relentless.
He breathed only when he had to, his nose and throat seared
by freezing air. His gums had contracted and all his teeth felt
ready to fall out.

He reached Li, rolled over and lay beside the unconscious
man. His eyes were closed, crusted with sleet : he looked
already dead. Marquis knew it was useless to shout; even a
cannon's roar would not have been heard by Li. The wind
roared through the yard, and immediately above them the
prayer-wheel shrieked its curse. He raised his frozen hand
and slapped it hard against Li's frozen cheek, and again and
again. The action brought some life back into Marquis's
fingers; it did the same for the other's face. The eyes blinked,
the head rolled a little, then Marquis felt the body beside his
stir. He shoved an arm under Li, pulling the Chinese on to
himself. He felt the hands clutch at his shoulders, the fingers
digging into him through the quilting of the anorak with all
the frantic strength of a man who wanted desperately to live.
He gathered his own strength, then began to inch his way back
through the snow, under the fury of the wind, to the doorway
to the tunnel. Above him, clinging to his back like some sort
of animal shell, Li took the full brunt of the wind. And though
he had risked his own life to save that of the Chinese, Marquis
felt a perverse pleasure in the thought of what Li, clinging
to his back, must be going through. It was some sort of
recompense for what the man, by being a man, had made him
go through. One wasn't Christ : there was always the drop of
resentment in even the purest charity.

The journey, only a few yards, seemed to take him hours.
Twice Li fell off him, twice he pulled him back on, cursing him
each time. The snow was smothering him and each time he
breathed his lungs caught fire. Once he lay still, sure then that
he was already dead. But his mind refused to die, and somehow
his dead limbs began working again. He reached the tunnel,
crawled into it and kept crawling till he was well down away
from the assault of the wind. He lay for a moment, coming
alive again, then he rolled over, dumping Li against a wall
that couldn't be seen in the blackness. He stood up, his
breath hissing, stamped his feet and slapped his arms against

his body, and slowly the blood started to flow again. He would live to die another death.

He went back up the tunnel, got his gun and torch and returned to Li Bu-fang. The Chinese was just sitting up as Marquis flashed the torch on him; he blinked and turned his face away, as lost in the light as he had been in the darkness. Marquis knelt down, ran his hands over Li's pockets, but could not find the pistol. The Chinese wiped the sleet from his face and the frozen mouth cracked in a tiny smile.

'It's outside in the snow.' He raised a hand, pushing back his cap, and tenderly felt the bruise on the side of his head. 'What hit me?'

'A prayer-flag. That must have hurt an atheist like you.'

Li smiled again, still with an effort. Then he stood up, swaying on legs that were still frozen. He leaned against the wall of the tunnel and looked steadily at Marquis in the beam from the torch.

'Do I thank you for my life?'

'You don't have to.'

'It's beginning to be a circle, isn't it? Colonel Singh saved your life from that leopard. Now you've saved mine. Who'll save his?'

'It's your turn.'

'He would never allow me to.'

'Would you want to?'

'No,' said Li slowly. 'You don't begin a war to save the life of your enemy.'

'Why did you begin the war?' asked Marquis, and saw the momentary dullness of puzzlement in the other's eyes. 'You don't really know, do you? They can never convince you generals with propaganda, can they? Not you, anyway.'

Li stared at him, his face stiffening again as if the ice were taking hold of it once more. Then abruptly he turned away and walked back down the tunnel, stiff-backed and stiff-legged, a man chilled by the storm and his inability to find an answer. Marquis slung his gun over his shoulder and followed him.

Singh, meanwhile, had been roaming the galleries and chapels, carrying his anger with him like a warming-stick. He was angry at himself, at Li Bu-fang and at the treacherous

hermit. What had Li said to the man last night, what con-
spiracy or threats had been woven in the language no one else
had understood? He tried to place himself in the situation of
being confronted by an Indian mystic. Would he have tried to
draft the man into service, would he have demanded that
country came ahead of self? He knew the answer, knew he
would have done exactly what he suspected Li had done.
Threatened the man.

He prowled the dark wind-ravaged galleries, the Sten gun
held at the ready, determined not to be caught off-guard again.
He had made up his mind to shoot on sight. Li was an
albatross round his neck and the necks of Marquis and his
party : all his presence brought was disaster of one kind or
another. He was no longer important in himself : in the
isolation of these mountains rank meant nothing, a captured
general was worth no more than a captured corporal. The
important thing was the papers : it was they, and not Li
Bu-fang, that he had to get out into India. He had no real
hatred of the Chinese as a man, but he would kill him as soon
as he saw him again. A dead enemy was the only one for whom
you had no responsibility.

Twice he had seen the porters flitting along the galleries
with their torches, dragging ragged banners of light after them.
He had no idea where Marquis was, but he hoped the
Australian had not come up against the Chinese. The big man
angered him at times, but he would not want him to be killed.
He was becoming involved with humanity, something he had
avoided all his life : surrounded by the misery of his countrymen, the only escape had been to turn in upon oneself or go
away to Europe, where the misery at least had a pretence of
comfort. Brought up in a history that had never placed a
value on a human life, he was suddenly and for the first time
suffering for the lives of other men. The years at Oxford were
at last showing their effect : they had weakened him, his father
would have said : made him part of the seventh continent,
the continent of man.

He was half-way down a long gallery when he saw the figure
come out of the doorway of a chapel. The man was lit only
from the side as the porters came up a side gallery towards
him, their torches throwing a light ahead to the alert crouching

figure. Singh could hear the shouts of triumph from the porters, echoing in the tall narrow gallery even above the howl of the storm. The Indian halted, brought up his Sten gun and waited for Li Bu-fang to move. Then the man came running towards him, stumbling as he ran, shouting words that had no meaning but had all the hysteria of wild threats. Singh waited while the man came on towards him, out of the light now, running through the gloom, one hand held out with what looked like a pistol in it. With a mixture of regret he felt unaccountable and of relief that he welcomed, Singh fired. He held the Sten gun hard against his body and pumped a full burst into the running man.

The man stopped as if he had run into an entanglement of wire. He reeled forward, hands out in front of him, then his legs buckled and he went down on his face. Slowly Singh walked forward as Nimchu and the other two porters came running down the gallery, their torches held high like torches of victory. They pulled up, lowered the burning brands and threw a red blanket of light over the dead man.

Wilkins lay with his face pressed against the stone floor, one hand clutching a bundle of dollar bills.

EIGHT

The storm died out during the night and the morning broke as a brilliance of mirrors. The wind had done its damage about the monastery, but it had also polished the sky and the mountains till each seemed to reflect the other. Distance was contracted in the virgin air and the mountains approached to stand like a rough-hewn wall of ice and rock around the ridge on which the monastery stood. Snow was banked in great drifts against the walls and a fresh fall just before dawn had made the ridge as smooth and bright to the eye as a vast stretched sheet. An eagle was the only blemish in the cold splendour of the sky.

Eve, eyes heavy from lack of sleep, was buckling the straps of her pack as Marquis came into the room where they had slept. He held Singh's pistol in his hand and was wiping snow from it with his glove. Snow was on his beard, ageing him more than the drawn cheeks and the dead dark eyes. Eve looked at him and wept inside for the pain she saw branded on him.

'The barrel's frozen up,' he said, but there was no concern or even interest in his voice: he seemed to have reached the point of complete indifference.

'He probably wishes the barrel of his other gun had been frozen, too. Have you talked to him this morning?'

'What the hell is there to say?'

'Do you blame him for what happened?'

'What's the use in thinking about blame?' He put the pistol aside and began to stuff his gear into his pack. They had already eaten, a breakfast that none of them had tasted, and now it was time for them to move on again. Nothing remained to be done but to dispose of the money and Wilkins's body. 'I've become a fatalist, love. What happened last night was in the cards.'

'A fatalist or a pessimist?' Then she bit her lip. 'I'm sorry, darling. I didn't mean that.'

He said nothing, but sat on his haunches looking at what he

held in his hand. 'Do you think it's worthwhile keeping this?' He held up the squashed polythene bag containing the now faded red poppy. 'Or should I bury it with Nick as his wreath? Or would he rather have a wreath of dollar bills?'

'You didn't have to say that.'

He shook his head. 'No, I didn't. I'm a mean bastard at times, aren't I?'

'At times,' she said honestly. 'But who isn't?'

Then Tom and Nancy Breck had come to the door. Their faces were yellow with their exhaustion and their eyes seemed ready to fall out of their sockets. They had kissed each other good-bye during the night, but each had kept his secret from the other. Their secret only increased their look of exhaustion.

'How are you going to bury Nick?' Tom Breck's beard was the same colour as his yellow face, hanging like shreds of flesh. 'You could never dig a grave in that ground outside. It's frozen solid.'

'We can't just leave him here,' Nancy said, shuddering at the thoughts in her mind. 'Not to rot.'

'He wouldn't rot in this cold,' said Marquis, dully practical. 'We could bury him under a cairn of stones.'

'Where do we find the stones?' Breck asked. 'There's two or three feet of snow outside.'

'We could take him to the end of the ridge and throw him down into the gorge.' Marquis liked none of what he suggested, but he could think of nothing better.

'Leave him to be picked clean by the birds?' Nancy shuddered again, her imagination too brutal in her fevered mind. She had been brought up to believe in clean orderly death : the church service, the cemetery burial, the proper display of grief. She shuddered again, gasping with shock, when Eve said :

'Why don't we cremate him?'

'How?' Marquis was beyond shock; he welcomed any suggestion. 'We used most of the wood to keep us warm last night.'

'You have to burn the money. We just can't leave it here.' Eve listened to her own voice putting the suggestion calmly and practically. But how callously practical could one be?

She listened to the stranger's voice as it went on: 'We have to do *something* about the money! Have you forgotten that?'

'I'd forgotten it,' Tom Breck said, and shook his head at how blank his memory had become. 'I'd forgotten those guys who are after us. We can't waste too much time!'

'But you can't burn Nick!' Nancy's dry throat made her voice a hoarse squawk. 'Some people don't believe in cremation.'

'It's not Nick's decision.' Marquis stood up, his knees creaking like those of an old man. He kneaded the polythene bag, like a piece of transparent dough, in nervous worried fingers. 'I'm a Catholic, we're taught not to have ourselves cremated. But we make exceptions. I think Nick would understand.' He looked down at the bag in his hand; his fingers had broken a hole in it. 'I just wonder whether he would understand about using the money to cremate him. He never had much sense of humour.'

'It's a pretty sick joke,' said Nancy.

'His death was a pretty sick joke,' Eve said gently. 'I'm sorry, Nan. But this isn't Bucks County or wherever it is. We're in a situation that has its own standards, that has nothing to do with the way things are done back home. I think Nick would want us to think of ourselves, not of him.'

Nancy stared at them all in turn, then she nodded dumbly. She had no strength left for argument: she had reached a new innocence, she was open for any terrible education that might be forced on her. Tom Breck put his arm about her and they leaned together, each needing the strength of the other.

'I'll get the porters started on the pyre,' said Marquis, and the unfamiliar word sounded like another sick joke. He twisted his mouth as if he could taste what he had said and went out of the room, calling in a cracked voice for Nimchu and the other two porters. He knew that they would not be shocked by what had to be done. Cremation was usual for adults in Bhutan. Although not by burning money: that would be a Western sophistication.

Singh and Li Bu-fang, the latter with his hands bound again, came out of their room as Marquis finished telling the porters what he wanted done. Both men, Indian and Chinese, had similar looks of painful thought, as if the events of the night had been a mould into which they had been forced, leaving its imprint on them like the recognisable features of two brothers. Neither of them showed much interest as they listened to Marquis instructing the porters; they seemed unaware of the hostile looks sliced at them by the three Bhutanese. At last Marquis turned to the two outsiders, the men who between them had brought about the tragedy that was to end in a few minutes with its bizarre ritual. He felt no anger at them this morning; that had all burned out of him last night. Instead he looked with sympathy at Singh, feeling closer to the Indian than at any time since they met.

'As soon as it's all over we'll get moving again.'

'I've thought it over.' Singh's voice was flat: Oxford had been buried with the rest of the irretrievable past. 'The general and I will stay here and wait for his men. I shall give you the papers, and you and your friends can go on.'

Marquis swore, all his anger coming back in a rush. 'What bloody good will that do? They'll kill you, then still come on after us!'

'I hope to hold them up long enough for you to get away. Perhaps I could hold them for the whole morning——' He looked with blank eyes at the porters as they ran past, their arms full of bundles of notes; then he turned back to Marquis, his voice as flat and pedantic as that of a staff officer giving the details of an army manœuvre. 'The ridge is all open country. I have a field of fire, if I stand on the north-east corner of the walls, of over two hundred degrees. With my own gun and Wilkins's '—he faltered a moment, opened his mouth and took a dry breath—' with the two guns I should have enough ammunition, used carefully, to keep them pinned down for several hours at least.'

The porters came running back, the only ones not made leaden-footed by emotion. They went into the chapel where the money was and a moment later came hurrying out again. This time they were carrying the dollar bills in blankets slung over their shoulders; they went by like peasants on their way to market. With a cash crop, Marquis thought. Their faces were expressionless, but as Nimchu went by he glanced with concern at Marquis. He had no thought at all for what was to happen to the dead Wilkins; but he worried for the sahib and his wife, who still lived. Especially for the sahib, whose great strength seemed at last to have run out and who now did not look as strong as the memsahib. He ran on, the money bouncing on his back, and behind him he heard the dry broken voice of the sahib crying in anger.

'Christ Almighty, do you think I'm going to give you up now? Do you think we've busted our guts out, lost Nick, gone through more hell than any of us dreamed of, to let you go now?'

'I'm not your prisoner, Marquis——'

'We're all prisoners! Can't you see that? Every bloody one of us, prisoners of each other. Ask this bastard here——' He gestured at the silent Li Bu-fang. 'He knows what I mean. He might deny it, but he bloody well knows what I mean!'

'We think differently——' said Singh.

'We don't think differently! Not in this—and you know it!' Marquis spun round, ending the argument with his broad back. 'Staying here is the easy way out, Colonel! You're coming with us, you're going to bloody well suffer like the rest of us!'

He went into the side chapel, began to pull one of the now half-empty cases towards the door, yelling to Tom Breck to come and help him, trying to deaden his mind, if only for a while, with work.

They started the fire in the snow-covered courtyard, beside the giant prayer-wheel which, bent and broken, lay like a big copper roller on a white lawn. The cases, when they were emptied enough to be moved, had been dragged out into the yard and their planks used as added fuel. Marquis had wondered if sufficient heat could be generated in the thin air to burn the body, but the blazing of the fire told him they could not be as high as he had thought. They had climbed up and down so many slopes and ridges in the last few days he had lost all idea of altitude; in any case the fact had become academic and he was not concerned enough to go looking for the altimeter. The dollar bills had remained dry in their tinfoil wrapping and they burned easily, going up in smoke with all the swiftness of a spendthrift's inheritance. There was no sound in the yard but the crackling of the wood and the hiss and roar of the flames.

Eve and Nancy, the latter reluctantly but uncomplainingly, had prepared Wilkins's body for the cremation. They had left the dead man in his anorak and pinned his hood up to cover his face; then they had slid him into the shroud of his sleeping-bag. Eve had for a moment considered saving the sleeping-bag and offering it to Singh, who had had to make do with blankets, which were much heavier to carry. But there were limits to which practicality could be taken; she felt sure that Singh would be more chilled in the sleeping-bag than in even the most ragged blanket. When the body was ready she called to Nimchu and Tsering and the two porters came in with two planks. They put the corpse on the planks, then carried it down the long gallery, past the blank-eyed placid gods, and out into the snow-covered yard.

'I don't think we all have to stay and watch this,' said Marquis. 'You can all go on and Nimchu and I will catch you up.'

'I'll stay,' said Eve, and Marquis, after one look at her, didn't argue.

'Which way do we head?' Tom Breck asked, looking out the open gates at the surrounding mountains.

Marquis nodded towards a distant spur and beyond it to a massif that stood out against the bright morning sky. 'I had a look at my map this morning. I think that's the last range we've got to climb.'

Nancy looked blindly in the direction in which Marquis was turned. Sick, exhausted, myopic, she could barely see beyond the gates; but like a blind woman, she knew the direction of home. 'Oh God, I hope so!'

Then she felt a sense of shame: she thought of Nick Wilkins, who would never make it now. She put out a hand to take Tom's, and both of them looked down at the man whom they had never really got to know nor to understand. But for whom they now grieved as if they had known and loved him all their lives.

'I feel we owe him a prayer or two,' said Tom Breck, and for the first time wondered if any prayers had been said over the bodies of his parents. He had prayed for them himself, but that had been months later and several thousand miles away.

'I'll say them for all of us,' said Marquis. 'I'll try to make them as undenominational as I can. In the meantime, get cracking. Better let Tsering lead you—he'll find the track.'

Tom and Nancy Breck bowed their heads above the dark bundle in the snow, grieving for a man who had suddenly become a brother, grieving for that part of themselves that had died with him. Marquis, looking at them with eyes that hurt, remarked, as he had at other funerals, that services for the dead were self-torture for the living : the dead were beyond it all, and all the prayers were for the comfort and penance of those who still lived. And angrily he told the Brecks to get started. Which they did at once, moving out of the open gates with Tsering and Chungma and trudging off without a backward glance, heading for a distant spur that blazed like a wall of glass under the just-risen sun.

Singh and Li Bu-fang were next to go. The Chinese had not spoken since he and Marquis had come back into the gallery last night to find the shocked and silent group gathered about the dead Wilkins. He had stood aside, like a stranger at a family bereavement, but gradually through the night their sense of loss had communicated itself to him. He stood with his bound hands in front of him now, looking more a man of prayer than an atheist; he bowed his head to the dead Wilkins, the man who had threatened to punch him up the snout, and regretted his passing. Then he looked at the burning money, then up at Marquis.

'At least Chiang Kai-shek didn't get it,' he said.

Marquis said nothing and looked at Singh, who now stood above Wilkins's body.

'I'll say my own prayers,' said the Indian, and bowed his head, torturing himself as no close member of Wilkins's family ever would have. At last he looked up, his face showing the strain of the rack of his thoughts. Not knowing Wilkins's God, he had committed the Englishman's spirit to one of his own gods, to Puchan, who guides the dead into the next world. Having killed the body, he owed the spirit a resting place.

'Leave nothing but bones and ashes,' he said, then nodded at Li and the two men turned and moved off out of the gates.

Marquis and Nimchu picked up the body on the planks and

approached the fire. The wood and paper were blazing now, giving off a singeing heat. The two men had to lean back, shutting their eyes, as they lowered the planks and the body into the flames. Then they stepped back, picked up more timber from the cases and threw it into the blaze.

'Go out to the gate,' Marquis said to Eve, 'and take a look through the glasses down the ridge. See if the Chows are in sight.'

Eve recognised that he was not only being alert and practical; he was protecting her from a sight he thought she might not be able to endure. Grateful for his considerateness, she took the binoculars from the top of his pack and went at once out to the gates. Behind her she heard him begin the Lord's Prayer, saying the words clearly and firmly above the hiss and crackle of the flames. It struck her that it was the first time she had ever heard him pray and it revealed a new facet of him to her. Prayers for her had always been a meaningless chant and she had long ago given up reciting them. But Jack spoke the words with belief. Somehow they did not sound strange on the lips that so often used only the vernacular and a vulgar vernacular at that.

She searched the ridge and the distant slope beyond but could see nothing that moved. She had a moment of hope that the Chinese might have given up their pursuit; but the hope melted as quickly as the snow under the fire behind her. Unless some natural disaster overtook them, the Chinese would not give up. The chase would go on while the mountains still surrounded them all and cut them off from the outside world. She looked up and around at the peaks, hated them for being another enemy. Then, having delayed as long as she could, she went back into the courtyard.

She could smell the burning flesh when she was yards from the fire, but she gave no sign that she had noticed it. She went and stood beside Marquis as he and Nimchu threw the last of the money on the flames. She could not distinguish the now almost-cremated body in the fire and she was glad of that. She watched the notes being thrown into the blaze, the portraits of Washington and Lincoln and Hamilton curling into ash in the blink of an eyelid. She wept dry-eyed for Wilkins, suffering for the thwarted, wasted life of the man, crying for him

at this last bitter joke that had been played on him, at the
dreams going up in smoke about the mind that was now beyond
dreaming.

At last she said, ' What are you going to do with—what's
left?'

' Nothing,' said Marquis. ' There isn't time to do anything.
If—when we get out into India, I'll write to Thimbu and tell
them what we've done and why. They can then put the
monks in the picture. When the monks come back here in the
spring, maybe they'll bury the bones.'

' All the money is gone, sahib,' said Nimchu, pushing the
fire together with a stick.

Marquis looked at the last of the blaze, at the shapeless
mass of embers at its centre. ' Poor bastard.'

2

There had been no signs of the hermit since he had disappeared last night and Marquis had not bothered to look for him.
But when Marquis, Eve and Nimchu had left the courtyard
and had begun to trek across the ridge, the man emerged
from a doorway, stood beside the dying blooms of the fire and
watched the disappearing strangers. His fear had left him and
he was once more sealed in the armour of his vision. Neither
the heat of the fire nor the cold of the snow touched him.
A coal burned inside him, but will was slowly extinguishing
that : a man with a vision of the future could not linger over
conscience for the past. Last night was already being forgotten :
memory and sin were expunged in the same effort of will. He
had yielded to threats, had given way to fears for the body
that he had sworn to ignore. He would have to pray harder
in the future, strain for a plane of contemplation from which
his mind would never return.

But he did not go immediately back into the temples of the
monastery. Moving mechanically, as if his body and limbs
had a conscience of their own and wanted to make some
recompense, he began pushing the fire closer together, bringing
it into flowering flame again. Nothing of the dead man must
be left on the bones. But he would leave here to-day, seek

further the placeless isolation of the mountains, because even bones could haunt.

When, half an hour later, Marquis called a halt and looked back at the monastery he could see nothing but the walled buildings standing like a becalmed ship in the midst of a still white sea. There was nothing to suggest the tragedy that had been added to the other ghosts within the walls.

But Nimchu, less affected by the death of Wilkins, with ghosts of his own to ponder on, had not been looking at the monastery. Instead he had turned to look back farther down the ridge and saw what he had expected. 'There are the soldiers, sahib!'

As soon as he turned his gaze away from the monastery Marquis saw the line of dark ants strung out along the white spine of the ridge. At this distance they did not appear to be moving, but even as he watched them he saw the line change direction.

'They've seen us!' Eve exclaimed, and at once picked up her pack and slung it on her back again.

'Us or the others.' Marquis picked up his own pack, nodded up towards where the six tiny figures of Singh and the others stood out like black beads against the bright breast of the spur. 'We're going to stand out like shags on a rock for another hour at least. Come on!'

They had rested by a prayer-flag that leaned drunkenly out of a cairn of stones half-buried by the snow. Nimchu touched the flag, then looked at Marquis and Eve.

'We are the ones who need prayers now,' he said.

They moved on, following the dark path trodden by the others in the glittering snow. The sun was clear of the eastern peaks, striking down at them through the rarefied air with a pitilessness that made Eve angry. It was no consolation to know that the soldiers farther back were also being subjected to the same burning, suffocating glare. Nature was supposed to be neutral, but it was stacking the odds against the fugitives. There were only nine of the pursued and still fifty or sixty of the pursuers. There would always be some of the latter left to finish the chase.

They stopped for a few minutes, took off their anoraks, then smeared their faces thickly with anti-sunburn cream. Even as she smeared the cream on her cheeks and nose, Eve could feel the burn already there. Despite her dark glasses her eyes ached from the glare of the snow. She was already dried out by the thin atmosphere and now she was being toasted alive. She was sweating, the last drops of moisture left in her, but it came out of her like blood. Her head was a hollow skull in which every pulse beat rang like the striking of a gong. But she did not complain, hid her exhaustion and pain behind the mask of the anti-sunburn cream. She did not want to add the weight of herself to the other burdens Jack already carried. True knowledge of oneself comes only through suffering, she had once read. Eve Marquis, old girl, she told herself, your education is about to be completed. You are about to graduate with honours in the subject of Eve Marquis.

'What are you giggling at?' Marquis said, looking at her worriedly.

'The benefits of education.'

'What?' He looked at her again, wondering if she was going to go the way of Wilkins.

But she just shook her head, smiled at him reassuringly and plodded on.

The early morning fall of snow had not hardened properly and under the fierce fire of the sun the crust had begun to melt. Walking became a torture that turned the muscles in their legs and thighs into rods that tried to burn their way out of the flesh. Every step was a stumbling agony as they drew their boots, like iron weights, out of the white bog of snow and put them down again in the same treacherous mess. Eve, conscious of the need to protect her mouth against the white-hot glare, breathed with difficulty through her nose, every breath adding to the echoes inside her head. Her mind had ceased to work and only instinct, the animal urge to survive, kept her going.

Marquis's mind was kept awake by the prod of danger. He was aware this morning of a heightened stillness; or was it his imagination? He looked up and around at the mountains: was he crazy or was there an air of waiting about them? Once in Tanganyika he had seen lions waiting like this for the release of a crippled gazelle that Marquis's bearers had brought into camp. There had been the same deadly patience, the same still menace. In the end Marquis himself had killed the gazelle, but he knew the lions had won.

He kept glancing up ahead to where Singh and the others had stopped to rest. The steep side of the spur on which they stood sparkled like a giant frosted window; and he kept shouting in his mind to the others to go on, wondering why they did not recognise the danger which threatened them. Tsering and Chungma should have known better, had been born with the thunder of avalanches in their ears. Why had they stopped to rest instead of climbing on up to the safety of the spur above them?

It was another twenty minutes before he knew. Singh and the others did not move in all that time, and by the time he, Eve and Nimchu came struggling up through the soft snow he was ready to explode at their stupid indifference to their danger.

He sat down, gasping for breath to blast out his temper, and Singh said quietly, ' Mrs. Breck can't go on, old chap. I'm afraid she's finished.'

Marquis raised his head from between his hands and stared across the blinding whiteness at the inert figure of Nancy. She lay flat on her back in the snow and Tom Breck knelt beside her, leaning over her to shield her from the assault of the sun. Her mouth was wide open and even from where he sat Marquis could hear her hoarse whistling breathing. Every now and again her whole body would twitch and she would jerk her arms; her legs would bend, then stiffen out in a quick kick. There was a moaning sound, but it was some moments before Marquis realised the moans came from Tom Breck.

He slid out of his pack straps, stood up and stumbled across to the Brecks. As his shadow fell across them, Tom Breck looked up, his dark glasses suddenly blazing like two small suns in the death's head of his face.

'It's no use, Jack.' His voice was shredded by despair; his world had come to an end. ' She can't go on.'

Marquis knelt down in the snow as Eve, fighting against her own exhaustion, came and knelt beside him. Both of them saw at once that there was little they could do for Nancy. Life had already begun to leave her, melting out of her like the snow in which she lay. The glare seemed to take all substance out of her and she looked no more solid than the pale blue bier of her shadow.

'Nan——' Eve said, but Tom Breck shook his head.

'She can't hear us. She's snow-blind, too.' Tears began to run down from behind the dark glasses, glistening on the yellow bone of his cheeks.

'It's not all over yet,' said Marquis, but wondered why he went through the mockery of hope. 'We'll get her up there to the top of the spur——'

His head jerked up as he heard the sound he had been dreading. The crack was like the blast of a gun, and he looked desperately around, trying to find the source of it. Then he heard the thunder and a moment later he saw the explosion of ice and snow falling down the face of a mountain a mile or more to the east of them. There was another crack, and a third: the mountains were beginning their barrage.

'Come on! We've got to get off this slope!'

'They've stopped!' Singh had been standing watching the Chinese soldiers far below through his binoculars. He turned as Marquis, taking up his own glasses, stood up beside him. 'Somehow or other they've brought their mules with them as far as this. But it looks now as if they're going to have to abandon them. They're taking all the gear off them.'

The Chinese had halted on a shoulder of the ridge. Between them and the base of the spur there was a shallow dip, a basin perhaps four hundred yards across. Through his glasses Marquis saw that the Chinese had yaks as well as mules, and all the animals were being hastily unloaded. Then he saw the small group of soldiers to one side, working feverishly on something that was quickly taking shape.

He swore savagely. 'The bastards are putting a gun together!'

Singh was staring through his binoculars. 'It looks like a lightweight mountain gun. Surely they're not going to try and shoot us off this slope——' Then realisation struck him and he looked back up the slope to where Li Bu-fang sat. A professional soldier, he could not hide his admiration for what was about to be done. 'You have a clever commander down there, General. If you survive what he's about to do to us, you should decorate him.'

Eve, aware of the tension felt by Marquis and Singh, had turned away from Nancy for the moment. 'What are they going to do?'

Marquis had already slung his pack on his back. He pushed her aside and picked up the unconscious Nancy. 'They're going to shell the slope above us, start an avalanche! Get weaving!'

But they had gone no more than fifty yards when they heard the first shell whistling through the air. Everyone but the porters dropped flat; Nimchu and the other two Bhutanese had never heard shells before and they had no instinct what to do. The shell landed thirty or forty yards below them and to their right, exploding dully in the snow. Marquis, lying beside the crumpled body of Nancy, saw the crack spread across the snow like a streak of blue-black lightning in a white sky. Then a whole slice of the slope slid away, slowly at first, then quickly gathering speed. Powder began to curl back, like spume, and in a moment the tons of snow and ice were thundering down the slope, tearing rocks out of the iron-hard earth beneath and taking them with them. Marquis watched the avalanche go, fascinated and frightened, waiting for the snow on which they lay to break away and follow.

But the crust here held. As soon as he realised they had been spared, he was on his feet again, picking up Nancy. The porters had not stopped moving and now everyone set off again after them. The snow was melting fast and everyone sank up to his knees with every step he took. Tom Breck, finding some unsuspected reserves of strength, had taken hold of Nancy's legs and was helping Marquis carry her. Eve was struggling, slipping and falling almost with every step, getting nowhere in her efforts to get there too fast. Chungma stopped, saw the trouble the memsahib was having, and began to come back down the slope to help her.

Then they heard the second shell coming. They all dropped flat, the porters too this time. It went over the heads of those strung out at the end of the line, a thin chilling shriek, more terrifying than the voice of any *sounday* or yeti. Eve, lying flat, her face pressed into the snow, looked up the slope through a screen of crystals in which the sun had spun rainbows. Through a spectrum of beauty she saw the beginning of death. The shell exploded, without sound it seemed to her, and a jet of snow rose high, then fell slowly, sparkling like a fountain of white glass. It settled and then she saw the crust beginning to break. The crack in the snow ran right across the slope above them, opening up like a wide malevolent grin just below Singh, Li Bu-fang, Nimchu and Tsering, cutting off the rear end of the line from those at the head. It flashed through her mind that if they had all been roped together, those above might have been able to save those below from being swept away. But it was too late now to have regrets for what had not been done. She felt the snow beneath her beginning to move and suddenly panic took hold of her. She got to her knees, then to her feet, began to run uphill. But it was as if she were on a treadmill; she went up and down in the same spot while the snow began to come down on her like a breaking sea. Then the snow curled over her and she could see nothing.

Marquis felt Nancy snatched out of his arms as the first wave of snow hit them. He had turned to face up the slope, had begun to run just as Eve had done. The snow hit him and he went into it bent forward; he had a flash of memory of himself going into the surf at Coogee just like this years ago. He had always been a strong swimmer and battling the breakers had been one of the pleasures he had missed since leaving Australia; but now he was not swimming for pleasure but to save his life. He swung his arms and kicked his legs, swimming uphill through a thick pounding surf of snow and ice, his eyes blinded, his lungs bursting. His eyes were closed but he had the impression that he could see the white whirling world that had swamped him: even his mind seemed full of the blinding choking whiteness. Rocks and ice kept hitting him, but he felt only the impact of them, not the pain they left behind: his mind and nerves were too concentrated on survival to feel pain. His arms and legs were ready to be wrenched from his body; his body itself felt as if it were splitting apart. He had stopped breathing and now all his senses had stopped; his arms and legs worked mechanically, like the wings and legs of a bird whose head has already been chopped off. The one thought still alive in his dead white mind was one of disbelief : this couldn't be happening to him, death wasn't for him just yet. Was this how everyone felt in the last moment, a final rebellion, a silent scream that some mistake had been made ? He opened his mouth to scream his own denial and miraculously gulped in air.

The breakers of snow went past and he fell on his face, his arms and legs still working but with nothing more to fight. He had lost his glasses and as he rolled over on his back the sun drove fists of fire into his snow-lashed eyes. He shut them quickly and lay spread-eagled, all the pain of the last few seconds suddenly bursting inside him. The strap of his binoculars-case was wound tight round his neck and so intense was the other pain, it was a moment or two before he realised he was choking. He tore at the strap, freeing his throat, and lay snatching his breath in great hoarse gasps. One strap of his pack had been broken, but the pack itself still hung from one shoulder, his anorak still caught in a strap loop. His gun had gone, but at this moment he did not miss it. He sat up, struggling out of the pack, and looked across the slope.

He would never know whether it was tears or the snow on his lashes that made his eyes run as he saw Eve scrambling across the slope towards him. He sat there with open arms and took her to him as she fell on him; they rolled back in the snow like lovers on some gay carefree picnic. Eve was weeping incoherently and he had no words that had any sanity about them. They held each other in a lunacy of relief and love, forgetful of everyone but themselves.

They broke apart as they heard Tom Breck crying : ' Nancy !'

They let each other go and stood up. As they did the other survivors also stood up, as if identifying themselves at a roll-call. Marquis looked up and saw Singh, Li Bu-fang, Nimchu and Tsering. Of Nancy and Chungma there was no sign.

Then Tom Breck cried again, more a scream this time, and Marquis looked back at him. The boy was standing with legs wide apart, arms stretched out in appeal, staring down the mountainside. Far below the avalanche was just settling under its cloud of snow in the dip between the base of the spur and the shoulder of the ridge on which the Chinese soldiers were grouped. The thunder of the avalanche came back up to the watchers and went past them till its sound was no more than a vibration on the thin gut-strings of the air. The cloud below settled slowly, like dying mist, and they all stood waiting, all of them silent but Tom Breck, who kept crying Nancy's name.

Then they saw the two dark shapes, some distance apart, in the rack of ice and snow. At the same time the Chinese soldiers must have seen them : half a dozen men began to move down off the shoulder of the ridge. And as they did Tom Breck started downwards.

'Tom, come back!' Marquis's shout was also a scream, thin and hoarse, like a cry of agony.

But Tom Breck was deaf. He went down on stiff stumbling legs, falling among the rocks and ice of the avalanche's rough path, but always picking himself up at once and going on down. There was something terrible and inevitable about his progress down the long scarred slope, like that of a rock that no amount of shouting and imploring from Marquis could ever stop. He was not running or glissading, but moving almost slowly, as if time no longer mattered, as if life were already over for himself and Nancy.

He was still fifty yards from Nancy's body when the Chinese soldiers reached it. Marquis, high up on the slope, took out his binoculars and watched with expectant horror as Tom Breck, still moving unhurriedly, staggered down towards the Chinese. They stood above Nancy's body, waiting for him, and when he was no more than twenty yards from them they shot him. Tom Breck stopped as if in surprise and was still standing when the crackle of the shots passed by the watchers on the slope. Then he took one step forward, an arm outstretched towards the dead Nancy, and fell face forward into the snow. Marquis took the binoculars away from his eyes, blind now with anger.

He looked wildly about for Li Bu-fang. 'Did you see what they did, General?' he screamed. 'That's the new China, General! Everybody's expendable! Including you!'

Li Bu-fang had watched the scene below in stiff frozen-eyed silence. The climb up the steep side of the spur had exhausted him and the yellowness of his complexion was now

accentuated; his sallow face had turned to a mask on which his
eyes looked as if they had been painted by a dry brush. The
three scars on his cheek looked like cracks in his flesh; one
waited for the flesh to peel back and expose the bone beneath.
He stared down at the three still bodies in the snow and the
moving figures beyond them, and to Singh, standing beside
him now, it seemed that the Chinese was not breathing. Then
the breath came, in tiny hissing gasps, like the beginning of
whispering. He took one step forward and Singh unslung his
Sten gun, waiting for the Chinese to start running down the
slope. But Li's step forward had been only to free his boot
from the depth of snow in which it was sunk. He turned and
without a word or a glance at Singh or the others began to
stumble up towards the crest of the spur, as if he too had
suddenly become a fugitive.

'They're going to shell us again!' The hissing whimper
turned into a thin shout. 'Hurry!'

Marquis slipped his pack over one shoulder, grabbed Eve
by the hand and began to struggle up through the snow.
Singh, Nimchu and Tsering were already stumbling after the
fleeing Li Bu-fang, all of them moving with the same desperate
awkward speed. They were slipping and falling, but somehow
none of them lost his balance and fell back down the mountainside. Each of them was straining his ears to hear above his
panting breath and pounding blood the whistle of the next
shell. The soft treacherous crust broke beneath every step,
grabbing at their legs, holding them back as best it could
while the soldiers far below raised the elevation of their gun
barrel and slid another shell into the breech.

But the first shell fell short. Marquis and the others heard
it coming but none of them flung himself down this time. It
landed thirty yards behind them and below them as they
struggled diagonally up the bright glare of the spur; its
fragments were buried at once in the thick glutinous snow that
a moment before had been trying to hold back the fugitives.
Another section of the slope broke away and went sliding
down, building up its thunder as it went, but none of the
party looked back. Their eyes were on the crest of the spur
fifty yards above them.

Dead of mind and limb, none of them would ever know how

they made it. They struggled over the top and out of sight of the soldiers below as the second and third shells landed on the slope behind them. They heard the growing thunder as more slides started and the crust of the slope went plunging down to the bottom. The echoes of the shots had started other falls on other slopes; the mountains reverberated with the barrage of avalanches. The air seemed to shiver all around them; the silence had never been assaulted like this before. The mountains seemed to be breaking apart: Nimchu's gods were proving mortal, dying in a chaos of thunder.

Marquis and Eve were tempted to fall down at once as soon as they clambered over the crest. But Singh shouted at them to keep going. Li, the other soldier, was still struggling on through the snow, heading at a tangent from his original direction across the main ridge that backed the spur up which they had just climbed. Marquis, bowing to Singh's and Li's experience, followed on without arguing, pulling Eve after him and shouting to Nimchu and Tsering not to stop. Two more shells came whistling over the crest, but they were wide of their mark. A third followed, but it was even wider: the Chinese were firing blindly, hoping for a lucky shot. They fired five more shells, working their way in a line along the back slope of the spur. But Marquis and the others by then were a hundred yards away, working their way slowly up the spine of the main ridge.

They climbed for another ten minutes, no longer hurrying, no longer able to hurry even if they had wanted to. Then they came out on to a flat ledge below a face of ice-sheathed rock. They all stopped without a word and sank down in the cold comfort of the snow. Their limbs were numb, nerve-ends paralysing the flesh like a hundred electrodes; their lungs burned so that every breath was a taste of fire; they would have welcomed the snow closing over them for the last long cold sleep of all. But death wasn't merciful: it retreated, left them to the tortures of living.

Marquis at last stood up, swaying a little, drunk with exhaustion and despair. From this ledge he could see down round the end of the spur to the bottom of the slope. He lifted his binoculars and looked back down through a mile of blue shining air. He saw the Chinese soldiers, strung out in a line, working their way along the base of the spur, looking for a way up past the scars, like bones laid bare, of the avalanches. Each successive slide of snow, ice and rocks had followed a different path from those before it. The Chinese, with their shelling, had engineered their own delay : it would take them hours to find their way up the spur.

Still with his binoculars to his eyes Marquis turned his head slowly, back to where the first avalanche had come to rest. Between the long glistening wound on the steep slope and the frozen wave of debris in the shallow dip at the bottom there was a wide stretch of snow that, from this distance, looked smooth and unblemished.

Unblemished but for the three bodies lying in the middle of it, like three punctuation marks in a white page from which all words had been erased.

NINE

'You'd better defect, General. When we get down into India, the colonel will put in a good word for you and you can join our side.'

Neither Li Bu-fang nor Singh smiled : each of them was beyond joking.

'Was it a shock to you, General?' Marquis went on. 'I mean when they started shelling us? One more life in the Great Cause. I don't think anyone particularly loves generals in our armies, but I've never heard of any of them being sacrificed in the way your blokes tried to get rid of you to-day. That's a pretty drastic way of being bowler-hatted, General.'

'Are you trying to anger me, Mr. Marquis, or frighten me?'

'I don't have to frighten you, General. Your own blokes did that this morning. And as for making you angry—you've got no right to any anger, General. We have the copyright on that.'

Eve, helping Tsering prepare the evening meal because she wanted to keep herself occupied and have less time to think and remember, listened to Jack baiting Li Bu-fang. There was a nervous grating edge to his voice that she had never heard before ; he was as close to hysteria as she believed he could come. She had been about to speak to him, to tell him to leave the unhappy Chinese alone ; then she had recognised that he was doing exactly what she was doing herself, trying to find some way to stop himself from thinking. He was talking the day out of himself, pouring the scarifying memory of it over the tormented Li Bu-fang, making himself suffer less by making the other suffer more. But she knew from experience that that would be only a temporary respite : suffering was a boomerang that always came back, and never more surely than from someone else who was also in pain.

Tsering was cooking the meal on the one small Primus stove they still had with them. There had been a spare one in Tom Breck's pack, but that had gone, along with both of Marquis's guns and some of the food. The stove was popping and flaring fitfully and Eve had to keep pricking it; if they had to climb much higher to-morrow she knew it would not work at all; breakfast in the morning might be their last hot meal. She did not dwell on the thought that it might be their last meal of any kind.

No fresh meat was left, and Tsering was warming up some tinned stew. They would eat this with tsampa cakes and follow it with more tsampa cakes soaked in honey; the craving for something sweet had increased and while they waited on the meal they were all sucking on some chocolate Nimchu had produced. None of them was really hungry; food didn't seem important to them now. But they were all achingly thirsty and they would end the meal with as much sweet tea as they could drink. Nimchu was packing snow into another pan. This would be melted down to produce the water for the tea, but it would be a long process and they might have to retreat to the haven of their tents before the tea was ready. Even hard-packed snow was four times as bulky as the water it produced and it might be half an hour or more before enough tea was made to satisfy them all. By then the sun would have gone and the cold would have driven them into their sleeping-bags.

They had been climbing all day. They had lost sight of the Chinese soldiers, but none of them had felt any rise in hope at that. They had not hurried but had plodded on, walking mechanically as if filling in time till the inevitable. They had begun to come upon an increasing number of crevasses and Marquis had stopped and told everyone to put on their crampons, the spiked metal frames that fitted to their boots and would give them a better grip. Then they had roped themselves together with Marquis leading, and moved on again, bound together physically now as well as emotionally. The mountains had once more settled back into their chilling silence, stood waiting beneath the silent neutral sky. In Eve's ringing chaotic mind the mountains had become no more than abstract patterns of glass, the fragments of some stained glass window that had once spoken a truth which was no longer available to her. She had begun to pray without realising what she was doing: prayer was not mere words, most of which she had forgotten anyway, but an appeal in the mind, a denial of self-importance. She prayed to a god who could have been the God of her childhood or could have been one of the mountains, one of Nimchu's gods : the white glare that surrounded her had penetrated her very being, so that she could identify nothing. Even when Jack, the only god she had worshipped in eight years, spoke to her she had difficulty in not dismissing him as a stranger, no more than a pale blue shadow in the white world of silence.

Marquis had called a halt here on this ledge at three o'clock in the afternoon. The ledge faced west and they would have the benefit of the sun for at least another hour. After that they would have to withdraw into their sleeping-bags and the cramped comfort of their tents. Already now the sun had begun to lose its warmth, was a cold red ball that threw dark blue shadows in which the air seemed to be turning into ice even as one looked at it. Everyone had stood up and was moving around, stamping his feet to guard against their becoming frost-bitten. To Eve, her mind more ordered now that they had escaped from the ordeal of climbing through the white glare, restored to sanity by her humour, the men looked like nervous expectant fathers, moving restlessly back and forth past each other as they argued.

'Why, General?' Singh had jerked himself out of his silence, had seen the merit of the therapy suggested by Marquis : blood-letting by talk. 'Why have you started this invasion of my country?'

'We are not invading India, Colonel. We are just reclaiming those parts of these mountains that belong to China.'

'Balls,' said Marquis, never given to diplomatic language. 'You don't believe that, General. What use are they to you?' He waved an arm around at the mountains. 'Do you honestly think you could use any of this country as lebensraum? And that's the only valid excuse you blokes have for wanting to break out of China.'

Li hesitated, then conceded a point. 'It is a good enough excuse, Mr. Marquis. How do you feed seven hundred million people when only ten per cent of our land grows food? In the district where I was born the fields have seen five thousand harvests. The Good Earth, as one of your Western writers once called it, is not so good when it has been worked so many times.'

' Well, why not be honest? Why all the bull about what belongs to you in these mountains? But you'll never raise a harvest on these slopes, mate.'

' Surely, old chap, you don't think my country can offer your people lebensraum? The only two things we have in common are famine and over-population. Are you suggesting we make an empire out of misery?'

Li shrugged, suddenly engulfed again by his own misery. The day had drained him of doctrine and dogma; the avalanches had taken part of him with them down the mountainside. Thirty years of belief had all at once been split by doubt; questions he had long denied himself had begun to assert themselves, had cracked the years of faith as the shells had cracked the snow crust on the slope of the spur. He was still a Communist, knew the socialist system was the only way his people could drag themselves out of the wretchedness that was their heritage; but he had become a man, had become something more than just a unit of society. And had begun to wonder at the ambitions of his leaders, a heresy that racked him as much as the physical labours of the day had done. His mind went back to yesterday: was his government like the beetle horde, bent only on destruction?

And behind all his doubts was the final doubt of himself. For in finding himself a man he had found all the weaknesses of a man. He had run from the shells and the avalanche as any craven selfish coward might have done.

They ate, drank their tea and went into their tents as the cold came in in sudden attack. The food and tea had warmed them and they took the warmth with them into the sleeping-bags: to feel warm, to escape the numbing bite of the cold, was one of the few comforts with which they could face the long night.

They had no air mattresses and fourteen hours on the hard bed of snow would be more torture than rest.

' Put your boots in the bottom of your bag,' Marquis advised Eve. ' Otherwise they'll be frozen stiff in the morning.'

They lay side by side in the gloom of the tiny tent, warm

in the only other comfort that was offered to them, that of each other. A bickering wind had sprung up, arguing with the ropes of the tent and slapping spitefully at the tied flaps. If the wind grew into a storm such as last night's, Marquis knew they were doomed. But he kept his despair to himself and looked at Eve, working the bones of his face into another disguise.

'I'm sorry we lost the guns. It's not many blokes who have lost their wedding present in an avalanche.'

Cautiously she said, 'Would you let me buy you another pair?'

'For sentimental reasons?'

'Yes,' she said, encouraged. 'And I know you got a lot of pleasure out of them. Even if we did fight about them.'

'What would I shoot with them? There's nothing in Kensington but starlings and lap-dogs. There's no fun in stalking a poodle.'

'Are we going to still live in Kensington?' Her heart gave a leap : were their journeys over? 'I thought you wanted to get rid of the flat?'

'You like it. We'll stay there.' It was easy to make the concession and just as easy to accept it : the past, which was Kensington and all the other places they had experienced, had already begun to rot in their minds. 'If I'm not made impotent by all this, do you want to have a baby when we get home?'

She laughed, making herself warm even more with humour. 'That's just like you. The last thing I feel like now is getting pregnant.' Then her laughter died and she felt cold again. 'I'm glad now we didn't have any children.'

'You wouldn't be here if there had been any,' he said, reading between her words.

'But you would have been. I wouldn't want a brood of fatherless kids.' She tried to laugh, but her throat was frozen. She began to weep, and he rolled closer to her, taking his arm from his sleeping-bag and embracing the quilted thickness of her. They sought security in their love, as if it were some sort of amulet. They were more conscious of themselves by being conscious of each other, and so were determined to go on living. The wind outside stopped bickering and went away, and Marquis, the Celt, saw it as some sort of omen. The tent grew dark, he drew his arm back into his sleeping-bag and they tried for sleep.

The cold woke them in the middle of the night. Eve was weeping with the pain and misery of it, and Marquis lay beside her, knowing he could do nothing to help her. He longed to bring her into his sleeping-bag with him, but his own bulk already filled it too tightly. He kept murmuring to her, nothing coherent : advice would have been useless and in the end would only have angered her by its stupidity. Instinct told her to rub herself, to thump her flesh and kick her legs in the confines of the bag : she didn't need to be told such things. He was doing the same things himself, struggling like a kidnap victim in the bonds of his bag, using up his strength and energy to stay alive to-night, ignoring what he would need to stay alive to-morrow.

It began to snow and after a while the sides of the tent billowed in under the weight. The tent became even smaller, threatening to smother them. The blackness itself seemed to thicken, and now they were struggling not only to stay alive but to stay sane. Each of them began to talk again, beating back madness and terror with the frail weapon of reminiscence.

' Remember that time in Mauritius, how lovely and warm it was there on the beach?' Her teeth chattered, mocking her words. ' I wanted to stay there forever. I wish we had.'

' As a kid I was always on the beach at Coogee. I can remember one day it was a hundred and eight in the shade. I burnt the soles of my feet.' He felt the burn again through the insulation of almost thirty years.

' We've never been to Australia. Will you take me there now?'

' If you pay the fare.'

She laughed, finding some warmth again. ' Darling, we'll never argue about my money again, will we?'

' When I burnt all that cash this morning, I realised how unimportant the stuff is.'

' I've said that for years.'

' But you've been rich all along. I had to wait till I was rolling in it to appreciate the point. I *was* rich this morning— for about half an hour.' He lolled in the memory of it,

Croesus with chilblains. 'I wish the old man could have seen me. Though he'd have been happier burning English quids.'

It was the longest night they had ever spent, but at last the blackness of the tent, and of the mind, began to fade. At the first glimmer of light Marquis struggled out of his sleeping-bag, pulled on his boots and dug his way out of the snow-banked tent. The morning was a world of blue, cold and beautiful and empty as he imagined space itself must be. Nothing moved, and while he stood entranced at the beauty of it all he had the feeling that he was looking at what lay beyond the grave. This was the territory of eternity which no one would ever conquer.

He stumbled through the snow to the porters' tent, woke Nimchu and Tsering and told them to get breakfast started. He woke Singh and Li Bu-fang, both of whom had somehow managed to sleep through the cold. Then he went back to his own tent and found Eve still lying in her sleeping-bag.

'Come on, love.'

'I can't feel my feet, darling.' He saw for the first time that she was weeping, with fear rather than pain. 'I'm dead as far up as my knees. Oh, darling!'

'Don't panic,' he said, but felt the panic tearing through himself.

He grabbed the bottom of her sleeping-bag and dragged her bodily out of the tent. He shouted to Singh, who came scrambling through the snow with a blanket. Marquis pulled Eve up out of the sleeping-bag, wrapped the blanket round her, then pulled down her socks. Her feet and ankles were the same pale blue as the morning sky, cold and stiff as the feet of a statue. If the colour of her feet had been darker, had been striped with white, Marquis knew it would have been too late.

He bit back the sob that belched in him. He pulled the socks up again, then turned and began fumbling with the frozen straps of his packs.

'What are you after?' Singh asked.

'Rope.'

'It will be frozen. Here.'

Singh turned to Li Bu-fang, who had come out of his tent and stood looking down with concern at the weeping Eve.

The Chinese guessed what was in the Indian's mind and lifted his bound hands; the rope had been kept warm and pliable during the night under Li's blankets and against the heat of his own body. All yesterday during their climbing Li's hands had been free; but Singh, apologising sardonically for his lack of trust, had bound them again last night. Now Singh untied the rope and handed it to Marquis. The latter took it and looked back at Eve.

'This isn't going to hurt at first, love. When it does, you can begin laughing. Because by then I'll have got the blood moving again.'

Then he began to lash at her stockinged feet and lower legs, quickly but methodically, like a professional sadist. The Indian and the Chinese stood and watched him, saying nothing, their anxiety for Eve showing plainly on their bare-boned faces. Marquis stopped for a moment to get his breath, and without a word Singh and Li dropped on their knees in the snow, each taking one of Eve's feet and beginning to rub it vigorously. The three men worked like this for some time, Marquis lashing with the rope and the Indian and the Chinese massaging. Then suddenly Eve let out a cry, of pain this time and not of despair.

Marquis stopped wielding the rope, and Singh and Li once again dropped on their knees and grabbed her feet and began to rub them. They pulled down her socks and could see the blueness slowly disappearing from her feet and ankles. The relief of all four, the man and wife and the two enemies, pulled them tighter together. Eve sat up, and the four heads leaned in, concentrating on the two feet that all at once seemed to belong to all four of them. Eve was weeping and laughing, and Marquis was holding her, laughing with her. Then Singh and Li began to laugh, and the warmth and the blood flowed through all of them.

Tsering and Nimchu came out of their tent with four cups of steaming tea and they, too, began to laugh. The cold dead silence of the morning was splintered by a beautiful sound, the human laugh.

2

It was late morning when they looked back and caught sight of the Chinese soldiers.

They had long ago lost the path of the trade route and were just heading south, hoping they might pick it up again leading up to a pass. They had crossed a glacier, negotiated the crevasse that separated it from the steeper ice and rock above it and were climbing a narrow couloir when Tsering happened to glance back and gave the warning.

'Soldiers, sahib!'

Marquis drove in his ice-axe, hung on to it and turned and looked back over his shoulder. He had been leading the climb up the steep narrow gully and had reached a section that was going to prove more difficult than anything they had faced so far. It was no time, he thought, for getting further bad news.

The Chinese had just reached the top of the glacier and were looking for a way across the crevasse. There were not so many of them now, perhaps no more than twenty; the Chinese commander had evidently decided on the gamble of a smaller party moving at what must have been a killing pace. At the rate they were going they would catch Marquis and the others within an hour.

Marquis cursed himself for not having set a quicker pace during the morning. But he knew in his heart that they had been moving as fast as they had been able. Eve's feet were no longer troubling her, but she had to be nursed; everyone had complained of the cold of the snow through which they had to climb and now everyone was afraid of frost-bite. Singh and Li Bu-fang were not experienced climbers and once the going had become steeper their progress had become slower and slower.

Marquis looked down at those below him on the rope. 'Okay, forget those bastards. Just keep your mind on your climbing. How do you feel, love?'

Eve was wriggling her toes, trying to keep the circulation moving in her feet. The close threat of frost-bite had frightened her more than the prospect of dying: she would not have wanted to live as a cripple. She looked up at her husband, forcing a smile. 'I'd rather be climbing Highgate Hill.'

He winked at her, then turned and gave his attention to the climb above him. The sun was blazing on his back and he could feel the sweat running out of him; but his feet still felt frozen in his boots. Climbing in the Alps was much different from climbing here in the Himalayas. In Europe there was always the danger of frost-bite, but the cold did not attack one's feet so continuously : there was always some feeling in one's feet, a sensitivity to danger when searching for a foot-hold. The stumps of ice he now possessed felt as clumsy and heavy as a hippo's feet.

He braced himself against the slope of the couloir, took out a piton and his hammer and drove the metal spike, with its ringed head, into the ice. He tested it, then looped the rope through, belaying it down to Eve, next on the line. That would hold him if he should slip while making his next step. He was breathing heavily, feeling the effect of working at this altitude, but he didn't dwell on the thought of how much strength he was expending. Nothing could be saved for the future : they were living from minute to minute now.

He punched in his ice-axe again, felt it take; then he pulled himself up, digging his crampons into the ice beneath his feet. He could hear the ice chips falling away beneath him, and once he heard Singh cry out, but he didn't look down. Slowly he worked his way up, paying out the rope behind him. It was not a difficult climb and he had attempted many far worse; but not after four such days as he had just experienced and not with the thought that there were men chasing him to kill him. By the time he reached the top of the couloir he was exhausted, worn out as much mentally as physically. He felt as brittle as the crust of snow on which he lay.

He sat up, digging deep into himself for reserves : the past years owed him something. He looked back down the steep narrow gully of rock and ice. He drove his ice-axe deep into the snow and ice beside him, belayed the rope round it and yelled down to Eve to begin climbing. She came up steadily, climbing beautifully with a minimum of effort; he watched her admiringly, not only as a climber but as a woman. God

Almighty, he was lucky! She had enough character for a battalion of Amazons, suffragettes and militant Irish washer-women. She came up beside him, lay panting on the snow and ice and he leaned over and kissed her.

'You'll do me, love,' he said, and she lay smiling at him, recognising it as the ultimate in an Australian husband's expression of love.

The others made the climb, Singh and Li Bu-fang both climbing slowly and with some clumsiness, Nimchu and Tsering both coming up with the same speed and natural skill as Eve had shown.

Marquis stood up while the others lay getting over their exhaustion. He took out his binoculars and looked up at what lay ahead of them. A long ridge ran up beneath great grotesque cornices, hanging waves of snow and ice that looked ready to crash down at any moment. Beyond the ridge there was a steep pitch of rock and ice that finished in what looked like a long broad ledge. The ledge ran back to a long slope that ran up to a narrow col; and in the gap in the mountains something moved. He steadied the binoculars, going blind for a moment with excitement; then his gaze cleared and he sucked in his breath. A prayer-flag, stuck in a cairn, fluttered in the wind at the top of the pass.

'There's the path!' He pointed as the others, his excitement communicating itself to them, stood up. 'If we can make it up that pitch there——'

'Pitch?' Singh had taken out his own binoculars. 'That sheer section? We'll never make it, my dear chap.'

'We've got to make it!' Marquis swore savagely. 'If we make it up that, we've beaten the Chows! We can start our own avalanche as they come along this ridge! All it needs is a burst from your Sten gun and that cornice will be on its way!'

Singh was still looking at the pitch through his binoculars. 'We could never climb up that face.'

'I'll get you up there!' Anger gave Marquis a strength he thought had gone. 'I'll get you up there if I have to drag you up dead! I've got you this far—I'm not going to bloody let you give up!'

Singh put his binoculars back in their case, then looked at Marquis. There was no arrogance left : the prince was dead.

'Lead on, old chap.'

Marquis had been prepared for argument; faced with such sudden acquiescence he could only grin and nod. He was still being educated in all the facets of leadership, that a philosophy was as necessary for acceptance of one's orders as for rebellion against them. But he still felt the weight of other men's lives. All his life he had looked with a satiric eye on men and now they were claiming their debt.

They started out along the side of the ridge, moving carefully. Marquis led them, chopping steps in the ice all the way, all the time acutely conscious of the overhang of snow and ice above them. The cornice shut off the sun from them and they moved through a long blue tunnel of shadow in which every sound seemed to be magnified. The shadow, accentuated by their dark glasses, contrasted exaggeratedly with the blinding glare from the slope on the other side of the valley above which they hung. The sun beat through the curled edges of the cornices, turning them blue, green, yellow; the ridge wore a necklace of the spectrum; the odd crystal broke off occasionally and came rolling down the slope, a reminder of the danger that the beauty disguised. Marquis chopped carefully with his axe, Tsering belaying him while he worked. Tsering had moved up to take Eve's place as second on the rope; if Marquis should slip, someone with strength would be needed to hold him till he could struggle back up the slope. It was freezing cold here in the shadow and Marquis began to wonder how Eve's feet were behaving. He could feel his own feet growing more numb, becoming clumsier. He was wearing a spare pair of dark glasses that were too tight; the side bars were beginning to bite into his cheekbones like knives of ice. He began to work faster, taking more risks.

He drove the axe in hard, hearing the crack as it hit rock. It shuddered in his hand and he almost let go. Then he heard Tsering's hissing gasp behind him and he looked up. He saw the cornice, ugly as a many-knuckled fist, break off and begin to fall. The sun blazed through the gap right into his face and he shut his eyes, angry for some unaccountable reason that he should die blind. He tensed, waiting for the ice and snow to hit him, knowing this time there would be no chance of swimming against it as he had swum against the avalanche. He heard the crumbling swishing sound, felt the rush of air and a spatter of ice splinters against his face. Then he opened his eyes and looked down at the tumbling mass of snow and ice far down the slope. He blew out, a slubbering sound like that of a horse, and looked back over his shoulder at Tsering and beyond him at Eve.

'I think we're going to make it,' he said, and everybody back along the rope nodded in agreement. They had reached the stage where every escape added to their fund of hope: despair looks for its own remedies.

At last they were off the ridge and immediately beneath the almost vertical pitch of rock and ice that led up to the broad ledge above. The climb would be no more than a hundred feet, but it would go up past a buttress of rock that would have them suspended over a sheer drop of more than a thousand feet. Marquis glanced up at it, then at the people with him, and his heart sank. Now they were beneath it the climb looked twice as difficult, even for an experienced climber like himself.

Singh sensed his dejection. 'You think it is too difficult?'

Before Marquis could reply, Eve said, 'It isn't going to be easy, but we can do it.'

He looked at her, wondering how she had guessed he needed her support. But it had been that way all along the way: this was the final decision and she was helping him make it. He looked at her gratefully and nodded. 'We'll make it!'

'We've got to!' She was afraid again, not of the climb but of dying at the hands of the Chinese. An hour ago her future had extended no further than the next step she had to take. Now, with the pass above them marked by the prayer-flag, life had once more taken on a long perspective. She was stamping her feet up and down, fighting the numbness that was taking hold of them. They were out in the sun again and she knew if she could keep moving she could perhaps hold off the frost-bite. But even another fifteen minutes here in the knee-deep snow would cripple her.

Marquis looked at Li Bu-fang. 'You want to try it, General?'

Li smiled. He was not the man who had begun this trek four days ago. All the calm confidence had gone and like the others he now clung to life only by the minute. But he could still smile: he had suffered too much in the past not to have some fatalism left. 'What choice do I have?'

'Damn-all, I'd say. I don't think your blokes care a damn about rescuing you. You might as well try your luck with us.'

Li looked back along the ridge: the soldiers were not yet in sight. Then he looked at Singh. 'If I refused to climb with you, Colonel, would you shoot me?'

Singh hesitated, then nodded. 'I'd have to, General. If I left you for your men to rescue, it would make the last four days pointless.'

'You would still have the papers.'

Singh patted his pocket, as if to reassure himself that the papers were still there. Education was a sham: there was always some knowledge that was denied you. Some brushed characters on paper: for all he knew, they could be the secret of the universe or a laundry bill. He prayed that the papers were not anything as trite as the latter. He had begun to build his own conception of the importance of the papers: even if they were never read in Delhi, never got out of these mountains, they *had* to be important. If they were not, then the lives that had been lost lost some of their value.

'Yes. But I left three hundred men back there in the mountains on the border. And there were Mr. Wilkins and Mr. and Mrs. Breck and young Chungma. I owe them something, General.'

'Meaning me?'

Singh nodded. Then he said, 'But I think you will come anyway. While you're still alive and still with us, you hope you can prevent me taking the papers back to India. Am I right?'

'We understand each other, Colonel. I do have to stay with you, no matter how I feel. There is an old Chinese saying: the trees want to be still, but the wind still blows.'

He looked at Marquis and the others and smiled. 'Not Charlie Chan.'

Marquis grinned, then he looked up at the glistening face of ice and rock. It hung above them like a threat, the iron helmet of a giant black knight : one could almost imagine a brain working behind the shining grey façade. He had had this reaction of fantasy before when climbing : there came a moment, when the final challenge was thrown down, when the mountain came alive. In the past it had been the moment he had welcomed, the justification for what to non-climbers was always a senseless, suicidal pursuit. It was the moment when he had faced the truth of himself, glimpsed the reflection of immortality that Man aspired to, that kept him going through generations of suffering, degradation and despair. But looking up now he felt none of the old excitement. He would not be challenging the mountain on behalf of himself. He would be defying it for the lives of five others.

He gave each of them their place on the rope : himself first, then Tsering, Eve, Li, Singh and last of all Nimchu, the most experienced climber after himself. He checked everyone's crampons, made sure the rope was secured properly to each climber, counted the number of his pitons against how many he reckoned he would need on the climb : then he was ready. He shut his mind to everything, the soldiers somewhere behind them, the mountains around, even the people behind him on the rope, and attacked the helmet of rock and ice.

He drove in the ice-axe as far above his head as he could reach, belayed the rope round it, then drove his crampons hard into the ice that sheathed the rock. He got a foothold, tested it, found it would take his weight; then he began to climb, Tsering paying out the rope from below as he inched his way up the dark frozen face. He was working his way diagonally up the pitch, finding tiny faults in the rock to give him toeholds. He stopped to rest frequently, exhausted not only by the climbing but by the effort of swinging his arm to drive in the axe. Even hammering in the pitons had become an effort that burned his arm and shoulder and made him pant; sweat blinded him and once he had to make two frantic grabs at a projection of rock before he got a hold. He hung there, shivering with exhaustion and fright, his face pressed hard against the cold unyielding rock. Then he gathered himself together again, digging for some of the iron in himself that he had once shared with the mountain, and went on.

He came to a buttress of rock, scrambled on the ledge beneath it and secured himself with a piton. Then he looked back down to the others and shouted to them to begin climbing. They came up so slowly that he wanted to scream at them to hurry; but that was the cardinal sin of climbing and he knew it. One always felt impatient when one was top man on the rope; and patience had never been one of his virtues. But he restrained himself, talking quietly and encouragingly to the others as they got nearer and nearer to him. Then Tsering and Eve were on the tiny ledge with him.

There was no room for any more and he looked down the rock face at Li, Singh and Nimchu. 'Hang on.' He managed a grin. 'Right now, General, you must be the highest ranking officer in the People's Army.'

Li clung to the face, held in by the rope. 'Just don't let me be demoted.'

Marquis looked back down along the ridge, saw the first of the soldiers appearing over the top of the couloir. 'That's up to your mates, General.'

'Get moving, darling,' said Eve, glancing fearfully back across the shining air to where the group of men was spreading in a dark stain on the bright glare of snow above the couloir.

Marquis pressed her arm, feeling it trembling beneath his hand. Then he turned once more to the ascent. The buttress of rock hung above him, sheer as a wall. It stretched up for perhaps forty feet, a great bulge like a broken nose in the face of the cliff. They would be exposed like flies on a wall once the soldiers got near enough to begin firing on them.

He began with his axe again, driving it into the ice and rock with all the strength he could muster. He reached up, took hold of the haft and pulled himself up, digging one knee into a slot in the rock while he kicked hard with his crampon to find a hold for his other foot. He felt the ice breaking away beneath each kick and he began to sweat, wondering if he would find a foothold at all. Then there was a tiny ledge under his boot, enough to hold him while he dragged himself up and roped himself to the axe. He took out a piton, drove it in and belayed the rope through it. He rested for a moment, feeling weaker than he had ever felt in his life before, aware as he had never been when climbing before of the great void at his back, the thousand feet of glittering blue air between him and the jagged ice-fall far below.

He pressed himself against the rock and with the axe chipped a nick in the ice to give himself a handhold. He reached for it with his left hand, felt his fingers slip, felt the panic freeze through him that all mountaineers fought against. Desperately he drew back his arm and somehow, with no leverage at all, managed to swing the axe and drive it into the rock. It held, and he hung on, adhering to the face more by willpower than anything else. He could feel his boot slipping on its tiny ledge of ice and his knee, jammed into the slot, was giving him agony as it took more and more of his weight. He was panting hard, his breath coming out of him like jets of steam. He was off-balance, caught where he could go neither up nor down. Out of the corner of his eye he could see Eve and Tsering just below him, but they were too far away to be able to help him. Taking his whole weight on his knee, feeling the pain of it shoot right up his thigh into his groin, he drew back his left foot and kicked desperately at the ice. The crampon went in, then slipped as the ice crumbled under it; he cried out as his knee went farther into the slot, feeling as if it were being sliced off . He kicked again, panicking now, blinded by sweat, his whole body losing all its co-ordination; then abruptly he felt the crampon take hold, another tiny ledge had been found. Slowly, carefully, he shifted his weight, praying that the new foothold would not give way. Every muscle burned in his flesh, every nerve was stretched to breaking point : he was a man of gelatine who might shatter at any moment. Slowly, slowly he let his weight move down through his left leg. He could feel his toes turning into claws in his boot, trying to hold on to the tiny ledge. Then his weight was evenly distributed between his knee and his foot : the ledge still held. Then just as slowly, holding his breath now he took some of the weight off the knee that felt as if it were embedded in jagged glass. He felt the ice ledge settle a fraction of an inch, then it hardened. He put his whole weight on it and let out a gasp of relief.

'All right?' Eve's voice was a hoarse whisper.

'Okay,' he muttered, and wondered how reassuring he looked, stuck like a spatter of drying mud against the face of the wall.

He looked up. The rock appeared to cut back in several feet above him, suggesting there might be a wider ledge there. He wished he had had more time to study the mountain face : he had never climbed like this before, not knowing what lay above him. Between him and the cut-back the rock was smooth and hard as a sheet of iron; he would never be able to get a grip on that surface. He leant his face against the patch of ice in front of him and looked down at Eve.

'Where are the Chows?' He could not look back down towards the ridge.

'They're all up on top of the couloir now. They'll be moving up along the ridge soon, I think.'

He cursed, then looked up again at the cut-back. He took off his dark glasses and awkwardly shoved them into a pocket. He took out his hammer and, still holding tightly to the axe, he drove a piton into the rock. He belayed the rope through it, then looked down at Tsering.

'Righto, Tsering. Hang on bloody tight.'

He committed himself to the piton. He withdrew the axe and held it almost at haft's length. He braced himself, foot dug into the ledge and knee jammed into the slot again. Then he swung his arm out and upwards in a wide circle, using all the strength he had in his shoulder. The axe swung up, punched into the ice on the cut-back and held. He hung there for a moment, splayed against the face, getting his breath, summoning up more strength. Without looking down he was aware of the others watching him; he could almost hear their silence as all of them held their breath. Somewhere he heard a crack : he didn't know whether it was a rifle shot or ice snapping off. It was immaterial : he was too close to death to worry about how he died.

He gathered himself, bending his legs a little to kick himself up as he pulled on the axe. Then slowly, taking all his weight on his arms, he began to pull himself up on the axe. He kept kicking with his crampons against the rock, but they made no dent in the hard face. He was hanging now from the axe, his feet scrabbling against the rock with no effect; if his grip slipped on the axe haft, if the axe itself tore out of the ice, he was gone. He could feel his arms being pulled out of their sockets; he couldn't hold on much longer. Then he felt something, ice or rock, give beneath the kick of his right crampon. He dug in his toe, found a grip. He took one hand off the haft of the axe and grabbed frantically at the cut-back, found a crack in the rock and hung on. He was safe as long as his strength held out. But he still had to pull himself up on to the cut-back or ledge, whatever it was.

He had stopped thinking, had become an animal needing an animal's strength. No amount of intelligence could help him here; the brute had to take over to save the man. He drew in his breath, finding it difficult suspended as he was: his lungs felt as if they were bound with tight straps. He began to draw himself up, slowly and with agonising effort. Inch by inch his face scraped up the rock. With the clarity of a man just before he pitches into unconsciousness he saw the veins in the rock, like reflections of the blood vessels in his own staring eyes, the tiny crystals of ice magnified till they shone like great tears: rock and flesh met in a kiss of hate.

Then his eyes were level with the top of the sheer face, he saw another handhold and made a desperate grab for it, hung on and with one last torturing effort pulled himself up and flopped over on to a flat ledge that, jagged and cold with ice, was as welcome as a bed.

He could feel his heart pumping madly, trying to burst its way out of his chest. Sweat was pouring off his face, dripping down past his eyes as he lay with his cheek resting on the pillow of his arm. He could feel the muscles in the arm quivering, and his stomach fluttering and contracting as if he were about to vomit. He sucked in air and blew it out in great whistling gasps: again he reminded himself of a horse. That's all I am, he thought: a bloody great nag good only for the knacker's yard.

At last he stood up, put on his glasses again against the glare, and shouted down to the others. He drove in a piton, belayed the rope and told Tsering to begin climbing. In ten minutes all of them stood on the ledge, more exhausted by the nervous tension of the ascent than by any physical effort:

the climb itself, with the aid of the rope, had now been comparatively simple. Singh and Li were beginning to look distressed, and Marquis noticed that both of them stood facing the wall of ice in front of them, their backs turned to the edge of the ledge and the terrifying drop below.

'How are you feeling?'

Singh shook his head, smiling weakly. 'This is an awfully stupid time to find out, but I've just discovered I have no head for heights. When we reach the top of that pass, will we have to go *down* sheer drops like this?'

Marquis grinned encouragingly. 'I don't think so. If that's the trade route, and I think it is, it'll be the sort of going that a mule or a yak can negotiate. You'll be all right, Colonel.' He looked at Li Bu-fang. 'What about you, General?'

'I'm finding the colonel and I have more and more in common. I share his dislike of heights.'

'I'm glad to hear it. Somehow or other I'd always thought vertigo, like ulcers, was only a capitalist disease.' He leant out on the rope, looking down at the soldiers. They had stopped at the far end of the ridge, evidently debating whether to continue on below the threatening cornices. 'Looks like your mates have got cold feet, General. Frost-bite of the nerves.'

Li risked a quick glance back over his shoulder, then turned into the wall again. 'They won't give up, Mr. Marquis.'

'No,' said Marquis quietly but angrily, 'I didn't think the bastards would.'

From here on the ascent was easier. The best route lay diagonally up the wall of ice that confronted them to a narrow chimney that ran straight up the rock face to the top. Once in the chimney it would be straight nursery climbing.

'I'll make it across to the bottom of the chimney,' Marquis said to Eve and Tsering. 'Then you two follow me and go on over me and up to the top.'

They were more exposed to the wind here than they had been farther down, but unless it strengthened suddenly it would not be a hazard. The sky had begun to cloud up and snow was trailing off the high peaks as the wind began its half-hearted assault on them. The sun was still striking straight on to the ledge where they stood and they could feel

the warmth of it being reflected from the wall in front of
them. That would be the only danger, that the wall of ice they
must traverse might be too soft for a secure hold.

Marquis began cautiously, chopping steps and stamping the
ice down hard as he went. There were plenty of handholds
in the ridged face of the ice, but he drove in pitons, trusting
that the ice would harden round the cold iron and hold them.
He had one or two anxious moments as the ice crumbled
under his foot, but he would quickly draw back, kick hard
and the crampon would sink in and stick. He came to the
last section of the wall, where the angle steepened so that
it was out of the vertical, creating a slight overhang. Here
rock showed through the ice. He swung the axe, felt it take
hold, swung himself on it over to a narrow ledge, settled his
feet in securely; then, still clutching the ice-axe with his left
hand, he juggled a piton and pushed it into a crack in the
rock, ramming it home with the hammer. He looped the rope
on it, working steadily now and without fumbling, knowing the
worst was over. Another piton, another step, a second piton,
a second step, then he had swung over into the bottom of
the chimney, leaning back against the rock and ice and grinning
triumphantly across at Eve and the others.

'We're home and dried!' he shouted, and his voice had
a note of triumph in it, the first for days.

Tsering came first, going past Marquis with his round face
wide open in a grin and climbing on up the chimney, moving
a little too fast and sending chips of ice and rock down on
the jovially complaining Marquis. Then he was at the top
and had secured the rope and was shouting with all his old
glee, sitting in the snow on the topmost ledge and making
rude gestures at the soldiers still standing at the far end of
the ridge.

Eve was next. As she went past Marquis he brushed his
lips against her cheek. She smiled and went on, using the
rope belayed to her by Tsering, moving even more quickly
than he had done but still managing not to disturb any ice or
rock splinters.

Then it was Li's turn. Marquis glanced down towards the
ridge and saw that the soldiers had now begun to make a

cautious move forward under the cornices. He looked back along the ice wall and shouted to Singh.

' As soon as he's half-way across, you start, Colonel!'

He was taking a risk having two novice climbers depending on the rope on such a stretch at the same time, but it was that or have them exposed to rifle fire before the second one could begin to cross. And behind them would be Nimchu, the man who meant more to Marquis than either of them. Though it might take the soldiers almost an hour to negotiate the ridge, even now they were only five or six hundred yards away, perhaps even less. At that distance it would be a lucky shot that might hit them from a single rifle. But concentrated fire from twenty rifles might find a target. It would depend on whether the Chinese soldiers would take a risk themselves, that of firing all their rifles while still under the threat of the cornices.

Li Bu-fang started towards Marquis. He had been carefully watching those who had come across before him and he did everything exactly as he had seen them do it. It was evident that he would never have been a natural climber, but there was a painstaking competence about him that Marquis, watching anxiously, found himself admiring. He remembered that the Chinese had always been good students at whatever subject they attempted; Li, a middle-aged one, was no exception. His face was tight with concentration and Marquis could hear his hissing breath, but he came on steadily while Marquis drew in the slack of the rope towards himself. Li had survived the Long March as a boy : he would survive this. Endurance had been a life-long habit.

Singh had also begun the climb. He had never been meant for mountain-climbing, and every step he took was as clumsy as that of a nervous drunk. He seemed to be having difficulty in fitting his body into the wall, seeming to stand stiffly away from it as if he did not trust the rock and ice. Marquis, looking beyond Li Bu-fang, could see the Indian's dark face contorted with concentration, effort and fear.

He was watching Singh when he heard the burst of rifle fire and felt the chips of ice and rock come raining down on him. He started, letting the slack of the rope run through his hands as they opened up in shock. He saw Singh flinch and bend in towards the wall, arching his back as if he had been punched there. Li stopped moving and pressed himself hard into the rock, shutting his eyes against the shower of splinters that fell on him. Beyond both of them Nimchu had flung himself flat on the ledge of the cut-back, still holding to the rope and shouting something that Marquis did not catch.

Marquis looked quickly down at the ridge. The soldiers were strung out in a line like a firing squad, but their rifles were raised to fire in line over each other's heads. They had fired the one burst and now stood, watching a cornice break off some fifty yards in front of them and go plunging down the slope of the ridge.

He looked back at the men on the rope. 'Come on!'

Singh, his face contorted in pain now, shook his head. 'I can't! I'm hit in the shoulder!'

Marquis could hear Eve shouting to him from the top of the chimney, but he didn't look up. Even as he began to snatch in the slack of the rope, there was another burst of fire: ice and rock fell past him, a chunk hitting his shoulder and almost toppling him off-balance. Out of the corner of his eye he saw another cornice break away, but the soldiers were still safe, still able to fire a third burst. He looked back along the wall, let out a curse when he saw the blood on Li's face.

'Take him!' Singh was screaming; he had been hit again. 'Don't let them get him!'

Somehow both men were still clinging to the wall. Marquis, still snatching in the slack, felt the rope catch on a projection below. He flicked the line, trying to clear it, meanwhile shouting to Nimchu.

'I'm going to pull the general across, Nimchu! Hang on!' He pulled savagely on the rope, but it still remained caught. He flicked another glance down at the soldiers: they had raised their rifles to fire again. They had not moved, but stood like a line of riflemen poised to fire a last salute. There was something to be admired about them, yet something to be hated. The cornice must eventually come crashing down on them, but they would keep firing till everyone on the cliff face was dead. Life meant nothing to them, not even their own.

Marquis cursed and looked across at Li. 'Can you make it on your own, General?'

Li Bu-fang shook his head as the blood ran down to blind him. Beyond him Singh was slowly losing his grip, his fingers slipping off the ice like the claws of a dying crab. Marquis swore again, jerked savagely once more on the rope, and it came free, spinning up towards him like a long snake. And in that moment Li Bu-fang flung himself backwards off the wall, taking Singh with him.

Marquis let out a yell, grabbed desperately at his axe and hung on, his heels dug in hard, as the rope whipped down and away from him. He saw the piton on which it was belayed shiver in the crack in the rock and he ducked his head away to avoid it as it came out like a bullet. But it held : it bent a little in the crack, zinging with vibration, but it held.

He looked across at the ledge, saw that Nimchu was still safe and felt the emotion choke him : the little man had become dear to him, someone he could not bear to lose. Then he looked down at Singh and Li Bu-fang hanging by the rope some twelve or fifteen feet below him. Both men were staring up at him, death already beginning to obliterate their features as life flickered out of them and their eyes turned to ashes. Singh had one hand caught in the front of his tunic, as if he was trying to get at the papers he had carried with him so far, but there was no strength left in his fingers to pull apart the buttons. Li hung backwards, both arms hanging loosely, his mouth open in what could have been a gasp, a snarl or even a smile.

'Cut the rope!' Singh's voice was only a whisper; the words frothed like bubbles on his lips. 'Cut the rope!'

And Li, beside him, nodded.

Marquis looked across at Nimchu. The porter had already taken out his knife, was looking at the Australian for the order : again Marquis had to admire the practicality of the simple mind. He took out his own knife and looked down at the Indian and the Chinese, men bound to him for the rest of his life, who would take his neutrality with them into their death.

'You poor bastards,' he prayed.

Then he nodded at Nimchu and began to saw on the rope.

Singh and Li Bu-fang went plunging down like dark rocks, whirling over and over in the bright shining air, their identity lost in the blink of an eyelid. Then the soldiers fired a third burst. Ice and rock flew off the wall between Marquis and Nimchu. Marquis ducked instinctively, then looked quickly down and let out a wild savage shout of joy.

The cornice above the line of soldiers had broken off. He saw the line of men break and try to run. Some of the soldiers slipped and went rolling down the steep slope. Then the cornice, a great wave of ice and snow, the sort of dumper he remembered from the beach back home at Coogee, fell down on the rest of the Chinese. The surf of snow and ice swept down the slope, taking the soldiers with it, gathering in the other men as it caught up with them, going on down in a rumbling thunder that came up to Marquis like the roll of an army of drums.

Then the sound died away, the cloud of snow settled. Marquis looked down, searching for some sign of bodies. There was nothing but the silent glittering wrath of snow and ice and rock.

3

It took Marquis, Eve, Nimchu and Tsering another three hours to reach the top of the pass.

Nimchu had safely made the climb across the ice wall, then he and Marquis had climbed up the chimney and fallen in the snow at the feet of Eve and Tsering. They had rested for ten minutes, then moved on, plodding silently on across the snow that was hard-packed and which didn't tire them as much as the soft snow lower down had done. They didn't talk about Singh and Li Bu-fang, but at odd intervals each one of them kept looking back over his shoulder. In his secret mind each of them knew that the Indian and the Chinese, Nick Wilkins, Tom and Nancy Breck and Chungma walked in the faint footmarks left behind in the harsh bright glare of the slope.

They came up to the prayer-flag leaning drunkenly in its rough cairn of stones. The wind was blowing hard through the pass and they stood leaning back against it, staring down to the south. From here the mountains sloped away in a series of gentle ridges. Far far away, but still with the naked eye, they could see where the snow ended, where the green promise of the hills of Assam began.

Marquis looked at Eve. 'One more night up here, that's all, love. Think you can make it?'

She nodded, felt for his gloved hand with hers. 'I can if you can.'

He looked at Nimchu and Tsering. 'It will be a long way home for you two.'

Both men smiled. 'I shall stop off and see my other wives,' said Tsering, the past already behind him, the future still as bright as ever.

'To get home is the important thing, sahib,' said Nimchu. 'When you get there, how long it takes doesn't matter.'

'Will you be afraid that the Chinese might come down and destroy your home?' Eve said.

Both men shrugged and looked back at the mountains. The peaks were wrapping their eastern shoulders in blue shadows; the western faces shone dazzlingly gold, like the faces of gods. Against the cloud-streaked sky they appeared as eternal as truth itself.

'The gods will take care of us,' said Nimchu, and his one good eye glittered in the dark bruise of his face.

I wish I had your faith, Marquis thought. He looked at the mountains, harsh and formidable in the cold burnished light, and wondered if they could withstand the giant awakening from his long sleep to the north of them. He was exhausted of hope as well as of strength; he had brought himself and the three others here to safety, but he would always look upon himself as having failed as a leader. Now Eve, with her love and her presence, drew the boundaries of his immediate world; what happened beyond them was more than he cared to contemplate for the moment. In the end what China did to the tiny lonely kingdom of Bhutan, even to India, might indeed lie in the lap of these shining snow-crowned gods. To guess would be as futile as trying to read the sound of the wind that blew from the north through this pass where they stood.

'I hope so, Nimchu,' he said. 'I hope so.'

Then Nimchu dug in the snow with his ice-axe. He stood

up, holding up a stone as if it were a nugget. He stumbled across the snow to the cairn, looked back at Marquis, Eve and Tsering and nodded, including them in his prayer; then he put the stone on the cairn and straightened the prayer-flag. He looked down the pass, at the footmarks already disappearing under the sweep of the wind; then he touched the prayer-flag, holding it for a moment between his fingers. The others saw his lips move wordlessly, then he turned abruptly and came back to join them.

They started off down the pass, heading south. Behind them the wind suddenly dropped and silence once more reigned: the sound of placelessness, the voice of Himalaya, the snow abode.

Fontana Fiction

Fontana is a leading paperback publisher of fiction. Below are some recent titles.

- ☐ KRYSALIS John Trenhaile £3.99
- ☐ PRINCES OF SANDASTRE Antony Swithin £2.99
- ☐ NIGHT WATCH Alastair MacNeill £3.50
- ☐ THE MINOTAUR Stephen Coonts £4.50
- ☐ THE QUEEN'S SECRET Jean Plaidy £3.99
- ☐ THE LEMON TREE Helen Forrester £3.99
- ☐ THE THIRTEEN-GUN SALUTE Patrick O'Brian £3.50
- ☐ STONE CITY Mitchell Smith £4.50
- ☐ ONLY YESTERDAY Syrell Leahy £2.99
- ☐ SHARPE'S WATERLOO Bernard Cornwell £3.50
- ☐ BLOOD BROTHER Brian Morrison £3.50
- ☐ THE BROW OF THE GALLOWGATE Doris Davidson £3.50

You can buy Fontana paperbacks at your local bookshop or newsagent. Or you can order them from Fontana, Cash Sales Department, Box 29, Douglas, Isle of Man. Please send a cheque, postal or money order (not currency) worth the purchase price plus 22p per book for postage (maximum postage required is £3.00 for orders within the UK).

NAME (Block letters)_____

ADDRESS_____

_____